Joshua Willis, a former Congressional staffer and trial lawyer for the last 25 years, wrote this book by blending his fascination of space, politics, and history. He is married and has two adult children. He lives with his wife in the beach community of Oxnard Shores, California. Joshua enjoys golf, snow skiing, cooking, and sailing.

*To the memory of my father, Kenneth Willis,
and grandfather, Herbert Willis.*

Joshua Willis

HEART ATTACK

AUSTIN MACAULEY PUBLISHERS™

LONDON • CAMBRIDGE • NEW YORK • SHARJAH

Ordering Information:
Quantity sales: special discounts are available on quantity purchases by corporations, associations, and others. For details, contact the publisher at the address below.

Publisher's Cataloging-in-Publication data
Willis, Joshua
Heart Attack

ISBN 9781641827829 (Paperback)
ISBN 9781641827836 (Hardback)
ISBN 9781641827843 (E-Book)

The main category of the book — Fiction / Thrillers / Suspense

www.austinmacauley.com/us

First Published (2019)
Austin Macauley Publishers LLC
40 Wall Street, 28th Floor
New York, NY 10005
USA

mail-usa@austinmacauley.com
+1 (646) 5125767

I would like to thank, first and foremost, my wife, Karen, who provided the inspiration for this book and who supported me throughout the writing process, including input at some of the oddest hours. In addition, I would like to thank all my family and friends who read a draft of the manuscript and provided valuable input, including, most of all, my father-in-law, Allen Rubenstein; as well as my mother and stepfather, Rachel and Irwin Levin; my brother, Aaron Willis; my good friend Dale Boutiette; and cousin Carol Holtzer. Also, I would like to thank Kenny Raffaelli for his advice and counsel about special forces operations. Lastly, I would like to thank my daughters, Kayla and Hannah Willis, for their unwavering support and confidence that they showed in their father while writing his first novel.

List of Characters

Jack Halliday – President of the United States
Karen Halliday – First Lady of the United States
Rich Hillary – Vice President of the United States
Anne Hillary – Wife of Vice President of the United States
Teddy Fitzpatrick – White House Chief of Staff
Jonas Frank – Deputy White House Chief of Staff
Nora Summers – President Halliday's Executive Assistant
Senator Henry McClintock, M.D. – Senator from Oregon
Senator Kayla Jackson - Senator from Louisiana
Senator Benjamin Boutiette – Chairman of the Senate Rules Committee
Congressman Richard Montgomery III – Speaker of the House of Representatives
Congressman Jedidiah 'Jed' Abel – Congressman from Iowa
Congressman Gary Schwartz – Chairman of the House Judiciary Committee
Senator Benjamin Boutiette – Chairman of Senate Rules Committee
Dr. Reuben Allenstein, M.D. – White House Doctor
J. Robert Peck – Chairman and CEO of Healthmed Inc. and Presidential Benefactor
Jerry Lanzella – Senior Vice President in charge of Sales and Marketing for Healthmed Inc.
Alexander Cain – Senior Vice President of MedSupply, Ltd
Mark Walker – Assistant Vice President for Technology for MedSupply, Ltd
Dr. John Malcomovich, M.D. - Chief Clinical Scientist Food and Drug Administration
Jake Redwell – NASA Administrator
Aaron Harbath – NASA ISS Mission Control Director Dr. Martin White - NASA Scientist
Commander James Thorson – NASA Astronaut at International Space Station

Cosmonaut Dimitri Korbatov – Russian Cosmonaut at International Space Station
Max Kallen – Special Agent in Charge of Office of the Inspector General at Kennedy Space Center
Mark Weisburg – NASA Inspector General
Jack Michaels – ISS Mission Control Director for the Canadian Space Agency
Commander Nick 'Nicky' Boucher - Canadian Astronaut
Stan Raffaelli - Attorney General of the United States
The Honorable Mark Stephens – FBI Director
Special Agent Frank Johnson – FBI Special Agent in Charge of the Washington D.C. Office
Uri Nimi – Deputy Director of Shin Bet
Hannah Willets – Senior White House Reporter for the Washington Post
Gene Betel – NSA Computer Analyst
Nassir al-Fazeh – Sunni Terrorist

Prologue
May 1, 1951

Somewhere Near the Lebanese/Syrian Border

In a remote village, approximately forty miles southeast of Al Qa, Lebanon, the wailing baby's howl pierced the quiet pre-dawn hours near the tent where Nassir was warming pita over hot coals. *The baby was to be the savior,* he thought to himself, *the child of two of the world's most renowned Muslim scientists.* The plan was foolproof. The Islamic World would finally achieve its rightful place amongst the world's superpowers. The *Western Devils* had swallowed up his Country whole, and now were in the process of establishing that Christian fool of a President, Chamoun, into power. Nassir was snowballing, he thought. Stay focused, he reminded himself.

At that precise moment, the birthing assistant exited the tent, holding a beautiful baby boy. Just like his parents, the infant boy had fair skin and light coloring. The birthing assistant smiled at Nassir who, unmoved by the sight of the baby, simply stuffed a handful of Pita into his mouth, scooped up the baby, and began his long journey westward.

February 5, 1955

Sioux City, Iowa

Years later, half way across the world, a woman would give birth to a healthy baby boy in a hospital outside Sioux City, Iowa. The birth was the culmination of a rough and turbulent pregnancy. After giving birth to the son of one of the leading Muslim clerics in the Middle East, however, Nassir's sister would raise a devout Sunni child who, most importantly, was an American citizen, born in the

11

United States. *The second part of his plan was now in place.* Nassir allowed himself the rare indulgence of a small smile.

Chapter One
April 1, 2017

The Oval Office, the White House, Washington, D.C.

The early morning sun bounced off the Resolute Desk, causing the Vice President to squint momentarily at the glare as the President entered the Oval Office.

"Good morning, Mr. President," began Vice President Rich Hillary in his thick Southern drawl. The Vice President was a tall imposing figure, standing six-feet four inches with the build of a professional athlete. To look at him, one would have no idea that he was a guest at some of the finest of the District of Columbia's local hospitals over the past few months.

"Good morning, Rich. What brings you here so early on a Saturday morning?" asked the President, curious as to why the Vice President might be awaiting him this early in the Oval Office without an appointment even though it was not uncommon given the nature of their relationship.

"Mr. President, you of all people should know it's never too early to address the issues confronting our Nation," smirked the Vice President, a bit too keenly aware that the White House taping system was recording this conversation, as well as others like it, for prosperity's sake.

"In any case," he said. "I understand that Senator Trist plans to go on 'Meet the Press' tomorrow morning to attack the Healthcare Bill that McClintock recently introduced."

He paused. "Jack, as you know, this Bill is critical for the millions of people who remain uninsured through loopholes in the Affordable Care Act." In this regard, Rich Hillary was preaching to the choir.

"Look Rich, we have been through this at least a dozen times," said the President, shuffling through a stack of papers on his desk. As he glanced up, however, the President immediately realized something was drastically wrong. The Vice President was sweating profusely, clutching his massive paws of hands just below his Adam's apple, at the base of his throat. Gasping for air, he twisted in a bizarre fashion like a crumbling marionette, ultimately coming to rest on one knee. Desperately trying to catch his breath that was noticeably strained, seemingly to no avail, the Vice President suddenly collapsed between the two light beige and caramel-colored couches in the middle of the room, which were left-overs from the Obama Administration. A loud thud reverberated throughout the office.

"Nora, quick, get a doctor in here," yelled the President.

"Excuse me, Mr. President," came the response.

"Nora, now! A doctor! It's the Vice President!"

Two Secret Service agents barreled through the side door to the Oval Office. Surveying the situation, the younger of the two agents jettisoned toward the Vice President's lifeless body which lay in the middle of the room while the older more senior agent surveyed the perimeter of the room. Speaking into a microphone under his blue blazer, he summoned additional help while the younger agent dropped to his knees and began administering CPR to the Vice President. The President, who by now, was on the floor squeezing the hand of his longtime friend and political ally for over twenty-five years, asked the agent administering CPR, "What is it, Gary?"

"I don't know, sir. It's hard to say, but he is not breathing, and I cannot find a pulse," gasped the agent between breaths and well-timed compressions on the Vice President's chest. He had a look of grave concern on his face when an army of individuals draped in medical uniforms raced into the Oval Office, accompanied by the President's personal secretary, Nora Summers.

"Reuben is on his way to GW. He will meet you and the Vice President there," she said. "An ambulance is out front now."

The medical crew and agents placed the Vice President's body on a stretcher, wheeling him out the South Entrance of the White House where an ambulance was waiting with its engine running. The President followed alongside the Vice President every step of the way and was just was about to enter the ambulance with the Vice President when the lead Secret Service agent for the President's security detail intervened.

"Mr. President, I don't think it's a good idea for you and the Vice President to travel in the same vehicle together," he said. "For security reasons," he clarified.

The President initially rebuked the agent, reprimanding him, "Damn it, Stan, this is my best friend we are talking about." The more he thought about it, however, the President realized that the Secret Service Agent was right, and relented. The Presidential motorcade followed in tow behind the ambulance carrying the Vice President.

George Washington University Medical Center, Washington, D.C.

Minutes later, the ambulance, and Presidential motorcade, arrived at George Washington University Medical Center, a hospital where many Presidents and Vice Presidents have sought medical treatment in the past, including President Reagan after the attempt on his life by John Hinkley, Jr., and Vice President Dick Cheney when he had his pacemaker installed.

Upon their arrival, the White House doctor, another close friend of the President, greeted the President and his entourage. Dr. Reuben Allenstein was the 'best of the best'. He was a graduate of Yale Medical School, not to mention the youngest professor to teach there, as well as at USC Medical School, who later became Surgeon General, only to later finally accept the post of White House physician to his good friend, and the former California Governor, Jack Halliday.

"What is it Reuben?" the President asked the doctor as Secret Service agents encircled the two.

"Preliminarily, Mr. President, it looks as if the Vice President's pace maker inexplicably failed, and he is presently in cardiac arrest due to a Myocardial Infarction. In plain English, he had a heart attack, sir. We will, of course, keep you posted, Mr. President, but right now, it does not look good," he said, rushing off to attend to his patient.

At that point, the President reluctantly pulled a secure cell phone from his breast pocket and placed a call to the Speaker of the House of Representatives, Richard Montgomery III. Congressman 'Dick' Montgomery, from the great state of Georgia, was only one of many from the Georgia Delegation, but he was certainly the pride and joy of the South. Raised a good Christian man, his strongest support was from a group known as the CBA, which was an acronym for Christians for a Better America. It was, in fact, a splinter group of the former Moral Majority. Congressman Montgomery was now entering his tenth term as a member of the U.S. House of Representatives, and over the last few months, seemed to vote against every initiative the current Administration put forth.

"Dick, Jack Halliday here," said the President.

"What can I do for you, Mr. President?" inquired the Speaker groggily. Pausing a moment, he added, "Especially at this ungodly hour." Evidently, he was not amused at being woken up at what appeared to be 6:27 a.m., even if it was the President of the United States on the other end of the line.

"I am afraid, Mr. Speaker, that I have some bad news," began the President.

"Yes, Mr. President?" said the Speaker, a bit more attentive now.

"Well, it's the Vice President," continued the President. "It seems as if he may have suffered a major heart attack and there may be a chance he will not make it," muttered the President, choking on the last two words as he uttered them.

The Speaker, unsure if he heard the President correctly asked, "Excuse me, Mr. President, what did you just say?"

Annoyed at having to repeat himself during this very emotional time for the President, he stated more tersely, "The Vice president has suffered a heart attack and it does not look good, I am sad to say."

"I am sorry Mr. President, but isn't this phone call a bit premature," inquired the Speaker, sensing where the conversation was heading. As a former history professor, the Speaker was all too familiar with the Twenty Fifth Amendment and knew that, under Section 2, should the current Vice President pass away, the President chose the Vice President's successor, but a majority of both houses of Congress had to confirm the nominee. That was unquestionably where the Speaker came into play.

The Twenty Fifth Amendment was ratified in 1967 when, following the Kennedy Assassination, Senator Birch Bayh realized that once Lyndon B. Johnson ascended to the highest office in the Country, there would be a glaring void in the Nation's second highest office to fill. Bayh, the Indiana Senator, and Chairman of the Senate Subcommittee on Constitutional Amendments at the time, was gravely concerned and rightfully so.

Before that time, there was only the 1947 Presidential Succession Act, which provided for a line of succession in case the President and Vice President died at the same time, or in case the President died and there was no Vice President, but there was nothing for when a Vice President died or was no longer in Office. As a result, there were sixteen vacancies of the position of Vice President in history, some of which lasted as long as four years until the next election, when the position was ultimately filled.

Consequently, Bayh's Subcommittee drafted Section 2 of the Twenty Fifth Amendment to rectify this Constitution oddity.

As drafted, however, the Amendment was riddled with several flaws that many Constitutional scholars have since acknowledged. For example, one flaw is that there is no accepted standard for Congressional ratification of the President's nominee. As it turns out, both Ford and Rockefeller were confirmed through respective confirmation proceedings in the House and Senate, but the Amendment itself provides no guidance in this regard.

Another, and perhaps even more troubling, flaw with the Amendment is that it permits accession to the Nation's highest office without approval from the general electorate at large, as Gerald Ford demonstrated when he served as both President and Vice President without ever having been elected to either Office.

The biggest problem, however, and no doubt the main reason for the President's call, is that it is susceptible to the whims of partisan politics potentially allowing the Vice Presidency to remain vacant for extended periods while contentious confirmation proceedings played out in the House and Senate. In the case of Nelson Rockefeller, for example, his Confirmation proceedings lasted 121 days. Unquestionably, that was where the Speaker of the House figured into the equation. He would be the one person able to rally support for any potential new Vice-Presidential nominee from both 'sides of the aisle' as there was a saying in D.C., that if you wanted to get anything done in this town, it had to first go through the Speaker's Office.

Sure enough, as the Speaker could have readily predicted, the President added, "Look Dick, I truly hope you're right, but should it come to that, I hope you will support whatever nominee this Administration puts forth to replace him, and not engage in political grandstanding, for the dignity of Rich, and the Nation," implored the President.

"Well, Mr. President, of course, I cannot say anything until I know who that person is."

"Let's hope it never comes to that," remarked the President somberly.

"Agreed," joined the Speaker.

Chapter Two
Seven Months Earlier,
September 22, 2016

West Plano, Texas

The limousines lined the driveway for almost a quarter of a mile, twisting through the wooded property for the length of almost six football fields in this small suburb outside Dallas. The home was an early Nineteenth Century style Victorian that from the outside, looked almost too modest for the grandeur of the scenic driveway preceding it. Amazingly, this was only one of many homes owned by its prominent owner. The inside of this palatial residence was virtually like a museum, unparalleled in its beauty. Lalique figurines lined the entryway, which opened into a spacious room with vaulted and hand painted wood beamed ceilings. The maple staircase was lined with early Impressionist art, including original paintings from Monet, Manet, and Degas. Directly to the right of the staircase, was an old-fashioned wood-built elevator that was the only item that looked as if it did not belong; at least, not aesthetically.

The evening's festivities were taking place in the Grand Ballroom and the Dining Room, which were just off to the left of the Grand Entry Hall. The Grand Ballroom's walls were a dark Mahogany and lined with presidential portraits from George Washington to Barack Obama. The Dining Room did not have its usual twenty-five-foot central dining table, but instead, had ten smaller round tables, with ten place settings on each. Still, there was plenty of room to spare. Near the servant's entry to the Dining Room, was a modest platform with a small ramp leading up to it. On it, were three chairs and a microphone. On each of the tables, the place setting included the finest Wedgewood China and Baccarat Crystal. At ten thousand dollars a plate, no attention to detail was spared.

The guests at this fund-raiser were some of the most powerful and influential people throughout Texas, including Congressmen, Senators, Judges, lobbyists, and many chief executives of large corporations. Perhaps the most prominent of them all, however, was unquestionably the evening's host, J. Robert Peck, Chairman and Chief Executive Officer of one of the world's largest medical device companies, Healthmed Inc.

J. Robert Peck was world renown for his philanthropy. At age twenty-five, he invented a computer chip that generated a large enough electrical current necessary to make heart defibrillators portable. As a result, the portable defibrillator is almost as common today as a stretcher was in the 'old days'. Having made billions of dollars in the medical device industry, Peck was well known for donating sizeable chunks of money to fighting disease, and sponsoring numerous grants for medical research, as well as making sizable donations to various political organizations. In this regard, it was widely believed that Peck's philanthropic efforts stemmed from his own unfortunate circumstances in life.

At age three, Peck contracted a rare life-threatening disease, which he eventually overcame, but which ultimately left him confined to a wheel chair since the time he was four. Nevertheless, despite his physical handicap, or maybe because of it, Peck always tried to overcompensate by being the best and brightest in his class. He did, after all, have a genius IQ of 175. He grew up in a very poor section of Dallas. By the time he was sixteen, he had graduated from Cal Tech with a bachelor's Degree in Mechanical Engineering. From there, he went East, and obtained his Master's and PhD from MIT; both of which, he held by the time he was twenty-three. For the next two years, he worked in the Silicon Valley, developing computer chips. It was during this time in California that he first met Jack Halliday and became interested in politics.

Shortly after forming Healthmed Inc. in 1984, at the ripe old age of thirty-three, Peck became a stalwart member in Party politics, doing everything he could for the 'cause', from making phone calls to touring various voting precincts and raising money. Yet, tonight was, by far, the biggest contribution he had ever made for the Party. Everyone here tonight was supporting the Jack Halliday/Rich Hillary Ticket.

"Good evening, Bob," said Jack Halliday as he approached the host of the evening. "Looks like a good turn out tonight."

"Sure does, Mr. Governor. I could not be more pleased."

"You should be. I've never seen anybody work as hard as you in organizing tonight's event. We certainly owe you a huge debt of gratitude. Thanks again for the use of your wonderful home this evening and all that you have done in organizing tonight's event."

"Don't mention it, sir. The truth is that I am just glad to put it to some good use finally. You know, I rarely make it down here as often as I would like. I only hope that all this hard work pays off, and I am addressing you next year at this time as 'Mr. President' in the Oval Office."

"Me too, Bob."

"By the way, have you seen Rich yet?"

"No, not yet, sir."

At that point, the guest of honor went off to find the emcee of the evening. After mingling for about an hour and half, the guests convened at their assigned dinner tables. After they were all seated, the host took center stage at the microphone, which was adjusted to the level of his wheelchair.

"Distinguished guests let me first begin by welcoming to you to tonight's Halliday/Hillary dinner. As many of you know, the upcoming election will be a close hard-fought battle. That is why it is essential that the Party has committed and dedicated individuals, such as yourselves. I thank each and every one of you for all of your generous donations for tonight's event, and more importantly, for your support for the Party, and for the next President and Vice President of the United States, Jack Halliday and Rich Hillary."

"Now, ladies and gentlemen, I am pleased to introduce you this evening to a man who has prided himself on hard work and the right for every man or woman to have as much of a chance as any to achieve the American dream. This was evident during his time at Harvard, while on scholarship, as well as throughout his private law practice which focused, in no small part, on making those conditions for the less privileged better. During his time in the Tennessee State Legislature, he was an ardent advocate for healthcare reform, which continues even to this day as a member of the United States Senate. He has long been a spokesman for the underdog and disenfranchised... Ladies, and gentlemen, I am proud to introduce to you the next Vice President of the United States, Senator Rich Hillary."

"Thank you, Bob," said the Senator from Tennessee as he took the stage and adjusted the microphone to his rather large frame. After speaking for just under thirty minutes on topics ranging from heath care to Social Security reform, Senator Hillary concluded his remarks reminiscing, "Now, many of you may not remember this, but it was about twenty-five years ago. I was a freshman Tackle for

Harvard in the big Harvard/Yale game and this senior running back got the ball and was supposed to go off my block into the end zone to win the game, and what does he do instead? He fumbles at the two-yard line. Ladies and gentlemen, that running back was none other than Governor Jack Halliday. Needless to say, he has gone on to score many political touchdowns as Governor of the great state of California, and no doubt, will do so as the next President of the United States. Distinguished guests, I am delighted to introduce you to the next President of the United States, Governor Jack Halliday."

Halliday went on to speak for about an hour; only, to conclude to an overwhelming round of applause and a standing ovation. The night's event was unquestionably a huge success.

Chapter Three
Eight Days Later, September 30, 2016

Somewhere over the Midwest

Governor Halliday and some of his top advisors were on a chartered jet flying back to California for some more campaigning while Rich Hillary was on his way down to the Florida Panhandle to meet with small business owners who were complaining about the easing of trade tariffs and trade restrictions that were flooding the markets with foreign competition, making it difficult for them to compete.

"I don't care what the polls are saying, we have to bring healthcare to the forefront of this Election. I'm telling you it affects everyone these days. Employers complain about the rising costs of insurance while a majority of the population remains uninsured. And, the Affordable Care Act has done little to alleviate the burden," complained Presidential Candidate, Jack Halliday.

"I understand that, Mr. Governor," said Teddy Fitzpatrick, Jack Halliday's Chief of Staff since his days as California Governor, who was presently Campaign Manager for the Halliday/Hillary 2016 Campaign. "All I am saying is that this particular group of business owners are more concerned about federal funding for infrastructure. The more highways that are built, the more revenue for them, and at the same time, the fewer accidents: A win, a win for everyone. Besides, this also happens to be the area where Matthews is the weakest, and most vulnerable. The prior administration didn't do much for his cause, either."

"Sir?" interrupted Nora Summers, Jack Halliday's longtime Executive Assistant. "You have a call from Mr. Peck," she announced.

"That's fine, Nora, I'll take it in here."

"Bob, how's it going? Thanks again for such a wonderful event last week," began Halliday.

"It was my pleasure, sir. I am just happy it was so successful. In any case, I just wanted to wish you luck campaigning in California."

"Thanks Bob. By the way, although I've known Rich most of my life, I must say that was a great suggestion of yours to put him on the ticket. We seem to be drawing bigger and bigger crowds since we put him on the ticket."

"Hey, don't discount your own political prowess there, buddy," said Peck playfully. "No, I know, I know," responded Jack Halliday agreeably. "I'm just saying 'good call.' Listen Bob, I have to run. Was there something in particular you wanted to discuss?"

"You know, Mr. Governor, I am the biggest supporter of universal healthcare, and improving the Affordable Care Act, but the more I think of it, I think you should downplay it during the campaign; make it your highest priority once you are in Office, just not now."

"Well Bob, as always, your timing is impeccable. Teddy and I were just discussing that very issue."

"Really, what was Teddy saying? I have always respected his opinion."

"Funny, just like you, he was telling me to downplay it during this campaign stop."

"What can I say, great minds think alike," responded J. Robert Peck.

"Anyways, thanks for the call. Got to go now."

"Good luck, Jack."

Immediately upon hanging up, Teddy Fitzpatrick blurted out, "What did he want?"

"Take it easy, Teddy, he actually agrees with you on the issue of improving healthcare. You know, he truly is one of the greatest philanthropists of the Twenty First Century, and a hero among the Party leadership. You should really give him a break." As the plane started its descent, Fitzpatrick's face gave way to a frown.

Redwood City, California

J. Robert Peck was looking over the numbers for the pace maker side of the business. After founding Healthmed Inc. on the discovery and distribution of the portable defibrillator, Peck decided the business should expand into other areas of medical device manufacturing, and so for a time, Healthmed Inc., expanded into the production and distribution of the insulin pump, used to treat Diabetes, as well as Prosthetics. Then, about three years into the insulin side of the business, Healthmed Inc. found its niche with the sale and production of pace makers. After a short while, that became the most profitable side of the business, causing the company to sell off the less profitable divisions, such as the insulin pump and prosthetic divisions and focus solely on the production and sale of pace makers and defibrillators. Presently, Healthmed Inc., has the largest market share in both those areas, both domestically and internationally, making it the largest medical device manufacturer in the world.

The intercom on Peck's desk buzzed and his personal secretary announced the arrival of Jerry Lanzella, Senior Vice President in charge of Sales and Marketing for the Pace Maker Division of Healthmed Inc. "Send him in," said Peck.

Lanzella entered Peck's enormous office that took up half of the entire top floor of the thirty-story modern industrial complex, which Healthmed Inc., owned and leased back to the Company. Peck's office had its own deluxe amenities, such as a 52 inch plasma screen, a modified gym, Jacuzzi and sauna (all wheelchair accessible, of course), a leather couch for guests, as well as a full-length bar, stocked with only the finest scotches and bourbons from all over the world, and a full floor to ceiling window with a view of the entire West San Mateo Valley. Peck motioned for Lanzella to have a seat in one of the two seats directly opposite his large glass desk. Lanzella obliged.

Once seated, Peck wheeled around from behind his desk so that he was directly in front of Lanzella, lifted some papers from the top of the desk in his hand and demanded, "What the fuck is this?" Lanzella, a bit taken back by his boss's frankness, didn't respond, at first. Then, Peck yelled, "I mean, what the fuck are these numbers," he said, throwing the entire stack of papers at Lanzella which scattered across the floor. He continued, "Are you fucking asleep at the wheel? What the hell am I paying you for? Can you answer me that!"

Lanzella was speechless at his boss's tirade. Finally, he mustered, "Sir, with all due respect, we have doubled sales of pace makers domestically from this time last year, and we are about 2,500 sales ahead of our target in last year's forecast, both domestically and internationally. We are doing great, especially if you look comparatively to where we were at last year when I signed on to this job. Quite frankly, I just don't understand where this is coming from, nor do I think it is deserved, Bob."

"Well, let me explain something to you, Jerry," Peck said, emphasizing each of the two syllables in Jerry's name, indicating that he did not appreciate Lanzella's informality. "When I hired you away from Medtropolus, you were supposedly this young hot-shot sales guy who not only had a knack for satisfying demanding sales plans, but far exceeding those sales plans. I'm just not seeing it though, Jerry. I need to see a much more dramatic improvement before the end of next quarter, that's all I can say."

Jerry began to speak, but Peck held up his hand to suggest that no further response was necessary and then said, "That's it Jerry. Thanks."

Lanzella, a seasoned executive, had never had an employer treat him so demeaning before. He just sat there, stunned for a moment before salvaging any self-respect he had and leaving Peck's office, hat in hand.

Chapter Four
The Inauguration of President Jack Halliday, January 20, 2017

The Capitol and Washington Mall, Washington, D.C.

As he strode to the podium to deliver his Inaugural Address, after being sworn into Office by the Chief Justice of the Supreme Court, Jack Halliday was all smiles.

He began, "Distinguished Members of the House of Representatives and Senate, invited guests, and fellow Americans, we enter the second decade of the Twenty First Century with a thriving economy, low unemployment, modest inflation, and a strong dollar; all of which, make America the world power it once was. Yet, at the same time, every American does not have healthcare coverage. Our children and schools are struggling. It is time we put money back into our people who made this country strong. Therefore, as promised, later this year, this Administration will be introducing a Universal Healthcare bill to close the loopholes in the Affordable Care Act that will make insurance coverage available for literally every American." This was met with a large cheer from most of those members of Congress, who, like the President, realized this was a critical issue facing the nation.

The President continued, "Also, by levying a small transportation tax on those vehicles which are not environmentally friendly, or in compliance with new stringent government regulations the EPA will soon be implementing, we will be able to put money back into the American infrastructure, while at the same time, reducing the effects of global warming. This is a win, win for everyone involved." Again, loud cheers.

"America can, and will, be restored to what it once was. It will, once again, be a leader in technology and a pioneer in the 'space race.' This Administration will launch three new highly sophisticated satellites during the next year. Each will contain the most sophisticated technology and will support a network that will facilitate even greater advancements in the fields of computer science, industry and military development. Such advances will be the result of government agencies working in conjunction with the private sector," touted the President.

After speaking for another forty minutes, the President finished his Inaugural Address to a standing ovation. Within minutes of the President concluding his nearly hour-long speech, which was considerably shorter than most, the political pundits were on the airwaves espousing their entirely contradictory views; each, putting their own spin on the President's remarks and what it meant for the nation.

Chapter Five
Three Days after Jack Halliday's Inauguration, January 23, 2017

The Oval Office, Washington, D.C.

Nora Summer's voice came over the intercom on the President's Desk. "Mr. President, Administrator Redwell from NASA is on the line for you, as you requested."

"Thank you, Nora, put him through."

"Jake, how's it going?" asked the President.

"Is everything proceeding as expected for the next launch?"

"Yes Mr. President, everything is going as expected," responded Jacob 'Jake' Redwell.

He was a heavyset man, in his mid-fifties, about 5'6", with a pale complexion, and balding on top. He had worked at NASA for almost his entire career, a lengthy 27 ½ years, but primarily as a relatively low-level scientist and public relations person. He was on track to be a career bureaucrat. That is, until about ten years ago when the Governor of California was touring the JPL plant, at which he worked, just outside of Pasadena. As head of their Public Relations Department at the time, he had the pleasure of touring the then Governor through the facilities. Thereafter, the two ended up staying in touch as they both seemed to share some strange connection. One of the first things President Halliday did after he assumed Office was replace the then acting Administrator of NASA with Jake Redwell.

"Great. When is it scheduled?"

"February 15th, sir."

"And everything is ready for that launch?" asked the President.

"Absolutely, sir."

"Jake, I cannot stress enough the importance that the next few launches go as planned, without any complications."

"I understand, Mr. President."

The President continued, "I mean, I campaigned as the 'Technology President' and that's just what I intend to do; advance technology. Like I said before, I want to have at least another 50 commercial and government satellites orbiting the Earth's atmosphere by the end of my first term to accommodate the influx of technology the new stimulus package is designed to promote."

"Mr. President," began Jake wearily, who never liked to disappoint his new boss. "There are certain safety protocols which must be followed, and as a result, certain timetables exist. Needless to say, we are doing everything to accommodate the deadlines imposed by your directive and have the launches occur according to schedule."

"Just a minute, Jake," interrupted the President. After a muffled conversation between the President and another person in the Oval Office, the President returned to the line, and abruptly ended the call a minute later.

Chapter Six
NASA Launch, February 15, 2017

Hollywood, Florida

The tall slender man hung up the payphone in the nondescript bar, paid the tab for his cheeseburger and milk, and got into his late model Buick. Preparing himself for the lengthy drive ahead, he lit a cigarette, put a Percy Sledge cassette into his old AM/FM cassette player and pulled out of the parking lot of the bar. He drove a couple of blocks and entered the I-95, heading North. After driving North for almost 3 hours, he exited onto Challenger Memorial Parkway, and drove for another couple of miles before turning right onto Columbia Blvd. Then, completing his journey, he drove for another five minutes before entering a utility road which led him to a guard station. After speaking briefly with the guard, the gate lifted, and he drove to his designated parking spot. He slid his identification card through an electronic entry key card device and entered the building.

John F. Kennedy Space Center, Merritt Island, Florida

NASA's Research Integration Office (RIO) coordinates with private industry, universities and the federal government to send private, and government sponsored, payloads to the International Space Station (ISS). Within just the last year, in fact, the federal government, working with private industry, approved both a private commercial lunar program as well as a commercial program to Mars. As a result, venture capital was the new force driving the space industry, and NASA's RIO suddenly found itself flush with money.

Today, was an important day for NASA's RIO. It was the scheduled launch to the ISS of one of the RIO's largest commercial private payloads, to date. Consequently, in addition to the usual scattering of media, there were a number of interested spectators, not to mention NASA personnel, who had gathered for this particular launch. Inside the Launch Room, it was uncharacteristically a bit hectic, as one might expect.

"Jimmy how does everything look?" barked Mike Sapinstein, a heavyset man in his late forties, who was the Launch Director for this launch.

"We are good to go," answered Jimmy Olson Sapinstein looked down at the Swatch watch on his wrist, and then up at the dozen or so monitors in front of him.

"Okay, let her roll." Countdown began.

"Hold on, we have a problem," yelled Martin Andropov, a recent emigrant from the former Soviet Union, whose thick Russian drawl was only outdone by the size of the individual himself. He stood a full 6'6" and weighed approximately 285 pounds. Countdown instantly paused. "I am showing exaggerated readings for the SatCom electromagnetic (EM) drive on Monitor Six, sir," reported Andropov, referring to the company's initial filing with NASA's RIO. Ever since a few years back, scientists discovered that EM drives could provide for the direct conversion of electrical energy to thrust spacecrafts without the need to expel any propellant, virtually all payloads to the ISS now included some sort of external EM drive, which in turn, required energy to power them. While the ISS gets most of its power from solar array wings, it also has twenty-four nickel-hydrogen batteries that can provide additional energy, if necessary. Presently, the reading for the SatCom EM drive was twice all the electricity the ISS's nickel-hydrogen batteries provided. In other words, devastatingly high.

Andropov's oversized fingers danced across the computer keyboard in front of him as if playing a concerto. Finally, he exhaled a huge sigh of relief that resonated throughout the entire room.

"Never mind, it is back to normal," he said. Countdown resumed.

Mission Control Center, Lyndon B. Johnson Space Center, Houston

Although launches to the ISS generally occur at the John F. Kennedy Space Center, in Florida, or at the Baikonur Cosmodrome, in Kazakhstan, operations for those missions are routinely coordinated through the Christopher C. Craft Jr. Mission Control Center, at the Johnson Space Center, in Houston, Texas.

Observing what Andropov had just seen on his monitor at Kennedy, the technician operating the keyboard in front of the

Mission Control Director, Aaron Harbath, at the Craft Mission Control Center, reluctantly reported, "Sir, there seems to be a slight irregularity with the EM readings for one of the payloads."

He pressed a few more keys on the keyboard, never taking his eyes of the monitor in front of him. Almost instantaneously, both he and his boss, who was now looking over his shoulder, were deeply concerned. The EM readings for the SatCom payload were fluctuating back and forth before ultimately settling on the same figure identified in the Initial Disclosure Form that SatCom filed with the RIO.

"What is it?" demanded Mission Control Director Harbath.

"I am not sure, sir," the technician reluctantly reported.

Harbath's expression immediately soured. "I don't understand," he said. "I thought all of the EM Drives were tested and rechecked last week."

"Yes, sir, that was my understanding too," agreed the NASA technician.

"Is it possible that the readings we are seeing here have been compromised or manipulated in some manner?" asked Harbath.

"I suppose so," responded the technician, quickly adding, "But I just confirmed with Andropov that they observed the same readings we did here, so it would have to be a system wide problem, sir."

Now Harbath was even more concerned. Given the amount of publicity this mission was receiving and what was at stake, Harbath decided not to go the Administrator or Inspector General with this information until he had more facts. So, he picked up his satellite phone, dialed a secure number, and moments later, was connected to an old friend.

Chapter Seven
NASA Launch, February 15, 2017

John F. Kennedy Space Center, Merritt Island, Florida

Max Kallen followed the tall lanky blonde man down the main staircase of the Central Instrumentation Facility (CIF), which houses the instrumentation and data processing operations for the Kennedy Space Center.

Kallen, a long time civil servant of the clandestine services was presently the Special Agent in Charge of the Office of the Inspector General ('OIG') at the Kennedy Space Center even though, technically, he remained on the Department of Defense's payroll, after what could only be described as a disagreement with his superiors - He punched the Deputy Director of the Central Intelligence Agency in the face!

While normally such antics could have gotten him hard time at Fort Leavenworth, some favors were called in given his heroic service to his Country that earned him two Purple Hearts, and a Silver Star, over the course of three tours of duty in Afghanistan and Iraq. Therefore, after serving a brief stint in the Brig at Fort Leavenworth, he went to the Federal Law Enforcement Training Center in Glynco, Georgia, where he received additional training in hand-to-hand combat, as well as surveillance, arrest and interrogation techniques. He also took classes in criminal law and procedure.

Immediately upon graduation, he joined NASA's OIG, whose agents are armed, have arrest authority and can execute search warrants, just as any other federal law enforcement officer. Presently, he was Special Agent in Charge of the OIG at Kennedy Space Center. That is where he met Mission Control Director Aaron Harbath two years ago.

' Kallen kept a safe enough distance between himself and the intruder, as he was trained so many years ago. After descending two flights of stairs, the man exited the CIF through the rear door. Kallen quickly followed suit, but immediately realized the subject was nowhere to be seen. Glancing in all directions, Kallen noticed a white Mercedes Sprinter van parked near the side of the building. Suddenly, there was a flutter of movement, both inside and around the van.

The blonde man, who Kallen recognized from inside, reappeared and was arguing with another much larger man. The other man had a military cropped haircut and elbow length tattoos underneath a white 'wife beater' tank top. Although, normally, a tweaker or fat slob might be seen sporting such an outfit, the man donning this particular outfit was none of those things. Muscles rippled from beneath his tight-fitting shirt, revealing a perfect six pack.

Kallen had to rely upon his well-developed lip-reading skills, over the course of his career, to try to decipher what they were saying. The best he could tell, the muscular man was angry about having to wait longer than expected, while the blonde man did not seem apologetic at all. In fact, just the opposite. It seemed as if the blonde man felt like he was doing the hulking one a favor. The conversation ended abruptly when the blonde man knelt down and reemerged holding a 12 x 12 square piece of electrical board that he had retrieved from a vent at the base of the building. He handed it to the other man who then loaded it into the van, shut the Sprinter door, and drove off. Meanwhile, the blonde man reentered the facility through the same door he had exited only a short while ago. Fortunately, before the van drove off, Kallen was able to commit two consecutive numbers from the license plate to memory.

Chapter Eight
Two Days after the NASA Launch,
February 17, 2017

Pebble Beach, California

"So, it looks like I have a new boss," said Peck's golfing partner for the day as they exited his handicap equipped golf cart prior to teeing off on the ninth hole of Spyglass Golf Course. Even with his disability, J. Robert Peck was a 15 handicap.

"Yeah, well I always knew Jack could do it," said Peck to his golf partner.

Dr. John Malcomovich, Chief Clinical Scientist for the Food and Drug Administration was a career bureaucrat who was presently enjoying this brief golfing excursion on the Monterey Bay, courtesy of his golfing partner. Peck's Gulfstream G550 was on stand-by at the Monterey Airport, ready to shuttle Malcomovich back to D.C. following their game.

Just as he was about to tee off in his specially equipped wheelchair, Peck felt a vibration in his pocket, grabbed his cell phone, and checked the number. Visibly irritated, he told Dr. Malcomovich, "I need to take this call. It's okay, you go ahead," he said, wheeling off the Tee Box and motioning to Dr. Malcomovich to tee off.

"Why the hell are you calling me on this line now!" demanded Peck.

"You know, this isn't easy," came the voice on the other end of the line, a bit shaky. "I can only get away so often and I am constantly worried about being detected."

"You don't need to worry about that! I keep telling you, I have everything covered," said Peck, which was what worried the caller the most. "You just stick to your end of the bargain. I need not remind you that you are being paid very handsomely for really a nominal task that, quite frankly, one of my 'techies' could have handled," he said, minimizing the caller's responsibilities. Peck waited, and then barked into the cell phone, "By the way, what the hell went wrong?"

"What do you mean?" asked the caller.

"I mean I understand there was a bit of problem the other day," Peck said

"You have to understand, with that size of the load, this is not as simple as we originally calculated."

"You damn well knew the size of the load when you first signed on to this Project. How quickly they forget," Peck said mockingly.

"As you well know, sir, theory is often different than practical application," said the man on the other end of the line defensively, fully aware of the high stakes involved here. "There are always glitches when one attempts to apply theory into reality." He paused. "There was simply no way I could have expected this. By the way," he continued, "you came to me, not the other way around."

"Never mind. I expect it won't happen again," barked Peck. "Remember, no mistakes," chastised Peck as he clicked off his phone, replacing it to his jacket pocket, and returning to his golf game.

A Week After the NASA Launch, Kennedy Space Center, Florida

The security guard was making his usual rounds as he had done now for the last three months since being reassigned to the Kennedy Space Center when he noticed what appeared to be a loose board at the bottom of a side wall in the main building of the CIF. He knelt down, gently pushed his hands against the loose board which, at first, made no movement whatsoever, but ultimately gave way once he played with it a bit. Once open, he saw what one would expect to see: dirt, rocks, cement and foundation joists beneath the sub-floor. Since he had not observed anything usual, he figured it would be more trouble than it was worth to report it to the OIG, so he simply placed the board back into place, radioed 'Maintenance' about fixing the broken board, and didn't give it a second thought. He then completed his rounds and went home for the day.

Ten Days After the NASA Launch

Kallen called in a couple of favors with some of his old contacts from his 'life before space' as he liked to refer to it.

"How is it going?" Kallen asked.

"Slowly," responded the analyst. "We have a couple potential leads which I will follow up on after I complete the initial run through." Proudly, he explained, "You see, I have generated an algorithm which calculates all possible matches for active license plates, and then cross-references it through all of the States' DMV offices. Once I have that information, I will narrow the search to the area where the vehicle was last spotted." Kallen simply rolled his eyes, unimpressed with the logistics of it all. The analyst continued working into the early morning hours.

Eventually, Kallen's old friend had a few possible matches for the description of the vehicle which he was then able to narrow down even more geographically until he limited it to two possible vans in the area on the day in question. One belonged to a Mark Sanchez of West Palm Beach. The other belonged to a Florida Medical Supply company out of Tampa, Florida. He tapped in a few more numbers on the keyboard running various algorithms that would decipher a better location and contact information for Florida Medical Supply. Nothing. He tried again. Still nothing. *That's odd*, he thought. Then, thinking about it a bit longer, he tried a different less often used algorithm. Sure enough, it worked!

He learned that the company that owned the van was a subsidiary of a holding company for Healthmed Inc., known as MedSupply Ltd. A brief search of its officers and directors revealed nothing of interest, but a brief search of the officers and directors of Healthmed Inc. did, however. It turns out that the founder and CEO of Healthmed Inc., was none other than the President's friend, largest fund raiser, and closest confidant, J. Robert Peck. At first blush, this fact seemed unusual, but the more the analyst thought about it, it made perfect sense. It was, after all, the American Way: "you pat my back and I pat yours." He decided it was probably nothing but would nonetheless let Kallen know about MedSupply Ltd., its parent company, and the ubiquitous connection between J. Robert Peck and the President of the United States. Then, it would be Kallen's problem.

Hart Senate Building, Washington, D.C.

Senator Henry McClintock was meeting with his key aides on healthcare when his Chief of Staff announced that the Vice President was on the telephone. He promptly excused himself and took the call in his office.

In Washington, the position of Chief of Staff requires an 'on hands' approach in almost every aspect of a Member of Congress'

Office. Jean Haney, Senator McClintock's Chief of Staff, was no exception to this Rule. A Washington lifer, Haney had initially been attracted to the Senator because of his commitment to serving the people of his State, and more importantly, to a cause that prompted his career in politics in the first place. Doctor McClintock had left a successful medical practice in his home state of Oregon to battle what he perceived to be a national crisis in healthcare in America. While practicing, he treated people on a daily basis who did not have insurance nor have any means to obtain the necessary amount of insurance they required. Fortunately, his flourishing private practice, due in no small part to his growing number of wealthier clients, allowed him to treat the neediest patients on a pro-bono basis. After witnessing this unfortunate scenario play out all too often, he put his frustration into action. He became an out spoken critic of the failed healthcare policies of the Reagan Administration, which prompted him to run for Congress in 1988, and then the Senate in 2000. After being elected to the Senate, he sought an appointment to the Committee on Health and Human Services, which at the time, was a relatively low-level appointment that was easy to obtain, even as a Freshman Senator. Now, more than eight years later, he chaired that very same Committee.

Once he returned to the staff meeting, after speaking with the Vice President, the Senator had a whole new aura of enthusiasm about the proposed Healthcare Bill that he and his staff were discussing. Proposed Senate Bill AB 76211 would effectively provide universal healthcare for all Americans by closing all loopholes in the prior Affordable Care Act. In order to achieve this laudable goal, it would place strict restrictions upon insurers, and would require all businesses to provide universal health insurance for their employees, with the assistance of subsidies from the federal government. Because the proposed Bill had little positive fiscal impact on a destitute economy that seemed to be re-entering a recession, however, the latter provision seemed to be the sticking point. Consequently, prior to the election of Jack Halliday and Rich Hillary, the subsidy portion of his Bill seemed doomed, but after speaking with his longtime friend and ally from the Senate, the Senator had a whole new aura of enthusiasm. He couldn't help but smile. For the first time in his twenty years in Congress, things were looking unquestionably brighter.

Chapter Nine
Approximately Two Weeks After the NASA Launch, March 1, 2017

John F. Kennedy Space Center, Merritt Island, Florida

While routinely scanning the security feeds from his laptop in his office, Kallen noticed the same Buick he had observed only a couple weeks earlier reenter the North Security Gate. With a couple taps of his mouse, he was able to track the vehicle to a parking spot near the rear of the Central Instrumentation Facility (CIF). The same tall slender man whom he had previously seen exited the beat-up car. His movements were slow and deliberate. *Clearly, a professional, or at a minimum, someone familiar with the intricacies of tradecraft,* figured Kallen. More worrisome, however, was the fact that the man had a key card that provided entry to the building. Kallen would later check on the Buick, hoping that whatever the mysterious man had planned inside would provide sufficient time to do so. In the meantime, Kallen needed to find out just what he was up to.

Once inside the CIF, the man proceeded down the long corridor that led to the central stairwell to the upper levels of the secure facility. The entryway to the stairwell was protected by a retina scanner on the outside of a heavy metal door located in the foyer of the stairwell, off the corridor where the man had just entered. Kallen was again surprised how easily the man passed through the retina scanner and entered the stairwell without a hitch. Allowing just enough time to pass before following the intruder, Kallen waited a moment before placing his eye upon the scanner. Moments later, he was inside the stairwell that led up to the Control Room, but rather than hearing the intruder's footsteps leading to the Control Room, as Kallen half expected, he was surprised to learn that the man had descended the stairs. Kallen followed. At the base of the stairwell, he observed the man stealthily enter the Engineering Room.

Knowing that there was little to no cover behind the Engineering Room door, Kallen bolted up the stairwell, racing for the OIG Security Room on the third floor. Once there, he deliberately slowed his pace, entered his security code and calmly entered the room in the same manner. The security personnel inside immediately looked up with grave concern on their faces at the unannounced visit of their supervising agent. On the table, was a half-eaten pizza with black olives on it. Kallen put them at ease by cracking a joke.

"Uh, what's up, sir?" asked the most senior agent, with a slice of pizza folded in his hand.

"Nothing," responded Kallen. "I am just following up on some research. There were some issues with the video surveillance algorithms I ran earlier so I thought I would come down here and check on them myself."

He walked over to the monitors, punched a few numbers on the keyboard and glanced inconspicuously down at the monitor. Kallen was shocked by what he saw, which was absolutely nothing. Nowhere to be seen was the mysterious intruder that Kallen had just observed enter the Engineering Room two minutes earlier. *That's odd*, Kallen thought, but figured he had seen his share of false video feeds before. He then jotted something down on a notepad next to the monitor where he was seated and downloaded the entire surveillance drive to a USB drive. Next, he bid farewell to his friends in the Security Room and decided now was as good a time as any to check on the Buick outside.

After Kallen left, one of the OIG agents commented to the others, "That is one bad ass!"

"Yeah, I heard he punched some spook in the face for providing bad intel that ended up getting him and his Special Ops team ambushed behind enemy lines. Half of his team was killed," remarked another.

"Not just some 'spook'. The fricking Deputy Director of the CIA," corrected the first agent.

"Yeah, one bad ass," they all agreed in unison.

International Space Station

The International Space Station (ISS) is a space research laboratory 249 miles above the Earth's surface where crew members, who are housed for extended periods of time, conduct various experiments in astronomy, biology, physics, and other micro-gravity disciplines. The ISS itself consists of a number of various pressurized modules, which provide housing for the crew members, as well as some external trusses, and other components. The backbone of the ISS is a long-pressurized corridor known as the Integrated Truss Segment (ITS), which has various external sites attached to it that accommodate multiple payloads.

 The Mobile Servicing System's (MSS) robotic arm, better known by its primary component 'Canadarm2', suddenly sprang to life and began moving in the direction of the newest payload arrival. Canadarm2's unplanned movement startled Cosmonaut Dimitri Korbatov, who was a guest at the ISS for the last two months now as he was not expecting the cargo to be unloaded until zero six hundred the following morning. Just as Korbatov was about to guide himself through the ITS where the other guest of the ISS, Commander James Thorson, was fiddling with controls, Korbatov's computer screen began to flicker. Due to budget cuts, the crew had been drastically reduced from its normal crew of six to just the two of them, at least until the next launch. Next, all the lights began to flicker too, and then everything went black.

Korbatov called out excitedly, in his thick Russian accent, "Jim, are you there? What is going on?"

There was a brief silence before Thorson's response came, "Yes, I am here Dimitri."

"I am not certain what is going on but am attempting to engage the back-up generator now."

Meanwhile, Korbatov pulled himself through the ITS in the direction of Thorson while the lights suddenly came back on again and so did Korbatov's screen too, but it was completely blank. Korbatov repositioned himself back in front of the screen when the lights began to flicker on and off again. Through his headset, he could hear Thorson muttering something about a multibillion dollar space station that was no better than his rundown apartment back home. Once in front of the screen again, however, the monitor began to flash and then came back into focus. The robotic arm in the loading area was now at a complete standstill. Korbatov pressed a few more keys, causing the monitor to scan the loading area and everything appeared normal, except the large payload that had just arrived was missing.

The Kennedy Space Center, Florida

Kallen exited through the side door of the CIF, between two abutting structures, and entered the parking lot where the late model Buick was parked conspicuously in the darkest section of the lot. The first thing he did as he approached the vehicle was to slip the GPS tracking device deep into the exhaust pipe. *The biggest mistake most people make is to place it where can too easily be found*, he figured. Considering that the last place their visitor would begin searching was the innards of his van's muffler, Kallen positioned the GPS device precisely where it needed to be. Once the GPS was in place, Kallen checked for alarms, which did not seem likely given the dilapidated condition of the vehicle. Nevertheless, after confirming the absence of any security features, he picked the driver's side door lock, and slipped in, carefully managing to stay below the level of the dashboard, out of view. Quickly, he went about his business.

Once inside, he instantly killed the dome light, opting for his small pen light instead. Next, he placed the covert listening device, more commonly referred to as a 'bug', deep into the springs of the passenger side seat cushion. Next, he began scanning the car's interior cabin for any loose papers, notepads or other items. Surprisingly, there were none. Instead, the car reeked of fried food and was littered with empty fast food bags, plastic cups and hamburger wrappers. There was a Percy Sledge cassette in the tape deck. Kallen had to smile. He could not recall the last time he saw a cassette player. Just as he was about to open the glove compartment, Kallen heard a noise and saw a shimmer of light in his peripheral vision. Instinctively, he dropped to the floor, slithered to the passenger door, reached up and opened it as gently and quietly as possible. Once outside the vehicle, he dropped to the ground, and closed the door behind him without making a sound. A minute later, the vehicle's engine roared to life. As Kallen rolled away from it, the Buick backed up, peeled out of its parking spot, and headed for the same security gate through which it had entered only twenty minutes earlier.

Chapter Ten
More Than Two Weeks After the NASA Launch, March 8, 2017

John F. Kennedy Space Center, Merritt Island, Florida

Kallen inserted the USB driver into his laptop. First, he pulled up the surveillance feed, which showed the same empty room he observed back in the Security Room while his comrades in arms were eating pizza, and later speculating about Kallen's questionable past.

Next, he reviewed the Visitor's Log. Once again, nothing. *That's odd*, he thought. *I know I saw him enter the Facility.* Kallen then ran a couple of different programs, cross referencing them with the 'Personnel Register' for Kennedy, which he had just downloaded to his tablet the night before. Still, nothing. *Well, he didn't just vanish into thin air*, Kallen berated himself.

Then, he remembered the new software his friends back at Langley had given him a while back in exchange for some background 'intel' he had provided concerning a 'high value target'. Kallen had never used it before, nor had any reason to, but now seemed to be as good a time as any. He trekked back down to the locker room and made his way to the back of the room. When no one was looking, he opened his locker, pushed back the false bottom, and pulled out a few CDs, wrapped tightly together with a black rubber band. After perusing them quickly, he pulled a single CD from the bunch, replacing the others back into the false bottom of his locker. Kallen returned to his laptop, inserted the disc and punched in a few keys on the keyboard. The screen sprang to life, displaying names, security clearance numbers, and social security numbers. Using another secure program, he then cross-referenced the list of all personnel at Kennedy, creating a macro to eliminate all non-personnel entering the facility. That limited the list to a surprisingly alarming number of fifty non-personnel who had entered the facility.

After briefly perusing the list, however, he immediately realized that most were part of a group tour of local school children. Once he eliminated the kids, their teachers, and their chaperones, approximately fifteen non-personnel had apparently entered the facility.

After cross referencing the maintenance logs and work orders, he was able to exclude all vendors, and outside contractors which whittled the list down further to just two individuals. Of those two, one was Air Force Major John Stanton, who although not technically an employee, was a constant presence at Kennedy, regularly overseeing test flights and conducting classified research for NASA.

By process of elimination, the other individual had to be his man of mystery: John Denton. As expected, Denton was not his real name. With a minimal amount of research, Kallen learned that a John Denton, age 25, died last year outside of Erie, Pennsylvania in a head-on collision. At the time of his death, he was on disability and receiving checks at a location outside of Scranton, Pennsylvania. No arrest records, and no fingerprints or identifying features. One thing was certain though; the Pennsylvania John Denton was not his guy as the picture on his driver's license showed a scrawny African-American male, listed at 5'6". The guy he saw was clearly Caucasian and stood over 6 feet tall. Wrong guy!

Kallen immediately began plugging away on his laptop keyboard. He pulled up the application for the mysterious John Denton to glean what he could from the information on his *secure* application. Then, he downloaded the video footage of the man entering the North Gate and paused it on the exact frame when he passed through the guard station. He magnified it to over one thousand times so that he could see even the most minuscule items inside the vehicle. He saw the familiar Percy sledge cassette he had previously seen inside the vehicle, along with a pack of Camel cigarettes, and a mobile phone. He enlarged the portion of the screen containing the mobile phone and was able to magnify it enough to read what was on the screen of the man's phone, as he entered the facility. Unfortunately, there was no useful 'intel' on it; just a screen saver of some 'Double D hottie' with her top off.

After that, Kallen downloaded the 'face shot'. Using the same global facial recognition program as the FBI's Next Generation Identification System, he cross-referenced it through all known law enforcement and military databases. This search proved to be a bit more successful. There were four potential matches.

The first one was a man named Martin Kohl; a German national, who was on the Department of Homeland Security's 'No Fly List' for what Kallen could best tell were questionable financial transactions with organizations that had dealings with Al-Qaeda of Iraq. Kallen's instantaneous hopes that he had found his man were soon dashed when he noticed that Kohl was listed as 5'8" tall with borderline albino skin tone. *Definitely not his guy*, Kallen thought.

Next up, was Fred Carson. He was in the FBI's database for armed robbery and was currently serving a fifteen-year prison term at Supermax Prison in Colorado. *Cross him of the list too*, figured Kallen. Then, there was an individual named Howard Kale, who showed up in the Miami-Dade Sheriff Department's arrest records for DUI. He was listed as 6'1" and 165 pounds. Kallen contemplated this for a minute before turning his attention to the last candidate: Peter Stern.

Stern was listed as 5'11" tall, and weighed 150 pounds, and was identified in the Army's database as a former military officer, with present contact information at a medical supply company in Southern Florida. *Probably not his guy*, figured Kallen, but just as he was about to return his attention to Howard Kale, something clicked. He recalled earlier tracing the van that left 'the facility' after its mysterious rendezvous with Mr. 'X' to a medical supply Company in South Florida. Sure enough, after a quick Internet search, Kallen confirmed that Peter Stern was a Senior Vice President with MedSupply Ltd., a subsidiary of Healthmed Inc., the same company his analyst mentioned when he gave him the report on the van's license plate.

Kallen immediately ordered a comprehensive 'People Finder Report' for Stern, using 'spook' software that integrated every viable search engine on the Internet using various key terms. The software then allowed the user to cross reference the search, using other significant terms, such as 'health', 'supply' or 'NASA', in this case, for example. Once it cross-referenced the multiple search terms, it would then prompt the user to input all know data concerning the individual, such as social security number, driver's number, address, and phone number. Then, it inquired about all known acquaintances, limiting all possible responses even further. At that point, a prompt requested a government identification number that required the highest security clearance level possible. After Kallen entered his government identification number, the program searched all Intelligence and Department of Defense databases, both classified and unclassified. Then, once the program completed its government search, it compiled all the information into useful categories paraphrasing the plethora of information obtained concerning the subject, with hyperlinks to the supporting documentation.

To be safe, as Kallen notoriously had a penchant for being, Kallen ordered 'People Finder Reports' for Kohl, Carson and Kale. Then, going the extra mile, doing that which even the most seasoned investigators would consider overkill, Kallen ordered 'Profiler Reports' for every employee of MedSupply Ltd., as well.

Chapter Eleven
Present Time, April 3, 2017

The Oval Office, Washington, D.C.

Sitting at his desk, President Jack Halliday was studying a list of potential replacements for the Vice President if it ultimately came to that when his Chief of Staff entered the Oval Office.

"Any word on Rich?" asked the President.

"No, not yet, sir. He remains in 'stable condition', and they continue to monitor his condition on a regular basis."

"Have you talked to Reuben?"

"Yes, sir, Mr. President. He says the prognosis is improving and he is trying to stay optimistic," answered his Chief of Staff. "How's the list going?"

"Uh, okay," responded the President, a bit distracted. He paused and then asked, "Are these the only candidates?"

"The only 'real' ones," responded Teddy. "Word has it that Bob Peck would also like to be considered as a candidate as well, but given his limited government experience, I don't think he could seriously be considered a viable option, Mr. President."

"Teddy, I must say that for me, Bob Peck makes a lot of sense with all that he has accomplished and done for the Party and our Administration. He did, after all, help us carry Texas."

"Come on Mr. President, you've got to be kidding," rebuked his Chief of Staff. "The man has absolutely no government experience whatsoever. What about Senator McClintock? He's on the list, and you both feel the same way about healthcare, sir."

"Yeah, Henry is not a bad choice. I just would like to keep all of my options open, that's all."

"Well, with all due respect sir, Senator McClintock, in my opinion, would make an excellent choice." Fitzpatrick continued, "In fact, some might say he could have had your job were it not for California, Ohio and Texas in the primaries." Immediately realizing he may have just over-stepped his bounds, Fitzpatrick swallowed hard, and simply smiled apologetically at the President.

The President paused for a pensive moment, and then continued, "I'm sorry, my heart and mind are just not into this right now, Teddy."

"Understandably so, Mr. President, but Speaker Montgomery will be expecting you to put forward a name shortly should the Vice President's condition take a turn for the worse, and you don't want to give them any possible ammunition that could possibly be used against you."

"All this talk is a little premature, don't you think? I mean, after all, Rich is still alive for God's sake! He deserves better than that. Even Dick said the same thing when I first notified him."

Teddy was silent.

With that, the President got up from behind his desk, stared out the window for a couple of minutes before returning to his desk to begin reviewing the list of potential Vice-Presidential candidates. Teddy Fitzpatrick was about to leave the Oval Office when Nora Summers suddenly burst in, tears streaming down her cheeks. She looked at the President, and simply shook her head.

The President buried his face in his hand and started sobbing hysterically. Somberly, he asked, "Did they say when?"

"No, just that he went peacefully, sir."

"Mr. President, I'm so sorry," offered Teddy Fitzpatrick. A moment of silence was shared between the three of them before Fitzpatrick suggested the President call the Vice President's widow to wish her his condolences.

The President, trancelike, regained focus and said, "I will," a single tear streaking down the left side of his cheek. "It is so weird. When I last spoke to Reuben, he said the Vice President was in stable condition, resting nicely. Nora, get me Reuben on the phone now," barked the President.

"Yes, sir," responded Nora, rushing out the door. Moments later, the President was speaking with the White House Doctor.

"I don't understand Reuben. You said he was making a recovery, and then all of a sudden, this happens! What went wrong," demanded the President, sorrow fueling his anger.

"Quite frankly, I've rarely seen this before, Mr. President. You are absolutely right. He did seem to be recovering well. All vital signs were normal, and he seemed to be in stable condition. Then, early this morning, his EKG showed a slight irregularity, so I ordered some additional tests." He paused, and then added, "You know about his pacemaker, right?"

"Of course," said the President.

48

"Well, generally, we would have immediately performed emergency surgery upon the Vice President's admittance to GW to remove the pace maker and replace it with another one, or one from an organ donor, but the Vice President was in such a fragile condition, it was not safe to do so. So, we were waiting for sufficient improvement in the Vice President's condition before scheduling surgery to remove and replace the pace maker with a new one. Based upon the improvement we were seeing, in fact, we were hoping to schedule his surgery for sometime early next week. Then, the EKG showed this irregularity, and just as the nurse came into his room to perform the tests I had ordered, the Vice President went into massive cardiac arrest. All attempts to revive him failed, I am sad to say." There was a brief silence on the line for a moment before Dr. Allenstein added, "Mr. President, I am so sorry. I know how close you two were."

"Thank you, Reuben."

The Oval Office, Five Minutes Later

The President, letting out a huge sigh, picked up the phone to call Anne Hillary. "Hello," cracked a voice on the other end of the line, obviously hoarse from crying for several hours.

"Oh, Anne," began the President, his voice beginning to crack, as well.

"Jack, I just can't believe it! Why," she wallowed.

"Anne," the President repeated, unsure whether he was able to shoulder the burden himself of the loss of one of his dearest friends, let alone comfort his widow at this very trying time. Regaining his composure, the President added, "You know if there is anything that Karen, I or the kids can do, just say so. In fact, I am on my way over now."

"No, that is not necessary. Thank you, Jack. We'll be fine," said Anne Hillary mustering all the determination of the gold medalist swimmer she once was.

"I mean it," reiterated the President. "Anything!"

"Jack, we'll get through this. I know we will. It will be difficult, no doubt," she said stoically. "All I ask is that you pick someone to succeed Rich who will finish all the hard work that you and he started together. I mean, ultimately, he paid the highest price one could pay, didn't he? But don't get me wrong," she continued. Jack Halliday knew right away that she was referring to her husband's lifelong battle, in politics, to achieve universal healthcare for every American, a goal the President was even more committed to achieving now than before.

49

The widow continued, "I am not bitter, Mr. President, believe me. He was a workaholic and an idealist, which is not a great combination especially when you are a politician, but that was who he was and part of the reason I loved him so much." She paused and started crying hysterically. Once the tears subsided, she said simply, "Anyways, that is how you can honor him, Mr. President, by selecting a qualified successor to finish what the two of you started."

Chapter Twelve
April 6, 2017

Arlington, Virginia

Following the Vice President 'lying in state' for two days in the Rotunda of the Capital, the day the President had dreaded had finally arrived - It was time to bury the body of the Vice President. The hearse carrying the body of the Vice President made the short jaunt across the River to Arlington Cemetery. The lengthy funeral procession followed, ultimately coming to a stop at the Vice President's final resting spot.

As a decorated Naval officer and veteran of one tour of duty in Vietnam (but, mainly because of his position as Vice President at the time of his death), the Vice-President was entitled to be buried at Arlington National Cemetery, which his family chose over being buried in his hometown of Chattanooga, Tennessee. The funeral ceremony was televised all over the world.

A twenty-one-gun salute followed the President's arrival. Once everyone was seated, the President then rose to deliver the eulogy for the Vice President, and one of his closest friends. He began, "Dear friends, the Hillary family, and fellow Americans, we are gathered here today to honor a true American patriot, and although it was only for a brief time, he was one of the best Vice Presidents this County has ever had, and one of the best friends I ever had." The President paused for a moment. Then, continued, "As many of you know, Rich and I first met in college, and immediately there was a connection. We then went our separate ways for a brief time, raising our respective families, but Rich was always the one who would call me and say Jack, I was just thinking of you and thought I would pick up the phone and say 'hi'; you know, that was just the kind of person he was, always thinking about other people and taking action. That, of course, led Rich to his career in politics. Always a committed advocate for the underclass, and most importantly the underinsured, he was a man on a mission, and it was not because of anything he personally had to gain. It was because it was the right thing to do, and that was all the mattered. He was a man of principle, and what fine principles they were."

The President paused again, realizing for the first time since he began speaking that he was now describing his close friend in the past tense. Once he regained his composure, he proceeded, "In all of his years in the United States Senate, he did not take a dime from lobbyists or Political Action Committees, making him free to follow his own ideals and conscience, which he continually adhered to, even in difficult times. And believe me, there were plenty of difficult times, but through it all, he managed to marry his high school sweetheart, raise two wonderful kids, and relish in his four amazing grandchildren. He was a good man. His legacy will always be remembered," the President concluded, glancing briefly in the direction of the Vice President's widow, Anne Hillary.

Once the President sat down, several close family members rose to speak, including the Vice President's children and grandchildren. Then, the President presented the American flag to the grieving widow personally, hugging and kissing her in the process.

As the crowd began to disperse, the President spoke with a few select individuals before entering the Presidential limousine and heading for Camp David.

Of those select few, the President made a special point of going out of his way to acknowledge his largest single donor, J. Robert Peck III. "Bob, thank you for coming. It means so much," said the President.

"Mr. President, really sir, my most since condolences," Peck consoled the President. "The Vice President was a dear friend to us all. Your words were so very kind," he said dabbing a handkerchief to his cheek.

"Thank you, Bob," but just as the President was about to pull away from Peck's wheelchair following this brief exchange, Peck brought him in closer and, in almost of a whisper, said, "Mr. President, I was wondering if I could get a few moments of your time later, if possible."

"Certainly, Bob," he said pausing momentarily, considering what he was about to propose. And even though many in his inner circle would later undoubtedly be unhappy with his decision, the President nonetheless offered, "Listen, Karen and I are heading down to Camp David for the weekend. Why don't you join us?"

"Mr. President, that really is not necessary. I just need a few minutes of your time."

"No, don't be silly. I insist. I will send Marine One to pick you up. I will have the White House Travel Secretary contact you to make arrangements," the President said walking away to greet other mourners.

Chapter Thirteen
April 6, 2017

In a Small Apartment, Outside Cape Canaveral, Florida

Poring over the 'Profiler Reports' he had printed earlier, Kallen read them intermittently with a report in one hand, and a beer in the other. Through his research, Kallen had learned that MedSupply Ltd., was not actually a medical supply company, but instead, was some sort of lobbying branch of Healthmed Inc., that lobbied for those prominent issues that impacted the Healthmed. Not lost on Kallen was the fact that the Company was in Florida instead of Washington, D.C. Apparently, MedSupply, Ltd., was comprised, in large part, of former lobbyists and Washington 'muckety mucks', as one would expect, but surprisingly, for reasons Kallen couldn't otherwise figure out, there were a few employees with classified backgrounds in the Intelligence Community on the payroll. More troubling, Kallen only learned this after entering his secure identification number into the Program.

One of those employees, it turns out, was Peter Stern, which was apparently a pseudonym of a pseudonym. His real name was Alexander Cain, and he was a former Sergeant in the U.S. Army's elite Ranger unit, with a dishonorable discharge for CUO or 'Conduct Unbefitting an Army Ranger' during his last tour of duty, in Reggah, Syria, fighting ISIS.

Kallen thought he recognized the name. He remembered that, when he served as Commander of the Naval Special Warfare Development Group or DEVGRU, better known as SEAL Team Six, he had a Luke Cain who served under him. He thought he recalled that Cain had a younger brother who was a Ranger in the 82nd Airborne Division a.k.a. 'the world's 911'.

Stern, or Cain or whoever he was, was employed as a Senior Vice President for Technology for MedSupply, Ltd. In addition to being a former Ranger, it appears the Army paid for him to attend

MIT to obtain his Bachelors and Masters from MIT in Computer Information Technologies.

He began working for Healthmed Inc., as an Assistant Vice President to the Chief Information Services Officer before being transferred to MedSupply Inc. One of the articles he read about Cain in his 'Profiler Report', printed from the San Jose Mercury News, had touted him as the rising star in the hottest Company in the Silicon Valley. Of course, there was no mention of his military background in the article; only his degrees and technology background were emphasized.

That's odd, Kallen thought to himself, while taking a swig of beer. *Why would a rising star be transferred to a lobbying subsidiary in Florida?* Almost immediately, he answered his own question, *Unless his location is significant for some reason.*

But, why would Florida be significant, especially, again, for lobbying purposes or for an up and coming IT guy, he wondered. Given the fact that he observed who he was now confident was Alexander Cain on the grounds of a secure Kennedy Space Center, he had to presume it had something to do with his mysterious appearance at the facility following the launch, but what could it be?

Almost absent mindedly, Kallen glanced down at the Washington Post sitting on the table. This was a little trick he learned from his former boss and mentor, the head of the National Security Agency (NSA) at the time; of course, that was before Kallen went back into the field for one very special assignment. He remembered his former boss saying, "When you reach an impasse in life, sometimes it helps to take a step back and look at the more parochial items life has to offer. Refocus," he would say.

He looked down at the newspaper. The headlines blared, '*Vice President Dies in Hospital. Search for Successor Begins*'. Even though he had moved here a while back, he still kept his subscription to that bastion of Washington liberalism, the Washington Post, to counter-balance it, he also had a subscription to the Wall Street Journal and the New Republic. He read each one every day. Nothing he recalled from the day's newspapers triggered anything for him. Instead, he made a mental note of Florida, and Cain, and moved on.

The next employee with an Intelligence background was Rick Marshall. Again, this was a pseudonym of a pseudonym. His real name was Mark Walker, and he was a former Chief Warrant Officer, U.S. Army (Ret.). Like Cain, Walker also had a background in computers, although not nearly as extensive as Cain's. During one of his postings, he was at NORAD, responsible for technology support at the Mountain Facility. MedSupply, Ltd., listed him as an Assistant Vice President for Technology. So, he was Cain's subordinate at the company. More significantly, based upon the photos in the file, Kallen was certain that Walker was the other guy from the van he observed arguing with Cain on the day of the launch.

Just as he reached for the next file, the telephone rang. Kallen immediately recognized the number.

"Hello," he answered.

"How is it going?"

Kallen proceeded to update the caller as to the results of his findings so far. "Forget it," blurted the voice on the other end of the line before he could finish. "What? What are you talking about?"

"Never mind that," said the caller excitedly, almost out of breath. "I am under a lot pressure to ensure that nothing impacts any of the upcoming launches. Therefore, unless you uncover something that potentially impacts any of the upcoming launches, you are to terminate your investigation, do you understand?"

Kallen reluctantly agreed. At least, that is what he would lead them to believe. But as with everything he did in life, he had every intention of completing what he had started.

Chapter Fourteen
April 7, 2017

Camp David, Maryland

The raging flames rippled through the large stone hearth in the middle of the room that warmed one of the world's most famous second homes, serving every President since Franklin D. Roosevelt to the present one. Seated next to The President and the First Lady, in his specially equipped wheelchair, was the man who, in no small part, had helped secure the election for the President, which allowed them to now enjoy this dramatic fire albeit under such somber circumstances.

"He was a tremendous patriot," began Peck. An un-permeated silence followed, lasting several minutes.

"And well loved and respected," Peck finally added. "He will be sorely missed."

"Thank you, Bob." After a few more cumbrous moments, the President asked, "So, what was it you wanted to speak with me about Bob?"

"I know it may be a bit too soon, sir, but have you given any thought to Rich's replacement?"

"I haven't, but I'm sure my staff has some ideas. Why?"

"Well, Mr. President, I know you have many fine candidates to consider which would both do Rich's memory honor, as well as make a fine Vice President. I just wanted to let you know that you may hear my name being bantered around,"

Oh boy, here it comes, anticipated the President. Much to his surprise, however, Peck humbly remarked, "I just want to let you know that I am officially taking my name off any so-called list."

Just then, Teddy Fitzpatrick entered the room. The President looked up at his right-hand man, and commented, "Teddy, your timing is impeccable. We were just discussing the possibility of Mr. Peck here filling the vacant position of Vice President of the United States of America."

Knowing what his chief aide was thinking, the President could only grin. The Chief of Staff rolled his eyes, but before he could say anything further, the President added, "Bob was just saying that he is taking his name off the list of potential nominees."

"Oh really, I did not realize he was on the list to begin with," Fitzpatrick said with apparent relief, but so as to not offend the President's guest, quickly added, "not that you wouldn't make an excellent Vice President, Mr. Peck. I just didn't realize your name was even under consideration."

"It's not," reiterated the biotech mogul. "I was just explaining to the President that there may be people bantering my name around and I wanted to make clear that, while flattered, I am quite content running my company and have no political aspirations whatsoever."

Fitzpatrick raised an eyebrow. For any other person, that would seem humble and the right thing to do, but knowing the philanthropist the way he did, Fitzpatrick was skeptical.

"Well, I would say you have done quite well for yourself Bob," interjected the President. "In fact, were it not for your abundant generosity, I think it is safe to say that we might not be sitting here today, for which, I am deeply grateful."

"Surely, you make more of it than it really is, Mr. President. I made some charitable donations and threw a couple of dinner parties: no more, no less." Again, for anyone else, such would seem unpretentious, but not coming from J. Robert Peck, one of the most influential men in American politics. There had to be something more, thought Teddy. Indeed, there was.

At that point, Peck shifted gears and inquired, "By the way, I was wondering which candidates you might be considering?"

Of course, you were, thought Teddy, but before he could quell any such inquiry, the President answered him. "Actually, you may have some good input on our current front-runner, Bob." Then, much to his Chief of Staff's dismay, the President blurted out, "We are considering Senator McClintock." There was a brief pause before the President added, "As you know, Bob, he is one of the leading proponents of healthcare reform."

Cringing at the fact that the President may have just shared too much information with an 'outsider' about a potential nominee that had not yet been properly vetted, Fitzpatrick quickly interjected, "Of course, talks are still only preliminary, and we are bantering several names back and forth, but nothing is final. Quite frankly, we have not even begun the vetting process. Consequently,

I am sure you can appreciate that these discussions must remain confidential, Bob. They do not leave this room, capiche?" he said.

Peck smiled ever so slightly at Fitzpatrick's crassness, remarking simply, "Of course. For what it's worth, I believe Henry would make a fine choice."

Attempting to lighten the mood, while at the same time hasten his friend's departure, the President commented, "Come now, enough of this talk. How is that golf game of yours going, Bob?" Looking at Peck in his wheelchair, Fitzpatrick was horrified that the President just made a bad joke in incredibly poor taste until Peck responded, "Not bad. It's improving, much like your approval ratings, Mr. President."

Both men laughed.

"Bob, I am sure you can appreciate that Teddy and I have important matters to discuss now," the President said excusing Peck. Recognizing his cue to leave, Peck responded, "Of course, Mr. President. Thank you again for having me here. Your hospitality has been really too much." He then abruptly turned his wheelchair and headed for the door, but not before embracing the President in a somewhat awkward arm lock causing the Secret Service agents in the room to stiffen a bit.

After he left, Teddy remarked, "You know, you really shouldn't be discussing potential nominees with anyone until our team has properly vetted them, Mr. President."

"Come now, Teddy, you worry too much. Bob can be trusted."

Meanwhile, aboard Marine One, J. Robert Peck's fingers frantically danced across his newly encrypted secure cell phone, and did not stop the entire twenty-five-minute flight back to D.C.

Chapter Fifteen
April 10, 2017

The Oval Office, Washington, D.C.

The President was massaging his temples when his Chief of Staff entered the Oval Office.

"That tough, huh?" he asked.

Shaking his head, the President simply remarked, "It's just that all of these candidates would make great nominees, Teddy."

"Of course, they would. That is why they are on the list in the first place. Right now, the task at hand is to evaluate, vet and select one of the individuals on that list. In that regard, however, I do have a bit of news. Of course, it is probably nothing, but we are checking it out now."

"Yes, Teddy, what is it?"

"Well, it's about Senator McClintock, sir. It seems that there was a complaint filed years ago with the Food and Drug Administration that 'Dr. McClintock', at the time, prescribed experimental drugs to individuals who were not authorized to receive such medication."

"I don't understand, Henry has not practiced medicine in over thirty years."

"Like I said, this was years ago, at a time when he was still practicing medicine."

"But, how come it is just coming to light now? I mean Henry has been through dozens of elections. How come no one else ever raised this issue before in any of those elections?"

"I don't know, sir. Like I said, we are looking into it."

"Yeah, do that, and do it right away too, Teddy. I am not going to let this railroad Henry's nomination in the slightest so let's get to the bottom of this immediately, okay?"

"Yes, sir."

"Our window of opportunity is closing here. I need to put forth a name soon. The Nation cannot perceive any instability with this Administration. I want everything you have regarding this matter by the end of the day, Teddy. Thank you," he said, excusing Fitzpatrick.

The Chief of Staff left the Oval Office while, all throughout the day, nervous pimple faced White House staffers gathered, organized, and devoured every morsel of information they could scrounge regarding the Senator from Oregon and his medical practice prior to entering politics. Couriers raced back and forth between the White House and the Food and Drug Administration Building. Still, by 3:00 p.m. that day, however, there was not much concerning the purported prescription Complaint with the FDA other than a memorandum from a doctor whose name was hard to pronounce.

Reaching what appeared to be an impasse, with time running out, Teddy Fitzpatrick picked up the phone and called over to the FDA. After speaking with a few nervous operators once he identified himself, the White House Chief of Staff was finally transferred to a Dr. Malcomovich. A barely audible "Hello" came across the other end of the receiver.

"Dr. Malcomovich?"

"Yes," responded the doctor weakly.

"This is Teddy Fitzpatrick, Chief of Staff to the President of the United States."

"Yes," responded the doctor, even weaker now.

"I have a couple of questions. As you may have heard, the President is considering certain individuals to replace the late Vice President, and during that process, a memorandum has recently surfaced that you apparently drafted some years ago."

"Yes," the weakest, by far.

"Well, it references a complaint against a doctor in the 1970s for prescribing a drug that the FDA had not yet approved, but it is unclear as to the drug prescribed, only the doctor who prescribed it."

"And who is that?" asked the doctor, uttering his first full sentence since the conversation began.

"You understand that discretion is required here, of course."

"Of course."

"The complaint concerns Senator McClintock."

"I don't understand," responded the doctor. "Mr. Fitzpatrick, as I am sure you are well aware, the Senator has not practiced medicine in nearly thirty years."

"Yes, I am well aware of that. However, once again, it appears that this memorandum, which you apparently authored some years back is just surfacing now, which also raises another issue altogether."

"Which is?"

"Well, doesn't it seem odd to you doctor that this Memorandum would appear now after all this time."

"I'm not certain I understand, Mr. Fitzpatrick. Perhaps, you could tell me what memorandum we are talking about and I can research the matter and get back to you."

"There is no time for that now," barked Fitzpatrick, growing increasingly impatient with Dr. Malcomovich. "You might say that this is somewhat of an urgent matter. As we have been speaking, a secured drop box has been set up in your government e-mail account which contains the memorandum we have been discussing. Please open it now."

As instructed, Doctor Malcomovich proceeded to open the newly created drop box in his e-mail account. Sure enough, in it, was a PDF document, which the doctor proceeded to open. The following instantly appeared on his computer screen.

From: Dr. John Malcomovich, M.D., Assistant Clinical Scientist To: Morris Krammer, Ph.D., Director
It has recently come to the Department's attention that several prominent doctors and psychiatrists throughout the country have been prescribing methylenedioxymethamphetamine, more commonly known as MDMA, a drug which the Department has not yet approved, in order to enhance communication in patient sessions and reportedly allow users to achieve insights about their problems. Some doctors have even gone as far as to describe it as 'penicillin for the soul'. However, recently we received a complaint from a Portland, Oregon woman who suffered severe side effects because of a drug her family physician, Dr. Henry McClintock, prescribed. Ultimately, she had to be hospitalized. Therefore, we recommend instituting further testing of this drug to determine whether it is safe for human consumption.

"Although the memorandum is undated, which is odd in and of itself, we believe it must have been written sometime in the Seventies since Dr. Krammer was head of the FDA from 1971 to 1977. Do you recall writing such a memo back in the Seventies, Doctor?"

"No, I do not. I must have written thousands of such memorandums during my forty plus years at the Department."

"You are telling me that, notwithstanding the recent popularity of the street form of the drug known as Ecstasy, you can't recall writing such a memorandum during your time at the FDA?" asked Fitzpatrick incredulously.

"No," the doctor said, gaining a little more confidence now. "I can honestly say that I do not. I am sorry I cannot be more help, Mr. Fitzpatrick."

"Oh, I don't know about that. I think you have been a tremendous help," said Fitzpatrick facetiously, figuring the doctor was clearly hiding something. "Just one more question, Doctor."

"Yes?"

"How come it is not dated? Doesn't that strike you as odd, Doctor?"

"Yes, as a matter of fact, it does. It has always been my normal practice to date all memoranda I draft. May I inquire how you obtained this Memorandum, Mr. Fitzpatrick."

Frustrated with Doctor Malcomovich's pomposity, Fitzpatrick simply slammed the receiver down in response.

Chapter Sixteen
Late Afternoon on April 10, 2017

The Oval Office, Washington, D.C.

The President was just finishing his conversation with the Speaker of the House about potential replacements for Vice President as the Chief of Staff knocked before entering the Oval Office. The President waived him in. Speaking directly into the speaker phone, the President commented, "Your objection is duly noted Mr. Speaker. Again, it is just a preliminary list."

Fitzpatrick could only smile, imagining the Speaker's reddened face upon receipt of the President's preliminary list of potential nominees to replace Vice President Hillary.

"No, no, I understand, Mr. Speaker. Thank you, I will be in touch shortly."

"Well, that seems like it went well," remarked Teddy, grinning sarcastically.

The President raised an eyebrow. "How is it going on your end?" he asked.

"Not much better, unfortunately. Malcomovich claims he does not recall writing the memorandum or why it was undated."

"You don't believe him," asked the President. Fitzpatrick shook his head. "So, what do you want to do?"

"Well, I have some ideas, but the first order of business should be to put out preliminary feelers through the Leadership in the House and Senate to determine whether they would even consider this an issue concerning Henry's nomination."

"Agreed. Have Jonas make some calls, will you. What are your other ideas?"

"In the meantime, sir, we should have the FBI investigate Malcomovich."

"Agreed, please place a call to Director Stephens Teddy," instructed the President. The Chief of Staff smiled, and abruptly left the Oval Office, racing for his own office, next door.

White House Chief of Staff's Office, Washington, D.C.

Back in his office, Fitzpatrick reversed the order of priorities he had just discussed with the President. Instead of first assembling a team to investigate the viability of a McClintock nomination, his first order of business was to place a call to Director Stephens of the FBI.

FBI Director Mark Stephens had spent most of his entire career in law enforcement, with the exception of a few years on the Federal Bench. After finishing law school at the University of Virginia, he became an Assistant United States Attorney, working his way all the way up to becoming the United States Attorney for the District of Columbia. He held that position until President Clinton nominated him as United States District Judge for the District of Columbia, and he received near unanimous Senate confirmation. In 2006, Judge Stephens retired from the Federal Bench. He was appointed as Director of the FBI when James Comey resigned following the whole election letter fiasco.

"Judge Stephens, Teddy Fitzpatrick here. Do you have a moment?"

Director Stephens never cared much about politics (especially Jack Halliday's) or how things were done in Washington, but he knew how the game was played, and he played along. "What can I do for you, Mr. Fitzpatrick?" asked the FBI Director.

Fitzpatrick then went on to describe the precarious predicament in which the Administration now found itself given the emergence of the mysterious Malcomovich memorandum. The Director agreed to assign one of his best agents to investigate the authenticity of the purported memorandum. Given the sensitive and, more apropos, political nature of the investigation, the Director decided to assign someone he could implicitly trust who he knew would be discreet.

Chapter Seventeen
Eight Weeks After the NASA Launch, April 15, 2017

In a Cramped Apartment, Outside Cape Canaveral, Florida

Coursing through the 'People Finder Reports' for a second time, Kallen was surprised to learn how many red flags he had missed during his initial review of the Reports. While it is true Harbath had told him to stop his investigation, Kallen was not one to fail to finish what he started, nor did he respond well to authority. Besides, he figured he could not rule out any future attacks without ruling out a past one, so he continued reading page after page about every employee of MedSupply Ltd.

By the time he finished during the early morning hours Saturday, and several beers later, he was confident that he had uncovered something. MedSupply Ltd. was in fact a Medical Supply lobbying company; that is, although at first blush, he thought he may have uncovered something, he really uncovered nothing at all.

While it was true that Cain (or Stern or whatever he called himself) had an impressive, albeit somewhat questionable military background, much like Kallen, there was not much else there. Also, it was not uncommon for companies to move employees laterally as Cain had done, thought Kallen.

Next, after hours of poring over those reports, he realized he didn't have a 'People Finder Report' for the second participant of that somewhat clandestine meeting at Kennedy was not among any of the employees of MedSupply, suggesting a possible dead end. Kallen, however, did not rise to the upper echelon of the intelligence community, in his past life before space, for accepting 'no' as an answer or taking the easy way out. He needed to probe further, and there was no better place to start than at the top. So, he pulled up everything he could on J. Robert Peck, Chairman and CEO of Healthmed Inc.

Almost immediately, Kallen was surprised to learn that Peck was born in a foreign American Embassy, the son of two career Diplomats. That was not the surprising part. What was surprising was the fact that the location of the Embassy was listed as 'Classified', and the names and positions of his parents were unlisted. Once Kallen entered his top-level security clearance code, he conducted various searches which led him to the conclusion that the Embassy where Peck was born, and where his parents were stationed, was the one in Beirut, Lebanon. *That was even more odd*, thought Kallen. Having a penchant for history and considering himself somewhat of a history buff, Kallen knew that there was no embassy in Beirut when Peck was born in 1951. Embassy status did not happen until the following year. Before then, there was only a U.S. legation team of six diplomats stationed in Beirut.

That might not be so unusual, thought Kallen, if Peck's parents were working for the offshoot of the OSS at the time, the relatively nubile Central Intelligence Agency that was created years earlier, under Truman. Given the Agency's relative infancy then, Kallen knew that it would not be uncommon for records to be doctored initially and later modified to be factually accurate once a particular objective was achieved, or target was compromised. Apparently, in the case of Peck's parents, it was possible that due to unforeseen circumstances, the correct information never made it into the file for some reason. At least, that was the simple explanation, but Kallen was not one for simple answers. He needed to dig further, and that was exactly what he was intended to do.

Chapter Eighteen
April 17, 2017

Chevy Chase, Maryland

Dr. Malcomovich noticed the conspicuous government issue sedan parked outside his Maryland townhouse from a quarter of a mile away as he drove the tree lined street. What he did not notice, however, was the FBI surveillance van parked around the block. As he exited his vehicle, the two Special Agents from the FBI's D.C. Office flashed their badges and asked if they could accompany him inside. He agreed.

After a few moments of small talk, the lead agent got down to business. "Mr. Malcomovich," began the agent.

"Doctor," interrupted Malcomovich.

"Excuse me," responded Special Agent Johnson. "It's Doctor Malcomovich."

"Right, Doctor Malcomovich," the Agent corrected himself, simultaneously rolling his eyes at his partner. "We understand that the President's Chief of Staff has been in contact with you about a note you wrote some years ago," offered Agent Johnson.

Feigning ignorance, at first, Dr. Malcomovich replied, "What?" and paused for a minute before responding, "Oh, that."

Agent Johnson raised an eyebrow and looked to his partner. I mean, who does not remember being contacted by the White House Chief of Staff, no matter what your position or how long you have been around Washington, thought Johnson.

"Yes, that." Johnson continued, "Do you have an actual recollection of writing that memorandum?" inquired Agent Johnson, while both he and his partner carefully observed Malcomovich's response and accompanying hand gestures. As a seasoned law enforcement officer, with more than twenty-two years' experience, this was where Agent Johnson earned his bread and butter.

At first, Malcomovich paused. Then, he proceeded to confirm what he told Teddy Fitzpatrick. Sensing he was lying, Special Agent

Johnson decided to throw a curve ball at him to see how Malcomovich reacted.

"Mr.," then correcting himself as if absent mindedly, "I mean, Doctor Malcomovich," continued Special Agent Johnson. "As you may have heard, we have a special device back at the office called a polygraph." He paused for a bit, and then added condescendingly, "You've heard of them, right?"

Malcomovich, confused, managed to sputter softly, "Yes, of course."

"Well, would you mind coming downtown with us now and taking one?"

"Agent," began the doctor.

"Actually, it's Special Agent," interrupted Johnson, smiling.

"Right. Anyways, as I was saying 'Special Agent', I do not like where this conversation is going. Do I need a lawyer?"

Using his standard line whenever someone asked him that question, Johnson responded, "I don't know, do you, Doctor? Is there something you are feeling guilty about?"

"Let's just say that I am not comfortable with what you are suggesting. Perhaps, it would be best if I contacted my attorney. If, after I speak with my attorney, you are still interested in me coming downtown, I am sure arrangements can be made at that time."

"Of course, I would be happy to send a car to pick you up," said Agent Johnson, teasing him a bit.

"It's okay, I am sure I will be able to manage," said the doctor, dead serious.

"Fine, suit yourself," said Agent Johnson. "Here is my card," said Johnson, handing him a card with the FBI logo on it with bold letters which read, "Special Agent in Charge, Washington D.C. Office."

As the two FBI agents walked down the pathway toward their Crown Vic, Johnson asked the other agent, "Was there anything wrong with my tone?"

"I thought you were fine," he said, shrugging his shoulders.

Later That Day, White House Chief of Staff's Office, Washington, D.C.

"Mr. Fitzpatrick, Director Stephens is on the phone," announced Fitzpatrick's longtime administrative assistant, who made the move to D.C with him earlier in the year.

"Thank you, Maria."

Without even greeting his caller, Fitzpatrick barked into the speakerphone on his desk, "So, what do you have for me?" Manners, or subtlety, were not some of his finer points.

"Good afternoon to you too, Mr. Fitzpatrick," responded FBI Director Stephens facetiously who did not appreciate being spoken to in that tone, whether it was from the White House Chief of Staff, or even the President, himself.

"Yeah, yeah, so?" pushed Fitzpatrick harder.

"Well, it is not so much what he said during our initial interview as what he didn't say, and more significantly, what he did afterwards."

"I'm listening."

"It seems that, after two of my top agents left his home, the surveillance van parked around the corner from his home picked up a call he placed to a secure number. I am going to play the tape now. 'You there? What the hell is going on? You said it was nothing, there would be no follow up or anything like that.' Becoming even angrier, Malcomovich shouted, "I am not going to calm down! I just can't believe it. If this comes out, it can ruin me!"

"Excuse me, Mr. Director," interrupted Fitzpatrick, "why is it we cannot hear what the person on the other end of the line is saying?"

"Well, that's the kicker! The number which he was calling employed such highly sophisticated encryption technology that my agents have been unable to determine what the other person is saying. Sir, we are talking military grade."

"Are you telling me he is speaking with someone inside the government or military?"

"I am afraid that is precisely the problem, sir. We do not know who is speaking with."

"Well, find out, and fast too," barked Fitzpatrick before hanging up.

Chapter Nineteen
April 18, 2017

The Oval Office, the White House, Washington, D.C.

Teddy Fitzpatrick burst into the Oval Office boasting, "I am pleased to report that we have solid information that the Malcomovich report is false, Mr. President." Before he could utter another word, however, the President, glaring at one of the television monitors in the room roared, "Are you watching this?" The President was the most animated Fitzpatrick recalls seeing him in recent years.

Uncertain what was unfolding, but more annoyed with himself for not being the one to bring it to the President's attention, he quickly came around to get a better view of what was on the television screen. The President was switching the channels back and forth between CNN and Fox. Then, he saw it. On display for the entire American public to see was the Malcomovich Memorandum he was just about to discuss with the President. A reporter could be heard in the background saying, "A Memorandum from the Food and Drug Administration has just recently surfaced about then 'Doctor', and now 'Senator McClintock', who is on the short list to become the next Vice President of the United States." The Fox correspondent snickered, correcting herself, "I mean was…" The President turned the sound off.

· "Did you know about this?"

"Not exactly, Mr. President, but as I was saying, FBI Director Stephens believes the Memorandum is not authentic."

"Teddy, you're missing the point. I learned early on as a young trial lawyer that you can't unring a bell that has been rung. Once the jury, or in this case the American people, hears this stuff about Henry, we can hope to mitigate the damage, but it will always be lingering out there." Sure enough, just then, Nora interrupted that Senator McClintock was on the line.

"Hank," began the President cautiously, picking up the receiver from speaker mode. "I know, I know, Teddy and I were just watching it," he said, referring to the present media blitz.

"This is bullshit!" yelled McClintock. "I am sorry, Mr. President," he continued, regaining his composure. "But I did not sign up for this."

"Come on, Hank this isn't your first rodeo. You know how the game is played. You've been through the ringer before."

"Yeah, well I've seen some pretty shady things in my time in D.C, but this pretty much takes the cake," complained the Senator. Clearing his throat, which sounded like it was cracking at this point, "Mr. President, I am calling to advise you that I am officially withdrawing my name for consideration for Vice President of the United States. I am honored you would even consider me, and I am sorry to have brought such shame to the Administration."

Now, it was the President's turn to cuss. "Bullshit, Hank! You're not getting off that easy. This is just a bump in the road. We have to fight this," the President urged his longtime friend, knowing ultimately the Senator was right. McClintock would have to go. ·

"Jack, I am tired," McClintock said, appealing to their personal friendship by not referring to the President by title, an otherwise unforgivable sin in Washington under any other circumstance. Finally, the Oregon Senator offered, "I have a family, Jack. It's not fair to them, especially at this stage in my life. For Christ's sake, it's not just my own kids I have to think about, I have grandkids too now. How do you think they are going to feel being asked about their grandfather being called the 'Drugstore Doctor', as I understand they are now referring to me. Please Jack."

The President figured he could not argue with that but was livid. He ordered a full-scale investigation into the leak and would have his staff issue a Press-Release later.

Redwood City, California

J. Robert Peck pushed the button for the private elevator adjoining his Penthouse Office Suite. Once the bell announced the elevator car's arrival, he inserted his key, the only one in existence (or at least so he believed), into the keyhole positioned at a level accessible for Peck's wheelchair. Once he heard that ever so familiar click, and the elevator door opened, he pushed the sole button on the console. Next, he placed his index finger on top of the keypad adjacent to the button he had just pushed and waited. It was a practice he had grown accustomed to over the last twenty-five years.

Recognizing the crisscrossing friction ridges of Peck's fingertip, the doors closed, and the elevator descended a quarter mile to a subterranean bunker containing some of the most technologically advanced communication equipment the world has ever known, at least the civilian word. Even though the bunker was initially constructed when the building was built twenty-five years ago, the communication equipment was updated every year, bi-annually.

When the doors finally opened after the lengthy descent, Peck approached a 72" monitor on the far wall where he inserted the same key he just used to summon the elevator into a separate keyhole, again at wheelchair level. Next, he placed his face directly in front of the retina scanner below the monitor, which completed its full retinal scan of Peck's right eyeball. Then, a series of numbers began flashing on the monitor, and after about a minute or so, a computer-generated voice came over the Bose speakers.

"Why the sudden advancement of the plan?" inquired the voice.

"It's just a small hitch, but I thought it was best to advance the time frame," responded Peck.

"And you did not first consult with us?"

Us, thought Peck. He hated that. He knew there was no 'us', but only one very omnipotent 'him'. Even though, in many ways, he was like a father figure to Peck, Peck never knew his true identity and never met him in person. One thing he knew for sure though was that there was no one else in charge.

, Peck spoke slowly and deliberately, "The FBI recently paid a visit to one of my sources who was beginning to panic. So, I decided to go public earlier than initially planned."

There was a silence before the voice on the other end spoke again, "Just to be clear, we did not plan anything. '*You*," he said, emphasizing the pronoun, "were given express orders: Orders, which were expected to be carried out. Remember," the voice on the line continued. "We made you what you are today, and just as easily can take that all away."

"Not true," countered Peck. "You need me for my relationship with the President, not to mention the vast financial resources I offer."

Peck continued, "Let's not lose focus. Yes, the timing of the release of the McClintock Memorandum was advanced, but the result will ultimately be the same. The President will have no choice but to withdraw his name from the Nomination. Then, the stage will be set."

"It better be. Just remember who is in charge here. No more mistakes or miscalculations on your part, understand?" Then, the line went dead.

After a moment, Peck returned to his Penthouse Office Suite.

The FBI Director's Office, Hoover Building, Washington D.C.

Two of the Agency's best cipher-tech analysts were standing before Director Stephens' cluttered desk attempting to explain the unexplainable.

"So, what you are saying is that, despite some of the most technologically advanced equipment on the planet, we are still unable to determine who Malcomovich was speaking to?"

The agents looked at one another before simply offering an uncomfortable nod. "Great!" yelled the director, slamming his fist into the stack of papers on his desk that scattered everywhere. Regaining his composure, and reshuffling the papers on his desk, the director continued, "Basically, then, what you are saying is that there is some political saboteur out there that is using communications equipment more sophisticated than the United States, or its Western Allies, possess?"

Once again, a disappointing nod and shrug of the shoulder by the analysts. "Okay, thank you gentlemen." The two analysts then left the Director's Office.

After they left, Stephens hesitated, dreading the next call he was about to make. Then, he finally pushed the button for his Executive Assistant.

"Mary, get Teddy Fitzpatrick on the line for me."

Moments later, he was connected to the White House Chief of Staff. "Good morning, Mr. Director. Do you have any news for me?"

"Yes, but unfortunately, none of it, good. We still have been unable to decipher who or what jammed the Malcomovich telephone call but are continuing our efforts in that regard." Then, reminiscent of a comment he himself had made only moments ago, the White House Chief of Staff said disgustedly, "So, what you are telling me is that the Agency that is charged with protecting Americans across this Country and throughout the World, with all the resources the U.S. Government has to offer, cannot decipher a single telephone call."

"Yes, sir, I am afraid that is exactly what I am saying, but I am confident that with enough time, we will be able to answer that question. In the meantime, we have other options available."

"What is that?" asked Fitzpatrick.

"We could press Malcomovich more. Based upon what I have seen so far, my guess is he will roll over and tell us what we want to know."

"Do it," Fitzpatrick said, ending the call.

Chapter Twenty
April 19, 2017

Rayburn House Office Building, Washington D.C.

The Congressman from Iowa entered his office, as he routinely had done for the last ten years. The cramped space was cluttered with papers and staff mulling over Committee issues and dealing with constituents' phone calls. He greeted his staff before heading into his office and shutting the door. He perused the articles from the New York Times, Washington Post and Wall Street Journal that his staff had selected for him from the day's editions. As expected, virtually all the highlighted articles dealt with the leak of the Malcomovich Memorandum. 'Oregon Senator Prescribed Illegal Medicine during Medical Practice in the Seventies', blared one headline. Another one read, 'Memorandum Surfaces Showing Oregon Senator, and Frontrunner for the Vice-Presidential Nomination, Prescribed Illegal Drug During the Seventies'. The last one read, 'FDA McClintock Memorandum All but Dooms Vice Presidential Nomination for Senator McClintock'. After reading all the articles thoroughly and skimming other highlighted portions of the papers, he placed a call to the Speaker of the House, a man with whom he had developed a close personal relationship over the last ten years since arriving in Washington D.C.

"Good morning, Mr. Speaker. I take it you've seen the articles about Senator McClintock."

"I have," was the response. "Most unsettling, I must say."

"Yes, indeed. He is a good man. Such a shame. Any ideas who will replace him on the 'Short List'?" inquired the Congressman.

"Well, I think it is still a bit premature, but from what I have seen from Halliday so far, I think it safe to presume it will be someone from the far left, which of course, we will fight, and fight hard."

"I would expect nothing less of you for your Party, sir."

As stalwarts for their respective parties, and their traditional beliefs, it was a given that the two Congressmen often did not agree politically. Nevertheless, they remained close personal friends.

"Now, if he was smart," continued the Speaker. "He would pick someone more moderate like you who can gather support from both sides of the aisle. I mean, after all, he knows he needs a majority of both Houses to confirm the next Vice President of the United States. In fact, I received an interesting call from the President when the Vice President first entered the hospital; call it a courtesy call, if you will. He was urging me to support any potential nominee for Vice President if it came to that, which clearly, it has now."

"Mr. Speaker, I am flattered that you would suggest me as a candidate for the job, but I hardly think I am in the running for the nomination." He laughed heartedly. "In fact, I don't even think I have been invited to the White House under the present Administration. Quite frankly, I'd be surprised if Jack Halliday even knows who I am."

"Oh, if he doesn't, he will now. I can assure you that," the Speaker said, as if a plan was taking shape in his head.

"Again, Mr. Speaker, I am flattered, but hardly think I am qualified for the position, having just been elected to my Fifth Term in Congress."

"Don't be silly, Jedidiah, you are more than qualified." Then, after a brief interruption on his end of the line, the Speaker abruptly said, "Sorry Jed, something has just come up. I have to run. Are we still on for lunch next week?"

"Of course," responded the Congressman from Iowa.

Chevy Chase, Maryland

The two FBI agents wandered down the same path they had meandered down only a couple of days earlier. Agent Johnson spoke to his partner, armed with an arrest warrant in hand. Agent Johnson was in the middle of his sentence when suddenly there was a huge explosion, accompanied by a thundering roar, throwing both agents to the ground. Orange and yellow flames illuminated the blue sky. The Malcomovich residence was consumed in flames. Billowing clouds of grey smoke shielded the sunlight this crisp winter morning creating a grey dreariness throughout the immediate vicinity.

A bit dazed and confused, Agent Johnson, stumbled to his feet and immediately checked on the other agent. Like Johnson, he was a bit shaken up, but ultimately, was fine. They radioed for back up, as well as other emergency vehicles.

Two hours later, after the corpse of Dr. John Malcomovich was removed from the charred remains of his suburban Maryland town home, arson and FBI investigators canvassed the property. It would later be determined that the fire was the result of a hidden slow and persistent gas leak. In fact, Malcomovich's utility records supported such a finding.

Normally, without evidence of arson, an autopsy would not be conducted, but Agent Johnson specifically ordered an FBI pathologist to perform one given the curious timing of the explosion. The findings turned out to be inconclusive.

The FBI Director's Office, Hoover Building, Washington, D.C.

Days later, Johnson briefed FBI Director Stephens in his office.

"So, let me get this straight, you and Marshall were approaching the subject's residence to serve, or at least threaten to serve," the Director corrected himself, "an arrest warrant when suddenly, there was an unexpected explosion, and Dr. John Malcomovich is later pronounced dead at the scene. Now, you're telling me it was ruled to be an accident?" asked the Director, incredulously.

"I don't know, I just don't like it Frank," the Director continued, shaking his head.

The Special Agent in charge of the DC Office simply shrugged.

"First, a panicked doctor makes an encrypted call to a number so secure that even our most sophisticated technology cannot determine who he was calling after a couple of FBI agents' visit unannounced. Then, just as those same agents reappear at his home to serve an arrest warrant, there is an explosion that is now being ruled an accident. I mean Frank, you have been an agent for almost as long as I have been a lawyer – doesn't that sound fishy to you?"

"Believe me, Mr. Director, I have exhausted all avenues during my investigation of the matter, going so far as to threaten a court injunction to the locals who refused to perform an autopsy after their arson investigators determined it was an 'accidental' cause of loss. They kept insisting that Malcomovich's utility records indicated a latent gas leak that had gone undetected for a while now. Finally, after I threatened to usurp the case, they relented, and agreed to release the body to us for one of our pathologists to perform an autopsy. I even used the Bureau's best pathologist, who is usually booked months in advance, for the autopsy. Unfortunately, she reached the same conclusion that the locals did: she determined that the cause of death was due solely to the gas explosion. There was no physical evidence to suggest otherwise, sir. That is, with the exception of severe third-degree burns covering the entire torso, arms, legs and head, as one would expect, there were no wounds to the exterior of the body that would suggest foul play prior to the explosion; no cuts, scrapes or abrasions. And, the interior of the lungs was consistent with the primary cause of death: respiratory failure."

Seemingly unconvinced, the director mustered only a "Hmm" in response.

Chapter Twenty-One
April 19, 2017

The Oval Office, the White House, Washington, D.C.

"Thank you for coming, Sam," said the President, greeting the Governor from Maine. "Of course, Mr. President," replied the Governor, shaking the President's and Teddy

Fitzpatrick's hands, in that order, as he entered the Oval Office.

"As you know, the Vice President's sudden and unexpected passing has left me in quite a bit of a 'pickle.'" That was the President for you, thought Fitzpatrick, using quaint vernacular expressions to describe a potential Constitutional crisis.

"Mr. President, we all mourn the Vice President. On a more personal note, I am very sorry for your loss personally, sir, as I know the two of you were close," responded Governor Haskins. "It was a terrible loss for the entire Nation."

"Thank you, Sam." The President paused for a moment. Then, continued, "Yes, in any case, Teddy and I were both saying that you would be a good candidate to replace the Vice President. I mean, given your experience on the Foreign Affairs Committee when you were a Congressman, you certainly have the foreign affairs experience, and now, for the last five years, you have executive experience too. Better yet, you did not make many enemies during your time in Congress, which I must say is an impressive feat, in and of itself, and will prove useful during the Confirmation proceedings." The President was doing such a hard sell that he could have easily passed for a used car salesman trying to dish off an old used Pinto to some unsuspecting buyer, except in this case, the President was selling the Governor on himself.

"Wow," said the Governor, a bit taken back. "I really am flattered, I truly am, but here's the thing, Mr. President, you and I are two different types of politicians. With all due respect, I tend to be much more of a pragmatist, and believe there is a lot of work to be done in Maine now. I know, it sounds crazy to say, 'Maine needs me', but it does. I would feel like I would be leaving a job unfinished there, only to return to D.C. to effectively accomplish nothing Yes, it is true that, in seven years, I might be a prime candidate for the Nation's highest Office." He hesitated before saying, "But that is not necessarily what I want. Mr. President, I want to finish what I started in Maine, sir, as cliché as that may sound."

Now, it was the President and his Chief of Staff who were momentarily taken back. They had, after all, carefully considered the Governor's background before making the offer, and were confident the Governor was going to accept the nomination. The awkwardness of the moment was short lived as Deputy Chief of Staff Jonas Frank knocked before entering the Oval Office.

"I am sorry to interrupt sir, but may I have a word with you," he asked his boss. Fitzpatrick grimaced at being interrupted at that precise moment. Nonetheless, he complied.

"Excuse me," said Fitzpatrick, following his Deputy out of the office.

Once in Fitzpatrick's office, Frank said, "I am sorry, sir, Director Stephens called and said it was urgent." Moments later, the White House Chief of Staff related to the Director of the FBI.

"What is that you just said, Director?" Teddy Fitzpatrick said in disbelief.

"You heard me correctly the first time, Mr. Fitzpatrick. Dr. Malcomovich was killed today in an explosion at his suburban Maryland town home as Agents were about to serve an arrest warrant on him. We are, of course, presently investigating the matter, and will keep you and the President updated as we get more information."

Fitzpatrick could only fall back in his chair, speechless.

Redwood City, California

Speaking from the secure communications center a quarter mile beneath the monstrosity in the West Silicon Valley that was the headquarters of Healthmed Inc., Peck exclaimed excitedly, "What the hell was that?" Then, remembering who he was speaking to, Peck curbed his tone dramatically, asking more calmly, "I mean, was that really necessary?"

"You question our methods, now?" asked the voice on the other end of the line.

Peck, again, thought it was curious – his use of the word 'our' when Peck knew, in fact, he was the only one calling the shots.

"No, but my source was secure."

"Was he?"

"Yes." Peck paused before continuing, "True, he became a little unnerved after that unexpected visit from the Feds the other day, but he was a source that I had cultivated over a long period of time. I am confident he would have been fine left to his own resources. Now, we have only raised suspicion with the questionable timing of his unseemly demise."

Silence. Then, abruptly changing subjects, the voice on the other end of the line asked, "What do you know about this Haskins fellow?"

"Should be a non-issue," Peck quickly replied. "He is a true 'bleeding heart liberal' who will take one for the cause."

Unfamiliar with Peck's use of the vernacular, there was an awkward silence on the line for a moment. Then Peck, recognizing his mistake, elaborated, "You see, he is an idealist who puts principles before ambition," said Peck, equally disdainful. As long as he believes there is more work to be done in Maine, he will not accept the nomination for Vice President. In his mind, he can accomplish what he needs to do in Maine, finishing what he started, and at the same time be in the same, or an even better, position to run for President in eight years."

"What if you have miscalculated and he accepts the nomination?"

Peck's irritation was growing every minute. Remain respectful, he reminded himself. "I have not miscalculated," he insisted. Playing it safe, he continued, "And if I have somehow misjudged the Governor, it certainly will not be hard to discredit him as I understand he was quite the ladies' man the last time he was in D.C."

"Don't you think it will be odd to have a second scandal in such a short period of time?"

"In Washington?" Peck laughed wholeheartedly. "Just another routine day in our Nation's Capital during political high season," responded Peck.

Chapter Twenty-Two
April 25, 2017

The Members Dining Room, Washington, D.C.

The two Congressmen sat at their regular luncheon table, as they had done for the last nine years, ever since the freshmen Congressman saved the Speaker's daughter from a freak accident in front of the Library of Congress. They were, without a doubt, the oddest couple in this town – one of the most powerful men in all of D.C., side by side with a virtually unknown Congressman from Iowa, laughing, and sometimes bickering back and forth like an old married couple. Their politics, constituency, upbringing and religious backgrounds couldn't be more different, but somehow, every Tuesday, there they sat at their regular table; the Speaker's Table.

Their strange bond began shortly after the Congressman from Iowa arrived in D.C. One day, while walking back to his office from the Library of Congress, a drunk driver lost control of his vehicle and careened over the barricades heading for a class of school children that were there visiting the Library. The Congressman reacted quickly, pushing a group of kids out of the way of the oncoming vehicle. It turns out that one of those kids was none other than the Speaker of the House of Representative's daughter. Many have since questioned the Congressman's impeccable timing of being in the right place at the right time. Nevertheless, an odd friendship developed between the young Congressman and the Speaker, which only solidified over the years.

Invariably, at least half a dozen different Congressmen would interrupt their meal, seeking to gain favor with the Speaker while, at the same time, lobbying for various bills they had recently introduced. Meanwhile, other than the curt obligatory greeting, the Speaker's guest would go virtually unnoticed.

During the last couple of weeks, the Congressmen's conversation always gravitated toward the hottest topic in politics.

"I understand that the President met with Governor Haskins last week," began the Speaker. "I wonder what they were discussing. Perhaps, federal funding for the new Planned Parenthood in Southeastern Maine," quipped the Speaker facetiously, furrowing a brow to see if he got the Junior Congressman's attention.

Not missing a beat, the Congressman from Iowa responded, "I think Governor Haskins would make a fine Vice President."

"Then, it's too bad he turned the President down," commented the Speaker.

"Why would he do that?"

"Other priorities, I guess. Not as glamorous as running the great State of Maine," said the Speaker, mocking the Governor, in part, for staying true to his values. "In any case, that leaves an opening for someone just like you who could rally support from both 'sides of the aisle'; someone who is young, healthy, and parries moderate views on both domestic and foreign policy."

"Again, Mr. Speaker, while I am certainly flattered, I don't believe I would make the best nominee."

"So, you keep saying," quipped the Speaker. "That is going to have to change. Anyways, I have my weekly call with the President this afternoon, and I am going to plant the seed in his head and mention your name."

Before the Congressman from Iowa could even voice a protest, the Speaker was already patting his hands up and down to quell any further discussion of the matter. "I don't want to hear it," he said. "Unfortunately, when I get an idea in my head, it sticks in a little brain cell, and there is no stopping me. Just ask my wife," joked the Speaker, who finished the last of the scraps remaining on his plate, and rushed off to his office while his companion, on the other hand, finished his meal leisurely, and left the building much the same way he entered; virtually invisible.

The International Space Station

Just as Commander Thorson was performing some rather routine atmospheric tests in the Internal Truss Segment (ITS), which is the main corridor of the ISS, the lights began to flicker on and off. It was at a critical time too. As a result, he could not get the proper readings on the test he had been working on for the last half hour (although, in Space, time is relative). Nevertheless, he was still pissed.

"Damn it," yelled Thorson. "Is that you, Dimitri?" he called out to his fellow ISS resident.

There was no response. Thorson stopped what he was doing, turned himself around and guided himself through the ITS toward the 'ELC', which was short for the Expedite the Processing of Experiments to the Space Station (EXPRESS) Logistics Carrier. The ELC was attached to the ITS and could accommodate multiple payloads through different external ports that attach to the ISS. Grabbing the bars to pull himself through the ITS corridor, Thorson checked each of the four payload stations. After that, he checked each of the various laboratories aboard the ISS. Cosmonaut Korbatov was apparently nowhere to be found. Next, he checked the sleeping quarters where he found Korbatov sound asleep.

Rule him out. That's odd though, he thought. First, the thing with the Canadarm2 robotic arm, and now this. Due to cuts in the participating countries' respective budgets, Thorson and Korbatov were currently the only residents of the ISS until another astronaut, from Canada, arrived next month. Consequently, all space walks were temporarily suspended. Thorson next checked the Command and Data Handling (C&DH) system, which is the hardware and software system that provides for all command, control, and data distribution for the Space Station's systems and payloads. After performing a routine check, Thorson could find nothing wrong with the C&DH. Nonetheless, he probed the CD&H further, but could find nothing out of the ordinary. He would report it to Mission Control, nonetheless, he figured.

Chapter Twenty-Three
April 25, 2017

Starbucks, Lake Merritt, Florida

After huddling over his laptop in his cluttered apartment for seemingly days now, Kallen needed a break. So, he went down the street to his local Starbucks, and plunged himself into one of those comfy leather chairs. He sipped his Skinny Late for a bit before cracking open the laptop. The screen pulled up the same news article Kallen had been reading before his left his apartment that day. It was about a three-year-old boy, the son of two American diplomats, who during the time his parents were stationed in North Africa, contracted a near deadly disease that left the boy confined to a wheel chair for the rest of his life. Because of the boy's illness, his parents were recalled from the Diplomatic Service, and ultimately, went to work for the State Department in Dallas, Texas. The article went on to describe how the boy, at a very young age, showed abilities well beyond his years.

Later in life, that boy would go on to attend Cal Tech, MIT and establish one of the largest medical device manufacturers in the world. It went on to discuss his philanthropy and involvement with politics, beginning in the early Eighties. All of this was pretty much standard public knowledge, and of course, all of it (and more) was included in Kallen's Profiler Reports. Kallen was nevertheless looking for any minutia which might trigger another possible avenue of research, but there simply wasn't anything there.

So, he decided to Google Peck's parents. Again, there was nothing much there that he hadn't already seen in prior articles or Profiler Reports. His parents were both from families that had emigrated to the United States while they were relatively young; his father from England, and his mother, from Persia, during the Shah's regime. Both had attended the finest schools and colleges. Because his father could speak multiple languages fluently, he was recruited for the Diplomatic Service at a young age. Peck's grandfather was a British Diplomat and Member of Parliament during their time in England. Peck's mother, who was pre-med at the time, accompanied her new husband at his first diplomatic posting in the Middle East. Consistent with what he had previously read, his father was part of the initial delegation of diplomats stationed in Beirut before it officially became an Embassy. *This seemed to explain the prior discrepancy that Kallen had detected earlier*, he figured. After all, a young diplomat with a pregnant wife might be less inclined to accept an assignment where there could be complications with his future child's citizenship. So, apparently, to protect unborn Peck's naturalization, the records were changed to reflect Embassy status in 1951. Very interesting, he thought.

Then, something else occurred to him. It was something he read earlier. He went back to the article, and there it was. Both of his parents had strong math and science backgrounds. His mother was pre-med and was offered a full scholarship to Harvard Medical School, at the time of his father's initial placement in the Middle East. It wasn't until years later that she herself would join the Diplomatic Service, after following her husband to various other assignments. Also, prior to attending college, his father had won a very prestigious statewide science competition. It may be nothing, but could certainly explain their son's innate capabilities, and enormous financial success.

It could come in handy later, Kallen figured, so he made a mental note of it.

The Speaker's Office, Cannon House Office Building, Washington, D.C.

"I understand, Mr. President," the Speaker said from behind his grand Louis XVI desk, anchoring the middle of his office. "Senator Jackson would make a fine choice. She is certainly well qualified. No one can argue with that, but there is someone else I would like you to consider." He paused for a moment before continuing, "I am sure you are familiar with my weekly lunch partner."

"I am," the President said cautiously.

Although the Speaker's weekly dining partner was somewhat unknown, their lunches together were no secret and hardly went unnoticed.

"Well, I think he would make a fine choice for Vice President, sir," the Speaker stated, with all the conviction in the world. There it was. Out in the open.

"Dick, correct me if I am wrong, but he is what... a second or third term Congressman?"

"Mr. President, he is presently serving out his fifth term, and has been instrumental on both the Judiciary and Armed Services Committees during his time in Congress."

"I'm sure he has," the President commented. "But what about name recognition, Dick?"

"Christ, Jack, you're not putting him on the ticket during an election. You only need a majority of support in both Houses. Rest assured, Mr. President, if he was your Nominee, I am confident I could garner enough support in both the House and the Senate to secure his confirmation as Vice President."

"Aren't you forgetting one small thing, Dick?"

"What is that Mr. President?"

"The Congressman's religion."

"Mr. President, if London can elect a Muslim Mayor, you certainly can appoint a Muslim Vice President. Besides, like I said before, he is not running on the ticket. All he needs to do is be confirmed by a majority of Congress."

"Well, it is certainly an interesting idea, Dick. One, quite frankly, I had not considered. Let me give it some thought," said the President. Ending the conversation with the Speaker, the President called out, "Nora, get me everything you can gather on Congressman Abel from Iowa, and get Teddy in here!"

Almost if on cue, Teddy Fitzpatrick entered the Oval Office.

"What do you know about Congressman Abel from Iowa?" the President barked.

Fitzpatrick's facial expression soured. "Not much, and I am afraid that is because there is not much to know." He hesitated before continuing, "The talk on the Hill is that he is fairly moderate and has generally supported Bills from both Parties. In fact, I recall he was particularly instrumental in the Conference Committee's meeting over Henry's recent Healthcare Bill."

"Then, why the sour look?"

"Mr. President, with all due respect, it's not what we know about the Congressman. It's what we don't know that concerns me."

Chapter Twenty-Four
April 25, 2017

Lyndon B. Johnson Space Center, Houston, Texas

"Houston, we have a problem," Commander James Thorson said over the Mission Control secure communications link.

Really, he couldn't be more original than that, thought Mission Control Director Harbath. He hoped it was nothing major, but Harbath had spent enough years with NASA to know better. "Yes, Jim, what is it? We're here," he responded.

"Aaron, as you know, we first had that thing with the Canadarm2's robotic arm's unexpected movement and the flickering lights shortly after the recent arrival of the newest payload," the Commander began. Continuing, he said, "I checked the C&DH System at the time and everything appeared normal. Now, just a little while ago, I experienced a similar surge, causing the same effect on the lighting within the ITS. So, I was just wondering if the monitors at Mission Control showed anything unusual."

"They are normal and have been so for the last forty-eight hours," Harbath advised him.

"Really, that's odd," Commander Thorson commented.

"Hold on for a minute, Jim," said Harbath. He bent over the set of monitors in front of him, consulted with the technicians positioned directly in front of them, and moments later, confirmed, "I am afraid that is accurate, Jim."

. "Well, maybe it is just a case of faulty wiring," Thorson suggested.

Then, changing the subject a bit, Thorson inquired, "Any update on when our two new roommates from the Canadian Space Agency will be joining us?"

"We are presently coordinating our efforts with the Canadians right now and hope to have the launch sometime this summer." Harbath added, "Right now, the target date is mid-July."

"Okay, well Cosmonaut Korbatov and I look forward to our new companions joining us sooner rather than later."

"Understood," Harbath said, signing off.

After that, he made one very important telephone call to his old buddy.

Chapter Twenty-Five
April 25, 2017

John F. Kennedy Space Center, Merritt Island, Florida

After hanging up the telephone with Harbath, Kallen was feeling rejuvenated that his investigation had again been given the 'green light'. For a change, Kallen was in a good mood.

Having finished scouring over the Profiler Reports he had printed earlier, it was time to turn his attention to the matter that prompted the investigation in the first place – the payload. There were three payloads on the last mission to the ISS. A rather large media conglomerate owned one, another one belonged to the government, and the third one was owned by a small satellite company, headquartered in Dallas, Texas, called SatCom Inc. Kallen was going over the 'payload specs' when suddenly his private cell phone sprang to life.

"I have the information you requested," came a voice very familiar to Kallen, one he had relied upon on numerous occasions. Boris Belitnicoff was Kallen's 'business techie'. Whenever a matter required an understanding of the corporate structure of a particular type of corporation or the determination of who were the real owners of a particular corporation, that was a case for Boris, and this was, no doubt, one of those cases.

It turns out that SatCom Inc. was privately held by a shell corporation, located in Eastern Romania. The problem was that, after the fall of Communism and the Romanian Revolution of 1989, Romania was not a country well known for its file maintenance system. In fact, generally, a small bribe to a government official was required to get any information out of the Romanian National Trade Register Office. The irony of this was that the Trade Office was under the direct jurisdiction of Romania's Ministry of Justice. Nevertheless, Kallen knew that Boris would be able to circumnavigate the bureaucracy of the Trade Office and obtain the required information, and that certainly appeared to be the case.

"SatCom Inc., is a subsidiary of a wholly owned Romanian shell company known as Luminex Inc., which we knew," explained Boris. "This is where it gets interesting though. Luminex, Inc. appears to be owned by a conglomerate of publicly traded companies, both here and in Romania, similar to a type of mutual fund. The interesting thing is that none of the various corporate entities own a controlling interest in Luminex, which means that, to control SatCom, there must be a voting bloc held by proxy. With me so far?"

"Yes."

"So, I pulled the Schedule 13d's from the SEC for all the publicly traded American companies that owned an interest in Luminex. This identifies all entities with more than a 5% ownership interest. Not surprisingly, there were none. I mean these guys are smart. If they want to stay under the radar as you say they do, they are not going to risk detection by having to file a form with the SEC due to the amount of stock they own. Instead, they are more likely to purchase just under 5% in each company to avoid the filing requirement, which means that, of the seventeen different entities that own Luminex, more than ten companies would have to have common ownership to constitute our voting bloc, right?"

"Yes, okay," Kallen said, following Boris' logic.

"Next, I pulled all the 10-K's for the publicly traded companies that owned an interest in Luminex, and cross-referenced them against one another, searching for matching terms in the filings to determine if any of the same names appeared throughout. Sure enough, one name appeared as a Senior Vice President in three of the seventeen companies." He paused, almost for effect, and then asked, "Does the name Alexander Cain mean anything to you?"

Kallen, of course, recognized the name as the true identity of Peter Stern, Senior Vice President of MedSupply, Ltd, whose older brother served under Kallen in the SEALS. It is odd, however, that he would use his own name, thought Kallen. Then again, maybe not. Maybe that was the purpose of the Stern pseudonym in the first place. Nevertheless, his involvement with those companies could mean only one thing. The mysterious shareholder of the companies comprising the majority voting bloc in Luminex, Inc., had to be none other than philanthropist and Presidential advisor, J. Robert Peck.

Chapter Twenty-Six
April 26, 2017

The Oval Office, the White House, Washington, D.C.

Two thick file folders were placed next to one another on the President's desk. The one on the President's left contained everything there was to know about the African American Senator from Louisiana, and the one on the right contained everything there was to know about the relatively unknown Congressman from Iowa, the Speaker's clear favorite choice.

Scanning the files, the Senator's background was quite impressive. She had been raised in a rural county in Central Louisiana and was home schooled. After gaining a bit of notoriety after having been a finalist for the National Spelling Bee as a teenager, she obtained an academic scholarship to Louisiana State University. After that, it was on to Yale Law School. Then, she returned home to run the Louisiana office of the Southern Poverty Law Center in New Orleans, where she litigated several seminal civil rights cases before becoming the State's first African American woman Attorney General. After two terms in that Office, she ran for and was elected to the Senate eleven years ago. No doubt, impressive.

On the right side of the President's desk, was the Congressman's file. His background was no less interesting, that was for sure. A single mother in the blue-collar section of Sioux City raised him while working two jobs. In high school, he was active in the debate club, even finishing in the National semifinals. As an undergraduate, he attended U.C. Berkeley, and then obtained a Masters in Social Work from the University of Southern California. Following college and graduate school, he settled in the Bay Area where he became a fixture as a community activist in East Oakland. Later, he returned home to Sioux City to care for his ailing mother. After several stints in local politics, he first ran for Congress in 2000. A long-term incumbent defeated him in both of his first two attempts, and he was finally elected to Congress in 2006. Presently, he was a member of both the House Judiciary Committee and Armed Services Committee.

"Did you see the part about his activities in college?" asked Teddy Fitzpatrick.

"So, he was active in the Student Union," remarked the President.

"Not just the Student Union, it was his affiliation with various Muslim organizations that concerns me."

Teddy certainly had a point there. Congressman Abel was a practicing Muslim. In past years, that might have seemed enough to doom any candidacy, but the truth of the matter was that times were changing. It turns out that the vicious rhetoric various candidates espoused during the last campaign, calling for a ban on all Muslims entering the United States, had the opposite effect. As a backlash to such hateful speech, Muslim Americans had rallied and increasingly become more accepted into mainstream America, but more importantly, into American politics, as well. Nominating a practicing Muslim as the Vice President of the United States would certainly highlight this Nation's founding principal of Freedom of Religion. On the other hand, however, there was still a lot of prejudice out there. It would certainly be an uphill battle. The only question was whether it was a battle worth fighting.

Abruptly changing the subject, the President said, "I am concerned that, given Senator Jackson's voting record in the Senate, we will not be able to garner the necessary votes in the House to win approval for her. Whereas, Speaker Montgomery has all but assured us the necessary votes in both Houses should we nominate Congressman Abel."

"Listen Mr. President, she certainly has a record to the left which could offend our 'friends' to the right, but I guarantee that our entire staff, and Party stalwarts, will work tirelessly gathering the necessary support in both houses to support her nomination, if necessary."

"I'm not certain that will be enough," commented the President. "We need to keep all options open at this point."

John F. Kennedy Space Center, Merritt Island, Florida

Kallen returned his attention to the 'specs'. Given the size of the SatCom Inc's payload, it was housed in the Japanese Experiment Module – Exposed Facility (JEM-EF) of the ISS, which is an external platform that can hold up to 10 experimental payloads at a time. Canadarm2, the robotic arm for the ISS, routinely maneuvers large payloads, over twice the size of SatCom Inc. payload, from the JEM-EF to other locations throughout the ISS. Given the electrical surge that prompted the investigation in the first place, Kallen decided to turn his attention to the electromagnetic (EM) drive within the SatCom Inc. payload. At first, there appeared to be nothing out of the ordinary there, but just as he was about to move on, he decided to double check the initial readings on the day of the launch. Much to his surprise, and consternation, the EM readings on the day of the launch appeared to be almost four times than that indicated in the initial payload disclosure form filed with the Research Integration Office (RIO), and more problematic, it was twice that which the JEM-EF and Canadarm2's robotic arm could support. *That could certainly seem to explain some of the problems Commander Thorson experienced*, Kallen thought to himself. He added that observation to a list of many, which now comprised the entirety of his investigation, filling a thick file folder on his desk.

Chapter Twenty-Seven
April 28, 2017

The FBI Director's Office, Hoover Building, Washington, D.C.

"We have tried informally to obtain the phone company's records, but they have been largely uncooperative, sir," said the Special Agent debriefing the director." He elaborated that, "Ever since the Bush Administration used their data to eavesdrop on domestic calls a few years back, this is the standard response." He continued, "And of course, that whole messy episode last year with Apple, forcing us to go to the Ninth Circuit over the San Bernardino shooters' phones, doesn't help either."

"I recall," said the director, who didn't need to be reminded of his predecessor's failures.

"In fact, the AUSA handling warrants says he is not even sure that we can establish 'probable cause' to obtain a warrant because they are not sure a crime has even been committed in the first place," continued the agent.

"What, that's ridiculous," bellowed the director, incensed.

"Sir, it seems that leaking *non-classified* information to the press is not a crime. More to the point, to the extent that the information Dr. Malcomovich purportedly leaked about Senator McClintock was false. If he did in fact leak the information, it would be an issue for the civil courts to resolve in a defamation lawsuit, not a criminal prosecution, sir. Unless we can establish that there was some sort of foul play involved with Dr. Malcomovich's death, any further investigation of the matter seems to have died with him."

"Incredible," said the director, disgustedly. Of course, he knew the law inside and out, having himself been a federal judge for so many years. "First, you tell me that we cannot track the call Malcomovich made after Agent Johnson's little visit, and now you are telling me that all other avenues of investigation seemed to have dried up, as well."

. "I am afraid so, sir."

"And it was one of our Pathologists that performed the autopsy of Dr. Malcomovich?"

"Yes, sir."

"And they found nothing suspicious that we could use in a declaration to get a warrant."

"No, sir."

"How about the Gas Company's records?"

"They were a bit more forthcoming, sir. They produced all the records for Malcomovich's property without a warrant."

"And there was nothing there?"

"I'm afraid that is the case, sir. Based upon all available evidence, there is nothing to suggest that the explosion at the Malcomovich residence was anything other than the result of a previously undetected gas leak."

Feeling a bit deflated, and once again dreading the next phone call he would have to make to the White House Chief of Staff, the director instructed the special agent to nonetheless 'Keep working on it'.

Redwood City, California

Following a routine that he had now grown accustomed to over many years, Peck waited for the arrival of his private subterranean elevator to the Penthouse Suite. Once inside, he inserted the key, pressed a button and the elevator car quickly descended. When it reached its final destination, a quarter mile below ground, Peck exited the car and initiated communications.

Once connected, Peck received the following greeting from the voice on the other end of the line, "What about this Senator Kayla Jackson?"

"Way too liberal to ever be seriously considered by a majority of both Houses," responded Peck. Then, having known the man behind the voice most of his adult life, even though he had never met him in person, Peck anticipated the next question, offering, "And, even should she somehow miraculously start to gain support in one, or both, Houses, we have our back-up plan."

"Is everything in place in that regard, just in case?"

"Yes." Peck truly despised being second guessed at every stage of the game. He had made it this far on his own, after all. He should be given the credit he rightfully deserved for his accomplishments and role in the fulfillment of the Ultimate Plan.

"What is going on with the FBI's investigation of the whole Malcomovich issue?" inquired the voice on the end of the line. *Interesting that he would callously refer to the murder of an innocent scientist as an 'issue'*, thought Peck.

"Nothing. My understanding is that it has ceased to exist due to lack of evidence."

"And how do you know this?"

"I have my sources."

"Wasn't that how we got into this whole problem in the first place?" queried the voice. *Damn*, the arrogance killed Peck, but he nonetheless remained calm, and responded simply, "As I said, the matter is resolved."

Noting that the length of the conversation had nearly reached its predetermined time limit, Peck advised his partner, prompting each to immediately terminate the call. Even though all communications were entirely secure, as the recent Malcomovich investigation had just demonstrated, all communications were predetermined to be a certain length, and took place on alternating dates, as an extra precaution to avoid detection. Nothing was ever repeated.

Chapter Twenty-Eight
May 1, 2017

The Oval Office, the White House, Washington, D.C.

Of the two interviews White House Deputy Chief of Staff Jonas Frank was able to schedule on such short notice, the first was with Senator Kayla Jackson. The attractive African American Senator waited patiently near Nora Summers' desk until she was finally escorted into the Oval Office.

The President reached for the Senator's hand, but before he could do or say anything else, the Senator was already embracing the President. "Mr. President, thank you so much for taking this opportunity to meet with me. I have always been a big fan of your gritty style of politics," she swooned.

The President thought to himself, *Okay, a bit forward for my liking.* Nevertheless, always the consummate gentlemen and politician, he responded in kind, "Senator, thank you for coming. I am only sorry we have not had a chance to meet earlier."

Almost immediately, and before the President could make the proper introduction, Senator Jackson turned to Teddy Fitzpatrick, and thanked him, as well. "Mr. Fitzpatrick, the feeling is likewise," she gushed.

Fitzpatrick politely accepted the greeting. When the Senator was not looking, however, he shrugged his shoulders, and rolled his eyes. The President waived it off discreetly and began his interview with the Senator.

"I think you probably have an idea why I have asked you here today."

Pretending to play stupid, which was not something she often did, Senator Jackson responded, "Actually, no Mr. President, why is it you asked me here today?"

"Well, as you know, given the Vice President's untimely passing, we must put forth a name for his successor, and Teddy and I thought you might make a good choice."

"I can understand that," she replied.

"You can?" asked the President and Fitzpatrick almost simultaneously, exchanging quizzical looks with one another.

"Certainly," she said, pausing. Then, playing the race card, she blurted out, "You want a young African American woman as the next Vice President."

The President and Teddy, immediately on the defensive, simultaneously shook their heads, vociferously denying such allegations. "Absolutely not," declared the President. "This is not a token nomination. In fact, in all honesty, I can tell you that it is just the opposite. You were selected based solely upon your qualifications and accomplishments to date. No consideration was given to your race or sex. Keep in mind, Kayla." He paused, and then asked, "May I call you Kayla?"

"Absolutely, Mr. President."

"Please, call me Jack," said the President, trying to defuse the tension in the room a bit. Rarely, in fact, did he offer visitors, or anyone other than the First Lady, the luxury of calling him by his first name. He had worked hard to get to this position and was going to enjoy all the perks that came with the Office. That included being addressed as 'Mr. President'.

The President continued, "As I was saying, Kayla, at some point in the future, we might be running for Office. That is not the case now, however, which means I am free to select the person I think would make the best Vice President, based upon qualifications alone, without consideration of their electability. The one caveat being that such an individual must be one who can garner support in both Houses. Believe me," he continued, "in politics, that is a rare luxury, and one of which, I fully intend to take advantage. To answer your question, that is why I have asked you to come here today."

"Well, Mr. President," she began. Then, correcting herself, "Uh hmm, I mean Jack. I am flattered, but I have to believe that, in all of Congress and throughout the country, there are other people more qualified than myself to be Vice President."

"You see, Teddy," remarked the President, looking at his Chief of Staff. "Humility, another admirable trait the Senator possesses."

Fitzpatrick agreed, nodding his head in approval. "Actually Senator, you would be surprised," interjected Fitzpatrick.

"Still, Jack," she began, but then paused. Her uneasiness at addressing the President of the United States with such informality was clearly apparent. So, the President interrupted, "If you are more comfortable addressing me as Mr. President, that is fine too," he winked at her.

"Thank you, Mr. President. As I started to say, the one caveat you yourself pointed out is that most of both Houses of Congress has to approve any potential Vice-Presidential Nominee."

Teddy and the President exchanged looks.

Then, she said what everyone was thinking, "I think I am hardly that person, wouldn't you agree?" There was an awkward silence.

The President spoke. "Look Kayla, I am not going to lie to you. That is one of our big concerns."

After that, they spent the next hour and a half going over her voting record on various bills, as well as any verbal attacks she may have made against other members of Congress. As expected, it was not good. So much so, that the President had to sheepishly inquire, "So, if we were to ask you to tone it down during the Nomination process, would that be something you could accommodate?"

She smiled. "Mr. President, I certainly understand your interest in that regard, but if you ask anyone who knows me, I tend to speak my mind." She paused, and then added, "Instinctively, that is. Clearly, if the Administration put forth my name as the Vice-Presidential Nominee, I would obviously do my best to temper my comments to make sure they coincided with Administration's Policy Points, but must admit, I tend to speak my mind."

Now, it was the President's turn to smile. "Understood, Senator."

Lyndon B. Johnson Space Center, Houston, Texas

"How are we coming on the upcoming launch with the Canadian Space Agency to the ISS," asked Administrator Redwell.

"We have been in constant contact with the CSA for the last several weeks," responded Mission Control Director Harbath.

"Just so you know, the President is riding me on this. Everything has to go as planned, you understand?" which was, in reality, no question at all, nor did Harbath understand it as anything other than a directive from his boss. At that moment, a thousand reasons were running through Harbath's head as to why he should inform his boss about the recent problems on the ISS. Instead, however, he chose to remain silent; in part, due to Harbath's resentment at the promotion of this career bureaucrat to Agency

Chief when there were others, including himself, who were far more qualified. They were just not Halliday's cronies.

"I don't need to stress the importance of the launch," continued Redwell. "I think you just did, sir," Harbath said.

"What are the latest communications we have had from Commander Thorson and Cosmonaut Korbatov?"

"I spoke with Commander Thorson at zero eight hundred, yesterday morning, sir."

He hesitated. He knew if ever there was a time to report the suspicious malfunctions with the lighting and Canadarm2's robotic arm, now would be the time, but Kallen said he was close to making a breakthrough. Wouldn't it be much better to have answers for the questions his boss would invariably ask? he figured.

"They are excited to have their new 'roommates' on board and look forward to their upcoming arrival," was all he offered instead, figuring it wasn't really lying to report on only half of the conversation.

"Okay, well keep up the good work, Aaron. Also, from here on out, I would like daily updates, okay?"

"Yes, sir," he said, hoping that Redwell did not pick up on the nervous tension that must have been apparent in his response.

After his meeting concluded, he promptly called Max Kallen.

Chapter Twenty-Nine
May 2, 2017

Video Conferencing Room, Kennedy Space Center, Merritt Island

Kallen noticed that Harbath seemed to be getting more and more frantic each time they spoke. He was making good progress, however. He just needed to fill in some missing pieces to the puzzle before he gave his final report to Harbath.

Even though his military background and time at NASA provided him with a minimal understanding of the numerous technical documents he had scoured over the last few days, he still had many unanswered questions. Fortunately, Harbath had arranged this video conference with one of NASA and the Jet Propulsion Lab (JPL)'s leading ISS scientists. As he watched the video screen, the picture of a short balding man in his late forties with thick bifocals came into focus.

"Thank you for taking the time to speak with me, Dr. White," began Kallen.

"Sure. Mission Control Director Harbath said it was quite urgent, Mr. Kallen," said Dr. Martin White.

"It is. By the way Dr. White, you understand that everything we discuss is strictly confidential, right?"

"Yes."

"Did you have an opportunity to review SatCom's initial filing with the Research Integration Office (RIO), and the data I forwarded you regarding the recent electrical surges Commander Thorson experienced aboard the ISS?"

"I did, and I must say it is quite troubling, to say the least. Keep in mind, Mr. Kallen, the amount of electricity we are talking about is staggering. There are eight miles of electrical wiring aboard the ISS. The surge was enough to strain the entire system affecting both the lighting and computer system, which is precisely what Commander Thorson experienced. That amount of electricity combined with the cloud capabilities of the OpenStack and the

GEO satellite in the SatCom payload could provide coverage over most of the United States, I am afraid."

"I'm sorry, I'm not following you," Kallen admitted. "Let me back up," said the scientist.

"In early 2008, NASA implemented OpenNebula, which at the time, became the first open-source software for deploying private and hybrid clouds for the federation of clouds. Then, in July 2010, Rackspace Hosting and NASA jointly launched an open-source cloud-software initiative, known as OpenStack. The OpenStack project was intended to help organizations offer cloud-computing services running on standard hardware. Initially, the early code came from NASA's Nebula platform, as well as from Rackspace's Cloud Files platform. In 2014, however, JPL contracted with SCAIR, a cloud management company, to create an abstraction layer on top of OpenStack-based Nebula One to act as a platform for application deployment, which can provide a high degree of elasticity for several multi-tier applications with varying operation system requirements. For example, JPL's Europa Clipper Mission, which will survey Jupiter's moon, requires multiple hardware refreshes over the fifteen years of the mission's duration. That, in turn, requires both electricity and cloud computing capabilities," continued the scientist.

"In other words, cloud computing and electricity have a symbiotic relationship," explained White. "The greater the amount of electricity, the greater amount of cloud coverage, and vice versa. As a result, it is not uncommon to see external electromagnetic (EM) drives on various satellite payloads for this, and other reasons as well, as you well know. But, the levels of the EM readings coming from the SatCom payload are enormous, which brings me to the payload itself." Dr. White pressed on, "The SatCom payload contained a long range Geosynchronous Earth Orbiting Satellite (or GEOS) that will eventually be placed into orbital position several hundred miles above the Earth's surface from the ISS."

Sensing he had lost Kallen, Dr. White further explained, "You see, Mr. Kallen, there are generally two types of communication satellites, which are still relatively new: GEOS and LEOS (or Low Earth Orbiting Satellites). LEOS are placed in orbital positions a few hundred miles lower than GEOS, and as a result, have less global coverage. GEOS, on the other hand, are placed in a higher orbital position, and can shoot 'spot beams' over the Earth's surface. This, in turn, provides for much broader global coverage. Based upon the SatCom EM readings I am seeing, combined with the cloud

104

computing capabilities of OpenStack. There could potentially be a huge threat to the global communications network, at large."

"And you are referring to the EM readings taken during the two surges the ISS experienced, not the figures that SatCom submitted in its initial disclosure form with the RIO, correct?"

"Correct."

"Doctor, is it possible that an external EM drive in the SatCom payload could affect the internal electrical wiring of the ISS in such a way that it causes the surges that Commander Thorson experienced?"

"Yes, it's possible," answered the doctor. Thinking about it further for a moment, he added, "In fact, didn't the Canadarm2's robotic arm independently move the SatCom payload?"

"Yes," Kallen acknowledged.

"Well, if that were the case, the surge Commander Thorson experienced could have occurred while Canadarm2's robotic arm was connected to the SatCom payload."

"Yes, Dr. White, but that begs the question; how did Canadarm2's robotic arm suddenly move on its own, in the first place?"

"I figured you might ask that," said the doctor, prepared. "So, I did a little research, and noticed that the SatCom payload was carrying the same type of software used, in part, to operate Canadarm2's internal communication drive."

"So, are you saying, Dr. White, that the software could be used to operate Canadarm2's robotic arm remotely?"

"Again, possibly, but it would have to be from a location that has a direct satellite connection with the ISS, such as a NASA facility, for example," offered Dr. White.

"So, if someone had access to a communication room at a NASA facility, they could operate the Canadarm2's robotic arm remotely, and move various payloads throughout the ISS?"

"Theoretically, it is possible. I have never seen it done myself," answered the scientist.

That would certainly seem to explain Cain's sudden unexpected appearance at the facility following the launch, Kallen thought to himself. *And, who better to operate such software than a former military operative who also just happened to have a Bachelor's and Master's from MIT in Computer Information Technologies.*

"By the way," added Dr. White. "I know that the report I received indicated that the SatCom payload was believed to be moved in the JEM-EF."

"Yeah," responded Harbath, wondering what he was getting at.

"Well, before this call, I double checked the positioning of all payloads and the SatCom payload was back in its original location in the JEM-EF." Reading Kallen's mind, he suggested, "Perhaps, when it was repositioned was when Commander Thorson experienced the second surge."

"That could very well be the case," answered Kallen, double checking the schematics to determine where exactly in the JEM-EF they were talking about.

"You know," continued Dr. White. "In reviewing SatCom's initial disclosure and proposal filings with the RIO in preparation for this meeting, I also noted that, strangely, no alternative financing was involved with the SatCom payload, which is highly unusual, I must say. Virtually every other application or proposal form I have seen submitted to the RIO, commercial or government, involves some type of outside financing, either by NASA or other branches of the federal government."

Actually, that made perfect sense to Kallen. If Peck was truly behind the unidentified source of electricity emanating from the SatCom payload, as Kallen now believed, he would not want any other entities involved because that could mean pesky disclosures and unwanted oversight. Certainly, he had enough money on his own to finance the project.

Changing the subject a bit, Kallen inquired next, "Let me ask you this, Dr. White, if we accept the proposition that the figures reflected during the two surges aboard the ISS are accurate, is it possible that the initial readings during the launch were somehow manipulated to mask the true wattage of the EM drive on the SatCom satellite."

"I guess, it is possible," answered Dr. White reluctantly.

That is, after all, why Harbath brought him in the first place. He had suspected all along that the readings were somehow manipulated during the launch, but had no evidence to support his suspicions. So, he asked, "Did you see any evidence of such manipulation?"

"Not specifically, no, but it would only be evident at the time of the breach itself."

Winding down the video conference, Kallen asked, "Well, Dr. White, I guess the million-dollar question is, what could be the purpose behind such a large EM Drive and the energy created by it?"

"Quite frankly, Mr. Kallen, that is what frightens me the most. As I mentioned earlier, we are talking about an enormous amount of electricity. Theoretically, in conjunction with the cloud computing capabilities of OpenStack, and the SatCom satellite's ability to shoot 'spot beams' from space. It could be used to shut down the entire infrastructure of at least half, or more, of the United States."

"That is what I was afraid of."

Chapter Thirty
May 2, 2017

The Oval Office, the White House, Washington, D.C.

The next of the two interviews White House Deputy Chief of Staff Jonas Frank scheduled was with none other than Congressman Jedidiah 'Jed' Abel from Iowa.

The Congressman waited beside Nora Summers' desk, engaging in small talk with the President's Executive Assistant, until Teddy Fitzpatrick summoned him into the Oval Office. Upon entering, the President came from behind his desk to shake the Congressman's hand.

"Congressman, thank you so much for coming here today," greeted the President. "Please, Mr. President, call me Jed," said the Congressman, taking the President's hand between both of his own. *Not really a shake*, thought the President.

"Okay, Jed. Based upon your weekly lunches with the Speaker, I presume you have a good idea as to why you are here."

"Well, Mr. President, as I have repeatedly told Speaker Montgomery, while I am flattered for the consideration, I am certain that there are other more well qualified candidates out there than myself."

"Don't sell yourself short, Congressman. Your background is quite impressive."

"Thank you, Mr. President. Once again, however, there are more qualified people out there than myself."

"Possibly," agreed Fitzpatrick.

The President shot him a glare, signaling his displeasure with the snide comment. "Listen Jed," began the President, retaking control of the conversation.

"We certainly appreciate all the support you have provided the Administration over the last few months with the introduction of recent legislation, and particularly, with respect to Senator McClintock's Healthcare Bill, in Committee."

The President paused before continuing, "Also, based upon the Speaker's glowing recommendation, we believe that you could prove to be a useful conduit to the 'other side of the aisle', which could not only help secure your possible nomination, but could also certainly help this Administration implement our vision for America."

"Again, Mr. President, there are others that I can think of that can garner the same broad support that you think I could rally, but who are far more qualified than myself."

"Humility is an admirable trait," said the President. "Sometimes. Look Jed, I'll be frank with you. We do have some concerns, but we are confident in your qualifications to serve as Vice President of the United States, if nominated."

"Concerns, sir?" the Congressman asked.

The President and Teddy Fitzpatrick exchanged uneasy glances. The President, putting the issue front and center, asked the Congressman bluntly, "So, we understand that you were involved with various organizations during the time you were at Cal, is that right?"

"Aha," said Congressman Abel, realizing that they were getting down to the real issue. "You mean, my religion, don't you Mr. President? That's what concerns you, isn't it?"

"Jed, I am only asking because we don't want any of your activism in college, or work as a community activist in Oakland, to come back and bite us in the ass during the nomination process." Silence. Then, "Now that we have brought up the elephant in the room, I am sure that there will be many questions about your religion."

"Look Mr. President, I am a very private man. I like to keep my personal and professional life separate as much as possible." He smiled, and then added, "As a Muslim American politician, however, that is often times easier said than done. I am not often afforded that luxury. Did I participate in Muslim organizations in college?" he asked, rhetorically. "Yes."

"Did I help raise money and awareness for the local Mosque in Oakland? Absolutely. I don't apologize for my activities, or my Faith," said Abel with conviction.

"Nor is anyone asking you to do that," quickly retorted the President. *Wow, these interviews were certainly not going as planned,* he thought. He looked to his Chief of Staff to say what needed to be said rather than it comes directly from the President of the United States.

On cue, Fitzpatrick stated, "We would like you to refrain from any public comments or support for Muslim organizations and religious activity, at least during the nomination process."

The Congressman smiled once again; this time, however, he was masking his true feelings at being asked to suppress his religious identity and affiliation.

"Mr. Fitzpatrick, as I said earlier, I am a very private man and will do my best to keep my professional life separate from my personal and religious beliefs, as I have routinely done during my entire time in Congress."

"That is good," Fitzpatrick and the President agreed.

After that, the three men spent the next hour and half discussing the Congressman's views on a range of issues. At the end of the meeting, the President asked the same question of the Congressman that he asked of Senator Jackson.

"Sir, if I am nominated, I will do whatever it takes to advance the Administration's position and will temper my comments so as to not spark unnecessary controversy," responded Congressman Abel.

Hmm, much better answer than Senator Jackson, thought the President.

Merritt Island, Florida

Figuring he better rule out any internal sabotage on the ISS itself, Kallen decided to review the Profiler Reports for the two current residents of the ISS, Commander James Thorson and Cosmonaut Dimitri Korbatov. Commander Thorson was what he expected: First, Naval flight school, and then, on to be a decorated combat veteran, leading to a brief stint as a test pilot before joining NASA. Once at NASA, he served on a couple Space Shuttle flights as Pilot before being promoted to Commander on his last mission. Last year, he was assigned to the ISS.

Korbatov, on the other hand, proved to be a bit more interesting. Before joining the Russian Space Agency, he was a Major at the Federal Security Service of the Russian Federation (FSB) in charge of satellites; spy satellites. That piqued Kallen's interest a bit further, prompting him to tap a few more keys on the lap top. That is where it got even more interesting. His program seemed to freeze up. A top-secret CIA program that was supposed to be virus proof seemed to have just contracted a virus when he was researching Cosmonaut Korbatov. *Interesting.*

Chapter Thirty-One
May 2, 2017

The Members Dining Room, Washington, D.C.

Like clockwork, there they were, at their normal luncheon table for their regularly scheduled Tuesday lunch.

"How did your meeting go with the President?" asked the Speaker.

"Probably, as best as could be expected," responded the Congressman from Iowa.

"Jed, I have known you for a while and I can always tell when you are holding something back."

The Congressman hesitated, and then added, "Mr. Speaker, as always, I appreciate your forthrightness. And, as always, you are right. The President and I discussed my religious activities in college, and in Oakland."

"Oh?" said the Speaker. No dummy, he always knew that would be an issue. "Did you mention how that could attract support for the Administration's policies with Muslim voters?"

"With all due respect, sir, I am not going to use my religion, one way or the other. It is something very personal to me. Besides, I am sure it is not the biggest voting bloc. Certainly, the Administration doesn't think so." Sensing the Speaker's disappointment, the Congressman added, "But that's not what matters here. It is a nomination, not an election, after all."

"Look Jed, I am not going to lie to you. It is true that with the rise of ISIS, there was a strong anti-Muslim backlash in this Country, but because of some of the remarks my colleagues made a couple years back." He stopped, thought about it, and corrected himself, "Well not even my colleagues really, but in any case, because of the potential ban on Muslims entering the Country, Muslims in this Country rallied, and all I am saying really is that I think it leveled the playing field somewhat."

"Absolutely, Mr. Speaker, but there are some out there whom you will never convince and their Representatives in Congress, here and in the Senate, will do everything they can to advance that anti-Muslim agenda."

"Hogwash," responded the Speaker gruffly.

The Congressman smiled. He had grown accustom to the Speaker's brusque manner over the past few years. The Speaker continued unabated, "I can tell you this Jed, if the President puts forth your name, and I certainly hope he does, I will tirelessly work the telephones to push your nomination through both Houses. That is exactly what I told the President too."

"Thank you, Mr. Speaker. I guess we will just have to see what happens," said the Congressman nonchalantly. His calm demeanor was in stark contrast to that of his lunch companion, which was another reason the two were such an odd couple.

Meanwhile, the Speaker devoured his steak sandwich while Congressman Abel simply picked at his salad, sitting largely in silence for the remainder of their meal. The Speaker was the first to leave the table while the Congressman briefly remained behind.

It is really happening, he thought to himself.

FBI Director's Office, Hoover Building, Washington, D.C.

"We have made some progress in the Malcomovich investigation, sir."

"Really?" asked the Director. He figured he was due some good news lately.

"Yes, well we still cannot determine precisely where the call was received because as was previously established, the receiving phone used an encrypted scrambler requiring an identical chip to unlock it to reveal communications to that particular phone. Nonetheless, because Malcomovich hastily placed his call, we were able to locate the nearest cell tower receiving the signal, which is in Redwood City, California."

"Oh?" said the Director.

"And, as you know," continued Special Agent Frank Johnson, the head of the D.C Office of the FBI, "we have been tracking Dr. Malcomovich's comings and goings over the weeks leading up to his death to see if there was anything out of the ordinary."

"Yes."

"Well, here's the thing: It seems that Dr. Malcomovich was the perfect employee. He rarely missed a day and was always early arriving to work in the morning and leaving late in the evening." Special Agent Johnson paused a minute before continuing, "Except for a day in mid-February of this year."

"Yes?"

"On that day, he called in sick, for the first time in several years. True, it was flu season at the time, but given the predictability of his daily routine, we checked the airports and train stations for that day. Sure enough, one of the counter girls in the commercial terminal at Reagan International recognized him. So, we pulled the flight logs for that day. It turns out that a Gulfstream G550, registered to MedSupply, Ltd, in Florida, had an unidentified passenger on it that day."

"I thought those flight logs are required to have the identity of everyone onboard the aircraft," interrupted the Director.

"Technically, they are, sir. With private jets, however, passenger lists can often be unreliable, especially given the FAA's laxity in reviewing such logs. In this instance, the Gulfstream flew from Reagan's commercial terminal to Monterey Bay, California, on February 17, 2017, which is not far from Redwood City, California, sir," noted Agent Johnson.

"Also, interestingly enough, the parent company of MedSupply Ltd., is Healthmed Inc., which is headquartered in Redwood City and whose Chairman and CEO is…"

"J. Robert Peck III," both said, simultaneously. "Would you like us to contact him, sir?"

"And have my ear chewed off by that weasel, Fitzpatrick, no thank you. You better get me a hell of lot more than that before I go to the President with this," demanded the FBI Director.

Chapter Thirty-Two
May 3, 2017

Shin Bet Headquarters, Jerusalem, Israel

The Deputy Director of the sister agency to the infamous Mossad, the Shin Beit, was busy reviewing the pile of paperwork that had gathered during his brief and unusual absence from the Office during his daughter's wedding when his assistant informed him he had a call from someone named Max Kallen. The Deputy Director immediately accepted the call.

"Max, *ma shlom chah*?" began the Deputy Director. "It's been a long time."

"*Shalom* Uri, *mazel tov* on Anat's wedding."

"*Todah*, Max." He paused, and then added, "Last I heard, you got yourself into a bit of a whirlwind of trouble with that thing with the Deputy Director."

"Oh yeah, that," responded Kallen nonchalantly. "Well, let's just say that I have been reassigned." He added, "Uri, listen I've been working on a certain file and need to know all there is to know about a John and Mary Peck."

Without missing a beat, the Shin Bet Deputy Director asked, "You mean the parents of the billionaire, J. Robert Peck?"

"That's right," responded Kallen. "Did you know that John Peck, his father, was part of the initial diplomatic legation to Beirut in '51 before it gained Embassy status?"

"Really?" responded Uri Nimi surreptitiously, not really answering the question. "Well, it appears he was," said Kallen definitively.

"Okay," replied Nimi, pausing for a moment. "Listen Max, I am not sure where you are going with this, but as the history buff I know that you are, you should know that, prior to the formation of the United Arab Republic ('UAR') in the late 1950s, there were a lot of splinter groups, comprised largely of Muslims and Druze Lebanese who opposed the rule of Christian President Camille Chamoun. Those groups later formed the UAR, which united Egypt and Syria until Syria left the union in the sixties." Nimi paused for a moment, and then continued, "And Max, I will tell you this, when I first started here as a young man, there were rumors that one of those groups had recruited some very high level American diplomats. This could correspond to around the same time frame you are talking about. Granted, they were old rumors by the time I started here," offered the Shin Bet Deputy Director, seemingly touting his own youth even though he was an elderly man at this point in his life.

"Uri, certainly you are not suggesting," began Kallen before Nimi interrupted. "Eh, eh, I'm just saying there were these rumors, none of which, any intelligence agency has ever verified, neither yours nor ours," protested Nimi. "I'm merely providing you with information. That is, after all, the trademark of our craft Max, isn't it?"

Understanding precisely what Uri meant, Kallen concluded the conversation by offering, "Absolutely Uri. *Todah. Shalom.*"

NASA's Jet Propulsion Lab, La Canada, California

The more he thought about it, the more anxious he grew. Dr. Martin White had been reviewing the figures for hours now. The amount of electricity in the SatCom EM Drive, combined with the cloud computing capabilities of OpenStack, and the ability of the satellite to shoot 'spot beams' across the United States, was troubling, to say the least. The tests he had repeatedly run only heightened his concerns.

The NASA scientist next turned his attention to another question Kallen raised during their video conference about the electrical manipulation of the SatCom payload during the launch. He reviewed the elevated figures that appeared on Andropov's monitors during the launch, and ran some other programs, cross referencing the original payload figures against the elevated figures, and then performed some additional calculations. After that, he pulled up all readings during the launch and studied them carefully. Based upon his calculations, it certainly seemed that some sort of manipulation had taken place during the launch. He double checked his numbers. There was no mistaking it.

Despite his initial instinct, and comment to Kallen that a breach could only be detected at the time of the breach, he was able to successfully recreate a virtual environment similar to that at the time of the launch. Then, he input the numbers into his calculations. Based upon those calculations, he concluded that there was definitely some sort of outside manipulation of the readings at the time of the launch. He had to report these findings, he decided. So, he logged off the computer, shut off the lights, and opened his office door; only to find none other than Mission Control Director, Aaron Harbath, standing in front of it.

"Can we have a word," asked Harbath, gesturing inside Dr. White's office.

"Certainly," said the JPL scientist reentering his office, turning the lights back on.

"Please, have a seat," said Dr. White, offering him the lone wooden chair in the cramped office.

"Thank you," said Harbath, taking the seat while Dr. White remained standing.

"I understand you had quite an interesting conversation with Mr. Kallen the other day." The scientist nodded.

Harbath smiled, and continued, "I know Mr. Kallen raised some disturbing possibilities." He paused. "I also know he told you everything you discussed was confidential, didn't he?" The scientist nodded again.

"Listen Martin, I know that your first instinct must be to report your findings through the chain of command, but Max is very close to completing his investigation, and we don't want to present an incomplete report, do we now?"

Dr. White had a troubling look on his face. "Aaron," he said addressing his boss by his first name as they had known each other over many years, "you have to understand, the figures he presented are astronomical."

"Leave it to a NASA scientist to use scientific adjectives," Harbath joked.

Dr. White was having none of it, however. His facial features remained unchanged, and he just stared at the Mission Control Director blankly for a minute before continuing.

"As I was saying, Aaron, the levels of electricity aboard the SatCom GEOS satellite, combined with the computing capabilities of OpenStack, give unfathomable range to the 'spot beams' that could be sent from SatCom's GEOS satellite. In fact, I fear that it could be enough to destabilize much of the country's communications network, or worse yet, could be used to generate some type of cypher attack on our infrastructure."

Dr. White pressed on, "Equally disturbing is the fact that I just verified that the figures that appeared on Andropov's screen during the launch were definitely manipulated to conceal the true levels aboard the satellite. That would seem to indicate sabotage. I am afraid your friend Kallen's suspicions may prove to be correct after all."

"Look Martin, I knew that you would be concerned after you spoke to Max, as I am too, believe me, but the best thing for now to do is let Max complete his investigation and then report our findings to Administrator Redwell. I also knew that, after you spoke to Kallen, you would be prompted to conduct further investigation which would only heighten your level of concern. That is why I came all the way out here to California, in person, to emphasize the importance of keeping this matter confidential, at least until we have all the facts in place, which as it stands now, we do not." Harbath looked White in the eyes, and asked, "Agreed?"

Dr. White was still unsure. "I don't know Aaron," he said, shaking his head.

"Trust me, Martin," Harbath said. Still sensing White's growing uneasiness, Harbath added, "That is a direct order, Martin."

Ultimately, Dr. White relented, nodding his head in agreement with his supervisor. Then, he said, "I need to speak with Kallen again."

"I'll arrange it," responded Harbath.

Merritt Island, Florida

After talking to his old friend Uri, Kallen got to thinking about the past. He was drawn to that particular night three years ago, in Southern Syria.

As Commander of SEAL Team Six at the time, he was notified that a very high-level target was confirmed to be in a remote village in Southern Syria. After more extensive briefing by the Secretary of Defense, the Chairman of the Joint Chiefs of Staff and the Deputy Director of the CIA, he would later learn that the target was none other than Abu Bakr al-Baghdadi, head of ISIS. With the help of Uri Nimi and Shin Beit, as well as a few highly trained Israeli Delta Force soldiers, SEAL Team Six, accompanied by a unit of Army Rangers from the 101st Airborne Division, made their way into Syrian airspace over the Golan Heights, flying at a very low elevation in two fully equipped Sikorsky UH 60 Black Hawk helicopters. Once the Black Hawks entered Syrian airspace, the Israelis retreated. The Black Hawks proceeded to land at the base of Mount Hermon in the Beqaa Valley, just east of Rachaiya al Wad.

From there, the SEALs and Rangers proceeded due North on foot while the Black Hawks left the Landing Zone (LZ) and retreated into friendly Israeli airspace. They were supposed to locate the target and perform the extraction about two and half kilometers from the LZ. Instead, half way into the extraction, they were ambushed. Given the sparsity of any viable cover, the soldiers immediately dropped, assumed the prone position, and returned suppressive fire while throwing both smoke and concussion grenades at the enemy positions. The firefight lasted just under five minutes. When all was said and done, however, half the members of his team were killed. Awaiting Black Hawk helicopters airlifted the remaining members of his team out to a nearby aircraft carrier in the Mediterranean.

Upon his return to the Pentagon, the first thing he did was punch the man in the face who was responsible for the bad intel they were given; none other than Deputy Director James Conklin. From then on, his fate was sealed.

Chapter Thirty-Three
May 6, 2017

Chief of Staff's Office, the White House, Washington D.C.

Deputy Chief of Staff, Jonas Frank, and his boss, Teddy Fitzpatrick, were busy going over the Administration's subtle overtures to a few select Members of Congress regarding the list of potential Vice-Presidential nominees.

"The response I am getting to Senator Jackson is largely negative," began Frank, "especially from many of the conservatives in Congress, such as Mariano and Trist, which is not surprising. What is interesting, however, is the similar feedback I am getting from some Senators on our side of the aisle. They worry she is way too liberal to effectively implement this Administration's policies. Many worry, quite frankly, what a Jackson Administration would look like should, g-d forbid, something happens to the President."

"What are they talking about?" blurted out Fitzpatrick. "The President is a young man."

"So was the Vice President, sir," Frank pointed out. Teddy Fitzpatrick shot his Deputy a dirty look.

"Hey, hey," he said, holding his hands up in feigned protest. "I'm just saying. Don't shoot the messenger."

Teddy Fitzpatrick looked back down at some paperwork on his desk, and without missing a beat, asked, "And, Congressman Abel?"

"Well, after most got over their initial surprise at such a potential nomination, it was mixed. Those on the other side of the aisle who had worked with him, like Seinz and Rivera, were impressed by his hard work ethic, and ability to grasp complex legal issues. Senators Johnson and Manheim appreciated his efforts in Committee on recent Bills, including his recent work on the Healthcare Bill. Also, many were impressed by his adept negotiating skills. But many, on both sides of the Aisle, were concerned about his lack of experience and the relatively short time he has been in Congress. By and large, however, more of the feedback concerning Abel was positive than negative."

Jonas Frank paused. Sensing something further was coming, Fitzpatrick looked up from his paperwork. "And?" Fitzpatrick demanded.

"Well, sir, there is the issue with Congressman Abel's religious beliefs and activities in college."

"Yes, what did they say?"

"In all honesty, sir, after the last few wars in Iraq and Afghanistan, and the whole thing with ISIS, they are quite concerned about possibly putting a Muslim in the White House. With good measure, I might add."

"Yeah, yeah, on that point, you are preaching to the choir, believe me, but the President seems to think that his nomination could go a long way for advancing religious freedom in this country, and could help end some of the backlash of Muslim prejudice. With that said, I hope you discouraged those Members from voting against a particular candidate based solely upon their religious beliefs and reminded them that doing so could have potential ramifications, even within their own constituencies."

"I tried, but quite frankly, many of the Members' constituencies might actually support such a bigoted position."

"By the way, what were the Members' concerns about his activities in college? As I recall, none of the organizations which he belonged to were that radical."

"That is true, but in many of their minds, any Muslim organization would be considered a 'radical' organization."

"Remind me again what the vetting of Jackson and Abel revealed."

"Nothing out of the ordinary. Jackson smoked some grass in college and got a public intoxication citation. Other than that, she is clean as a whistle."

"And Abel?"

"That's the thing. Other than his membership in the organizations we already discussed, there is really nothing else, with one possible exception." Frank paused before dropping the bombshell. "We did find an uncle in Lebanon in the early Fifties who had ties to radical organizations, but he is believed to have been killed during the Six Day War. Other than that, nothing."

Fitzpatrick considered this for a moment. Then, he thanked and excused his Chief Deputy. Moments later, Fitzpatrick briefed the President.

The Personal Residence, the White House, Washington, D.C.

The President awoke at two in the morning, which to his dismay, was becoming rather routine now. He snuck out of bed, trying not to wake the First Lady. Standing in front of the window, he rubbed his temples. Sneaking up from behind him, the First Lady gently placed her hand upon his back and shoulders.

"I'm sorry, I did not mean to wake you," he said. "You didn't. If you can't sleep, I can't," she said.

"It's just this whole thing with Rich's replacement," he said. "Every candidate is certainly well qualified, but some could be more effective for this Administration than others, and time is running out. I have to make a decision soon."

"Honey, this should be a 'no brainer' for you," she told him. "I know that you instinctively know what the right decision is, as you have continually proven to me time and again over the last thirty years. Just follow your instincts, dear. I know you will make the right decision. Do you remember when we first met?" she asked.

She came around to face him. Their eyes engaged. "You were this young hot shot corporate lawyer who wanted to change his practice area to environmental protection law, a relatively unknown area of law at the time. You thought your family would disown you. You thought I would not approve. Remember?"

He smiled at the memory. "I do."

"But, you made the switch. To this day, your parents still beam when they talk about their son, the Environmental Law lawyer, even though that son is now President of the United States. Also, remember right after that, your practice thrived; much more than when you were a corporate lawyer. In hindsight, it was the right decision and you instinctively knew it at the time. You knew what the right decision was back then, and I know you know what to do here too."

The President looked at his wife of almost thirty years, grateful for the love he shared with her. She had given up so much for him over the years, leaving a successful medical practice behind to raise their two wonderful children, and then helping her husband run for public office. A smart and competent woman in her own right, the First Lady was one of the President's most effective advocates and advisors.

The President smiled again at his wife. Thinking out loud, he continued, "The truth is that Henry would have been the best fit, and while I believe Senator Jackson and Congressman Abel could both be fine choices, they each have their own issues, which could hinder their ability to effectively serve as Vice President." The President sighed. "And, as much as it pains me to say this, I am not certain that the Country is ready for a Muslim Vice President," mused the President.

Reiterating a sentiment he heard earlier from the Speaker of the House, the First Lady commented, "If London can elect a Muslim Mayor, then the American people can accept a Muslim Vice President, believe me," she said.

Chapter Thirty-Four
May 7, 2017

John F. Kennedy Space Center, Merritt Island, Florida

Kallen was finishing up his second video conference with Dr. Martin White via Aaron Harbath.

"So, you have now positively confirmed that there was some sort of internal manipulation of the EM readings at the time of the launch?"

"Yes," responded Dr. White.

"Even though you initially told me you could only confirm it at the time of the launch, and not subsequently?" asked Kallen.

"Yes, and actually, what I said was that evidence of such manipulation would only be present at the time of the launch, but as it turns out, I was able to recreate a virtual environment equivalent to the one at the time of the launch, and made the appropriate calculations based upon the virtual recreation," answered the scientist. "I am quite sure these figures are accurate, and my conclusions are correct," he added.

Kallen pondered this for a moment. Then, he asked, "Were you able to pinpoint the exact location of the breach?"

"What do you mean?" asked White.

"Well, you recall we previously discussed the possibility that the Canadarm2's robotic arm could have possibly been operated remotely, right?"

"Yes,"

"So, my question is, was the manipulation within Kennedy or outside it?"

"I was not able to determine where the manipulation occurred, only that such a manipulation did, in fact, occur."

"Okay, thanks for the information Dr. White."

"I just thought you should know, that's all."

"I appreciate it. You have been most helpful, Doctor."

They concluded the video conference, and both went back to their respective offices.

Once back in his office, Kallen decided to focus his attention on their surprise visitor on the day of the launch, the mysterious Alexander Cain, now that it had been confirmed that there was indeed some sort of manipulation of the EM readings. He replayed the video feeds of Cain's visit, and again, nothing showed their visitor.

Next, he pulled up the information concerning delivery of the SatCom payload to the NASA facility. It turns out that a company called Space Freight, Inc. delivered it, which Kallen knew was a common carrier for Kennedy Space Center. In fact, the more he thought about, Kallen recalled that he had dated an Executive Sales Assistant for Space Freight, Inc., a few years back. *A real cutie*, he remembered. *Sharp as a whistle too*. If only he could remember her name. Then, it came to him, *Sally Waters*. He would definitely have to give Sally a call.

Redwood City, California

Peck took his private elevator from the Penthouse Suite to his secure subterranean communications center below the surface of the massive Healthmed Inc. facility. Once there, he followed his normal routine to make contact.

Peck began the conversation, "My source tells me that all is leaning in favor of our nominee. He said that, despite concerns about his religion and college activities, which we expected, he fared much better with members of Congress than Senator Jackson. In part, due to her liberal voting record, but also no doubt based, in part, on the Congressman's relationship with the Speaker."

"Oh, really? Does your source also inform you that the woman infidel Senator will be withdrawing her name effective tomorrow for 'personal reasons'?"

"What?" exclaimed Peck, furious. "No! You shouldn't have done that. It will draw too much attention, especially after the whole McClintock/Malcomovich fiasco, which by the way, still remains under investigation despite your assurances otherwise."

"Did your source also indicate that they identified an uncle of Congressman Abel who was allegedly killed during the Six Day War?"

Oh. So that was what this was all about. Peck immediately realized his mistake. Silence.

"In any case, it's done," said the voice on the other end of the line. Silence again.

Peck considered this for a moment. Then, the voice on the other end of the line continued, "All this dissension and questioning of our methods," he said. "We are well aware of your sources and the status of the nomination, which is why we took the measures we did."

Peck realized, at that point, that they were not his sources, but rather, were in the employ of the caller on the end of the line.

He simply offered, "We could have resolved it short of that."

"Sure," came the response on the other end of the line.

With that, the call concluded.

Chapter Thirty-Five
May 8, 2017

The Oval Office, the White House, Washington, D. C.

"Yes, Senator Jackson," answered the President after Nora Summers announced the call.

After listening to the Senator a few moments, the President responded, "No, certainly, Senator, I understand. I cannot say that I am not disappointed, but I appreciate your honesty and the seriousness with which you considered the potential nomination." He hung up the phone, feeling somewhat deflated. He summoned Teddy to the Oval Office.

As he entered, the President remarked, "And then there was one." Fitzpatrick gave the President a quizzical look.

"Senator Jackson has just withdrawn her name for consideration for vice president for 'personal reasons.' Is it really such a terrible position to have?" asked the President rhetorically. Fitzpatrick remained silent. He let the President vent.

"There used to be a time when the Vice Presidency actually meant something. I mean, if all goes as I expect, that person could certainly be president in seven years."

Having got what was bothering him off his chest, the President turned his attention to the issue at hand. "Well, I guess that leaves our mystery man from Iowa," he said, referring to Congressman Jedidiah 'Jed' Abel. "Actually, of all the candidates, I must say that I liked Congressman Abel the best," continued the President. "I am just not sure whether America is ready for a Muslim Vice President." He paused and added, "I guess we will find out."

"With all due respect, sir, Congressman Abel is not our only option. There were plenty of other names on the list I gave you."

"Come on Teddy, at this late stage, after all the vetting we have done, he is the only viable candidate we could put forth at this point. Congress, and the Nation, expect me to put forth a name soon. It has already been way too long." Fitzpatrick could not quarrel with that.

With that settled, the President said into the intercom on his desk, "Nora, get me Congressman Abel on the line."

Space Freight Inc. Warehouse, Cape Canaveral, Florida

Kallen approached the heavyset woman behind the front desk with a very serious look on his face. Flashing his NASA Inspector General Badge, Kallen spoke authoritatively, "I need to speak with a Sally Waters regarding an ongoing NASA investigation."

"May I inquire what the nature of this investigation is," asked the woman behind the desk curiously.

"Actually, I need to speak with Ms. Waters directly."

"I am sorry, but Ms. Waters is no longer with the company," she informed Kallen. That presented a problem he had not considered. He was trying to keep the nature of the investigation, or even the fact that an investigation was ongoing, confidential, and knew Sally would be discreet. Now, that she was out of the picture, he realized he had revealed too much to the counter clerk already. Thinking quickly on his feet, he recalled that Sally worked in the Government Compliance Department, and knew that all vendors that worked with the Kennedy Space Center were required to maintain an annual certificate to make, and pick up, deliveries. Relaxing his shoulders a bit and letting out a big grin to try to ease the tension in the room, he said, "It is really nothing, we are just checking all the vendors' annual compliance certificates. Do you know if yours is current?"

She immediately relaxed, smiled, and offered, "I believe so. Let me get Kim." A few minutes later, a middle-aged lady with pointed rimmed glasses came out from behind a corridor of offices which lined the hallway. She was carrying something in her hand, which sure enough, turned out to be that year's annual NASA compliance certificate. Kallen looked at it, typed something into his phone, thanked the woman and exited the building.

Driving back to the Office, Kallen called a man who his good friend and corporate maven, Boris Belitnicoff, referred. As it turns out, Boris not only knew everything there was to know about the makeup of corporations, he knew many of the people who ran some of the larger ones, as well. Kallen was now calling John Patterson, Executive Vice President for Cloud Star, Inc., which was a cloud computing consulting firm.

Max wanted to learn more about the potential interaction between the electricity aboard the SatCom payload and its potential effect on cloud computing capabilities. He spoke with Patterson for the entire thirty-minute drive back to the Kennedy Space Center across town. Back in his office, the gravity of the situation hit him like a ton of bricks. It was far worse than he could have ever imagined.

Chapter Thirty-Six
May 9, 2017

Rayburn House Office Building, Washington, D.C.

The Congressman from Iowa picked up the telephone after being informed that President Halliday was on the line.

"Good morning, Mr. President."

"Good morning Jed. I am pleased to say that, after a long and tiresome search, Teddy and I believe there is no better candidate than yourself for Vice President of the United States, Mr. Congressman."

"Wow, I am honored and humbled, Mr. President. Honestly, I am."

"No, I mean it Jed. I am truly excited about this."

"Well, sir, I must first discuss it with my family, of course, you understand?"

"Of course," responded the President.

The Congressman hesitated before asking, "Mr. President, do you mind if I ask you a question?"

"Certainly."

"Do you have any reservations about nominating a Muslim Vice President?" asked the Congressman bluntly.

Now, the President paused.

"Listen Jed, I do have some concerns," remarked the President candidly. "Also, as Teddy and I mentioned when we met at the White House, we would prefer that during the confirmation process, you not emphasize that part of your 'personal life', as I recall you phrased it."

The Congressman smiled to himself, and offered the following response, "Yes, sir, and as I said when we met, I have always tried to keep that side of my life separate from my professional life and will work extra hard to do so during the confirmation process."

"Thank you, Jed. Obviously, there may be some initial backlash from the ignorant and misinformed, many of whom surprisingly are in

Congress, but I am confident that with the Speaker's help, we will be able to get you confirmed as the next Vice President of the United States."

"I certainly hope so and will do everything in my power to make that happen."

"Great, I would like to announce your nomination tomorrow morning at a press conference in the Rose Garden. Please meet me in the Oval Office beforehand at 8:30 a.m."

"Certainly, sir. And, Mr. President, I will not let you down." '

"I know, Jed. See you tomorrow morning, and please be prompt."

"Of course, Mr. President."

Lyndon B. Johnson Space Center, Houston, Texas

Aaron Harbath listened intently as Max Kallen briefed him on the investigation so far. Kallen described their mysterious visitor on the day of the launch, and again two weeks later, whom he later identified as Alexander Cain, a former Navy SEAL and graduate of MIT with advanced degrees in computer science.

Next, he described Cain's partner, whom he later identified as Mark Walker, retired Chief Warrant Officer from the U.S. Army. Kallen told Harbath how both were using pseudonyms to conceal their true identities, and noted how both individuals worked for MedSupply, Ltd, which also owned the van the two used on the day in question. MedSupply, Ltd, he explained, was a subsidiary and lobbying branch for the huge medical device conglomerate, Healthmed Inc., which was owned by none other than philanthropist and Presidential advisor, J. Robert Peck.

Then, he explained what Boris discovered about SatCom Inc., and how J. Robert Peck effectively owned that company too, through a series of dummy companies incorporated in Romania. After that, he described Peck and his parents' mysterious backgrounds, conveying the story that Uri Nimi had told him about how the United Arab Republic ('UAR') compromised two high level American diplomats in the early fifties. Again, that was around the same time that Peck's father was stationed in Beirut, before it officially gained Embassy status, Kallen pointed out. Harbath listened intently.

Finally, Kallen described the manipulation of the wattage for electromagnetic (EM) drive for the SatCom payload at the time of the initial launch, and what was behind the Canadarm2's sudden movement of its robotic arm. He specifically stated that, based upon his conversation with Dr. White, he had confirmed that there was some manipulation of the wattage readings for the SatCom EM drive at the time of the launch.

Furthermore, and even more disconcerting, he confirmed that the SatCom payload contained an external EM drive with more than 4 times the wattage identified in the initial RIO, which combined with the cloud computing capabilities of OpenStack, could shut down virtually the entire infrastructure of the United States. He also explained how Cain operated Canadarm2's robotic arm remotely, using the same software used to run Canadarm2, and how Cain surreptitiously entered the NASA facility on the day of the launch, and again, two weeks later. Then, he described how he had been unable to rule out internal sabotage by the Space Shuttle's only other occupant besides Commander Thorsen, Cosmonaut Dimitri Korbatov who it turns out was a former member of the successor agency to the KGB, the FSB, specializing in spy satellites.

When he finished, Harbath just sat there, stunned for a bit.

Then he said, "Great, so basically, what you are saying is that you know something bad is going to happen, but you just don't know what, or when!" yelled Harbath. "Are you kidding me? I can't go to my boss and tell him that his boss's best friend is secretly trying to sabotage the entire United States: I just don't know how, when or why. I need more!"

"That is all I have."

"Get more," Harbath demanded, slamming the phone down into the receiver.

Chapter Thirty-Seven
May 10, 2017

The Rose Garden, the White House, Washington, D.C.

"Ladies, gentlemen, members of the press, and distinguished guests," began the President. "It is with great pleasure and pride that I am pleased to announce that, after careful consideration of several well qualified candidates, this Administration has selected the next Vice President of the United States of America." He paused before announcing, "Congressman Jedidiah Abel from the great state of Iowa," who was standing to the President's right.

Almost immediately, there were hushed gasps amongst those gathered in the Rose Garden that sunny Wednesday morning. The President nevertheless continued unabated, "Congressman Abel rears from a hard-working blue-collar family outside of Sioux City. As a young man, he worked his way through college and graduate school, attending both the University of California at Berkeley, and the University of Southern California for graduate school. Then, after returning home to Iowa following a brief time in the San Francisco Bay Area, he held several positions in local politics before being elected to Congress in 2006. Since being elected to Congress, Congressman Abel has demonstrated that he is an effective coalition builder, and in fact, he proved to be instrumental in the Conference Committee's consideration of the recent healthcare legislation that Senator McClintock of Oregon put forward. It is for these reasons, and because I generally like the man a whole lot, that I submit his nomination to the United States Congress for confirmation as Vice President of the United States."

Immediately, the Press Corps' hands shot up, each reporter calling out, "Mr. President, Mr. President!"

The President glanced all around the room. This was mostly for show since everyone in the room knew he was about to call on; Seth Roberts, Senior White House Correspondent for the Los Angeles

Times. He then pointed to the reporter to his immediate right, calling out his name, "Seth!".

"Yes, thank you, Mr. President, meaning no disrespect to the Congressman, but do you think he has the necessary qualifications to hold the Office of Vice President?"

Thankfully, his 'go to guy' had lobbed him a soft pitch, as expected, and the President was about to hit the ball out of the park.

"Well the easy answer to that question, Seth, is that if I didn't think so, I wouldn't have nominated him, now would I have? But the real answer to your question, Seth, is that he has been an active Member of Congress for the last ten years, during which time, he has been instrumental in the passage of several very important key Bills. So, absolutely, I have no doubt he will be an effective member of this Administration. Next question!" The President scanned the room once again, settling on a female reporter to his left. "Hannah?"

"Thank you, Mr. President," responded Hannah Willets, Senior White House Reporter for the Washington Post. "The question I have is for both you and the Congressman. First, Mr. President do you intend to use the Vice President to conduct foreign affairs, and if so, Mr. Congressman, what foreign affairs experience do you have that leads you to believe you can be effective in that regard?"

"Well, to answer the first part of that question, we hope that Vice President Abel, in conjunction with Secretary of State Stein, will work as an effective team to implement this Administration's foreign policy. With that said, I am pleased to turn the microphone over to Vice Presidential Nominee, Congressman Jed Abel."

"Thank you, Mr. President," began the Congressman. Having previously studied every single member of the White House Press Corps beforehand, he responded, "Well, Ms. Willets, that is an excellent question, and let me answer it this way. As you may or may not know, I am currently the next ranking member to the Chairman of the Armed Services Committee, having served on the Committee my entire time in Congress. As such, I certainly have learned the importance of a strong military, both here and abroad, which in turn, means the appearance of a strong United States of America, at a minimum. At the same time, however, I recognize the benefits that diplomacy can play in foreign relations in this ever-changing world landscape with increasing conflicts that often times can be resolved short of military intervention. So, yes, I believe I can be an effective representative in that regard on behalf of this Administration, and on behalf of the United States."

He waited for a minute before adding, "But that wasn't really what you were asking, was it Ms. Willets?" Willets looked confused.

"You were asking whether I was going to be a puppet, like virtually every Vice President who has preceded me or whether I am going to be an active, and effective member of this Administration, weren't you? And, the answer is the latter, I hope." He smiled, and then so too did Willets, easing the brief bit of tension in the room.

Pleased with the exchange so far, the President retook control of the podium, and said, "Next."

Hands once again shot up immediately. Figuring he had used up most of his safety net, he scanned the room for what he perceived to be the least confrontational reporter from the other side. Then, he saw John Sampson's hand amongst the sea of waiving limbs. Sampson, Senior Fox Correspondent, was his best bet he figured.

"John," said the President pointing to Sampson.

"Mr. President, thank you. Congressman Abel isn't it true that you are a practicing Muslim, and if so, how will you be able to reconcile that with the foreign policy we are discussing here today which obviously will be focused on fighting the insurgence of radical Islamic groups, such as ISIS?" There it was, the elephant in the room. The President tensed as Congressman Abel approached the microphone.

"Let me first thank you Mr. Sampson for bringing up what was certainly on everybody in this room's mind. And, let me answer it by noting that you used the term 'radical Islamic groups', and referenced the now infamous ISIS, which instinctively draws visceral reactions from the American public, but the thing to remember is that radical Islam is such a small percentage of those practicing Muslims in the world. To fear all Muslims because some are bad seeds is like suggesting that all Hindus are bad because some have committed atrocities against my Islamic brothers in India or that all Jews are bad because the Jewish Defense League perpetrates attacks against Arabs. I believe that such analogies are apropos in answering your question, Mr. Sampson, to show the simple flaw in the logic and the distorted view which spurs hatred in this country and abroad. That is, to state it bluntly – I am not a terrorist because of my religion nor are all practicing Muslims terrorists. So, yes, I believe I will be able to deal effectively with those radical groups that threaten the safety of the United States, whether it is ISIS abroad, or homemade revolutionary groups in Oregon. My religion has no bearing on that, one way or the other."

After that exchange, several additional questions followed along the same lines and the Congressman answered them in much the same manner that he did Sampson's question – very well. This continued for about another twenty minutes or so before the President ended the press conference.

Overall, he was very pleased with the way things had gone. Quite frankly, he thought it could not have gone much better.

Chapter Thirty-Eight
May 11, 2017

Special Agent in Charge Frank Johnson's Office, Hoover Building, Washington, D.C.

Having hit a dead end regarding Peck's involvement with the SatCom Inc. payload, Kallen thought he would check his law enforcement sources to see whether there were any ongoing investigations involving Peck or Healthmed Inc. Given the subject of his investigation, he figured it was best to be discreet, however. So, he made the long drive from Florida to meet with Frank Johnson.

He waited patiently outside the busy office of the Special Agent in Charge of the D.C. Office of the FBI. Things had not changed that much from the last time he was there. Agents hustled back and forth through the corridors of the top floor of the Hoover Building.

Glancing down at the newspaper in the waiting area outside Agent Johnson's office, the headlines blared, "President Halliday nominates first Muslim as Vice President." Then, the door to Agent Johnson's office suddenly opened, and a woman in a red dress came flying out, like a woman on a mission. Behind her, Johnson came to the doorway immediately filling the doorway with his large frame.

"Well, well," he bellowed. "If it is none other than Max Kallen, what do we owe this honor, Commander?" he said extending his hand.

Taking his hand, Kallen responded simply, "Hello Frank. Good to see you. By the way, it's just Max now, or OIG Agent Kallen," remarked Kallen

"Come on in, Max." Once inside, Johnson offered Kallen a seat opposite his desk, which he promptly took. "Correct me if I am wrong, but I think the last time you were here was when we were on the Anti-Terrorism Task Force together?"

"Yeah, a few years back."

"Oh yeah," said Johnson, realizing it was before the well-publicized event which ultimately cost Kallen his job and led to his current position with the Office of the Inspector General, failing to have picked up on it before.

"Anyways, what brings you around here, Max?"

"I am investigating for NASA some irregularities that occurred during the launch back in March. I don't know if you know this, but a subsidiary of the health giant, Healthmed Inc. owns one of the payloads. Consequently, my investigation has led me to door step of none other than billionaire, J. Robert Peck." Kallen paused for a minute, and then said, "So, I was wondering whether the FBI had any ongoing criminal investigations involving either Healthmed Inc. or Mr. Peck."

"Why not go through normal channels?" asked Johnson

"Well, here's the thing, Frank, it is technically 'off the books'. The Inspector General and NASA Administrator do not know about it yet."

Special Agent Frank Johnson considered this for a moment, trying to decide how much to share, before offering, "Actually Max, as always, your timing is impeccable. We do have an ongoing investigation regarding the explosion at Dr. Malcomovich's residence. Malcomovich was the former chief scientist at the FDA, whom you may have heard about recently."

"Yeah, I think I recall reading something about that," said Kallen, remembering that he had recently perused an article about that very subject not too long ago. "Weren't you one of the agents on the scene?" Kallen asked.

"Actually, I was."

Johnson continued, "But, as I was saying, we found out that Dr. Malcomovich traveled on a Gulfstream G550 Peck owned to play golf in California back in February. We also determined that he made an encrypted call to an undisclosed number shortly after we initially interviewed him, and as it turns out, the receiving cell tower is in Redwood City, California, right near the Healthmed headquarters."

"Why were you investigating Dr. Malcomovich if I may ask?"

"Actually Max, at this point, I would like to keep that part of our investigation confidential since it involves an ongoing investigation."

"Understood, on a need to know basis only. Say no more, but if you don't mind me asking, doesn't it seem odd to you that Healthmed Inc. would be wooing the Chief Clinical Scientist at the FDA?"

137

"Well, other than possibly violating some internal FDA ethics policies or procedures, there is nothing per se illegal about Malcomovich's little golfing excursion. What does concern us, however, is that so far, we have not been able to break the code for the encrypted call. The technology involved is so sophisticated that we will likely be unable to decrypt the call without assistance from the service provider, and as you may know, ever since the whole Apple debacle last year, companies are often challenging court orders and subpoenas for such information. Without their assistance, it is not as easy as it looks on TV."

Max agreed. "And, once again, you can't get into the details of the initial interrogation or why you were investigating Malcomovich, in the first place?"

"I'd rather not."

Sensing Kallen's disappointment and recognizing the fact that he owed Kallen from the time they were on the Task Force together when Kallen saved his ass from a stupid 'rookie' mistake, he added, "Look, if your investigation pans out further, and you can provide greater details into the nature of your investigation, I can make a formal request to the Director for you."

"Thanks Frank, I appreciate that."

"Sure, Max."

After that, they spoke about Johnson's family, and his two college bound kids, and beautiful wife, who was also a federal agent, with the ATF.

Of course, Kallen had no immediate family to talk about, having been a ward of the State before joining the Navy at eighteen. And since that time, his relationship with women amounted to nothing more than a series of one-night stands such that there was no family for him to discuss.

Redwood City, California

Speaking from his secure subterranean bunker, Peck boasted, "It has come to fruition."

"You speak as if he is already Vice President," challenged the voice on the other end.

"Well, it should be a foregone conclusion," bragged Peck confidently.

"Is it now?"

"Yes, I would think so. Between my connections, the Speaker's, and the President's connections, I would think we have it all well covered," he said.

"Would you now?"

Peck thought to himself, *Stop with the questions already.* The arrogance of the caller was galling enough, but to have every statement turned into a question was frustrating beyond belief. Nevertheless, knowing better to say anything else, he responded simply, "Yes."

"You better hope so." The line then went dead.

Department of Homeland Security, Washington D.C.

Once he left Frank Johnson's office, Kallen visited another friend at the Department of Homeland Security (DHS). Jack Seymour was head of the Cyber Unit at DHS. Kallen had to find out more about the potential ability to shut down the infrastructure of the United States remotely using the EM hard drive in the SatCom payload.

After waiting a few minutes, he was shown into Seymour's office. Kallen explained his concerns to Seymour without revealing the precise nature of his investigation. Seymour listened intently before explaining that each utility company has a private security code which must be entered before one could even gain access to the facility's computers. That meant that, even if hackers could crack one security code, they would have to break literally tens of thousands different security codes to shut down much of the United States' infrastructure. Then, one would have to input each code manually, which could take literally hundreds of man hours.

Also, in addition to the initial password, many utilities have their own security features which could provide another hurdle for any potential saboteurs. Clearly, DHS has already considered this potential scenario and ones like it before. Based upon what Seymour was saying, it seemed far less likely or feasible than it did before his visit to DHS, which was somewhat comforting to Kallen. If they were not planning to shut down the infrastructure of the United States, however, what were they planning to use the extra electricity in the SatCom EM drive for?

Kallen was determined to find out.

Chapter Thirty-Nine
May 12, 2017

Speaker's Office, Cannon House Office Building, Washington, D.C.

The Speaker was frantically working the telephones, calling every Party member in the House of Representatives to garner support for the President's nominee for Vice President.

"Janis, get me Howland on the phone," he barked from behind his big mahogany desk.

"Sir, didn't you speak to his Chief of Staff a half hour ago?" answered his AA. After thinking about it for a moment, he realized she was right. "Never mind." He had been working the telephones all morning, and yesterday afternoon too.

Although back in the day, during some of his earlier campaigns, and House battles, he could work the telephones better than anyone, he was not as young as he used to be. It was clearly taking a toll on him, but he lobbied for his friend to the President, and would not let either of them down now. Nevertheless, he was clearly not looking forward to the next call he needed to make, to Congressman James Tapper from the Second Congressional District in South Carolina, outside Columbia. They had known each other over thirty years and he did not need to pick up the phone to know what Tapper's Opinion would be of Nominee Abel.

"Jim, its Dick Montgomery here," he began.

"I wondered how long it would take before you called. Either I was not high on your list of calls or you dreaded having this conversation. My guess is the latter."

"Listen, Jim, before you start in on him, let's look at all he has done during his time in Congress."

"Don't you mean his 'brief time in Congress'? Dick, I have known you a long time and have never seen you skirt an issue like this before. He is a frickin' Muslim, for crying out loud! How can you seriously put one of them in such a position as Vice President of the United States?"

"Jim, you are right. We have known each other a long time, and I have never seen you act like this before. I mean, listen to yourself. How can we put 'one of them' in power? Although we have had our disagreements over the years, I have never known you to be a bigot or buy into stereotypes, but that is exactly what you are doing now."

"Because I put the security of the United States over one's religious beliefs?"

"No, because you are ignoring the very principles this Country was founded upon."

By now, the Speaker's voice had raised to such a level that his staffers outside his closed office door could hear him. "For Christ's sake, Jim, are you forgetting about the First Amendment and the ideals upon which it was based: Freedom from religious persecution amongst them!"

"Just because I believe someone has the right to practice their own religion does not mean I have to put someone whose religious beliefs call for an attack on this Country and other civilized Western countries into a position of power," countered the Congressman from South Carolina.

"Does their religion really so dictate, Jim? I didn't realize you were an Islamic scholar," the Speaker said facetiously. "Look, I may not be either," he added. " But at least I know better than to make such sweeping generalizations based upon a few bad seeds."

"A few bad seeds? That is what you call them, Al Qaeda and ISIS? I call them terrorists, and we certainly do not need a Caliphate here in the U.S. or anyone trying to create one."

"Come on, Jim, you have worked with Jed in the past. Do you really think he is the person you are describing?"

"No, quite frankly, that is what makes it so difficult for me, Dick. You are right. I do know him, and I like him, but how can one ever really know?"

The Speaker, the President and J. Robert Peck would all have dozens upon dozens of conversations like this with other Members of Congress over the course of the next couple of weeks.

Public Library, Cape Canaveral, Florida

After visiting his friends in Washington, Kallen decided he needed to investigate the Malcomovich angle a bit further to see if he could determine why the FBI was investigating Malcomovich in the first place. If he could figure that out, then maybe he could find the missing link in his investigation. The first thing he did at the library was pull up every article he could on Dr. John Malcomovich. Apparently, Malcomovich was involved in some type of smear campaign involving Senator Henry McClintock and was accused of releasing a doctored memorandum suggesting that the Oregon Senator prescribed illegal narcotics when he was a practicing physician in Oregon in the Seventies. *That's interesting*, thought Kallen. Did Malcomovich's little golf game with Peck, and subsequent call to a cell tower in Redwood City have something to do with the smear campaign of Senator McClintock, Kallen wondered. Remembering that Johnson said the trip was back in February of this year, it seemed unlikely since that was well before the death of the Vice President. The telephone call to a secure line in Redwood City following the FBI's interrogation, however, was more problematic. Kallen thought about what possibly could have the basis for the FBI's interrogation of Malcomovich. Although there could be some potential civil liability, it was, after all, not a crime to publish a false memorandum from decades earlier. *Could Peck have somehow been involved with the smear campaign of McClintock, and if so, what could possibly be his motive for doing so*, wondered Kallen. One thing was for sure: Peck appeared to be a man of many faces lately. First, healthcare tycoon, then NASA partner, and now, political operative.

Chapter Forty
May 17, 2017

The Members Dining Room, Washington, D.C.

As usual, the two Congressmen enjoyed their weekly lunch together. "So, how are your calls to other Members going?" asked Congressman Abel.

"Much the same way the President's conversations are going, I imagine," responded the Speaker.

"I have been making calls of my own," the Congressman added.

"For some reason, I doubt they are saying to you what they are saying to the President or myself. In any case, we knew it would be an uphill battle, but we are prepared to fight it. You just keep your head up and continue to prepare for the upcoming hearings."

"Of course. Thank you, Dick."

"By the way, how is the family dealing with all the hoopla surrounding the nomination?"

"They are dealing with it as to be expected."

"That is good. It is only bound to get crazier from here on out."

"We expect nothing less. Believe me, we are prepared for that too."

"Good, glad to hear."

Their conversation continued for a good twenty minutes or so, and as usual, other members of congress interrupted their lunch at least half a dozen times. This time, however, they were expressing their greetings to the Congressman from Iowa instead of the Speaker of the House of Representatives.

Administrator's Office, Lyndon B. Johnson Space Center, Houston

Harbath decided it was time to come clean to his boss, at least to a certain degree. Kallen, with the help of Dr. White, had confirmed that the EM readings were manipulated at the time of the launch, and that the SatCom payload contained in excess of the wattage stated in the disclosure form filed with the RIO. He could share this with Administrator Redwell during one of their weekly briefings, he figured. Redwell listened to Harbath patiently.

When Harbath finished, Redwell, being the career bureaucrat, was asked, "Okay, so what does it all mean?"

Harbath couched his response cautiously, stating the obvious, "Well, of course, we are still investigating all possibilities, but one thing is certain the payload aboard the ISS contains a dangerously high level of electricity." Then, offered, "Sir, there is some concern that that level of electricity, combined with the cloud computing capabilities of OpenStack, could pose a security threat to some, or most, of the Country's infrastructure."

That got his boss's attention. "Okay, I will contact SatCom and find out what is going on," responded Redwell.

"It is not that simple, sir." Harbath then explained SatCom's connection to the President's close friend and chief advisor, J. Robert Peck.

"Who is heading the investigation on our end," asked Director Redwell.

At that, Harbath hesitated because he had not gone through normal channels. Normal channels would have been to contact NASA's Inspector General, Mark Weisburg, to conduct the investigation. Instead, Harbath had contacted Kallen because he was operating under the radar at the time. Finally, he confessed, "Max Kallen, Special Agent in Charge of the Inspector General's Office (OIG) at Kennedy, sir."

"What?" asked Redwell, noticeably confused. "Why isn't Mark handling the investigation?"

Here, Harbath improvised. "Because Kallen was the on-site agent in charge for the OIG at the time of the launch at Kennedy when the elevated EM readings were first detected," he responded.

Now, the truthful part: "And, because of what was at stake, I thought it was best to conduct a preliminary investigation through Kallen before alerting Mark." Harbath proceeded to describe Kallen's background and the set of unfortunate circumstances that led to his current position within the NASA hierarchy. At that, Redwell frowned.

"So, what do you suggest we do now," asked Redwell.

"I suggest that we don't contact SatCom; at least, not until we can rule out any potential sabotage. In the meantime, let Kallen finish his investigation, which I understand is nearly complete, and determine where we go from there."

Redwell thought about it for a minute, and ultimately agreed with Harbath's proposal. Aaron turned to leave the room when Redwell commented, "And Aaron, by the way, you weren't exactly forthright with me when I requested daily briefings, were you?"

"Sir?"

"I mean you concealed this whole investigation from me from the get go, didn't you?"

As a non-scientist, Redwell often liked to use colloquial phrases. In turn, Harbath liked to respond in the same manner. "With all due respect, sir, there was nothing to report until I knew what was up."

"Aaron, you should have come to me earlier with this information. Once the investigation is complete, I will expect your resignation after the CSA launch, just to make sure everything goes smoothly with that launch. I will also expect you to work with your successor to ensure a smooth transition thereafter, understood?"

"Yes, sir."

Harbath turned and headed out of the Administrator's office.

Chapter Forty-One
May 18, 2017

Oval Office, the White House, Washington, D.C.

The President finished his fifth phone call, and it was only a little after seven in the morning. Unfortunately, most of the calls progressed in the same manner. Initially, the Members would rave about what an effective consensus builder, and how personable, the Congressman was, but the conversations would invariably conclude with the Senators and Congressman expressing concern about his religion and politics in, and shortly after, college.

Just then, Nora informed the President that J. Robert Peck was on the telephone. "Bob, how's it going?"

"Mr. President, I am sorry I did not call sooner, but I just wanted to let you know what a fabulous choice I think you made in selecting Congressman Abel for Vice President."

"Quite frankly, Bob, I wish more members of Congress saw it that way."

"Well, I wanted to let you know that I will do all I can with the numerous Congressmen I have helped get elected."

"I must say Bob, I hope you are having more success than we are."

"If it is his religion and political activism in college that you mean, I have heard some of the same concerns you have, but most of these guys are such whores that just the threat of pulling funding for future campaigns will make them practically lobby on his behalf."

"Well, we can certainly use all the help we can get," the President remarked. "Have you reached any opposition that you believe you cannot overcome?"

"It is hard to say. Still too early, but I don't think there is anything we cannot overcome. Otherwise, we would not have put his name forward."

"Good point, Mr. President," Peck commented. "Well, if I can ever be of assistance, Mr. President, let me know."

"Thank you, Bob," offered the President.

He concluded the conversation, just as Teddy Fitzpatrick and Jonas Frank entered the Oval Office.

"I just got off the phone with your favorite person, Teddy," commented the President. Fitzpatrick raised an eyebrow.

"Bob Peck," said the President, answering the facial expression on Fitzpatrick's face.

"Look, I have nothing against the guy," said Fitzpatrick defensively.

"Anyways, what is going on?" asked the President.

"You want to share the good news with him," asked Fitzpatrick to his Deputy. Jonas Frank said, "I just got off the phone with the Senate Majority Leader, who has pledged his support for Congressman Abel."

"Oh really," asked the President. "What did that cost us? Did you have to sell our soul?"

"All he asks in return is that the Administration support the Budget Committee's recommendations on cuts to Social Security and other entitlement programs."

"Are you kidding me? Tell me that you didn't cut that deal Jonas? Please tell me you didn't. And if you did, who authorized it because I sure as hell didn't! Nor would I have," added the President.

Frank's face reddened. He went from 'hero' to 'zero' in a matter of moments.

"I did," interjected Fitzpatrick, coming to the rescue of his underling. "Think about it, Jack."

Teddy Fitzpatrick was one of the few individuals to address the President by his first name. Still, rarely, he took advantage of such a privilege. In this instance, however, he clearly felt it was appropriate.

"It is only for next year's Budget, and after that, we can factor a CPI multiplier into all future budgets to make up for the short-term difference in the interim," explained Fitzpatrick.

"That is great Teddy," he said facetiously. "Except for the fact that it presumes we will not encounter any opposition from our own Party, or the people who put us here in the first place, when we announce our support for broad budget cuts to the very programs that affect the people who voted for this Administration. Or worse yet, it could embolden our opposition, who could retain both houses again next Fall, which is not what I signed on for, nor is what is best for this Country. Oh, and by the way Teddy, the next time you decide to make such a unilateral compromise with such huge implications, you may first wish to discuss it with the person who actually runs the Country," said the President, admonishing his Chief of Staff.

Clearly, the President was not happy. There was an awkward silence for a moment before Jonas Frank excused himself. Fitzpatrick broke the silence, adding, "I'm sorry, Mr. President, I may have overstepped my bounds, but I only did what I thought was best to secure the Congressman's nomination."

"I know Teddy. I just don't want to give away the shop away, especially if it is not necessary."

"But the Majority Leader's support is huge, sir."

"I know that. All I am saying is that we need to be smart about this. His support is not the only way to secure the nomination and I do not want to sacrifice the ideals that got us here in the first place to do so."

Redwood City, California

Once in front of the secure communication center beneath the Healthmed complex, Peck initiated the call.

"Status," inquired the voice on the other end of the line.

"We are encountering some opposition, based primarily on his religion and political activism in college, but that was expected."

"And?"

"And my source informs me that, although the President was not happy about the deal they made, we now have the Senate Majority leader on board, which should help secure a significant number of votes in the Senate. With the Speaker and the Majority leader, we should be in good shape."

"And what is the status of the FBI's investigation?"

"Dead, I believe."

"I want confirmation."

"The Malcomovich investigation was closed a while ago. The only thing outstanding is his cell phone call, which they will never crack," clarified Peck.

"Again, confirmation."

Peck was infuriated, but nonetheless, simply responded, "I will get confirmation." With nothing further to discuss, the call concluded.

Peck took the elevator back up to his penthouse office suite.

The FBI Director's Office, Hoover Building, Washington, D.C.

Agent Johnson just finished briefing the Director that the investigation into Dr. Malcomovich's mysterious phone call had hit a dead end. Ultimately, they could not decipher where the call to the Redwood City cell tower eventually went, and therefore, were closing their investigation.

Upon his return to his office, Agent Johnson's secretary informed him that Max Kallen had called. He returned Max's call.

"Twice in one week, Max. What do I owe this unexpected pleasure?"

"Frank, last time we spoke, you indicated that you could not disclose the nature of the initial investigation into Malcomovich, but perhaps, if I asked questions, you could confirm one way or another. That way you would not be officially disclosing anything related to an ongoing FBI investigation."

Boy, leave it to a former covert operative to skirt the rules, thought Johnson, who responded, "Max, once again, your timing is impeccable. I just finished briefing the Director that we were closing our investigation. So, fire away."

"That investigation didn't have anything to do with a purported smear campaign of Senator McClintock, did it?"

"Wow, you haven't lost your touch one bit, have you? Actually, it did."

"And since when did the FBI get involved in politics?"

"Hey, you worked for the government long enough to know that when the request comes from the top, that is when the FBI gets involved. My understanding is the President's Chief of Staff had a 'hard on' to prove that the whole Malcomovich memorandum was a fake, which appears to be the case."

"Any reason why the Chief of Staff was so interested?"

"I imagine it had something to do with the Vice President's successor."

"Anything ever pan out?"

"No, just as we were going back to interview him is when the explosion occurred."

"And the Bureau concluded that there was no foul play involved with the explosion?"

"That's correct Max, and believe me, we investigated everything. We even had our own pathologist do the autopsy."

"Hmm," Kallen mumbled to himself

"By the way Max, if you don't mind me asking, why are you so interested in Peck besides one of his payloads being sent to the ISS? I mean it does not seem so unusual that a billionaire with interests in healthcare and manufacturing, who is well connected politically, would be sending payloads to the ISS, does it?"

"Maybe not normally, Frank."

After deciding that information sharing was a two-way street and Frank had been quite forthcoming so far, Kallen went on to brief Johnson about the particulars of his investigation. Besides, by doing so, Kallen knew that Frank Johnson would keep him in the loop once the 'higher ups' got involved.

When he finished, Johnson could only say, "Jesus Christ, Max that is incredible. You must allow me to take this to the Anti-Terrorism Unit. If what you are saying is true, this poses a direct threat to the Security of the United States. Also, if we can tie Peck to the potential sabotage with the SatCom payload, then I may be able to get the required surveillance to link him to the Malcomovich death, as well. I mean, based upon what you have told me so far, we certainly have more than enough probable cause to get a warrant from Magistrate Wallace in a few hours."

"That's the problem, Frank. You can't go through the normal channels just yet as the investigation remains under the radar at NASA. Once I get approval from those in charge at NASA, we can open an official investigation. Also, I don't know if we want to tip our hands so soon to Peck who has billions of dollars to fund a cover up and tie us up in Court for years."

At that point, Johnson's demeanor changed dramatically. He became Special Agent in Charge of the D.C. Office of the FBI, and said, "Max, you better get it and get it quick! You just informed a federal agent of an impending terrorist attack on the United States. You understand I have a duty to report it and open an investigation, if necessary."

"I do. All I am asking is that you delay just a bit longer before doing so."

"You've got forty-eight hours before I take this down the hall," said Johnson.

Chapter Forty-Two
Early Morning Hours, May 19, 2017

Kitchen of the Personal Residence, the White House, Washington, D.C.

"Up in the middle of the night eating cereal, honey? Something must be wrong," commented the First Lady as she entered the private residence's kitchen. "Let me guess, this doesn't have anything to do with your nominee for Vice President, does it?"

The President let out an exasperated sigh.

"The confirmation hearing before the Senate Rules Committee is scheduled to begin next week, and you would not believe the hateful rhetoric I am hearing from both sides of the aisle about Congressman Abel's religion and his past community activism. Christ, you would think he was a member of Al Qaeda, not an elected Congressman to the House of Representatives."

"You knew this was going to be a tough battle when you made the nomination, and Jack, I have never known you to be one to shy away from a fight."

"I'm not. I just don't want to tarnish the Country's image with a blood bath of hateful attacks on the Congressman during the confirmation process, which I expect the other side may unduly prolong, seeking to derail the nomination like the Democrats did in the Seventies."

Forever being the student of history, the President knew how long it took to get Senator Nelson Rockefeller confirmed after newly confirmed President Ford appointed him. He also knew how ugly and contentious the hearings before the Rules Committee were, but that was following Watergate, he reminded himself.

"And what part of that did you not expect when you put his name forward in the first place," asked the First Lady.

"I only worry it could get a lot uglier here on out."

"You know, honey, when I first started my practice, I made a promise to myself that I would never second guess any diagnosis or treatment plan I made because otherwise, I would be second guessing myself all the time. I would not be the best doctor I could. Now, by comparison, you are the leader of the Free World and if you start second guessing yourself, you will be one of the most ineffective ones this Country has ever had. The Country will wallow in your own indecisiveness, which will thwart any progressive measures your Administration puts forward. You must have faith in yourself and trust that you have the best possible staff so there is no room for doubt. You said both you and Teddy believe in Abel and know he will make a fine Vice President. You must trust that assessment and go into these hearing on the offensive, not the defensive. Be the fighter that I know you are, always have been, and will continue to be," she admonished the President.

The President smiled and said simply, "I love you, honey."

She replied, "I know, as you should."

They finished his bowl of cereal together and returned to the bedroom, where they fell asleep in each other's arms.

Max Kallen's Office, Kennedy Space Center, Merritt Island, Florida

"I am telling you, I am very close," said Kallen to Harbath.

"Listen, your investigation may be coming to a close sooner than you think."

"What do you mean?"

"I mean I spoke with Redwell and came clean, and he asked who was heading the investigation on our behalf and I indicated you instead of Weisburg." He paused, and then continued, "Let's just say he was not happy about that."

"Why did you do that?"

"I had to," Harbath replied.

Good thing he filled Johnson in on the investigation, he figured, as it now looked like his involvement in the investigation may soon come to an end. As always, however, Kallen had something up his sleeve. He had a plan, but first, it was his turn to come clean with Harbath about his little chat with the FBI, which he did.

Now, it was Harbath who exclaimed, "What! Why?"

"In conducting my investigation, I use all resources at my disposal, and that it turns out, is one of them."

"Damn Max, you knew this entire investigation was under the radar, and now the FBI will be conducting a formal investigation within forty-eight hours."

Figuring this was his way in, he said, "Listen Aaron, if you keep me on the investigation, I can act as a liaison between the

FBI and NASA, but if you turn this investigation over to Weisburg, there is no telling where it will lead or what they may find out. At least with me on board, we can still keep taps on what they know and the status of their investigation. Without me, however, who knows where it will lead."

Knowing that his days were limited at NASA, Harbath thought about it for a moment, and said, "Just get me what you can Max, and keep me in the loop."

Chapter Forty-Three
May 22, 2017

Dirksen Senate Office Building, Room 226, Washington, D.C.

As the Senators milled about their seats with their respective aides shadowing them, the chatter in the room was deafening. Congressman Abel was in the forefront of the room, flanked by Teddy Fitzpatrick and other key aides for the Congressman and the White House. Behind them, were members of the press from virtually every media outlet in the world.

Having occurred only twice before in history, there was no established mechanism for confirmation proceedings under the Twenty Fifth Amendment. Initially, when Gerald Ford was nominated in 1973, the major procedural question to be worked out was which committee would handle the nomination in each chamber. In the House, it was quickly decided that the Judiciary Committee would have jurisdiction. In the Senate, however, there was vigorous debate between members who wanted to establish a special committee to consider the nomination and those who wanted to refer it to the Rules Committee. The conflict was subsequently resolved when Senate Republicans joined with the Democratic leadership and gave the Rules Committee jurisdiction.

So, Congress followed the lead of both last two confirmed Vice Presidents for the third nominated Vice President in history. They began the confirmation hearings before the Senate Rules Committee. Thereafter, the entire matter would be put to a vote on the Senate Floor. At the same time, or shortly thereafter, the House Judiciary Committee would conduct its own separate hearings, and make a recommendation to the entire House, at which time, the entire House of Representatives would vote on the matter.

"Good morning Congressman Abel, members of the media, distinguished guests, ladies and gentlemen," began Senate Rules Committee Chairman, Benjamin Boutiette from Nebraska. Boutiette was a long-standing member of the Rules Committee. A

154

former Federal Prosecutor, he was known for his tough questioning of individuals who appeared before the Committee.

"Good morning, Mr. Chairman," answered the Congressman.

"Before we begin, I should advise you Congressman that you are entitled to legal representation throughout these proceedings."

"Thank you, Senator, I am aware of that and have declined such representation."

"Sir, you are not a lawyer by training, are you?"

"I am not."

"Well, it might not be a bad idea given the nature of these proceedings and the significance of what is at stake."

"Thank you, Senator, but once again, I am quite comfortable without representation at this time. Should that change for any reason, I will let you know."

"Okay, well let's begin Congressman, shall we?"

"Absolutely, Senator."

"The Rules Committee is convened here today to act upon President Jack Halliday's nomination of Congressman Jedidiah 'Jed' Abel to serve as Vice President of the United States because of the vacancy the unexpected and untimely death of Vice President Richard Hillary caused. Congressman, you understand that today's proceeding are only the beginning of what could involve multiple hearings, numerous witnesses, and is expected to take place over the course of a number of days, with several written questionnaires to follow?"

"I do."

After that, the Committee Chairman read his prepared written statement, followed by the Ranking Member of the Committee. Then, it was Congressman Abel's turn.

"Okay, before the Committee begins its questioning, we understand that you have prepared a statement you would like to read."

"I do Senator, thank you. Mr. Chairman, Committee Members, distinguished guests and members of the press. It is with great honor that I humbly accept the nomination of Vice President of the United States. Growing up the son of a single working-class mother, I never in my wildest dreams ever thought I would be sitting here today for one of the biggest job interviews in my life. It is a testament to the ideals this Country was founded upon, including the American Dream that with a little hard work, diligence, and perseverance, anything is possible."

The Congressman continued, "More importantly however, it is the embodiment of one of the most fundamental Constitutional Principles and the reason that this Country was founded in the first place: freedom from religious persecution. The fact that I, a practicing Muslim, would be a nominee for the Second Highest Office in the land in this era of fear and discrimination against many of my faith, is truly amazing. Believe me, I am thankful for such an opportunity. And, while it is true that as with any religion, there are a few fanatics who preach jihad, do not allow the few to taint the many. We are a nation based upon the principles of religious freedom. Now, as you consider my nomination for Vice President, it is time to put those principles into action. Do not allow the fears of the minority dictate the future of a majority of this great nation. In the past, our nation has been tarnished when we have given into the whims of the few. Do not let it happen again."

After that, the Congressman went on to detail his accomplishments in Congress, his ability to work with both parties to implement important legislation and concluded with a brief description of his background. By now, of course, every Senator on the Committee was familiar with his background having received a detailed package concerning Congressman Abel beforehand.

Once Congressman Abel had concluded his opening remarks, Senator Boutiette responded, "Thank you, Congressman."

Next, the Chairman turned the proceedings over to the Ranking Minority Member of the Committee, Senator Alan Mankins from Maine, for his initial questioning of the witness. Obviously, the Chairman, who controls the order of the Senators' questioning of the witness, was saving his own examination (or perhaps, more appropriately, cross examination) of Congressmen Abel for the conclusion of the hearings. Needless to say, this was most unexpected.

Senator Mankins, who himself seemed surprised about the order of questioning, nonetheless began stating, "Good morning, Congressman Abel. You are entering your fifth term as a Congressman, is that correct?"

"Yes, Senator."

"And do you think that is sufficient time in Congress to one day possibly assume the highest Office in the land?"

"With all due respect, sir, President Obama served less than half of a term as a United States Senator, just under three years, as opposed to my ten years in the House. Respectfully, that seemed to be enough for him."

"What is it exactly that you believe qualifies you to be Vice President, Congressman?"

. "That is an excellent question Senator, and one which quite frankly, I have to admit, I was expecting in some form or another, but when you think about it, what really qualifies anyone to serve in the Nation's second highest Office?" He paused to let his rhetorical question sink in.

Then, continued, "As we all know, the nomination of Vice President is far too often a tool for political expediency. For example, when a Presidential candidate needs to win States where his polling numbers are low, he may nominate a candidate to secure those states. Now, for a change, the President has the luxury of picking someone he believes is most qualified, and best suited, for the job. Again, I am humbled he has selected me."

Regaining his focus, he continued, "But, you asked what qualifies me to be Vice President, Senator, right? And first and foremost, it is my ability to promote bipartisanship consideration of controversial legislation, which is a quality that would behoove any Vice President, especially as President Pro-Tempore, and the tie breaking vote, in the Senate. Also, given the nature of relationships I have developed in the House, I am confident that I could be an effective conduit to promote the policies of the current Administration, as any good Vice President should be able to do."

Clearly, that was an indirect reference to his relationship with the Speaker of the House, a relationship he had meticulously nurtured over his tenure in the House. From there, the questioning by the Ranking Member on the Committee went pretty much the same way throughout, with the Senator throwing soft pitches to the Congressman who ultimately made a good case as to why he should be Vice President.

Max Kallen's Office, Kennedy Space Center, Merritt Island, Florida

Calling hours before the deadline SAC Johnson had given him, Kallen began, "Frank, Max Kallen here."

"Max, old' boy, what do you say?"

"Okay, Frank. I've been given the green light to bring the Bureau in if necessary but listen to me. If the FBI or the President's Chief of Staff believes there is a link between the purportedly fraudulent Malcomovich Memorandum and the derailed McClintock nomination, which now appears to be the case, then someone in the

White House must have leaked the information concerning the FBI's investigation of Malcomovich, right?" said Kallen.

"Okay, I am with you, Max. So, what do you suggest?"

"I suggest that, instead of obtaining a warrant through normal channels, we obtain one through FISA."

He was, of course, referring to the United States Foreign Intelligence Surveillance Court (FISC), also known as the FISA Court, in which case, each application for a surveillance warrant (called a FISA warrant) is made before an individual judge of the court. When the U.S. Attorney General determines that an emergency exists, however, he/she may authorize the emergency employment of electronic surveillance before obtaining the necessary authorization from the FISC so long as they apply for a warrant within 7 days after authorization of such surveillance.

"What purpose would that serve," asked Johnson.

"Well, for one, it would keep things under taps for a bit, and if your boss can get the AG to sign off, we could begin surveillance of Peck as soon as reasonably practicable."

Kallen apparently knew that from 1979 to 2004, only 4 FISA warrants were rejected. "More importantly," Kallen continued, "it would allow us to operate under the radar for the time being without necessarily involving the White House and risking a further leak, at least for the initial seven days before seeking a warrant."

"Excuse me Max, but aren't you forgetting something?"

"What do you mean?"

"Well, first there is no foreign national in the US requiring surveillance, as is generally the case for such warrants, but more importantly, how do you expect us to get the AG to sign off without involving the White House?"

"That is where you may need to use your finesse a bit, buddy."

"That seems like a tall order my friend, especially if you knew the Attorney General. He is not generally the type to take independent action on his own without keeping the President in the loop."

"We just need one week and then we can file the warrant requests," responded Kallen. Johnson thought about it for a minute and agreed with his past terrorism task force colleague.

Now, the tricky part was selling it to his bosses.

Chapter Forty-Four
May 22, 2017

Dirksen Senate Office Building, Room 226, Washington, D.C.

Once the Ranking Committee Member, Senator Mankins, finished his questioning of Congressman Abel, Chairman Boutiette called on one of his cronies to begin questioning the Congressman.

"The Committee recognizes the Senator from Oklahoma, Senator Jansen," acknowledged the Chairman.

Jansen wasted no time.

"Thank you, Mr. Chairman," began the Senator. "Congressman, you acknowledged in your Opening Statement that you are a practicing Muslim, is that right?"

"Yes, that is true, and I am proud of my faith."

"Well, let's explore that a bit, shall we?"

"Okay."

"In college, you were involved with Muslims for a Better America, is that right?"

"Yes, Senator."

"What exactly was the purpose of that Organization?"

"Well Senator, it peacefully promoted education about Islam in an effort to combat the rhetoric that was being promulgated by some of our most ardent critics at the time."

"That sounds like the answer of a politician."

"Well Senator, I do not know how to respond to that. I am a Congressman, and thus, by definition, also a politician and that was my response."

"Very cute, Congressman."

"I am sorry Senator, I don't mean to be 'cute'. I am just answering the questions posed to me by the Committee."

"Again, the answer of a politician," responded the Senator. "Congressman isn't it true that this peaceful group disrupted commerce and threatened the Public's safety by staging a 'sit in' at one of the main on-ramps to the Interstate 880 in Oakland?"

"No Senator, what is true is that the Organization staged a lawful protest at a site that the City of Oakland pre-approved, issuing city permits for the demonstration. Nobody was hurt, and while it may have proved inconvenient for some Bay Area commuters, I am proud to say it worked. Attacks against Muslims in San Francisco and Oakland went down by almost as much as 40% following the Demonstration."

"How about attacks by foreign Muslims against the United States, has that gone down in recent years?"

"In fact, it has, Senator. Of course, it depends upon what study one uses, but I believe that statistics clearly support the proposition that Pro-Islamic Fundamentalist attacks against the United States have gone down in recent years."

"Including ISIS and Al Qaeda?"

In response, the Congressman answered affirmatively reciting various statistics to support his position. Clearly, he had prepared well. In fact, this response was almost verbatim as he had practiced with Teddy Fitzpatrick and Jonas Frank in the dress rehearsal for these proceedings hours previously. Fitzpatrick, who was watching the proceedings via CSPAN from his Office, had a big smile on his face. The back and forth between Senator Jansen and Congressman Abel went on for a while until the Senator abruptly changed the subject matter of his questioning, making it more personal."

"Congressman, isn't it true that your uncle is a well-known Muslim terrorist whose whereabouts is currently unknown by most intelligence agencies worldwide?"

"Senator, as I suspect you well know, I have never met my uncle, and did not even know of his existence until I ran for Congress ten years ago. My mother wanted me to be prepared for whatever my opponents might throw my way, just in case. The fact of the matter is that I imagine the intelligence agencies of which you speak probably have a better idea of where he is than I do."

"So, you are telling this Committee you do not now or have never known Nassir al-Fazeh?"

"That is correct. I know of him only from what my mother has told me, but I have never met him, nor am I familiar with any of his activities. And quite frankly, do not even know if he is alive."

"Well, let's consider that for a moment. Born Nassir al-Fazeh, in Southwest Syria in 1931, he became a founding member of the United Arab Republic in the Fifties. Once Syria left the UAR in the Sixties, he disappeared off the charts for a while until he re-emerged as a senior advisor to Yasser Arafat and the Palestinian Liberation

Organization in the Seventies. Then, identified as a known associate of Osama bin Laden in the Nineties, he went on to become a leading figure in forming Al Qaeda of Iraq, and is now believed to be a senior advisor to the leader of ISIS, Abu Bakr al-Baghdadi. My god man, if we were ever talking of a resume of a terrorist, your uncle probably has the best one I have ever seen."

"Your point is, Senator?" asked the Congressman.

"My point is that such a man could be a blood relative of the future Vice President of the United States, and that to me, Mr. Congressman, is a terrifying possibility."

Abel decided to go on the offensive. "Shame on you, Senator! I just told you that I have never known, nor had any affiliation with this so called 'uncle' of mine, and that I did not even know if he is alive. Nonetheless, you paraded his background before this Committee in a pitiful effort to promote fear and hatred against those who may happen to share my same religious beliefs. You are grandstanding, Senator, plain and simple. Shame on you," admonished the Congressman.

With that, all hell broke loose. The Senators hurled a mix of insults and questions at the Congressman and each other causing the Chairman to bang his gavel several times. It made for high theater in the Dirksen Committee Meeting Room that fine day.

Chief of Staff's Office, the White House, Washington D.C.

Meanwhile, Teddy Fitzpatrick and his deputy, Jonas Frank, were watching the televised hearings on CSPAN in Fitzpatrick's Office cringing at the site of the raucous that was transpiring in Dirksen Senate Office Building. It is true that they told Abel to go on the offensive, but never could they have imagined that the Congressman would publicly accuse one of the most respected Senators on the Committee of 'grandstanding' before all the American public to see, even though that was clearly what he was doing.

"For Christ's sake, couldn't he have been subtler than that," barked Fitzpatrick to Frank.

"Actually, I like it," responded Jonas Frank. "It shows he is no wussy."

"Wussy? That is the type of vocabulary they teach at Princeton these days?"

"No, it's the type of vocabulary that comes with being a Congressional Staffer for more than a decade. Anyways, as I was saying, I think any member of Congress watching these proceedings will appreciate Abel's chutzpah."

"I don't believe it, first using the word 'wussy' and now using a Yiddish word to describe a Muslim Congressman. Amazing," said Fitzpatrick, shaking his head in disbelief.

"As I was saying, it is that kind of leadership that I believe Members of Congress, and more importantly, their constituencies, are looking for in a Vice President."

"I certainly hope so. Let's just make sure to go over ways he can rehabilitate himself later when we meet with him this evening, okay?"

"Yes, sir."

Chapter Forty-Five
May 22, 2017

Lyndon B. Johnson Space Center, Houston, Texas

Following the plan Kallen had laid out, Harbath, with his boss's blessings, contacted his counterpart at the Canadian Space Agency ('CSA'), Jack Michaels, who was the CSA ISS Mission Control Director.

"Jack, Aaron Harbath here."

"Hello, Aaron. How are you?"

"Good. Hey Jack, I'm calling about the upcoming launch in July," advised Harbath.

Without getting into specifics, he said, "It turns out there have been some technical problems with the ISS's wiring that have caused some irregularities in the JEM-EF."

Not missing a beat, Michaels interjected, "You're referring to the Canadarm2's sudden unexpected movements last month, I take it."

A bit taken aback that Michaels was aware of the situation, but not surprised, Harbath responded, "Yes, well we have been monitoring the situation and are concerned that it may have been more than an aberration."

"Oh?" inquired Michaels.

"Yes, it could be a recurring problem. We are hoping that Commander Boucher has some background in electronics," he said, referring to the astronaut the CSA had selected to be the next visitor to the ISS in just under two months.

"Well, let's just say we don't expect him to be wiring up any worldwide recordings of Space Oddity," Michaels said, referring to Commander Chris Hadfield's recording of David Bowie's Space Oddity from the ISS a few years earlier.

"Seriously Jack, we were hoping that Commander Boucher had some electronics background, which we did not see in his paperwork. Otherwise, we would strongly urge you to reconsider your decision to send Boucher to the ISS."

"Amazing," exclaimed Michaels. "You have known about this for what, at least a couple of months now, Aaron? And you come to me with this now, less than sixty days before the scheduled launch, raising this nonsense! Does Administrator Redwell know about this?"

"Of course," said Harbath, incensed at the insinuation that he was doing something behind his boss's back, even though that was exactly what he had done earlier.

"Listen Jack, you have to understand that we would not be asking if we did not think this thing with the Canadarm2 required a specialist in the field's immediate attention."

"Quite frankly Aaron, I don't know if Commander has any background in electronics and would not otherwise be inclined to find out this late in the game."

However, Harbath's request was not truly a request as much as it was a demand because, as with most things in life, it all comes down to a matter of money. Canada's three main contributions to the ISS are the Canadarm2, the mobile base system, and Dexter (the Special Purpose Dexterous Manipulator, also known as the Canada Hand). Over the last twenty years, Canada has contributed about $1.4 billion Canadian dollars to the ISS program, in total, whereas, comparatively, during that same period, the United States has spent between 1.5 and 2 billion dollars *a year* on the ISS program. Thus, prepared to play the 'money card' and pull rank, if necessary, Harbath repeated his request.

"Again, Jack, we would really appreciate if you could update us as to Boucher's background in electronics, or possibly consider a suitable replacement if necessary."

Michaels thought about this for a minute. Realizing Harbath was playing the money card, he ultimately agreed to investigate Boucher's background and get back to Harbath.

Redwood City, California

Peck was fiddling at the control panel to the secure subterranean communications center for a couple of minutes before the call actually went through and the first words from the other end of the line in Arabic, roughly translated, were, "How is this whole fiasco unraveling before our very eyes?"

"My sources within the Administration inform me he was instructed to go on the offensive," replied Peck; also, in Arabic.

Peck, as it turns out, was fluent in nine languages.

"On the offensive, yes agreed, but that was too much." The voice continued, "He has just given the Senators a reason to further explore the Congressman's 'mysterious uncle', as if they did not already need one. You assured us this would not be an issue nor a problem. Yet, it clearly has become both," fumed the voice on the other end of the line.

Peck had heard him upset before, but never like this. He was livid.

"Rest assured, it is under control. Senior Administration Officials are meeting with him right now to go over damage control that may be necessary."

"And that is supposed to instill confidence in me?"

"It is all that can be done for the time being," replied Peck. "Again, confidence?"

Realizing they were nearing the pre-programmed time limit for the call and reaching the limit of arrogance he could no longer further tolerate from the caller, Peck decided it was time to conclude the call. "We will speak again in a couple of days," said Peck.

Taking his cue, the caller said, "I hope you have better news for us at that time." The line went dead, and moments later, Peck made his way back up to his penthouse office suite.

Chapter Forty-Six
May 23, 2017

FBI Director's Office, Hoover Building, Washington, D.C.

"So, Frank. What exactly is the 'federal emergency' that justifies issuance of this FISA warrant?" asked the FBI Director.

"Sir, following the NASA launch last February, NASA's Office of the Inspector General has been conducting an ongoing investigation that has confirmed some sort of electronic manipulation during the launch itself, which combined with cloud computing technology, we fear could have broader implications for an attack on the Nation's infrastructure." True enough so far.

"And, sir, it has been linked to a Peck owned corporation." Also, true enough.

"That, combined with what we already know about Peck, the Malcomovich leak, and the doctor's ultimate untimely death, would certainly justify issuance of a federal subpoena."

True again. Now, however, is where it gets a bit sketchy.

SAC Johnson continued, "And we have confirmed intelligence that a foreign entity was behind it." Not so true, even though technically, it was a foreign owned corporation.

"Sir, more importantly, we also are concerned that there may be an internal leak within the Administration at the highest-level that could tip off Peck about issuance of a subpoena, which would all but assure destruction of the critical evidence we need for a federal prosecution. That is the reason for the AG pre-warrant surveillance request."

True.

At that point, the FBI Director simply glared at Johnson, not happy about how he was skirting the issue. So, he asked again. "So, Agent Johnson, what exactly is the 'emergency' that requires the pre-FISA Warrant surveillance?"

Okay, time to cut the shit and come clean with his boss, thought Agent Johnson. "Well, sir, technically, there may not be an 'emergency' in the true sense of the term, but this matter requires the utmost discretion, and based upon the very high level internal breach within the Administration, we are again concerned about Peck destroying vital evidence once he learns of issuance of the FISA warrant. Thus, we need the pre-warrant surveillance in order to gather intelligence on where the best locations are to execute the warrants, and also, to artfully craft the description of the items specifically sought in the FISA warrant."

He paused for a moment. The Director looked up from the paperwork on his desk that he was perusing during the conversation. He raised an eyebrow as if he knew more was coming.

Sure enough, Agent Johnson reluctantly continued, "But the real hard part is getting the Attorney General to sign off without telling the President."

"Come again," said the Director.

"Well, sir, like I was saying, we are concerned that there is a leak within the highest levels of the Administration, and if the Attorney General tells the President about the pre-warrant surveillance, it will get back to Peck."

"Who exactly is this 'leak' we are talking about? You don't expect it is the President himself?" asked the Director.

"Well, not directly, but given the relationship between Peck and the President, it is not outside the realm of possibility that the President could have inadvertently conveyed confidential information to his friend and largest supporter, but no, we do not believe it is the President. We have reason to believe that the breach has occurred at the highest level of his Administration, however."

"So, again, do you have any names you believe could be the 'leak'?"

"No, not specifically, but we believe it could be one of the President's most trusted advisors."

"So, based upon some innocuous conspiracy within the ranks of the President's most senior advisors, I am supposed to ask the Attorney General to betray the President's trust, and keep the President in the dark about surveillance on his one of his closest friends?" asked the Director. "Let me ask you this, Frank, do you really believe that if the President was informed of the need for the pre-warrant surveillance, and just what was at stake, as you suggest, he would tip off Peck?"

"Like I said before, sir, maybe not directly, but again, to the extent that we believe it is some unknown source within his Administration, the need to keep the President in the dark is due to the need to keep his advisors in the dark, at least for the time being. Look, I don't even need the full seven days; just a few days, and then we can seek a full FISA Warrant."

The Director thought about it for a moment, and then grumbled, "I will speak with the Attorney General."

West Wing Meeting Room, the White House, Washington, D.C

"No really, it was good Congressman. We just think you need to tone it down a bit," advised Teddy Fitzpatrick at the beginning of the daily debriefings that were scheduled to last throughout the duration of the Committee's hearings.

"Perhaps, something a bit more conciliatory when the questioning resumes," he suggested. "Maybe even an apology." '

"Excuse me?" asked Abel, a bit irked.

"I'm sure Teddy did not mean an apology," interjected the First Lady, who was there as an advisor too. She had, after all, successfully navigated her husband's numerous campaigns for public office. Also, tonight, she was there to play the role of Senator Beth Reschel who would begin the questioning following Senator Jansen the next morning.

"Just something a little more subtle," suggested Karen Halliday.

"Thank you, Mrs. Halliday, but I was instructed to go on the offensive, and I thought that was the perfect opportunity to do so."

"It was, and you did a fine job," commented the First Lady.

"All Teddy was suggesting was that, tomorrow morning, if you are able to do so, perhaps just take a more respectful tone, Congressman. By the way, please call me Karen, Congressman," said Karen Halliday.

"Okay, Karen. Please call me Jed. I appreciate the suggestion, but can you be more specific?" requested the Congressman.

"I'm afraid, Jed, I cannot, because, of course, we do not know where the Senator's questioning may lead. I am afraid it was more of a directive than anything else. In these situations, it is imperative that one understand the primary objective and adapt accordingly," she said.

"Look, I'm not a lawyer," she said raising an eyebrow in the Chief of Staff's direction, "but from what I understand, when a lawyer prepares a witness to testify, sometimes they imply a subtlety in tone or an implicit understanding of where the line of questioning is leading, and that is all we are suggesting here. Also, hold your ground," she instructed.

"For example," she continued. "The Senators may try to twist your words out of context by rephrasing a previously answered question in terms of 'So what you are saying is', but it is important to stick what you previously said and reiterate it as much as possible to drive home the point you are making. In the end, the Committee, and their viewing constituency, should not be thinking about the question, only your answer. Got it?"

He smiled. "Got it," he said. *Damn, she was good.*

She continued, "Now, getting back to what we were discussing in the first place. When Senator Jansen finishes his questioning in the morning, Senator Beth Reschel from Vermont will begin questioning. Believe me when I tell you, I have met Senator Reschel and she is unpleasant on her best day. So, with that in mind, let's keep a respectful tone, and begin a test run, shall we?"

"Certainly, Senator Reschel."

"Good. Good morning Congressman," began the First Lady.

"Good morning, Senator."

"I think it has been firmly established that you are Muslim, right Congressman."

"Yes Senator."

"Do you mind telling this Committee whether you are Shia or Sunni?"

"Pardon me, Senator? What does that have to do with anything?"

"Remember, keep your patience and bury your indignation, Jed," instructed the First Lady, temporarily stepping out of her role as Senator to do what she was there for, which was to advise the Nominee.

"Excuse me, but I do not see what that has to do with anything," responded the Congressman.

"Quite frankly, it has everything to do with what the American people are most concerned about, which I will elaborate upon in a minute, but you are missing the point, Jed."

She paused and thought for a minute, and then asked the Congressman, "Did you ever see the movie Animal House?"

Abel shrugged his shoulders and said, "Um, yeah sure."

"Do you remember the scene, during hazing, where Kevin Bacon is being paddled and responds, 'Thank you, sir, may I have another'?"

He nodded.

She proceeded, "Well, the fact of the matter is who knows what she is going to ask, but your job as the nominee is to sit there, take it, and smile and thank her and get ready for the next thing she can throw at you, okay?"

The Congressman nodded.

"Great, now as I was saying, it has everything to do with what the American people are most concerned about because, in their minds, at least, those that understand the difference, they want to know which terrorist group to associate you with: Hezbollah or ISIS/Al Qaeda."

She continued, "Your job, Mr. Congressman, is to establish that it is neither. Since we both know that you, along with a majority of the Islamic world, are Sunni, you can steer the conversation away from which terrorist organizations are affiliated with the different branches of Islam by simply pointing out that one of the United States' closest allies in the Middle East is a country that shares your beliefs. I am, of course, referring to Saudi Arabia, but the point Congressman, is that you are in the driver's seat. By emphasizing that the United States has allies who are Sunni, you have instantaneously made yourself a friend instead of a foe in the Committee's eyes, and more importantly, their Constituents, who will no doubt be weighing in on this critical vote."

Fitzpatrick grinned, in awe of the First Lady's natural political acumen. *Damn, she was good*, he thought too.

The evening continued with the First Lady interjecting tidbits of advice in between the mock question and answer session into the wee hours of the next morning, when the Congressman finally had to excuse himself to go home and get some sleep before the next day's hearing.

Chapter Forty-Seven
May 23, 2017

John H. Chapman Space Centre, Longueuil, Quebec

Jack Michaels was studying the file for Commander Nick 'Nicky' Boucher. Nowhere in the file did it indicate that he had any background in electronics.

"Mary, please schedule an appointment with Commander Boucher ASAP."

"Yes, sir," came the prompt response.

For the next half hour, Michaels gathered as much personnel information he could about Commander Boucher. At 3:00 p.m., there was a knock on his door.

"*Oui?*" inquired Michaels, without inviting his guest into the office. Nevertheless, in strolled Commander Nick 'Nicky' Boucher.

"You wanted to see me, sir," inquired the Commander, in French, even though it was clearly his second language.

Instantly picking up on the Commander's lack of fluency with Quebec's preferred language, the ISS Mission Control Director for the CSA remembered his manners, and said in English, "Yes, please come in, Commander."

"Please call me 'Nicky', sir. With my life in your hands for the next year or so, I figure that it is best that we be on a first name basis, don't you?" Before Michaels could respond, Boucher continued unabated, "Anyways, all my friends call me Nicky. So, please just call me Nicky, sir, okay?"

Michaels sat there for a minute before mustering, "Uh, sure."

Boucher's down-home folksy style was not that with which the Mission Control Director was accustomed. As 'Nicky' pointed out, however, they were going to be relying upon one another for the next year, so he better get used to it. Quickly too.

"Anyways Commander," then, correcting himself, "I mean Nicky, the reason I asked you here today is that the ISS recently experienced some electrical malfunctions, and our friends down

South were hoping that you might have some background in electronics to help resolve the problem. In reviewing your file, however, I didn't notice any. So, do you have any background in electronics, Nicky?"

"Absolutely, sir," he said.

Michaels brows furrowed, "Oh, really? You do?"

"Certainly, if you consider working construction with my dad before joining the RCAF."

Michaels face soured, "Oh. I think they were looking for more formal training."

"Well, I have built, and rebuilt, 200-amp breaker boxes with my dad when we were building homes from scratch in the early eighties."

"Really?"

"Sure, it is simple. Just connect the copper tips of the hot wires to the breakers and the neutrals to the bus bar," he said, with an air of confidence as if he, indeed, knew what he was talking about.

Now, he had piqued Michaels' interest further. Michaels asked again, "Really?"

"Sure," said Commander Boucher, nonchalantly. "What exactly are we talking about?"

"Well, NASA's concerns are not entirely clear at this point, but certainly, your experience can only prove invaluable, I'm sure."

"Thank you, sir. Will there be anything else?" He added, "If not, I am already late for our zero-gravity training."

"No. Thank you, Commander. That's it."

Max Kallen's Apartment, Outside Lake Merritt, Florida

"You have forty-eight hours," bellowed Frank Johnson.

"What happened to seven days?" asked Kallen.

Johnson repeated, "You have forty-eight hours." He continued, "And, the Attorney General is going to brief the Director of National Intelligence, who will then decide whether to bring the President up to speed."

"Okay."

"Do you have any idea where you want to start, Max?"

"Absolutely," responded Kallen, almost immediately.

He had given this a lot of thought over the last couple of days. "In addition to the full works for the Healthmed facility in Redwood City, I would request similar surveillance for MedSupply, Inc.'s headquarters in Tampa, Florida, and SatCom Inc. in Dallas, Texas."

'Full works' meant the full realm of all available FBI electronic eavesdropping equipment being set up in non-descript vans outside the subject locations; which in turn, would allow the authorities to monitor all verbal communications within a five-mile radius.

"Additionally, individual surveillance should be set up for Peck, of course, and two executives for MedSupply, Inc.: Peter Stern, whose real name is Alexander Cain, and Rick Marshall, whose real name is Mark Walker. Both are former military."

"Geez, anything else? How about surveillance on the Prime Minister of Canada while we are at it," remarked Johnson, facetiously.

"Frank, seriously, I would not be asking if I did not believe such surveillance would yield useful intel." He paused. Then added, "Especially on such a narrow window we have."

"Touché," thought Johnson.

Chapter Forty-Eight
May 23, 2017

Dirksen Senate Office Building, Room 226, Washington, D.C.

Chairman Boutiette began the day's proceedings with a crack of the gravel, and a brief lecture to both the witness and his fellow Committee members about the gravity of the proceedings before them. He admonished them how the proceedings were going to be conducted with dignity and decorum befitting the same, at all costs. This meant no further outbursts or pre-rehearsed sermons.

With that said, Chairman Boutiette turned the proceedings over to Senator Jansen, whose questioning was surprisingly far tamer than the day before and concluded within a half hour.

After that, Chairman Boutiette announced, "The Chair recognizes the distinguished Senator from Vermont."

"Good morning, Congressman," began Senator Reschel from the great state of Vermont.

"Good morning, Senator."

Not shying away from controversial issues, the Senator began, "Congressman, I would like to begin by asking, what are your views on a woman's right to have an abortion?"

Before responding, Congressman Abel tried to recall the answer they had rehearsed hours earlier in the 'prep session'. However, he could not remember the precise way he was to phrase his response. Nevertheless, having spent decades counseling wayward girls in the Oakland area, he had grown to be somewhat of a reluctant advocate for women's rights, even though it went against the core of his religious beliefs. The Congressman had spent many nights trying to reconcile these two conflicting beliefs. Finally, he had come to terms with the position he had long since advocated.

"Senator, let me begin to answer your question by stating that I am a bit old fashioned in my beliefs in that I believe that young people should first, and foremost, abstain from engaging in sexual relations until they are married. Recognizing, however, that this may not be so practical currently, as a pragmatist, I realize that there must be a concerted campaign to educate our youth about these core values. Recognizing that these ideals are not being embraced by America's youth today, I believe the next best thing is education regarding contraceptives, and then public access to health care facilities."

"'Public access to health care facilities' – What does that even mean? Congressman, with all due respect, answer the question! Yes or no?"

"If all the other steps I have outlined should fail, an adult woman should have the right to choose any legally available options concerning her own health care, and as it presently stands, that includes procedures for abortion. So yes, Senator."

He paused intentionally. Recognizing this an opportunity to exploit the divergence between his religious beliefs and his beliefs as a politician, he elaborated further, "In fact Senator, this is a prime example of me not allowing my religious beliefs to control my opinions as a duly elected legislator."

Good use of the 'duly elected legislator', thought Fitzpatrick to himself, watching the Hearing from his West Wing Office.

"And what if people don't have access to the same resources you are touting, Congressman," countered the Senator. "For example, I am from Vermont where a good part of my constituency lives in rural areas that do not have access to the information or health care facilities to which you refer. What do you tell them, Congressman?"

Carefully considering his response, the Congressman figured that he could gain a few conservatives, as well as liberals, by preaching States' rights concerning healthcare education, while at the same time, emphasizing the merits of the McClintock Bill to close the loopholes of the Affordable Care Act (ACA) to make healthcare available to all. So, he responded, "First, and foremost Senator, let me emphasize that I believe the issue of healthcare education is primarily a State's responsibility, but under the new McClintock Bill, funds will be made available to those States with clinics in rural regions, such as your own, to promote proper sex education for the Nation's youth, as I mentioned earlier. I might also add Senator that, under the new McClintock Bill, which codifies last year's Supreme Court holding in *Zubick v Burwell*, such increased coverage applies to not only those in rural regions, but to those individuals who work for employers who have religious beliefs against abortion, like myself, providing a blanket of coverage for the nation, as a whole.

"Wow, what a politician's answer if ever I heard one," remarked Senator Reschel. "Congressman, let me ask you point blank, if you were President, would you appoint Justices to the Supreme Court that would overturn Roe v Wade?"

Throwing her colloquial tone back at her, he said, "Wow, with all due respect Senator, that is a loaded question if I ever heard one." He continued, "The only way to answer that is to say that I have no idea how some later appointed judge to the Supreme Court might rule on some hypothetical case in the future."

Senator Reschel's questioning went on throughout most of the day, and except for that hiccup in the beginning, things went pretty smoothly after that.

Aaron Harbath's Office, Lyndon B. Johnson Space Center, Houston

"Thank you for getting back to me so quickly Jack," said Harbath.

"Sure thing, Aaron," replied Jack Michaels, the ISS Mission Control Director for the Canadian Space Agency. "Listen Aaron, I spoke with Commander Boucher and it turns out he does have some background in electronics. As we speak now, he is also undergoing more extensive training in electronics. We are confident he will be able to address the situation upon his arrival to the ISS."

"Okay," said Harbath, hesitating a bit before adding, "Do you mind if we speak with him."

"Sure," responded Michaels. "When?" he asked.

"As soon as we can. Also, Jack, just to be clear, we need someone with a significant background in electronics. The whole mission may depend upon it." Recognizing his slip, he regretted it the minute he said it.

"Excuse me Aaron," interrupted Michaels. "What 'mission' are we talking about exactly?"

"Sorry Jack, that was a slip of the tongue. I generally refer to most of our ISS launches as 'missions' around here."

Michaels responded, "Uh, okay."

Abruptly returning to the subject of Boucher, he added, "So, you will arrange a conference call with Commander Boucher for later today or first thing tomorrow morning?"

"Sure, Aaron."

The call then concluded, but Michaels still wondered what Harbath meant by the term 'mission'. He knew Aaron Harbath to be a very careful man who rarely made a 'slip of the tongue'. For that reason, he would have to keep a close eye on this 'mission'. He intended to be on that conference call later, and if necessary, he would involve the Canadian Security Intelligence Service (CSIS), which is the equivalent to the CIA, in order to determine what the Americans were up to, and why it was so important that Commander Boucher have some type of background in electronics.

Chapter Forty-Nine
May 24, 2017

Redwood City, California

The FBI surveillance team had set up its base of operations in a commercial plumbing van one and a half miles away from the Healthmed facilities in what was primarily a residential neighborhood so as not to attract attention. They had been there the entire morning and most of the afternoon, as well.

"How is it going?" asked Agent Johnson, who had just arrived on the FBI Falcon 900 from D.C.

"Slow and quiet," answered Special Agent Gonzalez, the onsite Agent in Charge.

"We have been here all morning, and other than routine business chatter, we have had no progress regarding any of the subject entities or individuals. Particularly troubling is the fact that we have had no communications whatsoever from Peck's Penthouse Suite, which of course, suggests some type of routine sweeping device or scrambler. Based upon my experience, however, it is not uncommon for a CEO of a major corporation like Healthmed Inc. to take such measures to prevent corporate espionage. In fact, I would have been surprised if there wasn't any such devices or security for Peck's office, but what concerns us most is the level of sophistication of the devices we have encountered. We are talking about military grade," he said.

"And that surprises you, Agent Gonzalez?"

"No, not surprised, but certainly concerned," he said. "I guess we won't know anything for sure until we execute the FISA Warrant," added Gonzalez.

"My CI tells me it is essential we gather as much intel before the Warrant issues. Otherwise, we believe critical evidence will be destroyed."

"That does not seem likely. At least, not at this location. I might also add, sir, that based upon our review of the public records, it appears there is a subterranean portion of the facility, only accessible from Peck's office. We have set up devices in the direct vicinity of this underground room, but with no success, much the same way when we tried to eavesdrop on Peck's office. Once again, this seems to suggest that the underground facility is equipped with the same type of devices in Peck's office."

"Duly noted, Gonzalez. How about the wire taps in Peck's office? Any luck there?"

"No, pretty much the same there too," Gonzales advised Johnson.

Med Supply Headquarters, Tampa, Florida

The agents stationed outside the MedSupply Headquarters in Tampa, Florida were not having much better luck than their counterparts in Redwood City. They were monitoring the internal communications of MedSupply, and Alexander Cain and Mark Walker, in particular. Both, having been former military, were obviously good at concealing their communications. Also, they both probably had the same type of sweeping devices that were blocking communications at the Healthmed facility.

But, then Cain got sloppy. He ran an errand, and while speaking on his Apple iPhone 7, the agents picked up a conversation he was having with someone whose communications were blocked on the other end. All they could make out was what Cain was saying, not the other party. "Yes, all tests have confirmed the ability to maneuver the robotic arm when everything is in place," Cain said. "What is happening with regard to timing on your end?" There was a brief pause while the other voice responded.

"Yeah, yeah, I know. I'm not telling you how to conduct your business," answered Cain. "All I am saying is that I need to know from an operational standpoint." There was a long silence while the other party spoke for an extended period.

"Okay, okay. Got it. Like I said, the Canadarm2 is good to go."

"Wow, did you just hear that?" asked one the agents who was eavesdropping on the conversation. "Did he actually just reference it by name?"

"Sure did," responded the other.

"You got that on tape, right?" asked the first agent.

"Yep."

"That is going in an affidavit for a warrant for Cain's iPhone."

"Sure is," agreed the second agent.

SatCom Inc. Headquarters, Dallas, Texas

Meanwhile, the FBI agents conducting the pre-FISA Warrant surveillance of the SatCom facility were having about as much success as their counterparts at t h e Healthmed and MedSupply locations before the Cain slip up. Then, they too caught a break. A telephone call from Jerry Lanzella at Healthmed to the Executive Vice President of Operations for SatCom, Gerry Kramer, was intercepted. In it, Lanzella could be heard questioning Peck's ability to effectively run Healthmed.

"Listen to me Gerry, I am only coming to you because I have nowhere else to go," Lanzella said.

He continued, "Peck is really losing it. He has gone off the deep end. Just last year, in fact, he lambasted me for no apparent reason but to exercise his machismo. Then, just last week, he displayed the same inappropriate conduct with a member of my staff. As you are a member of the Healthmed Board of Directors, I thought I should bring it to your attention. Quite frankly, it has been festering with me for quite some time."

Kramer let Lanzella vent a bit longer before cutting him off to say he would investigate the matter.

Chapter Fifty
May 24, 2017

Dirksen Senate Office Building, Room 226, Washington, D.C. and Chief of Staff's Office, the White House

Senator Reschel finished her questioning of Congressman Abel Wednesday morning, and the Committee took a brief recess until the afternoon when the liberal Senator from Massachusetts, Senator Levin, began questioning the Vice-Presidential nominee.

"Good afternoon Congressman, could you please describe your relationship with your staffer, Mira Cervantes, for this Committee," began Senator Levin.

"Excuse me, Senator?"

"Congressman, do not be coy with this Committee. You heard the question the first time. What is the relationship between you and Ms. Cervantes?"

"What is he doing?" yelled Teddy Fitzpatrick to his chief aide as they watched the proceedings unfold on CSPAN, as they had been doing for the past few days.

"Senator, as I am sure you well know, Ms. Cervantes is my Chief Administrative Assistant, and has been for the last four years. Our relationship is entirely professional. I don't know what you are suggesting, nor do I appreciate your connotations otherwise."

"Where the hell is he going with all this?" bellowed Teddy Fitzpatrick to Jonas Frank.

"I am not sure, sir."

They both continued to watch the proceedings a bit longer before Frank said, "Wait a minute, sir. He seems to be handling it just fine."

Then they both paused, smiled and laughed aloud.

"I don't believe it. Son of a bitch," exclaimed Frank and Fitzpatrick simultaneously.

The Senator had just successfully pulled off one of the oldest political tricks in the book. Based, in part, upon the Latin phrase *circulus in demonstrando*, one asserts something that is untrue, so they can later prove it is untrue and look like a hero while doing so.

In this case, the Senator raised the spectra of an inappropriate relationship between the Congressman and his chief staffer which he knew was false and readily disprovable so that he could later disprove it with hard facts. That reinforced the pious nature of the Congressman for all of Congress, and the Nation, to see.

Brilliant, thought Jonas Frank.

Teddy Fitzpatrick's face immediately soured. He was a control freak, after all, partially due to his ADHD. So he did not like surprises.

"He was supposed to run any soft pitches through this Office first. Didn't you tell him that?" Fitzpatrick reprimanded his Deputy.

Unsure why his boss was not relishing what could only be described as promising testimony by the Congressman, Frank responded, "Of course, I did."

"Well, apparently he didn't get the memo," said Fitzpatrick facetiously. "Make sure it does not happen, again," he instructed.

Deflated and a bit perturbed, Frank responded, "Yes, sir, will do."

Redwood City, California

In the secure subterranean facility, Peck picked up the yellow receiver in the room to initiate contact. Within a couple of seconds, he was connected to the voice he had grown accustomed to over a lifetime now.

"It was a set up," explained Peck. "The Senator tossed him a non-issue about a purported affair he knew was false, so the Congressman could dispute it and come across smelling like roses."

"That seems like a big gamble. Why were we not advised of this previously?"

"My source tells me the President and his staff were uninformed about it as well."

"So, now we have freelancers?" asked the voice on the other end of the line.

"I would not characterize them as 'freelancers', but certainly the Party, at large, has a stake in the outcome."

"You better regain control of this whole fiasco, and quickly too," came the response on the other end of the line.

"Understood," said Peck.

John H. Chapman Space Centre, Longueuil, Quebec

Commander Nick 'Nicky' Boucher and Jack Michaels spoke via a secure video conference link with Aaron Harbath and an electrical engineer from NASA. The video conference lasted approximately a half an hour, during which time, Boucher detailed his background in electronics. Extensive questioning from the NASA electrical engineer followed. Although ultimately generally unimpressed with Boucher's knowledge of electronics, the engineer concluded it was sufficient for the task at hand. After that, Harbath concluded the call with the usual pleasantries.

Unbeknownst to Harbath, the Canadian Security Intelligence Service (CSIS) had been monitoring the video conference. Similarly, unbeknownst to Michaels and Boucher, Max Kallen was also monitoring the call from his office at the Kennedy Space Center.

Following the conference call, Michaels spoke with his main contact at the CSIS, Pierre Sands, who was listening in on the call.

"What did you think?" asked Michaels.

"Well, it seems rather innocuous to me. Nothing seemed out of the ordinary on their end. On our end, I think Commander Boucher performed admirably. He certainly impressed me, but as my wife likes to remind me, I am about as handy as 'shit on a stick' so anyone could impress me with their technical knowledge."

"Yeah, well it's not Boucher's qualifications that concerns me. It is why they are so concerned about sending someone to the ISS with a background in electronics in the first place. As I mentioned, last time I spoke with Harbath, he referred to it as a 'mission'."

"He didn't do it this time."

"I know, but that does not make me any less suspicious."

"It sounds like you should be working for us my friend," responded Sands, half joking and half serious.

"Seriously Pierre, should we open an active investigation, or can't you at least make some calls?"

"I'll see what I can do," said Sands.

John F. Kennedy Space Center, Merritt Island, Florida

Following the call, Kallen spoke to Harbath.

"Well the engineer, Sanders, seems to think Commander Boucher has sufficient training and background in electronics to do what needs to be done to the upon his arrival to the ISS, what do you think, Max?"

"If he is good with it, I am fine with it," said Kallen.

"Okay, we will proceed with the launch as scheduled. When do you think we should brief Boucher on the objective at hand?"

"As soon as possible I would say."

"Okay, agreed," said Harbath.

Oval Office, White House, Washington, D.C.

In the Oval Office that day, Teddy Fitzpatrick, the Attorney General, Stan Raffaelli, NASA Administrator, Jake Redwell, NASA Inspector General, Mark Weisburg, FBI Director Stephens, and Special Agent in Charge of the D.C. Office, Frank Johnson met with the President.

After Agent Johnson finished a thorough debriefing, and Weisburg and Director Stephens completed some follow up, the President asked, "So, basically, what you are saying is that, based upon some wild theory by a rogue intelligence Officer, I am to believe that one of my closest friends and longtime political allies, not to mention one of the greatest philanthropists of the Twenty First Century, is trying to destabilize the infrastructure of the United States. And based upon that, we are to issue national security subpoenas for not only for his primary business, and one of the Country's largest corporations, but two of its subsidiaries, as well; all, in a search for something that probably does not exist in the first place. Is that what you are telling me?" demanded the President. "Incredible," he said, shaking his head.

"Mr. President, with all due respect, Max Kallen is no rogue intelligence operative. Rather, he is a hero and may be one of this Nation's finest intelligence agents. Granted, he may have done something he probably should not have done years ago, but nevertheless, we have also independently confirmed each of the various facts supporting his theory. I mean, except for the suspected murder of Dr. Malcomovich."

Agent Johnson added, "More importantly, Mr. President, as a result of our pre-FISA surveillance of the subjects, we have gathered credible evidence indicating that there was indeed some electrical manipulation during the launch of SatCom's satellites to the ISS, as well as subsequently, Mr. President."

"I knew I didn't like that guy from the beginning," mumbled Teddy Fitzpatrick under his breath.

"Please Teddy," the President rebuked his Chief of Staff.

Sensing the President's reluctance in issuing the necessary FISA warrants, both Attorney General Raffaelli and Director Stephens cautioned about how not doing so could have potentially dire ramifications for the Country. They further cautioned that it could not appear as if the President was placing his friendship over the national security interests of the Country.

Following that, Director Stephens went on to lay out the planned execution of the FISA Warrants. Ultimately, the President reluctantly agreed.

Chapter Fifty-One
May 26, 2017

Dirksen Senate Office Building, Room 226, Washington, D.C.

The questioning went smoothly for most of the morning, with the grandstanding to a minimum. The Speaker of the House was in attendance this morning, an unusual occurrence for normal Senate hearings. Given that this was only the third time in history the Nation had held hearings to approve a Vice Presidential nominee, however, nothing could have said to be 'ordinary' about any of these proceedings. The Senators questioned the Congressman extensively about his finances, his views on the use of executive privilege, the Supreme Court and taxes.

Following the morning session, Congressman Abel and the Speaker retreated to the Speaker's Office. A couple of the Speaker's staffers brought in lunch from Hank's Oyster Bar. The Speaker assessed how things went that morning. The Congressman thanked him and proceeded to inquire about the Speaker's family. After that, they exchanged pleasantries, and the Congressman thanked the Speaker for taking the unusual step of attending the morning's hearing.

"It is important for those members of my Party in the Senate to see my support for your nomination," said the Speaker. "Besides, it just isn't the same watching it on CSPAN."

The Congressman raised an eyebrow, and the Speaker just smiled.

Redwood City, California

The FBI swarmed the Healthmed facility, armed with search and seizure and surveillance FISA warrants. Accompanying them, were agents from the Department of Homeland Security and Special Agents from NASA's Office of the Inspector General, under the command of Mark Weisburg.

At least fifty federal agents, and NASA security personnel, entered the building, dispersing floor by floor throughout the inside. At times, they escorted employees from the building so that they could conduct unadulterated searches, but more importantly, so they could place electronic eavesdropping devices throughout the building.

When the agents first arrived at the facility, and later arrived at Peck's Penthouse Suite, an army of attorneys greeted them. After Agent Johnson presented the FISA Warrant to the lead attorney in Mr. Peck's office, he perused it and handed it to Peck, instructing him to make his office available for the federal agents' search of his office.

"We would also request that Mr. Peck remove himself from the premises while we search his office," advised Agent Johnson.

"Well, obviously, you can request whatever you want Agent Johnson, but that is not going to happen," responded Peck's smug lead attorney. "To the extent that you intend to seize any items pursuant to this Warrant, we do not intend to rely upon any inventory your agents may provide without independent verification, nor are we required to do so. So, unless, Mr. Peck interferes with your search or seizure, he is entitled to be present, under the Fourth Amendment, and will stay."

Peck's attorney continued, "If you want to have the U.S. Attorney go before Judge Anderson and explain how a man in a wheel chair prevented you from conducting an effective search and seizure of his property, in the name of National Security, by all means go ahead." Peck did not like that last remark. He motioned for his attorney to bend down, and he whispered something in his ear. Afterwards, the attorney turned a bright shade of crimson. Peck motioned to another attorney, who picked up where the other one left off.

"I am sorry Agent Johnson for my colleague's remarks which, while legally accurate, may have been unnecessarily confrontational. The bottom line is we are staying while you and your agents conduct your search."

"Fine," Johnson relented.

After a couple of minutes of searching the Penthouse suite, Johnson inquired about the elevator, which of course, he already knew about.

"What is this?"

"It's not working," Peck grumbled out loud, the first words he had spoken since the agents had arrived in his office. His attorneys all glared at him at one time.

"Excuse me?" asked Agent Johnson.

"He said it is not working," responded one of the attorneys motioning for Peck to remain quiet.

"Yes, but that does not really answer my question, does it?"

"I am sorry Agent Johnson, but with all due respect, unless you are interrogating my client, I do not believe that he has to answer your questions." Johnson looked at the attorney and smiled.

"Come on, counsel, you and I both know that is not true. So long as I am conducting an ongoing open investigation, your client has a duty to cooperate and tell the truth during all active government investigations. Just ask the former Sheriff of Los Angeles County about that," smirked Johnson.

"It's okay, Larry," said Peck moving his wheelchair closer to where his attorney and Johnson were standing, near the elevator.

"To answer your question Agent Johnson, it is an elevator that leads to what I believe is some type of shelter for a natural disaster or act of war that I had the architect add when the facility was first built, but in all honesty, I can't recall. It has been ages since I have been down there, and like I said, it is not working and hasn't worked for years."

Johnson studied Peck, and then said, "Oh, really? Well, we are going to need to have one of our engineers take a look. In the meantime, no one is to enter this area which will now be restricted. I am going to have to have an Agent seal it off."

"Absolutely not," barked the lead attorney.

Again, Peck raised a hand to his attorney, and said, "It's okay, but please do your best to expedite this matter Agent Johnson."

"Of course, sir," responded Johnson immediately suspicious about how cooperative Peck was being under the circumstances.

"Do you have a key?"

Peck wheeled around to his desk, opened a drawer and presented Agent Johnson with a key. After a couple of attempts, Johnson concluded that the elevator, in fact, was not working.

He positioned an agent just outside the elevator until an engineer from the FBI's San Francisco office could get there to fix the problem and access this so called 'shelter'.

Chapter Fifty-Two
May 27, 2017

The White House, West Wing Meeting Room, Washington, D.C.

No rest for the weary. Even on a Saturday, the Congressman and White House Staff were preparing for the closed-door Senate hearings the following week. Teddy Fitzpatrick led the meeting, but his deputy, Jonas Frank, and the First Lady were also present.

"If you thought last week's hearings were tough," Fitzpatrick began, "that is nothing to what you are about to experience next week during the closed-door hearings. We can fully expect the Senators to probe everything about your finances, both past and present."

"Rest assured Mr. Fitzpatrick, there is nothing of much concern there; simply, because I am not a wealthy man, nor do I live extravagantly or beyond my means."

"Well, that is good to hear Mr. Congressman, but that is not all they will be focusing on, believe me," interrupted Jonas Frank.

"Oh?" said the Congressman inquisitively.

"Mr. Frank is right," confirmed the First Lady.

"They will want to know not only about your finances, but everything about all your close relatives' finances as well. As you know, we previously provided the Committee with your tax returns for the last ten years so anything in there is fair game, and we do not want any surprises. So, let's start there."

They spent the next hour and half pouring over the Congressman's tax returns, and then switched gears, focusing instead on the Congressman's personal life.

"Congressman, I apologize for prying, but the Senators will undoubtedly do so as well. That said, are you presently seeing anyone?" asked Fitzpatrick.

"Mr. Fitzpatrick, you know that I am a widower, my wife having passed away last year. So, to answer your question, I am not currently seeing anyone, nor do I expect to do so anytime soon. With my present schedule, I barely have time for anything other than prayers and work."

"Well, it would probably be best if you didn't start dating anyone now, at least, until the confirmation proceedings are concluded," interjected the First Lady.

"As I said, Ms. Halliday, I have no intention of doing so, nor any free time to do so even if I so desired."

"Good," said Fitzpatrick.

The next area they discussed was, once again, his political activism during college.

Finally, the subject of his long-lost uncle was revisited. "We also have to be prepared for a full-frontal assault concerning your uncle in these closed door proceedings. We have provided you all the intelligence reports concerning Nassir al-Fazeh, so you can be fully advised as to what information the Senators will have," advised Fitzpatrick.

"We are concerned that you must do even more than in the open sessions to distance yourself from your estranged uncle. So, when the subject comes up, you need to answer their questions completely, but in a manner seemingly disgusted to have to revisit issues which in your mind, and the mind of the Senators and American people, should be a non-issue since you never met the man, nor have you had any contact with him your entire life," said Fitzpatrick.

"So, when you are asked about him, remain firm in your conviction that this is a non-issue, which is clearly being politicized," further advised the First Lady.

Fitzpatrick turned to his Deputy and then asked, "How are we doing with the Senate polls?"

"Mostly positive," responded Frank.

"And our efforts lobbying the individual senators?"

"As expected," confirmed Frank.

Turning back to the Congressman, Fitzpatrick said, "Continue to project an air of confidence no matter what they may throw at you during these closed sessions, just as you did last week during the open hearings, okay Mr. Congressman?"

"Understood, Mr. Fitzpatrick," confirmed Abel.

After that, they went over a few final matters. Just as they were about to conclude, the door opened unexpectedly and in walked POTUS himself, in sweats and jogging shoes.

"Mr. President, we were just concluding the meeting," advised Fitzpatrick.

"Great, I just wanted to stop by and tell you myself what a great job you have been doing, Jed. Keep it up."

"Yes, sir, Mr. President."

The First Lady smiled, the President excused himself, and the meeting concluded.

West Plano, Texas

The private Gulfstream G550 landed at Addison Airport, outside of Plano, Texas. The Bentley Limousine was already waiting to pick Peck up. Immediately, it whisked him away to his home in West Plano.

Once there, he entered the wine cellar, chose a bottle of red wine and positioned it just right so that the palm reader could read the palm of his hand and the eye reader in the cork could read his eyeball. Once the sensors approved his palm and eye recognition, the wall at the end of the room turned to allow entry into a hallway that led to an elevator, much like the one at the Healthmed facility, to which, the FBI was presently attempting to gain entry.

He couldn't help but smile at the thought that, after the FBI's engineer got the elevator running again, they would be confronted with precisely what he had a described – an outdated bomb shelter, devoid of any electronic or communications equipment whatsoever. The elevator arrived, and he descended into an identical communications center as the one that previously existed at the Healthmed facility, this eventuality having been previously considered.

Within minutes, he was connected to the same dark voice he had known for his entire adult life. "Did you not know about the FISA warrants before they were issued?" asked the voice on the other end of the line."

A pause.

"No, of course not."

"You continue to disappoint."

Another pause. "Were it not for our sources advising of what was coming, we would not have been able to clean the bunker in time. Don't fail us again," the voice on the other end of the line instructed. Click. The line went dead.

Peck was fuming. Yes, it was true that Peck's source had not informed h i m of the issuance of the FISA warrants in advance. Once he learned of them, however, it was Peck's team that 'cleaned' the bunker before the FBI arrived. Next time, he would remind the voice on the end of the line that he still had a vital role to play. Peck then retreated from the bunker beneath his Texas mansion to the luxurious amenities above ground.

Chapter Fifty-Three
May 29, 2017

Quantico, Virginia, Forensic Science Research and Training Center (FBI Laboratory)

After the U.S. Attorney's office obtained a search warrant for Cain's iPhone7 based upon the pre-FISA warrant surveillance, the FBI laboratory analysts were able to unlock the phone (which was seized during the execution of the FISA warrants) using the fingerprints the government had on file for Cain from his military service.

Then, because one's voice is translated into a series of bits and converted back into sound when speaking on one's phone, service providers can record the digitalized voice data, which working in conjunction with the cloud, can be stored and streamed later. As a result, working with Cain's service provider, the FBI agents were able to download virtually every communication that took place on that phone except for one number. Again, with regard to that particular number, they could only track what Cain was saying, not what the other party to the conversation was saying, as was the case with the calls for Dr. Malcomovich.

One conversation that occurred on February 17, 2017 to a mobile cell tower close to Pebble Beach, California was particularly interesting. The transcript of the recording read:

> "CAIN: You know, this isn't easy, I can only get away so often and I am constantly worried about being detected.
> OTHER PARTY: Blocked.
> CAIN: What do you mean?
> OTHER PARTY: Blocked
> CAIN: You must understand, with that size of the load, this is not as simple as we originally calculated.
> OTHER PARTY: Blocked
> CAIN: As you well know, sir, theory is often different than practical application. There are always glitches when one

attempts to apply theory into reality. There was simply no way I could have expected this. And by the way, you came to me, not the other way around."

"Seems pretty incriminating to me," said one of the FBI Agents assisting the Analyst downloading the contents of Cain's iPhone.

"I'll run it upstairs," she said.

Lyndon B. Johnson Space Center, Secure Conference Room "C"

Deep in the bowels of the Johnson Space Center is a secure meeting room, which is a drab no frills space with faux mahogany wood paneling, a conference table and some chairs around it. Nothing else. Nevertheless, the room was supposedly as secure as the Situation Room.

On this day, its occupants included NASA Administrator Redwell, Mark Weisburg, Aaron Harbath, Max Kallen, Dr. Martin White from JPL, Jack Michaels, and Commander Nick 'Nicky' Boucher from the CSA. Following Aaron Harbath and Max Kallen's detailed briefing, CSA Mission Control Director, Jack Michaels, inquired, "So, what is it exactly that you expect Commander Boucher do once he gets to the ISS?"

Dr. White then explained precisely what would be required to disengage remote access to the ISS and return the ISS wattage to normal levels.

"Sounds easier said than done," commented Commander Boucher.

"That may be the case Commander, but frankly, you are the best shot we have now. Keep in mind, we will all be relying upon you."

"Wow, no pressure there," joked Boucher, in part, to relieve the tension in the room. It didn't work. No smiles around the conference table.

"Now that you understand the seriousness of the situation, Commander, maybe you can appreciate why we were so interested in your background in electronics," explained Aaron Harbath.

"I certainly do," offered Boucher.

At that point, Administrator Redwell regained control of the meeting. "Gentlemen, I want you to know that this mission has the approval of the President and other high-level government officials. Presently, the FBI is investigating Mr. Peck, Healthmed SatCom, and other Peck companies. Thus, it is imperative that this information not leave this room and be given the highest security clearance available. It is my understanding that the President will be briefing the Prime Minister directly," he said to Michaels and Boucher.

"Thank you for taking the time to come to Houston, gentlemen."

Chapter Fifty-Four
May 30, 2017

Dirksen Senate Office Building, Room 226, Washington, D.C.

During the morning session of the first of three closed door sessions, the Senators thoroughly vetted Abel's financing of every one of his campaigns, going all the way back to student council in college through his recent re-election to the House of Representatives, just last year. The Senators also probed every investment he had ever made, good or bad, over the last thirty (30) years. They pored over every reason for the investment, how he found out about it, and whether it was successful in the end.

The next subject was school. Believe it or not, they started at grammar school and continued through graduate school. They asked him about his study habits and whether he ever cheated in school.

Really, you think they could do better than that, Abel thought to himself.

After the morning session, the Congressman retreated to the inner sanctum of the Speaker's office before heading off to the Members' Dining Room for the two Congressmen's weekly lunch together. They enjoyed a relatively peaceful lunch together; probably, because the other Members of Congress were worried about interrupting two of the most powerful people in D.C. presently. Whatever the reason, their lunch was quiet, which was precisely what Congressman Abel needed; a brief respite before returning to the fire.

After lunch, it was back to the wolves. Literally. When Congressman Abel re-entered the Hearing Room, the Senators were practically foaming at the mouth. Apparently, it was time for the good stuff: gloves off!

Sure enough, the first question was, "Congressman, earlier we explored your contact, and purported lack of contact, with your estranged uncle Nassir al-Fazeh, but what do you know about your other relatives' contact with him, starting with your mother, his sister?"

Not wanting to bring his mother into the proceedings, which was seemingly becoming more of an inevitable possibility, Congressman Abel responded, "My understanding is that she, like me, has not spoken to him during my lifetime. They too are 'estranged' as you so aptly referred, Senator."

"How about any other relatives," pried the Senator.

"Senator, as you sat through the entire last week of hearings, you know that it is only my mother and me. I have no other 'relatives' as you suggest."

"Very nicely done," thought Deputy Chief of Staff, Jonas Frank, sitting in the back of the room. He, of course, would promptly report back to his boss following the hearing.

The questioning continued throughout the rest of the afternoon with the subject of his estranged uncle coming up twice more, but with much the same effect: nothing, or very little, at a minimum. It was a tough day and the Congressman performed admirably.

FBI Headquarters, Hoover Building, Washington, D.C.

Special Agent Johnson was comparing the transcript of the telephone call the lab had just downloaded from Cain's iPhone to that of the conversation during the mysterious Malcomovich excursion to Pebble Beach.

"Amazing, it matches up perfectly. So, it is safe to assume that Malcomovich's host is the same person with whom Cain is having this conversation, right?" asked Johnson, more rhetorically than anything else. The agents with whom he was speaking at the time simply nodded. "Well, we certainly have enough to bring Cain in for questioning and find out who he was talking to and what he was talking about." Again, the agents just nodded. Johnson thought about it for a moment, and then said, "Okay, do it." The agents left the office. As they did so, he picked up the telephone to inform the Director.

Hours later, Alexander Cain was seated in Interrogation Room 'I' at FBI Headquarters in Washington D.C., with the FBI Director and other senior level FBI agents positioned on the other side of the two-way mirror in the middle of the room. Max Kallen and Mark Weisburg were also viewing the interrogation through a secure video conference monitor, at Kennedy Space Center.

Frank Johnson entered the interrogation room and took a seat directly opposite Mr. Cain and didn't say a word. Neither did Cain. They sat there in silence for a good three minutes, but it seemed like thirty. Then, Special Agent in Charge, Frank Johnson, broke the silence.

"I understand you have requested counsel, whom we are waiting for, but don't worry, those high-priced attorneys usually take their sweet ass time getting here. More to bill you, I guess," Johnson said. Cain just grinned.

"Or should I say, rather, more to bill your benefactor."

"One of the perks of working for corporate America in one of the greatest countries in the world," smirked Cain.

"Smug bastard, isn't he," commented Director Stephens from behind the two-way mirror. All at once, his underlings agreed in unison. Kallen smiled. Just like his brother, he thought.

At that moment, the door to Interrogation Room 'I' flung open, and in barged a heavyset man in a three-piece suit.

"Speak of the devil," joked Johnson. "Counselor," he said, greeting the new participant to the interrogation.

"Wow, none other than SAC Johnson himself. What have you done Alex to warrant such special attention?" asked the attorney facetiously.

"I don't know, we were just discussing your billing practices, Jack," said Cain.

"Oh really, does Agent Johnson require the services of an attorney?" asked the attorney, playing along. "Don't worry, Alex, I don't think he could afford me on that civil servant's salary of his."

"Boy, they are just having a grand old' time, aren't they," said Director Stephens, unamused.

"Well, instead of wasting the taxpayers' money with your ridiculous banter back and forth, why doesn't Mr. Cain tell us," but then Agent Johnson stopped mid-sentence and said, "Strike that. Let me back up a minute, is it Mr. Cain or is it Mr. Stern?"

"I think you well know by now, Agent Johnson, that my client's real name is Alexander Cain."

"Well then, Mr. Cain, perhaps you can tell us why you also go by the pseudonym of Peter Stern?"

When the attorney began to answer, stating, "I did not realize it was illegal to use a pseudonym," Johnson held his hand up and said, "Uh-uh, Counselor, you are familiar with the drill. I let you answer the first one, but we are not going to do this anymore. You can ask me to clarify my questions if necessary or instruct your client regarding those questions, but you may not answer those questions for him. Should you continue to do so, we will have you removed and replaced by a federal public defender." When the attorney started to protest, Johnson interrupted him, got up from his chair, left the room and returned with two FBI agents.

"Well, what is it going to be counselor?"

With the threat of possible removal, the attorney quieted down, and Johnson proceeded with his interrogation as the two other agents left the room. "Now," began Johnson, "back to my original question. Why is it you use Peter Stern as a pseudonym, Mr. Cain?"

"Well, when I left the military, they recommended that I do so given the sensitive nature of the operations in which I was involved during my stint in the Army."

"Was that how you would refer to it? As a 'stint in the Army'?"

"Well, given that they paid for my education, as I am sure you are well aware, Agent Johnson, I guess it was a bit more than that."

"And was your employer aware that it was a pseudonym when you were hired."

"Well, since they required that I present them with paperwork from the military, I imagine they are fully aware of that, sir."

"Has anyone at MedSupply or its parent company, Healthmed ever discussed the issue of your true identity with you or addressed you by your real name, Mr. Cain?"

"I am not certain I can recall a particular instance of that occurring, Agent Johnson," answered Cain.

At this point, the attorney interjected, "Excuse me SAC Johnson, I am not certain why this line of reasoning is relevant, especially since my client has yet to be charged with anything, and last time I checked changing your name was not illegal, and certainly, not a federal matter, in any case."

If it is done legally, thought Johnson to himself. Nevertheless, ignoring the attorney, and continuing undeterred, Johnson kept his focus on Cain. He asked his next question.

"Besides 'the army made me do it," is there any other explanations you would like to offer at this time for the reason you use a pseudonym, Mr. Cain," asked Johnson.

After about an hour of the 'preliminaries', as Johnson liked to think of them, he got down to the meat of the matter. "Mr. Cain, do you recall any conversations you may have had with anyone in the area of Pebble Beach earlier this year?"

Cain laughed out loud, a big hardy laugh. "Sir, you do realize that Healthmed is in the Silicon Valley, in Redwood City, don't you? And that half of the executives with whom I deal with there have weekly tee times at Spyglass?"

"So, that is a 'no' then Mr. Cain, you can't recall?"

"No, it is an 'I've had many conversations and have no idea about the particular one to which you are referring' Special Agent Johnson."

"Indeed, if you have a particular conversation in mind, Agent Johnson, perhaps you would like to share that with my client and me," offered the attorney

Again, ignoring the attorney, Agent Johnson asked his next question. "Of those conversations with executives on the golf course, which you just mentioned, were any of those conversations with Healthmed's CEO, J. Robert Peck?"

"It is possible, I can't recall specifically. Like my counsel said, if you have something in mind, why don't you go ahead and show me."

Not wanting to play into his hand and let him take control of the interrogation, Johnson was not going to introduce a copy of the telephone transcript just yet.

Abruptly changing the subject, he said, "Mr. Cain, can you tell me if you have ever entered a NASA facility under your pseudonym or using any other aliases."

"I am quite certain I have not," responded Cain.

"Are you sure about that," asked Johnson raising an eyebrow. "Absolutely, sir."

Hmm, thought Johnson, who wasn't ready to confront him with Kallen's findings just yet. Switching gears again, he asked, "Mr. Cain, of any of those numerous calls with executives on the golf course, did any of them involve discussing the size of the SatCom satellite that Healthmed was sending to the International Space Station from a secure NASA facility?"

"I don't know what you are talking about," he said.

On the other side of the two-way mirror, Director Stephens reiterated, "Smug bastard."

At that point, the attorney figured he better earn part of that $600 an hour fee, and offered, "Unless you have anything further Agent Johnson, other than commentary, I believe we are done here."

"Actually, I do counselor, and I will say when we are done here."

Johnson proceeded with another hour of questioning without showing him a single document, and then concluded the interrogation, stating, "Thank you, gentlemen. Now, we are done. You are free to leave, Mr. Cain, but I wouldn't make any plans to leave the country anytime soon."

"Well, considering that you have not charged my client with any crime nor notified him that he is a 'person of interest' or 'suspect' in an ongoing investigation, I would say he is free to do as he pleases SAC Johnson," countered the attorney.

Johnson simply got up and exited the room, closing the door behind him and entering the room next door to consult with the team assembled there as well as connected via secure video conferencing. The general consensus was that, other than being an arrogant prick, which of course was not a crime, they had no grounds to hold him for further questioning or to issue an arrest warrant, unless of course, they wanted to put together a case against him based upon Kallen's investigation. That was the subject of discussion. The 'nays' carried the day with the rationale being that they did not want to play their trump card too soon, and already had the evidence they needed should, and when, they decided to pursue that option.

In the meantime, they would continue to conduct further surveillance on him, both electronically as well as with alternating surveillance teams.

Chapter Fifty-Five
June 7, 2017

The White House, West Wing Meeting Room, Washington, D.C.

Having just narrowly passed the Senate by a tally of 53 votes in favor of Congressman Abel versus 47 against, the brain trust was again hard at work, preparing for the next battle in the House of Representatives.

"The Senate vote was way too close for comfort," theorized Teddy Fitzpatrick aloud. "We want to avoid that in the House. I mean, based upon pure arithmetic, we should be fine unless..." Teddy Fitzpatrick paused mid-sentence, looked awkwardly at the Congressman, and added, "Unless there is something we do not know about."

"Rest assured, Mr. Fitzpatrick, at this stage, there is nothing you do not know about me, especially after all the vetting I have been through." After a brief silence, he continued, "Although, I think it is safe to assume that our opponents in the House will again raise the issue of my estranged uncle."

"Absolutely," agreed everyone in the room.

"So, the question then becomes how to dispel the myth once and for all," asked the Congressman. Everyone agreed that this would be the primary hurdle in the House.

Fitzpatrick turned to his deputy, and barked, "Get me both the NSA and CIA reports of al-Fazeh's purported death in 2007." Then, he turned toward the Congressman and asked, "Congressman, will you agree to make your phone records available for the last five years?"

The Congressman shrugged his shoulders. "I guess so, if you really think that is necessary."

"Gentlemen, it seems we should go on the offensive as opposed to looking for ways to dispel any connection between the two," offered the team's newest participant; none other than the Speaker of the House of Representatives himself. "By the way, Teddy, I recall the al-Fazeh reports you are talking about and remember they were clearly inconclusive," added the Speaker.

"Nonetheless, it can't hurt to have the information readily available. I have a little saying Mr. Speaker, 'Data is king.'" The Speaker did not say anything, but clearly did not appreciate the Chief of Staff's condescending tone. It was an 'ultimate ego fighting championship.'

"Both are good suggestions," offered the First Lady, attempting to smooth the waters.

"In addition, Mr. Speaker, you obviously need to work with all of your connections in the House."

"Of course, that goes without saying, Ms. Halliday," responded the Speaker. "My staff and I have been tirelessly lobbying on behalf of the Congressman from the day the President first put his name forward. In fact, let's not forget whose idea it was to nominate Congressman Abel in the first place," reminded the Speaker.

"Well, now is more critical than ever," offered Teddy Fitzpatrick. They all agreed, and the meeting concluded.

John H. Chapman Space Centre, Longueuil, Quebec

Commander Nick 'Nicky' Boucher was beginning to believe that he woke up in a different person's body; the body of a full-fledged member of the Quebec Chapter of the International Brotherhood of Electrical Workers. When he was not studying electrical currents, he was in a lab splicing wires and connecting fuses. Before, when he said he had toiled with hooking up fuse boxes with the family business, it was nothing like what he was learning now. He was fully and completely engrossed with electricity, from all aspects. He felt like he was back in school again. One thing was for sure, he did not sign up for this when he signed up to be an astronaut. Anyways, he might as well make the best of it, he figured. Day in, and day out, he continued with his studies, labs, and his typical astronaut duties. All of a sudden, Jack Michaels unexpectedly entered the lab just as Boucher was about to enter the zero-gravity simulator.

"Nicky, we know you are being asked to take a lot more on with this mission." Damn, there was that word 'mission' again, thought Michaels to himself. He continued, "but I can't stress the importance enough here. If, what the Americans truly believe is the case, then it goes without saying that diffusing whatever is causing the extra wattage aboard the ISS could be one of the single greatest accomplishments in terms of both of our nations' security?"

"Of course, sir," said Boucher. The significance of what was at stake, however, was not lost on him.

"Jackson tells me you are picking up the electrical engineering aspect quite well."

"Yes, well it is far more extensive than I could have imagined, in all honesty."

"As one would no doubt expect. After all, we do not know what you will encounter up there so we have to be prepared for a variety of different scenarios."

"Of course, sir," Boucher said.

"I have been in touch with Director Harbath and NASA's security team who, on a regular basis, are continuing to monitor the situation. They have been providing updates as information becomes available. Also, we are informed that the FBI is conducting a pending criminal investigation of Healthmed, its subsidiaries, and some of its high-level executives, but to date, nothing has panned out."

Boucher looked at his boss curiously.

"Look Nicky," Michaels continued. "I just want you to know that you are not in this alone. There are lots of people, and agencies out there, working to solve the problem. We will have your back at all times."

"Yes, sir," responded Boucher.

Chapter Fifty-Six
June 15, 2017

Lyndon B. Johnson Space Center, Secure Conference Room "C"

Max Kallen and Mark Weisburg, and half a dozen FBI agents, were poring over the dozens of documents Kallen had gathered or generated during his initial investigation in the make shift task force room at Johnson Space Center, in Houston, Texas. Also, on the 72" flat screen monitor in the middle of the room, the videotaped interrogation of Alexander Cain was playing over and over. In addition, they had the FBI transcripts of all recorded Cain conversations since the interrogation.

"One thing is for sure, he has been one careful son of a bitch since they brought him for questioning," commented Weisburg, reviewing one of the transcripts of the FBI recordings.

"No doubt," responded Kallen, looking at one of the surveillance tapes of Cain, on his laptop. He suddenly stopped the video, and moved it in slow motion, frame by frame. In it, Cain could be seen walking his dog behind a small tree with lots of dead branches on it. Although he is not holding any type of cellular phone, he clearly appears to be having a conversation with someone by the odd gestures and tilts of the head he is making. Kallen notes the time on the still frame and immediately scrambles to find a transcript of a recording matching that date and time. Curiously, there are none.

"Mark, take a look at this, would you?" Kallen showed Weisburg what he has discovered. "Don't you think it is odd that there is no corresponding transcription of any recording on that date at that time?" Weisburg looked, and then looked through the transcriptions. Kallen had done a rough calculation, and added, "By my calculation, that should be within the range of the van, shouldn't it?" Kallen was, of course, referring to the FBI van that was positioned within a quarter mile of Cain's residence in Florida. Weisburg did some of his own calculations and concurred with Kallen. Kallen picked up the phone and spoke with SAC Johnson briefly. Moments later, FBI agents descended upon the Cain residence, armed with search warrants which they knew they would not need as the subject was not home at the time. They proceeded to the backyard where Cain's German Shepard immediately gave them a warm welcome, but they were prepared. One of the agents was a trained dog handler for the FBI and was able to subdue the aggressive canine. Once the dog was under control, the agents headed toward the subject tree. Shortly thereafter, it was confirmed that the tree was embedded with a scrambler to prohibit electronic eavesdropping which was removed and replaced with an amplification device that would allow agents to better hear all conversations within a proximity to that tree.

West Plano, Texas

Peck was in the secure bunker at his Dallas mansion for less than a minute before the secure line lit up and he picked up the receiver. The voice immediately came over the line, accusatory.

"You barely succeeded this time around. It better not be as close next time."

"Larger playing field," responded Peck. "Incidentally, the subject of our old friend's fears appears to be a subject of concern for the upcoming hearings, my sources inform me."

Silence for a moment. Then, came the response. "Noted."

So frustrating, thought Peck. What the hell does 'noted' mean? Was there further action required of Peck? Would Peck ever be informed of the solution? Probably not. The voice on the other end of the line then said flatly, "And the FBI?"

"Not a concern," said Peck. "We have taken extra precautions."

"And Cain can be trusted."

"Absolutely. I vetted him myself."

Again, on the other end of the line, nothing. Then, "Let's hope so," and click.

Peck sat there momentarily in his wheelchair before taking the elevator back up to his luxury world above. He ordered that the limousine be brought around for his return flight to California.

Chapter Fifty-Seven
June 20, 2017

2237 Rayburn House Office Building, Washington, D.C.

The House Judiciary Committee Chairman called to order the first hearing in the House of Representatives regarding the nomination of Congressman Jediah Abel for the position of Vice President of the United States.

Chairman Gary Schwartz from California was a tall, heavy-set man with a high whiny squeaky voice that could become grating on a person if they had to listen to it for extended periods of time. Recognizing this inherent flaw, he kept his opening remarks brief.

Then, much like he did in the Senate, Congressman Abel provided some brief opening remarks before Chairman Schwartz, who unlike his colleague in the Senate, began the questioning of the Congressman before turning it over to the Ranking Member on the Committee.

Like his colleagues in the Senate, Chairman Schwartz focused much of his questioning on the Congressman's political activism in college, his finances and of course, his nefariously estranged uncle. The questioning lasted about an hour and a half and was, for the most part, dull and redundant.

Once the Ranking Member began questioning, however, it became a bit more interesting. With much less theatrics than his colleagues in the Senate employed, the Congressman from Wyoming covered many of the same areas, including religion and any ties to radical organizations. Once again, Congressman Abel performed admirably, thought Fitzpatrick and Jonas Frank who were watching in the Chief of Staff's West Wing Office via CSPAN.

At the noon recess, the Speaker and Congressman Abel had their weekly lunch together, and as a sign of the Speaker's support for the nominee, they did so publicly in the Members Dining Room.

"You are doing great, Jed," offered the Speaker.

"I suppose," said the Congressman halfheartedly.

"There were a couple of trick questions by Congresswoman Zydell, but surprisingly, not as bad as in the other Chamber," remarked the Speaker.

Again, "I suppose so," from the Nominee.

"Just keep your calm demeanor as you have been doing," instructed the Speaker.

"Yes, believe me, I have been well coached."

"I know you have, but sometimes it just helps to have a friendly reminder," said the Speaker smiling, trying to keep the Congressman's spirits high before he returned to the afternoon session of the Judiciary Committee Hearings.

Over the last couple of years, the two Congressmen had grown close in a strange way. They understood each other's moods and penchants. Congressman Abel looked up from his plate of food and smiled too. The two Congressmen finished their lunch, conversing over their families and the wonderful season the Nationals were having behind Strasburg's pitching and Bryce Harper's offense and defense.

Following lunch, Abel returned to the Rayburn House Building for further questioning by the Judiciary Committee. That promptly concluded in the afternoon at 4:30 p.m. Afterwards, the Congressman attended the routine evening cocktail parties various lobbyists and Political Action Committees hosted, which was no doubt a much-fancied perk for many of the unpaid interns working on Capitol Hill.

SAC Johnson's Office, Hoover Building, Washington, D.C.

Special Agent in Charge Frank Johnson had just finished briefing the Director as to the status of the ongoing wiretaps, electronic surveillance and physical surveillance in connection with the Healthmed investigation when another agent on the newly created task force entered his office. She said, "Excuse me boss, but we may have found a needle in a hay stack."

"Pardon me," said Johnson. He was in no mood for games.

"Sir, in looking through the pre, and post, FISA warrant recordings, we may have found a potential CI," she said, referring to a confidential informant.

"Excuse me," responded Johnson, still not amused, but his interest piqued more.

"Sir, it turns out that a very high-level executive at Healthmed has been disgruntled for quite some time and has questioned Peck's ability to lead the company to other executives."

"So, does he have any pertinent information to our investigation?"

"Maybe, maybe not, but he could be our way into the Company. It could potentially help facilitate access to other members of the Company who may have the relevant knowledge we need who are willing to cooperate."

Johnson thought about it, and then asked, "Okay, does this 'needle' have a name?"

Now it was the agent's turn to say, "Excuse me," missing the 'needle' reference altogether. Finally figuring it out, she said, "oh yes, his name is Jerry Lanzella, Senior Vice President in charge of Sales and Marketing for the Pace Maker Division of Healthmed Inc."

"Okay, and what is your plan for getting Mr. Lanzella talking?" asked Johnson.

"Well, he is disgruntled. Perhaps, the presence of an ongoing FBI investigation will increase his willingness to assist the United States Government. It certainly can't hurt to ask and gage his willingness to cooperate. In the meantime, we will run all databases to see if there is anything we can come up to use which might also make him a bit more cooperative."

"Sounds good," said Johnson.

Chapter Fifty-Eight
June 24, 2017

Lyndon B. Johnson Space Center, Secure Conference Room "C"

Kallen enjoyed the silence of the large conference room on a Saturday morning. As usual, he was its sole occupant this morning. Suddenly, a strange beeping sound broke the silence. Strangely, it was not coming from his cell phone. Rather, the beeping was coming from a private beeper in his briefcase that notified him he had a special encrypted message in a secure inbox that only a few people knew about from his old intelligence days. He immediately stopped what he was doing, dialed into the secure inbox and was surprised to hear a message from his old friend, Uri Nimi, Deputy Director of Shin Beit. He promptly returned Uri's call.

"Uri, Max here. Shalom. What is so urgent that you called on the beeper line?"

"Max, I have been following the confirmation hearings, and you will probably hear this from your people soon enough if you have not already." Uri paused for a moment, immediately realizing his mistake.

He quickly added, "I mean, if you still keep in touch with any of them."

"Uri, it is okay. What is it?"

"Well, I know there has been a lot of talk about the Congressman's estranged uncle, Nassir al-Fazeh."

"Yes?" asked Kallen.

"There are reports coming in as we speak of a drone attack southeast of Damascus. Al-Fazeh is believed to have been in one the subject vehicles." He then added, "It was not us, so if it was not you guys, it was probably Iran or Assad."

"Very interesting, Uri. Thanks for the tip."

"No problem, if you want, I can send you the reports."

"Yeah, that would be great, thanks. Seriously Uri, *todah*."

"*Bevakasha*."

Max immediately called one of his old contacts at the NSA, only to be redirected to the CIA's Middle East Division where some mid-level analyst was spewing standard media PR bullshit. Finally, Kallen got so frustrated, he picked up the phone and called his old friend and mentor, the former head of the NSA. Like Kallen, he had been out of the intelligence community for some time, but still had some contacts. He made some calls, and as it turns out, because the subject vehicle was carrying explosives at the time, no identification could be confirmed. There was, however, strong evidence that al-Fazeh was in the vehicle at the time of the attack.

The White House, Oval Office, Washington, D.C.

A few hours earlier, the President, having received his President's Daily Briefing, or PDB as it is more commonly known, was also briefed by his national security team about the drone strike that purportedly killed the Islamic terrorist known as Nassir al-Fazeh. Also present was Teddy Fitzpatrick and Jonas Frank.

"So, it wasn't us?" asked the President.

"No, sir," responded the Chairman of the Joint Chiefs of Staff. "And the Israelis?"

"No, sir, Mr. President," answered his National Security Advisor. "We believe that, given his extensive ties to various Sunni movements, it could have been Iran's Ministry of Intelligence and Security, aka MISIRI. Based upon his recent affiliation with ISIS, however, it could also have been Assad and his Russian backed forces."

The President turned to his Director of National Intelligence, and asked, "Bob, what is your best call?"

"Mr. President, everything points to Iran."

"Doesn't the whole timing of this attack strike you as odd, Bob?"

"What do you mean, sir?"

"I mean al-Fazeh has been the subject of hot debate during the recent confirmation hearings of his estranged nephew, and now, there is suddenly this drone strike?"

"Sir?"

"I mean, Christ, I can just see the bloody headlines tomorrow, 'Administration Orders Drone Strike to Quiet Opposition During Congressional Hearings.'"

"That is why we must shut this down now, and immediately issue a press release about the drone strike, indicating that neither us nor the Israelis had anything to do with it," interjected the political wunderkind, Fitzpatrick.

"That will buy us some time, at least temporarily," added Fitzpatrick. "In the meantime, we need to confirm who was responsible and whether al-Fazeh was indeed in the vehicle. Also, we need to brief Congressman Abel immediately, so he is ready for this during the hearings."

"Agreed," said the President, turning to his Director of National Intelligence and Joint Chiefs Chairman. "I want everything we have up to the minute regarding the strike and confirmation concerning al-Fazeh's presence in the vehicle. Run it through both Teddy and me first, okay?"

"Yes, sir," they responded simultaneously.

"Okay, next item of business is to notify the Congressman," said the President aloud as if he were speaking to himself. He picked up the phone on the Resolute Desk and said, "Nora, will you have Congressman Abel come to the Oval Office immediately."

"Yes, sir, Mr. President," responded Nora Summers.

Chapter Fifty-Nine
June 26, 2017

2237 Rayburn House Office Building, Washington, D.C.

Even two days after the initial reports of the demise of Nassir al-Fazeh surfaced, confirmation of the terrorist's death had yet to be confirmed. Nonetheless, it was a hot topic of discussion at the next House Judiciary Committee hearing on Congressman Abel's nomination. The mysterious timing of the event was the focus.

"Yes, I would agree [sir or madam], but as you heard in the confidential briefing this morning, neither I, nor our government or close allies had anything to do with it," became the catch-phrase of the afternoon.

After the third or fourth time, the Committee Chairman realized he needed to do something to restore order. He took a brief afternoon recess, during which, he discussed with other Members the need for them to limit further questioning on the matter since it was not productive and tending to drag the hearings out longer than necessary, not to mention was a subject concerning National Security.

Chairman Schwartz's little pep talk apparently worked. Following the afternoon recess, the questioning revolved around religion, family and finances. Once again, Congressman Abel performed admirably, with only a few tense interactions with Committee Members from the other party flaring up now and again.

In response to one question, he stated, "Keep in mind, Madame Congressman, that the victims of a vast majority of radical attacks are Muslims. As a Muslim, I believe we can, and must do, more to stop our youth from being allured by false promises, and instead, show them the ineffectiveness of the radicals that will only lead to the deaths of more Muslims."

In the end, he came out of the day's hearing pretty much unscathed. He knew deep down that it was due to the intense preparation he had undergone. Indeed, the Administration was forthright with all the information it had concerning the attack. Meanwhile, Fitzpatrick, the First Lady and others had worked hard, peppering him with questions and answers so he would be prepared for the next Committee hearing. As a result, he certainly was. *If things continued the way they were going, the hearings should be over in a few more days and then a full vote in the House,* thought the Congressman. Perhaps, that was just wishful thinking on his part, however. Just as the wheels of justice could sometimes be slow in coming, the wheels of Congress were known to be notoriously much slower.

Following his day on the Hill, Congressman Abel returned to the West Wing of the White House for further preparation with Jonas Frank, and Teddy Fitzpatrick. The First Lady was curiously absent from the meeting this evening. Perhaps, duty called, figured the Congressman. The session went late into the night. The Congressman then returned to his Foggy Bottom condominium for a couple hours of sleep before returning to the Judiciary Committee hearing room the next day.

West Plano, Texas

Having heard the reports, Peck was a bit curious as who might be on the other end of the line once he was connected in his secure bunker below his Dallas mansion. He did not know what to expect.

So, when a new voice he never heard before came over the line, he was not surprised. The voice was much calmer but spoke with just as much authority as his predecessor. He explained that, for the time being, he would be Peck's 'handler'.

Alternating speaking in English and Arabic, he indicated that it was of no concern to Peck what happened to his previous contact. Although this would seem to suggest more of the same arrogance he previously had to endure, Peck realized that was not the case as the conversation progressed. It soon became clear that this individual was appreciative of Peck's contributions to 'the cause', and impressed with Peck's intelligence and achievements. He told Peck that recent developments should not affect the time schedule, and things should progress as originally planned.

Peck, in turn, updated him on the status of the FBI investigation, which he said was progressing according to plan, and Cain's recent interrogation where Cain had kept quiet. The voice on the other end of the line instructed Peck to close 'any loose ends', and although he agreed to do so, Peck was not sure what he meant. Keeping within the scheduled call time, the call concluded with the caller offering the following advice, "There is a saying in your country, I believe, which is to 'keep your friends close and your enemies closer'," he said in Arabic. Funny, in Arabic, it seemed to be somewhat lost in translation.

Following the call, Peck returned above ground to his mansion. Instead of heading for the airport, however, as he regularly did, he took a slight detour. He took the wood elevator that was directly to the right of the maple Impressionist lined staircase up to his office. Once comfortably seated behind his grand desk, he powered on the computer, entered a password, and began searching various data bases regarding potential adversaries. Disappointed, and weary at the size of the list, he soon relented. He would resume the search tomorrow from Healthmed's headquarters.

In the meantime, he poured himself a sifter of sixty-year-old single malt scotch, sipped it, and fell asleep in his leather chair in the mahogany paneled office.

Chapter Sixty
July 1, 2017

Launch Pad, Baikonur Cosmodrome, Kazakhstan

Given the urgency of the unusual circumstances surrounding the mission, and the quick progress that Boucher had made in his study of electronics, the launch was advanced a couple of weeks. Although the launch was occurring in a foreign land, the hoopla surrounding the launch of the first Canadian to the ISS since Commander Hadfield in 2012 was still grandiose. Just like Hadfield, Boucher was tasked with operating the Canadarm2, and performing robotics tasks, but unlike the astronaut before him, Boucher would also be tasked with servicing the Remote Power Control Modules (RPCMs), which are the circuit-breaker boxes that control the flow of electricity through the ISS's secondary power distribution system; the idea being, to create a backup electrical system that only Boucher could access while at the ISS, and then shut down the primary system which was breached. Then, he would deal with the issue of deactivating the SatCom payload. *First things first.*

Boucher had arrived in Kazakhstan a couple of weeks early to meet his colleague and traveling companion, Cosmonaut Yuri Valenshek, as well as familiarize himself with the Russian language, culture, and technical aspects of the spacecraft in which they would be flying. They would be traveling to the ISS in a Soyuz TMA-M Spacecraft. Recently, this had become the primary source of travel between Earth and the ISS, at least until some of the existing flaws with the Falcon Spacecraft are worked out.

The Soyuz Spacecraft consists of three modules: The Orbital Module, which contains the life support system equipment, and is the crew's living quarters traveling to the ISS. Next, is the Descent Module, which is where the crew sits in a reclining position during ascent, orbital maneuvers, and re-entry. Lastly, there is the Instrumentation/Propulsion Module, which contains oxygen tanks, electrical and thermal control systems, computers, thruster jets, infrared sensors, external radiators, and solar array attachments. Notably, both this Module and the Orbital Module separate from the Descent Module after undocking from the ISS and burn up in the atmosphere upon re-entry.

A small passenger bus transported Boucher and Valenshek to the launch pad at the Baikonur Cosmodrome in Kazakhstan. Both NASA and CSA ISS Mission Control teams were monitoring the launch from the Johnson Space Center in Houston, and the John H. Chapman Space Centre, in Longueuil, Quebec, without their respective Directors, Harbath and Michaels, who were present at the launch site in Kazakhstan. After the standard checks were conducted and confirmed, the countdown began, as normal. "Ten, nine, eight…" Lift off.

At approximately twenty-eight miles above the Earth's surface, and a minute fifty-five seconds into the flight, the Bailout Thruster separated from the rest of the Soyuz Spacecraft. Mission Control director Michaels was closely monitoring the screens in front of him, in direct communication with the rest of his team thousands of miles away. Then, three seconds later into the flight, and thirty miles above the launch site, the first stage of the launch vehicle separated from the Spacecraft, as scheduled.

Suddenly, things went horribly wrong. Reminiscent of the Space Shuttle Challenger disaster in 1986, the entire Spacecraft burst into flames disintegrating into a huge ball of fire, smoke and debris. The explosion could be heard up to forty miles away and the plume of smoke was visible from the ISS itself. Michaels and Harbath watched in horror as this tragedy unfolded. It would, of course, be sometime before they knew whether this was due to a mechanical defect or the result of a terrorist act, but Aaron Harbath, Jack Michaels, and Max Kallen all nonetheless had their suspicions.

Chapter Sixty-One
July 3, 2017

SatCom Inc. Headquarters, Dallas, Texas

The newspaper was sprawled out over the Executive's desk. The headlines blared, "No New Details in Mysterious Soyuz Spacecraft Explosion, Astronauts Confirmed Dead."

His secretary notified him that agents from the FBI were there to see him. A bit flustered and confused at this unexpected visit, Jerry Lanzella promptly responded, "Send them in." The FBI agents were shown into a lavish office with spectacular views of downtown Dallas. Behind a big glass desk was a well-built man in his late forties with a receding hairline who stood as they entered the office. He offered the FBI agents the two empty seats opposite his desk, and neatly folded the newspaper that was laid out on the desk.

"What is this all about?"

"Well, Mr. Lanzella, as you know, we recently served warrants on Healthmed Inc., all of its subsidiaries, as well as some of its executives."

"I am aware of that," responded Lanzella.

"Well, it turns out that, in reviewing some of the documents that were seized from the SatCom and Healthmed facilities, the Securities and Exchange Commission, who is also assisting with the investigation, noted some questionable trades you and some people in your department made."

"Really? That is outrageous!" exclaimed Lanzella, although he was growing more concerned by the moment. The agents were bluffing, but as was evident from his facial expression, Lanzella was clueless. *Bingo*, the 'tell', noticed the agents. The truth of the matter was that Lanzella, and some people in his department, had made some trades during 'blackout periods', when trading was prohibited, but for the most part, they all had lost money. Thus, it would be hard to prove a successful insider trading case against any of them. Nonetheless, based upon the noticeable concern that was evident on Lanzella's face, that was news to him.

"Yes, well it appears that you and some people in your department traded during some express 'blackout' periods."

"First of all, I very much doubt that," said Lanzella, now on the defensive. "But, in any case, what does that all have to do with the National Security matters I understood the FBI to be investigating in connection with the issuance of the warrants in the first place?"

"Well, in actuality, very little," responded the more senior agent of the two FBI agents. Continuing, however, he explained, "but as law enforcement officers, we are obligated to investigate all potential criminal activity, including insider trading." Letting it sink in a bit, he added, "And that is what brings us to you, Mr. Lanzella." Again, another pause. Then, more confrontational than before.

"The SEC lawyers tell us they can make an airtight case against you and others for insider trading, or at a minimum, withholding information from federal authorities, in violation of 18 U.S.C. § 803, if you are not forthright with us now."

Finally, Lanzella asked the all too often posed question when being questioned by federal agents, "Do I need a lawyer?"

The more junior agent responded as she had often heard SAC Johnson respond to that question, "I don't know Mr. Lanzella, do you? Is there something you are feeling guilty about?"

Lanzella held his gaze at the younger female agent.

Just as he was about to pick up the intercom on his desk to have his secretary contact the family lawyer, the older agent immediately diffused the tension in the room and stated, "Look Mr. Lanzella, it does not have to come down to that. You might be able to help us out with something else we are investigating, in which case, we would urge the US Attorney's Office for leniency, or depending on the extent of cooperation, that even all charges be dropped entirely." Silence, for a moment.

Then, Lanzella spoke up inquiring, "What exactly is it that you are investigating that requires my assistance?"

The older agent responded calmly, "Your boss."

At that point, the younger agent offered, "Mr. Lanzella, we know that you have been unhappy with Mr. Peck for a long time now."

Lanzella arched his eyebrows.

"Oh really, how do you know that?" asked Lanzella.

The younger agent continued on, "That is not important right now! What is important is that you might be able to assist the FBI with an ongoing investigation implicating National Security."

"And how exactly is that? You know, to this day, no one has ever explained to me the nature of the investigation for which my company, and its parent company, were subpoenaed or just how national security interests 'are implicated'," he said.

The two agents went on to detail a story that was half true, divulging that the federal government was concerned that a hostile foreign agent may have 'compromised' the recent satellite SatCom sent to the ISS. Beyond that, however, they would not give further details.

In the end, the FBI agents gave him forty-eight hours to notify them whether he would be willing to act as a 'confidential informant' for the FBI.

Chapter Sixty-Two
July 3, 2017

The Situation Room, White House, Washington, D.C.

The President, Teddy Fitzpatrick, the Attorney General, Stan Raffaelli, NASA Administrator, Jake Redwell, NASA Inspector General, Mark Weisburg, FBI Director Stephens, and Special Agent in Charge of the D.C. Office, Frank Johnson, were all gathered in one of the thirteen secure rooms comprising the Situation Room, beneath the Oval Office. These were the same individuals who had gathered in the Oval Office more than a month earlier to discuss a potential breach in the nation's security, on a scale never seen before. And, in a most unfamiliar theater: Space.

Also, the President's National Security team was present. This included his National Security Advisor, the Secretary of the Department of Homeland Security, the National Intelligence Director and the Chairman of the Joint Chiefs of Staff. Also, because the launch was a joint mission between Canada and the United States, the Secretary of State was present when she otherwise may not have been present.

"God Dammit Jake, I want to know what the hell went wrong, and I want to know now," barked the President. He was livid, the maddest Jake Redwell had ever seen him. Unfortunately, Jake had no answers for the President, nor did, quite frankly, anyone in the room. Unabashedly, the President continued his tirade.

"I was supposed to be the President to bring space to the people and this happens on my watch. Now, it is two days later, and I still have no answers."

Coming to the defense of the NASA Administrator, the Secretary of State offered, "Mr. President, for what it's worth both Foreign Minister Dupree and I have been having difficulty obtaining information through our Kazakhstan counterparts."

The National Security Advisor promptly chimed in, "That's true, Mr. President. Information has been slow to be forthcoming out of Kazakhstan, to the say the least."

"Is that so," the President asked incredulously. "Well, then let's cut the shit, shall we," the President said. "The bottom line is: Was this a terrorist act or not?"

Momentary silence in the room, and then the President's gaze focused on his DHS Secretary, who in turn, looked to the National Intelligence Secretary. The Homeland Security Secretary finally spoke up and said, "I am sorry to say, sir, but it is still too early to tell. Significantly, no organization or terrorist group has claimed responsibility for the explosion, which would tend to indicate it is not because if it were, someone would have claimed responsibility for the attack by now. Of course, we have ground crews working feverishly at the site, but as Secretary Stein just indicated, Kazakhstan is not being very forthcoming. As you know, although a member of NATO, and despite good relations with President Narcayez in the past, Kazakhstan currently leases the 6,000 kilometers of land comprising the Baikonur Cosmodrome space launch site to Russia, and therein lies the problem, sir. While our crews have been allowed access to the site, they are not being permitted to retain or return evidence from the wreckage."

"You leave President Narcayez and Putin to me," said the President. "But I will tell you this, I want answers as soon as our people have the access they need." Then, turning directly to FBI Director Stephens and Agent Johnson, he said, "And I want to turn up the heat on the Peck investigation. Where are we on that?"

Director Stephens turned it over to Agent Johnson.

"Mr. President, we are making progress, and are pursuing one lead through a confidential informant within Peck's organization. If it turns out the Peck, or someone working for him, was involved in the initial sabotage that prompted the investigation in the first place, then he would be the prime suspect in any sabotage related to Soyuz explosion, I imagine."

"Have we confirmed his involvement with the initial sabotage?" asked the President.

"Technically, yes, but do we have enough to bring an indictment? Of course, I would defer to the Attorney General on that, but I would say probably not at this point, sir," interjected the FBI Director.

Attorney General Rafaelli said, "I would tend to agree with Director Stephens' assessment, Mr. President."

"Well, now is the time to hammer them," said the President.

"Like I said, I want answers and I want them now. If he was involved in the initial launch, we should know that by now. I want arrest warrants, and I want them now," demanded the President.

"Yes, sir," responded the Attorney General dutifully.

"Do we have any idea what they intend to do with the increased power to the satellite if they are successful?"

"We are still investigating all possible avenues, including a potential attack on the Nation's public utilities or infrastructure, Mr. President," responded Director Stephens.

After that, the President returned his attention to the Soyuz explosion. Redwell went through the details that were known, which at that time, was very little.

The meeting concluded five minutes later.

Chapter Sixty-Three
July 10, 2017

United States Senate Chambers, Washington, D.C.

The House Vote on the nomination of Jedidiah Abel as Vice President of the United States was delayed a week due to the Soyuz tragedy.

Ultimately, however, Congressman Abel was confirmed as Vice President by a vote of 236 to 199. That meant that, even though it was by the slimmest of margins, he won some members over from across the aisle. A day after the vote, Congressman Abel resigned as a Member of the United States House of Representatives to Iowa Governor, Sid Healy.

As was the case the two prior times in history with Ford and Rockefeller, the Chief Justice of the United States Supreme Court swore in Congressman Abel as Vice President in the Senate Chambers.

Presiding over the ceremony was the President Pro Tempore of the Senate. He began, "The Senate, by vote of 53 'Yeas' to 47 'Nays', on June 6, 2017, having confirmed the nomination of Jedidiah Abel of Iowa to be Vice President, and the House of Representatives having confirmed Jedidiah Abel of Iowa to be Vice President of the United States by a vote of 236 'Yeas' to 199 'Nays', there has been compliance with Section 2 of the Twenty Fifth Amendment. In accordance with the laws of the State of Iowa, Congressman Abel has tendered his resignation to the governor of that State. Therefore, I ask, currently, that the Chief Justice administer the Oath of Office."

The President Pro Tempore of the Senate next turned to the senior jurist, and said, "Mr. Chief Justice."

Notably, instead of a bible, Congressman Abel asked that a Koran be used at the swearing in ceremony, and so it was.

The Chief Justice began, "Please raise your right hand, and place your left hand on the Koran in front of you, and repeat after me, 'I, Jedidiah Abel, do solemnly swear...'" The Congressman repeated it. "That I will support and defend the Constitution of the United States..." The Congressman repeated it. "Against all enemies, foreign and domestic, that I will bear true faith and allegiance to the same; that I take this obligation freely, without any mental reservation or purpose of evasion; and that I will well and faithfully discharge the duties of the office on which I am about to enter: So, help me God." The Congressman repeated it and with that became the next Vice President of the United States.

Following a few congratulatory remarks, the newly minted Vice President took the Podium with the President looking on behind him.

"Distinguished Members of Congress, Mr. President, Mr. President Pro-Tempore, Mr. Speaker, and honorable guests. Today is just another example of the Constitution working effortlessly in this great democracy of ours, which makes this Country the greatest one on Earth. The Twenty Fifth Amendment, enacted just over fifty years ago this year, provides an effective mechanism for an efficient transfer of power during times of crisis such as the death or resignation of a Vice President. Today, it worked, just as it did with Vice Presidents Ford and Rockefeller about forty-five years ago. And, in record time too, I might add. So, keeping with my new position of being seen but not heard, I will keep it brief." Laughter erupted in the Chamber.

"But seriously folks," the Vice President continued. "This Administration is on track to close all of the loopholes in the Affordable Care Act and provide comprehensive health care to every American. I, as part of the Halliday Administration, certainly intend to do everything in my power as Vice President to make that happen. And, despite the recent tragedy last week, we have made some of the greatest inroads of any prior Administration regarding space exploration and our Country's unwavering support for the International Space Station, and the vital work it performs, year after year. As Vice President, I will ensure that we continue down along this path, not despite of the recent tragedy, but because of it. Those astronauts will not have died in vain."

He continued to speak for another ten minutes resulting in a standing ovation and room full of cheers.

Damn, he's good, thought the President.

West Plano, Texas

Peck was livid. Who the hell did this new guy think he was!

"You had no right to do that, dammit!" blasted Peck.

"Excuse me," came the calm and even paced response from the other end of the secure line.

"You've been in the game for all of five minutes now, and you saw fit to kill those astronauts without even a consultation with me or others."

Again, the response, "Excuse me."

"This is going to raise way too much heat. If you don't think there will be a comprehensive investigation by NASA, CSA, and the FTA, not to mention Congressional hearings, you are sorely mistaken."

"Excuse me."

Okay, now this was becoming more and more frustrating, thought Peck. So, he decided to try a new approach.

"Perhaps, you can enlighten me as to what you were thinking when you blew the Soyuz from the sky, killing that Canadian astronaut and Russian cosmonaut?"

"First, our sources inform us that the Canadian astronaut was more than that." He paused. "He was sent to the ISS, in part, to diffuse some of our handiwork." That is more of a Western expression, thought Peck. Things did not seem to be going as they had long been planned. More and more, things seemed to be reactive instead of proactive, worried Peck.

"Second, it is not your place to question the directives you receive. You are part of something larger than yourself. Don't ever forget that!"

Peck had to do everything he could to remain calm. He responded that, "I always remember that, and have for quite some time," reminding the voice on the other end of the line who was around longer than the other.

"Your continued loyalty and commitment is duly noted," responded the voice on the other end of the line. Changing the subject, the caller said, "You saw the ceremony, I take it?"

"Yes, of course, his remarks were articulate and well received, I believe."

"Agreed."

Acknowledging that the time limit for the call was quickly approaching, the caller instructed simply, "Keep the course, and all will be fine."

Peck felt like telling his counterpart the same, but instead, simply terminated the call, and returned to his mansion upstairs.

Chapter Sixty-Four
July 17, 2017

SAC Johnson's Office, Hoover Building, Washington, D.C.

"How is our CI panning out," asked Agent Johnson.

"So far, he has only given us information pertaining to price manipulation of some products in Healthmed's Pace Maker Division. He claims to have no knowledge of the satellite Divisions of Healthmed," explained the younger FBI Agent.

"Doesn't sound like a very good CI to me," surmised Johnson.

"Give us a bit more time. I think he knows more than he is letting on. Certainly, he has access to individuals and files within the company, which may ultimately prove to be very beneficial. If nothing else, given his level within the Company, he has to have access to its subsidiaries even if he claims otherwise."

"Remind me what this invaluable asset expects in return for this plethora of information he is supposedly providing," asked Johnson facetiously.

"He believes that the government will not press charges against him and some of his colleagues for some questionable trades they made, which was pretty much of a bogus case anyways."

"Sounds like we need to press him harder."

"We're on it, sir," she said as she left her boss's office.

After she left, Johnson's Administrative Assistant informed him he had a call from Max Kallen.

"Max, what's up," asked Johnson as he picked up the receiver.

"Just checking in on the status of the investigation," said Kallen. "Weisburg seems to be intentionally keeping me out of the loop. Guess, he feels a bit threatened by me."

"Ha, ha." Johnson laughed out loud. "That would be an understatement. I would say he has good reason to be, wouldn't you?"

"I'm not after his job, believe me."

"I know that, but it doesn't sound like he does," said Johnson, still chuckling.

"Anyways, I'm not calling to debate my future career plans with you, Frank. Can you please just give me a quick update," asked Kallen.

"Yeah, well we have been poring over all the subpoenaed documents and found a weak link within the company who we have been pressuring to come up with some information, but so far, it has yielded no viable intel."

"Anything more on Cain?"

"No, after he lawyered up, we haven't gotten shit. The AUSA has been busy fighting off motion after motion his lawyers keep filing."

"What about any word on confirmation of al-Fazeh's demise or anything new on the Soyuz investigation?"

"Surprisingly, no. As for al-Fazeh, I expect that, given the inter-agency cooperation for which your buddies in the CIA are notorious, I expect it might be quite some time before I hear anything."

Damn, he did it again, thought Johnson. He immediately regretted referencing Kallen's 'buddies in the CIA' once he said it. In any case, Kallen did not say anything so Johnson let it pass but reminded himself to be more careful about his continued social 'faux pas' in the future.

"As for Soyuz, I would think that would be more in your area, wouldn't it?"

"Yeah, well you know how that goes. Once again, I am getting nothing from that weasel Weisburg or any of the other higher ups. Even Harbath has clammed up on me for some reason."

"Well Max, what I hear is that Russia is making it increasingly difficult to get access to the site, as well as letting information out of Kazakhstan, which leases the Baikonur Cosmodrome space launch site to Russia."

"I can't imagine that sits too well with the President."

"Nope," Johnson mustered.

"Well Frank, please keep me in the loop and update me as to any new developments."

"Sure thing, old buddy."

The President's Dining Room, the White House, Washington D.C.

The President, the First Lady and the newly christened Vice President were all gathered around an informal dining room table in the President's Dining Room, formerly known as the Prince of Wales Room.

"I'm sorry we did not get to do this sooner after your swearing in ceremony Jed, but as you know, things have been a bit hectic around here, "said the President cutting into the one kilo Florentine steak sitting in the middle of the table.

"I certainly understand, Mr. President."

"Please Jed, call me Jack."

"Uh, okay Jack," said the Vice President, a bit uncomfortably.

Easing a bit of the tension in the room, the First Lady, who was more familiar with the Vice President, having spent many evenings preparing him for the Congressional hearings, made a toast. "To the new Vice President," she said raising her class of J. Davies 2012 Jamie Cabernet Sauvignon.

The President and Vice President raised their glasses and clinked too.

"I look forward to this new partnership," added the President. "And, I mean it, I want this to be a true partnership. In fact, I have a briefing tomorrow morning dealing with the Soyuz explosion, and I want you to be a part of it. You should also be receiving a copy of the PDB too," he said, referring to the President's Daily Briefing.

"Yes, sir."

"Great, it's settled then. Be in the Oval Office tomorrow morning, at 8:00 a.m."

After that, they enjoyed a lovely carnivorous meal, followed by Brandy and a cigar for the President, but not the Vice President. The topics of discussion that evening ranged from opera, politics, and gardening to another disappointing season for the Washington Redskins.

Shortly after midnight, the Vice President retreated to Number One Observatory Circle, located on the grounds of the United States Naval Observatory, where Vice Presidents and their families have resided since Walter Mondale, in the Seventies.

Meanwhile, the President and First Lady retreated to the Personal Residence for some presidential love making.

Chapter Sixty-Five
July 18, 2017

The Oval Office, White House, Washington, D.C.

Many were summoned to the Oval Office that hot muggy summer morning. There was NASA Administrator Redwell, NASA Inspector General, Mark Weisburg, the Vice President, the Director of National Intelligence, the President's National Security Advisor, Teddy Fitzpatrick and Jonas Frank were all meeting in the Oval Office. Deputy NTSB Administrator Melvin Hankins also joined them after making the short trek down from L'Enfant Plaza.

Laid out in front of them were a series of photographs, accompanied by reams of data, buried in stacks of paper. Administrator Redwell began the meeting explaining, "These photographs here," he said, pointing to a set of photographs, "were taken from our team of investigators at the crash site in Kazakhstan. I believe Deputy Hankins will concur that the scattering of debris, combined with soil tests conducted at the crash site itself, indicate that the explosion initiated in the cryogenic helium chamber, like the Space X Falcon explosion last year at Kennedy; the main difference is that this explosion does not appear to be due to a mechanical breach, as was the case with the Falcon. Instead, we have reason to believe that an incendiary device strategically planted in the cryogenic helium chamber caused this explosion."

"You see, Mr. President, cryogenic propelled rockets, like the Falcon and Soyuz spacecrafts, require some type of on-board pressurant gas, such as Helium, to assist with propulsion. The Soyuz spacecraft consists of three separate and distinct modules: The Orbital Module, the Descent Module, and the Propulsion Module. The Propulsion Module, which is supposed to separate from the Descent Module after undocking with the ISS, is divided into three compartments; the intermediate, instrumentation and propulsion compartments. These compartments contain oxygen tanks, electrical and thermal control systems, computers, thruster jets, infrared sensors, external radiators, solar array attachments, and a cryogenic helium chamber to assist with propulsion. Given the timing of the explosion, at just 118 seconds into the flight, after the first stage separation, and the distinct scattering pattern reflected here," he said pointing to the photographs, "we believe a device, possibly implanted in the wall of the cryogenic helium chamber, detonated at the time of the initial separation."

Administrator Redwell looked up from the photographs, first to the President, and then to Deputy NTSB Administrator Hankins, who promptly chimed in, "That is correct. Our analysts concur with that assessment, Mr. President."

But, it was the Vice President, not the President, who spoke up first. He asked, "Why are you so certain it occurred in the helium chamber as opposed to other parts of the Propulsion Module?"

Taken a bit by surprise, not so much by the question, but more so, by who was asking it, Administrator Redwell hesitated before responding, "Well, Mr. Vice President, given the near incineration of that particular Module and this distinct scattering of debris, reflected here," he said pointing to another area of severe debris in the photographs, "it would appear to have occurred in the upper chamber of the Propulsion Module, where that chamber is located, sir."

"And, how can you be so certain that an incendiary device caused the explosion as opposed to a breach in the Helium chamber, like the Falcon last year?" asked the Vice President.

Again, the fact that it was the Vice President, not the President, asking the pivotal questions seemed curiously strange to the individuals assembled there, but no one said anything. The President, Teddy Fitzpatrick and Jonas Frank just sat there, apparently in a self-congratulatory mood, confident they had made an excellent choice for Vice President.

"The rate of acceleration throughout the upper modules was increased a hundred-fold compared to last year's explosion, sir," responded Deputy Hankins.

"Additionally, this debris scatter right here," said Administrator Redwell pointing to a couple of the photographs in the middle of the table, "contain chemical elements in the soil which suggest a titanium chemical interaction with Helium resulting in this discoloration you see here," he said.

"Titanium is the preferred outer covering of the types of incendiary devices we have seen in the past, especially military grade," explained the President's National Security Advisor.

"Has anyone claimed responsibility for the attack if that is what we truly believe it was," asked the President for the first time during the meeting.

"Not yet, Mr. President. Quite frankly, that is what is so surprising. By now, we should have heard something from some group claiming responsibility, but nothing; not even the regular 'loonies' have claimed responsibility," interjected the National Intelligence Director.

"Sir, we do have good reason to believe this attack was not targeted at the United States or Canada, but rather, our intel tells us Russia may have been the target. It could have been either Pro-Ukrainian forces or Chechnyan rebels, we believe, sir," added the National Security Advisor.

"Why is that," asked the Vice President.

"Putin was lauding this mission to the ISS, and in particular, Cosmonaut Valenshek as a national hero. If someone wanted to attack Russia or Putin, that would certainly be one way of doing it, and the fact that no one has claimed responsibility suggests to us that may precisely be the case."

"Really, that is what we are going with?" asked the President incredulously.

"I mean we were specifically sending Commander Boucher to the ISS to remedy what we believe to be a terrorist plot. Now, you are telling me that you believe this explosion was unrelated to that plot because Putin was hyping his own guy."

The President gave his National Security Advisor and Intelligence Director a hard scowl. Teddy Fitzpatrick made a mental note to himself.

The President took charge and demanded to his National Security team, "I want all satellite images over Kazakhstan from the day of the launch to this very minute."

"Next, get Stan, and Director Stephens, to apply the pressure on Peck," said the President to Fitzpatrick, who nodded in acknowledgment. "If he was involved, he will likely make the critical mistake we need when the pressure is on."

Everyone else agreed. The President then turned to Redwell and said, "Jake, I want all thermal topography of the launch site from three weeks prior to the launch to yesterday."

"Yes, sir."

Turning back to Fitzpatrick, he said, "And have Secretary Jensen meet Foreign Minister Demeitrov in Kazakhstan, at the crash site. I will brief him on his way there. Have him take Air Force One."

With that, the meeting ended.

Chapter Sixty-Six
July 20, 2017

SatCom Inc. Headquarters, Dallas, Texas

The three unmarked Crown Victoria sedans screeched to a stop outside SatCom Headquarters, sirens blaring. Six FBI agents jumped out of the vehicles with arrest warrants in hand. Minutes later, they exited the building with Jerry Lanzella, and four other SatCom executives, in handcuffs.

Lanzella was placed in the lead vehicle with the Special Agent in charge while the remaining suspects were placed in the other vehicles. In the lead vehicle with Lanzella, was FBI Special Agent Julio Gonzales.

"What is this all about?" demanded Lanzella. "We had a deal."

"That deal was contingent on us receiving valuable information that we could use, none of which has apparently happened so far. What can I tell you? I guess the U.S. Attorney believes he has enough to prosecute you, and your fellow cohorts back there, on insider trading charges."

"Bullshit! I demand to speak to the Agent in Charge."

"Mr. Lanzella, if you haven't realized, you are under arrest on federal charges. You are in no position to make any demands," responded Agent Gonzales.

"I demand to speak with my attorney then," responded Lanzella.

"You will be given an opportunity to call your attorney when we get downtown."

Lanzella looked down. He was not willing to go to jail for that piece of shit, he thought. Thinking about all his options, he blurted out, "what if I am willing to wear a wire?"

Gonzales shrugged his shoulders, "Eh, probably doesn't matter at this point. The way the suits see it, I imagine, is that you probably could not get useful information even if you tried. That is why you are where you are now."

Lanzella did not say anything, still considering his options at this point. He thought long and hard about the type of information his handler had sought. Finally, he offered up, "What if I could get Cain for you? That's who you want, isn't it? I mean besides Peck. We all heard about his arrest and interrogation."

Now, Lanzella had piqued Agent Gonzales' interest a bit. Not wanting to play his hand too soon, Agent Gonzales shrugged it off and said, "If you heard about his arrest and interrogation, then what makes you can you can give us more than we already have, Mr. Lanzella?"

"His boss and I work closely together. I know that, with his help, I can get you what you need."

Even though highly unprofessional, Gonzales could not help but let out a guttural laugh. The man in handcuffs beside him was desperate, but really had nothing to offer in return. He was grasping at straws. Having worked the White-Collar Division of the Bureau for five years, Agent Gonzales had seen all of this before. Grown men, earning millions of dollars a year who cower at the first sign of trouble. In fact, it was ironic; because he played it safe, he really had nothing to offer. As a result, he was worthless when 'trouble' reared its ugly head.

Once he contained himself, Gonzales just said, "We'll see. Of course, you can raise it with the 'powers that be' when we get downtown."

With that, he flicked the siren on and pulled into traffic.

Healthmed Inc. Headquarters, Redwood City, California

Meanwhile, at roughly that same time, FBI agents were descending upon Healthmed's headquarters, armed with an arrest warrant for Peck, the charge: defrauding the United States government with its NASA RIO filing for the SatCom launch. Upon their arrival, a team of attorneys greeted the FBI agents outside Peck's office and informed them that Mr. Peck was currently overseas and would not be returning for another week. They indicated that he would voluntarily surrender to agents at the Dallas FBI Field Office at that time. The agents considered their options, and ultimately left empty handed.

Moments later, Special Agent in Charge Johnson and Director Stephens were on the telephone with Attorney General Raffaelli, updating him as to the status of the investigation and what transpired during execution of the arrest warrants.

"Why wasn't the timing of the Peck warrant better planned?" asked the Attorney General.

"I am sorry, sir, but there was no way our agents have anticipated a sudden unplanned business trip," responded Agent Johnson.

"Are we sure it was unplanned?"

"Sir?" asked Director Stephens.

"I mean is it possible information was leaked to him about the impending warrants?"

"Not from us, sir," said Director Stephens defensively.

"Nor was I suggesting that, Mark. All I am saying is that we should investigate that possibility. In the meantime, is there any reason we cannot wait another week?" asked Raffaelli.

"Other than the fact that your boss wants us to exert pressure, no," responded Director Stephens.

"Let me worry about that," countered Raffaelli.

Somewhere over the South Pacific Ocean

Peck was reached on his satellite phone after dozing for a while on the flight from Australia to Hong Kong. He spoke with his attorneys for a bit before promptly terminating the call and initiating another. On a secure satellite phone, he began by demanding, "The timing has to be moved up." Peck went on to explain the details of the telephone call he just ended.

"Not going to happen," responded the voice on the other end of the line. "We will stick to the initial plan, and not vary from it for any reason," said the voice in a determined confident tone. "The attorneys will keep you out of jail long enough for execution of the final plan to come fruition." *Again, 'fruition' – not a term commonly used in the Middle East*, thought Peck, prompting his curiosity further about this new leader. In any case, they had come this far, and the voice was right on both counts. So, it was decided. Peck would turn himself in upon his return.

Chapter Sixty Seven
July 24, 2017

The Oval Office, White House, Washington, D.C.

"Jed, I need you to go the Hill to lobby for AB 76211," said the President to the Vice President. Teddy Fitzpatrick was seated to the right of the Vice President while Deputy Chief of Staff Jonas Frank flanked the Vice President's left side. The President sat behind the Resolute Desk. "Use all of your connections, including most importantly, those you have made with the Speaker," he said.

"Of course, sir."

"The passage of this Bill, Mr. Vice President, is critical to closing all loopholes in the Affordable Care Act," added Fitzpatrick.

"Absolutely, I understand, Mr. Fitzpatrick. You will recall that, during my initial interview, we discussed this, and I was on board then, and I remain committed to doing all I can to help pass the Bill and advance the Administration's objectives. As you both probably know by now, I am scheduled to have my weekly lunch with Speaker Montgomery tomorrow. I will raise the issue with him at that time."

"Great. What is the next order of business Teddy?" asked the President.

"There is the SatCom investigation, Mr. President," responded Fitzpatrick wearily, unsure whether they should be discussing it in front of the newly minted Vice President. Sensing his hesitation, the President assured him, "It's okay, Teddy. I want Jed on board with everything that is going on around here. Not only have I come to value his input, but he should be up to date on all matters involving National Security."

Fitzpatrick proceeded, "The SatCom warrants were executed. As expected, the FBI's informant vigorously complained, insisting that he speak with the Director himself."

"And Peck," asked the President.

"He is out of the country, sir, and not due back for another few days, at which time his attorneys have indicated he will surrender to agents at the Dallas Field Office."

"Excuse me, sir, are we talking about the billionaire, J. Robert Peck," inquired the Vice President.

"Yes, sorry, Jed. Let me back up." The President then proceeded to debrief the Vice President on all that transpired from the initial SatCom launch back in February to the present.

"Incredible," was all the Vice President could muster.

Then, putting two and two together, he inquired, "So, if we were sending Commander Boucher to the ISS, in part, to fix the problem with the Canadarm2 and electrical currents, what are we going to do now that that does not appear to be an option any longer?"

"Since we believe the timing of any planned attack could be imminent, especially based upon our findings that the Soyuz explosion does not appear to be an accident, our only option is to train Commander Thorson to do what needs to be done."

"Excuse me, Mr. President, correct me if I am wrong, but didn't Commander Boucher undergo extensive training concerning the ISS's electrical system in the weeks preceding the launch?"

"That's true," answered the President.

"So, if time is truly of the essence, with an attack believed to be imminent, what makes you think Commander Thorson can familiarize himself with the system in time to prevent the attack?"

"Believe me, we know it is not great Jed, but it appears to be our only option at this point," responded the President.

Changing gears a bit, the Vice President asked, "What is the latest on the drone attack in Syria?"

Immediately, both the President and Fitzpatrick raised an eyebrow. Sensing what they were thinking, the Vice President quickly added, "Relax, it is a natural question if we truly consider the Soyuz explosion to be a terrorist attack."

"Our national security team is still considering all possibilities," responded Fitzpatrick. "No definitive word one way or the other," he added. The meeting adjourned shortly thereafter.

John F. Kennedy Space Center, Merritt Island, Florida

"Any word on the cause of the Soyuz explosion yet?" asked Kallen to Harbath over the secure inter-NASA conferencing system between the Johnson and Kennedy Space Centers.

"You know Max, I am not at liberty to disclose that information. It's classified."

Okay, I will access it myself later, thought Kallen to himself.

"Alright then, what are they going to do to fix our little problem aboard the ISS," inquired Kallen.

"It looks like a thorough debriefing and crash course in electrical engineering for Commander Thorson is what they have planned."

"That's it," belted out a clearly frustrated Kallen. "That's their grandiose solution."

"Believe me, it's not great. They know that, but it's all they have at this point."

"Let's hope the Commander is a quick learner," remarked Kallen. "Let me ask you this Aaron, is there any concern about internal leaks within NASA or the Administration? I mean it seems that, ever since this investigation has been given a green light, we have hit a road block at virtually every lead. They somehow always know when and where we are coming."

"I don't know, Max. Above my pay grade," remarked Harbath.

"It is something that should be seriously considered," advised Kallen.

"Again Max, right now, my focus is on regaining control of the Canadarm2 and shutting down any remote capabilities at the ISS. I will let others, who are more capable than myself, address the security concerns."

Yeah, like me, thought Kallen to himself.

"You or Administrator Redwell haven't discussed it with Weisburg?"

"No, they may have discussed it, but I was not privy to that conversation."

"What is going on with coordinating the investigation with the CSA?"

Feeling a bit like he was being interrogated, Harbath demanded, "Stop Max. You know I can't tell you that."

Kallen, equally exasperated, complained, "Hey Aaron, don't forget, it was you who got me involved in this whole mess. I didn't ask for this!"

"I know," said Harbath. "And believe me, both I and the country are grateful for all that you have done, but since the Soyuz explosion, this investigation has taken on a whole new dimension, with a slew of others involved."

Kallen did not like being kept out of the loop, especially since he knew that the investigation would not be where it was today were it not for him. He made a mental note to raise the issue with Johnson next time they spoke, raising the specter that there was a leak at the highest level of government.

"Okay, thanks Aaron. You have been most helpful," said Kallen facetiously.

The next call Max Kallen placed was to none other than Special Agent in Charge Frank Johnson.

Chapter Sixty-Eight
July 25, 2017

The Members Dining Room, Washington, D.C.

"So, has he included you in the inner circle yet?" asked the Speaker curiously, as he sipped his tomato bisque.

Playfully, the Vice President remarked, "What do you think?"

"I think he would be a fool not to do so."

Emboldened with a new sense of confidence since becoming Vice President, Abel smugly agreed. Then, he simply smiled.

Sensing an appropriate segue, the Vice President said, "You know Dick, speaking of the inner circle, I am sure you are aware that AB 76211 is about to pass the Senate and go to Conference in the House."

"I am aware," responded the Speaker.

"Well, the Administration believes it is critical that the Bill end up on the President's desk for his signature."

"Of course, Jed, but just because we have this kinship of sorts, please don't confuse that with political support. We obviously have very different political perspectives, to say the least," commented the Speaker. "I have a real problem with some of the Bill's main provisions not to mention the quarrel I have with Obamacare, in the first place," he said, referring to the vernacular for the Affordable Care Act.

"I understand that Dick," he said, intentionally using his name as opposed to his title. "However, this Bill will fix all that is wrong with Obamacare and the Affordable Care Act. It will make it so the healthcare is available to every American who could not otherwise afford it. Certainly, that cannot be a bad thing," he said, making a case for the Bill's passage.

"At the expense of the American taxpayer," said the Speaker of the House of Representatives. They continued back and forth for a bit, and then the Vice President wisely changed the subject.

"Are you and Martha still planning that trip to Montreal next month?" asked the Vice President.

"As a matter of fact, we are. I can't tell you how much I am looking forward to it."

"I imagine you would be. I certainly would welcome any opportunity for a bit of rest and relaxation, especially over the last few months."

"No doubt," said the Speaker, as they clinked their glasses of ice tea.

Over the Pacific Ocean Somewhere Between Japan and Hawaii

"That is what their grand plan is?" asked Peck somewhat in disbelief, but at the same time, satisfied that it would simply be too little too late to foil their objective. He was once again speaking on his secure satellite phone aboard the company's Gulfstream jet.

"Apparently so," was the response from a secure line within the White House.

"Well, it will never work in time," Peck said.

"Let's hope so."

"We will, of course, employ counter measures, if necessary."

"If you say so. What is our time frame?"

"It is quickly approaching, but it may need to be advanced," responded Peck.

"Okay, keep me advised."

"Of course."

Chapter Sixty-Nine
July 27, 2017

SAC Johnson's Office, Hoover Building, Washington, D.C.

"That's his offer?" asked Johnson to Gonzales. "He is going to roll on Cain?"

"That is what he said, sir," responded Agent Gonzales.

"Do we even have any idea what that means? Do we know, for example, what he has, if anything, on Cain?"

"No, sir."

"Doesn't sound like any better deal than his useless intel so far," said Johnson. Gonzales shrugged his shoulders.

Then, Johnson's Executive Assistant interrupted the meeting to inform him that Max Kallen was on the line.

"I have to take this call," Johnson said to Gonzales as he picked up the line. Gonzales left the office.

"Max, how is it going?"

"That is precisely what I would like to know," fumed Kallen, who then proceeded to unleash a tirade about how he was being kept out of the loop and needed more information on the status of the investigation. After Johnson agreed to do so from the FBI's end, Kallen then shared his theory about a leak within the upper echelons of the government.

"Think about it, Frank," pleaded Kallen, making his case.

"First, you guys are investigating Malcomovich when he suddenly goes up in flames, quite literally," noted Kallen. "Then, during the vetting of a little-known Vice-Presidential nominee, a drone attack purportedly kills his estranged terrorist uncle who was the subject of hot debate at the Confirmation hearings. Next, there was no surprise when the FISA Warrants were issued. And, most recently, we now apparently believe the Soyuz explosion, which was carrying an astronaut to the ISS to fix our little problem, was an act of intentional terrorism. It doesn't take a genius to figure out that someone must be leaking information," theorized Kallen.

Johnson's interest was piqued. "So, what would you suggest we do about it, if anything," asked Johnson.

"I have a plan," Kallen said.

"I thought you might."

After Kallen finished sharing his plan with Johnson and ended the call, Johnson called Gonzales, and said, "Let Lanzella know we may take him up on that offer. In the meantime, I have a flight to catch."

Hollywood, Florida

Using a secure satellite phone this time instead of his I Phone7, Cain spent most of the conversation listening, and even though the caller could not see it, he was nodding his head. It was nearing midnight and he had been in the dive bar most of the evening.

Finally, Cain asked the caller, "And the codes are still valid?"

"Yes."

"Same spot?"

"Yes."

"And the lenses?"

"They're on the way."

"The laptop?"

"The same."

"Timing?"

"Now, but be careful, especially given the heat."

"Copy that," said Cain, ending the call.

Addison Airport, West Plano, Texas

Once the secure satellite call was finished, the Gulfstream G550 began its final approach to the dimly lit airfield through the cloudless night. On the ground, a swarm of attorneys engulfed Peck, who was immediately ushered into the awaiting 2017custom-built Bentley Limousine. Meanwhile, parked directly behind the limousine, about two hundred feet on the tarmac, was a car with its lights turned off. In it, were two FBI agents, just in case Peck had second thoughts about going anywhere other than the Dallas Field Office upon his return.

Nevertheless, the limousine proceeded directly to One Justice Way, as planned, with the FBI agents following closely behind them the entire way. Upon his arrival to the FBI's Dallas Field Office, Peck was greeted by none other than Special Agent in Charge, Frank Johnson, who notwithstanding the late hour, had chosen to make the three-hour twenty- minute flight from D.C. just for this meeting, or more appropriately, for this interrogation.

Peck was then ushered into a long rectangular room with a two-way mirror on the right wall and a table with four chairs around it in the middle of the room. The FBI agents who accompanied him and his lead criminal defense attorney to the room promptly excused themselves and left the room, leaving Peck and his attorney to sit in the room by themselves. Not only had his attorney thoroughly prepared him for this, Peck was no idiot; he knew they were being watched. For that reason alone, not a single word was spoken between Peck and his attorney until Johnson entered the room almost fifteen minutes later.

Johnson did not waste any time. He sat down directly opposite Peck and his attorney and jumped right into things. "Ever hear of a Dr. Malcomovich before?"

"Isn't that the poor fellow at the FDA who recently had that most unfortunate accident," responded Peck, toying with Agent Johnson.

"You never met with him or spoke to him before his death?"

"For heaven's sake, is that what this is all about," cried Peck. "I could have saved you all a lot of time. I know nothing about that whole fiasco."

"Don't worry Mr. Peck, time is a luxury that fortunately we have so get comfortable, as I think we are going to be here for a while."

Sure enough, over the course of the next several hours, an exhausted but thorough Agent Johnson grilled Peck on a range of topics including Peck and Malcomovich's little golfing trip last year, Peck's questionable corporate structure to avoid SEC disclosure requirements, and his employment of two former military operatives and their suspicious activities. Occasionally, Peck's lawyer would interject a question here and there seeking clarification of a question which Johnson would largely ignore, choosing instead to repeat the exact same question he had just asked with no modification whatsoever. Not only was this a deposition technique he learned as a young attorney, it was also an interrogation technique designed to show the subject who is in charge. In this case, that little game went on for about three and half hours, with no bathroom breaks, until Johnson finally stood and turned to leave the room.

Just before his hand grabbed the door handle, with his back to Peck and his attorney, he said, "I'll be back. Don't go anywhere," he joked smugly.

Once he left the interrogation room, he entered the room next door, where the United States Attorney General, the Director of the

FBI, the NASA Administrator and Inspector General were all present. The general consensus was that, although some rather unseemly matters were discussed, they did not have enough to prosecute Peck. Johnson re-entered the interrogation room deflated. Immediately, Peck realized he had won, at least this round. He left the Federal Building and was on his way home to his West Plano mansion five minutes later.

Chapter Seventy
July 28, 2017

Eisenhower Executive Office Building, Washington, D.C.

The Vice President placed the phone call from his main office in the Eisenhower Executive Office Building as opposed to his other office in the West Wing of the White House. The phone call he placed was to Senator Trist in an arduous effort to lobby support for Senator McClintock's Healthcare Bill.

"Senator," he said, "Jedidiah Abel here."

"Mr. Vice President," the Senator said, addressing the former Congressman by his newly minted title, causing the Vice President to grin a bit.

"As you might expect, I am calling about Senate Bill AB 76211," explained Abel. "Yes, sir," said the Senator. "And, as I told your predecessor and Senator McClintock, it is riddled with problems."

"I'm listening," said the Vice President.

The Senator then proceeded to detail all the Bill's deficiencies. The Vice President listened patiently before stating, "I understand Senator, but we have a limited window of opportunity here." The Vice President then went on to tout the merits of the Bill before ending the conversation.

After that, he called several other high-ranking members of Congress. Just before noon, the Vice President was informed that Teddy Fitzpatrick had made the brief stroll over from the West Wing and was now waiting to see him, without an appointment.

"Send him in," instructed the Vice President, to his Executive Assistant.

"I hear you have been a busy beaver, Mr. Vice President."

"What do you mean by that Teddy?" asked the Vice President. Again, that was one of the perks of being Vice President, Abel mused to himself: It was no longer Mr. Fitzpatrick, but 'Teddy'.

"Well, my sources on the Hill tell me you have been busy calling everyone from Senator Trist to Congressman Schwartz to rally support for Senator McClintock's Bill."

"I have," acknowledged the Vice President.

"Well, kudos to you. The President will be pleased."

"I hope so. Like I said before, I am willing to do whatever I can to help the team," rallied the Vice President.

SAC Johnson's Office, Hoover Building, Washington, D.C.

Following his fruitless interrogation of Peck, a bleary-eyed Agent Johnson arrived at the office a couple of hours after landing at Reagan International on the Agency's Falcon 900. He had just enough time to stop at his Foggy Bottom apartment, shower and change clothes before heading into the office.

Working on only a couple hours of sleep during the return flight, he called Agent Gonzales. "What did he say?" asked Johnson, yawning.

"He said, generally, he did not have access to that information, but given his seniority in the Company, he would try using his password to download all calendar information for Healthmed Inc. and all of its subsidiaries, including SatCom and MedSupply Inc. If that does not work, he said he would employ the old-fashioned method."

"What is that?" asked Johnson.

"His secretary will ask Cain's secretary."

Johnson laughed out loud. "Remember, it must be done discreetly," he said.

"Absolutely. Understood, sir."

"When do we expect to have the information?" Johnson asked.

"As soon as possible, sir."

That was the correct answer. As it turns out, the secretary network proved fruitful indeed, providing vital information on Cain's whereabouts. The rest was simple deductive reasoning.

Hollywood, Florida

Cain stuffed the remnants of the Big Mac in his mouth, scooped up some fries, plopped the Percy Sledge CD back into the audio cassette player, and headed North. He recalled making the trip before, months earlier. The Turnpike was more crowded than usual.

At this rate, it would take well over three hours, thought Cain to himself. Cain turned up the volume and settled in for the drive.

Sure enough, he arrived in Titusville just over three hours later. He checked in at the Budget Motel on Washington Avenue, which was within a half hour drive of the Kennedy Space Center.

"Will that be cash or credit?" asked the clerk.

"Cash," Cain said, as he handed him five one hundred-dollar bills, which was more than six times the amount for a single room. The clerk immediately perked up; eyes wide open and a huge smile on his face.

"I like my privacy," Cain simply said.

"Absolutely, sir. No one will know there is a soul in that room."

"Now, and in the future," confirmed Cain.

"Yes, sir."

"Great," said Cain displaying all his pearly whites.

Chapter Seventy-One
July 29, 2017

John F. Kennedy Space Center, Merritt Island, Florida

Cain entered the Central Instrumentation Facility (CIF), at the Kennedy Space Center, through the same gate he had previously used only a few months earlier. There were no issues entering the facility. As planned, he pulled into the same parking spot he had previously used. He paused a minute before exiting the vehicle. Then, he approached the side door, swiped his card, entered the building and proceeded to the retina scanner. As he approached, however, Cain thought he saw something in his peripheral vision. Nonetheless, he kept moving towards the secure door with the retina scanner.

Suddenly, a deafening siren sounded. Cain immediately turned, only to be confronted by six military policemen with their M-16s leveled precisely at the upper part of his chest. Cain knew the drill. He interchanged his fingertips above his head and proceeded to lie down face first, as instructed. The last thing he remembered was the flash of the butt of one of those M-16s being smashed against his head.

When he awoke, he was in a lone cell with steel bars in a room with a steel door that had no handles on it from the inside. His hands and feet were in shackles. No other person was in the cell or in the room, but there was a camera in the corner of the ceiling which he quickly realized was following his every movement. Moments later, the steel door opened, and two MPs entered the room accompanied by a well-built man with a military crew cut in a navy suit with no tie. The MPs and the Suit remained outside the cell.

"How is it going there, Tiger?" asked Max Kallen, the Suit. Cain just glared at him.

"You know, when I was with Team Six, I had a Luke Cain under my command," continued Kallen. "He mentioned that he had a younger brother who was a Ranger in the 82nd Airborne, named Alex. That wouldn't happen to be you Mr. Stern, would it," asked Kallen, grinning.

Cain just continued to stare at him, saying nothing. Kallen nodded to the MPs who then opened the cell door and grabbed Cain, lifting him to his feet and dragging him out of the cell. They proceeded to drag him out the steel door, down a long cement corridor until they reached a plain metal door. The MPs opened the door, secured Cain into a metal chair opposite a metal table, locking his leg shackles to the base of the chair, and his handcuffs to the table in front of him. The MPs then left the room and Kallen and Agent Johnson entered the room.

As with all interrogation rooms, there was a two-way mirror in the middle of it, behind which was quite a crew, to say the least: the FBI Director, the Director of Central Intelligence, the Attorney General, the Chairman of the Joint Chiefs of Staff, NASA Administrator Redwell, and NASA Inspector General Mark Weisburg. The interrogation was also being videotaped live, and transmitted through secure channels to the Oval Office, where the President, the Vice President, Teddy Fitzpatrick and Jonas Frank were all watching intently.

Unbeknownst to all watching, Kallen's participation in this interrogation was the result of a tireless lobbying effort by his close friend, Frank Johnson, who believed it was only fitting given that Kallen was the one who uncovered the suspected terrorist plot in the first place.

Kallen and Johnson sat in the two chairs opposite Cain.

"Mr. Cain, this is FBI Special Agent Johnson who will be assisting here today." Kallen paused, and then said, "Oh yeah, I forgot, you two have met before, haven't you?"

"I want to speak with my attorney," Cain immediately demanded. Johnson and Kallen both looked at each other quizzically before Kallen broke out laughing. Frank joined Kallen. "He thinks he is going to be prosecuted by the Feds, Frank," laughed Kallen. "Oh no, brother," said Kallen, shaking his head, but still laughing in a more controlled manner now. "You were caught red handed entering a secure government facility with false credentials carrying a lap top with all sorts of classified programs on it."

Kallen continued, "Because of your military service, you are going to be tried for Treason in a military court." Cain's eyes bulged. Kallen clearly had his attention now.

He proceeded, "In the meantime, you will be leaving for Fort Leavenworth, Kansas, in about twenty minutes. Once there, you will be given an opportunity to speak with your attorney, a First Lieutenant, Molly Henderson, from the Judge Advocate General, I believe. The reason she can't come any earlier, I understand, is because she is busy attending her law school graduation somewhere out on the West Coast."

"You bastards," blurted Cain.

Kallen then turned to Johnson and said, "Frank, I am not an attorney, but you are, right?"

"I was."

"Do you know what the penalty for treason is?"

"Well, I am no expert, but I believe the last time I checked, it could carry the death penalty," Johnson responded.

"Wow, it would be a pity to perish for such a piece of shit like Peck, who we know put you up to this in the first place," said Kallen.

Cain was listening. He knew, after all, that the prospects for success in a military court, with a rookie lawyer, were dim to nil, at best. That was if he even made it out of the Brig without first being killed or silenced. From then on, it was just a matter of negotiation between Cain and the Government, for which Johnson was the point man for the government. One hour later, they had a deal in place. From that moment on, Cain would disappear off the grid forever.

Chapter Seventy-Two
August 1, 2017

The Members Dining Room, Washington, D.C.

"Congratulations," said the Speaker, as he and the Vice President ate their lunch at the regularly appointed time and place. Things had not changed since Abel became Vice President.

"What do you mean," asked Abel.

"I hear that you have been busy rallying support for McClintock's Bill in the Senate, and from what Senator Trist tells me, you may have converted some of the undecideds to vote in favor of the Bill. Of course, you have not convinced him."

Abel rolled his eyes. "Converting that man would be like you converting me to Christianity," he said smiling.

"Hey, watch it there," said the Speaker jokingly. "Seriously, I understand that you have become quite an effective advocate on behalf of the Administration."

"If that is the case, then I would be happy, but some might say it is still too early to tell," remarked the Vice President.

"I don't know about that," responded the Speaker. "In any case, maybe it was not such a good thing recommending your name for consideration," he said, halfway in jest.

"You knew my politics then, and you know them now. My positions remain unchanged. If I can help the Administration advance its agenda, then that is what I fully intend to do," said Abel.

After that, feeling as if he was preaching to the Speaker, and recognizing that he was no longer campaigning for the job, Abel changed the topic of conversation to a familiar one; the Speaker's family. They continued their conversation for another twenty minutes before the Vice President excused himself to meet with some other Senators in a further lobbying effort for Senator McClintock's Bill.

West Plano, Texas

"I am afraid we have hit a setback of sorts," said Peck to the caller after being connected in his secure bunker beneath his West Plano mansion. He continued, "My sources tell me one of our significant assets has been compromised."

"How serious is it?" asked the anonymous voice on the other end of the line.

Peck continued, "Not serious. It could have potentially been devastating, but fortunately, I took precautions. We will be fine," he said.

"I hope so," said the voice on the other end of the line.

"We will," Peck assured him. Pausing a bit, he added, "But we may want to advance the schedule a bit, to be sure."

"No, unless absolutely essential, we will stick with the plan," said the voice. *Spoken like a true bureaucrat*, thought Peck - *Afraid to take risks!*

"I think the circumstances may so warrant and believe it should be given due consideration."

"Noted," was all the voice on the other end of the line said.

Sensing the time limit for the call was quickly approaching, Peck simply stated, "I will keep you updated."

"We expect nothing less," said the voice before the call was terminated within the designated time. *"Hmmm, just as arrogant as his predecessor,* thought Peck to himself before retreating upstairs to tidy up and heading back to Northern California on the G550 to catch up on some things back at the office.

Secure Computer Room, Kennedy Space Center, Merritt Island, Florida

In a secure computer laboratory in the Central Instrumentation Facility (CIF) at Kennedy Space Center, Cain was doing his thing. Typing away with an FBI Analyst and a member of NASA mission control, watching over his shoulder to ensure that he did not create any firewalls that would prevent the system aboard the ISS from being accessed remotely, as he had done before. Director Stephens, Frank Johnson and Max Kallen were also present. Impressed by what they were observing, the government employees just sat there stupefied. At times, Cain would narrate as he navigated his way through page after page of Code.

"Peck thought he was so smart. He thought he would put his own firewall back in the program, so he could shut me out at any time in case I became compromised." Cain looked up, smiled and said, "I guess he really is a smart guy, after all. Anyways, I switched the firewall, and by typing these five keys, will permanently shut Peck and his cronies out of the ISS system."

"Do it," instructed Stephens.

Cain proceeded to type 'FUPECK'.

"There, his systems are now disabled," advised Cain.

"Will he know they have been disabled," asked Kallen.

"Not unless he suspects something and checks on them. There is no automatic notification when a change has been made."

"But as soon as he learns of your detainment, we can presume that will be the first thing he does, if he hasn't already done so," added Johnson.

"Which raises the specter of whether he has beaten us to the punch and changed the code before you had time to access it," suggested Kallen.

"That was one of the first things I considered, and expressly checked for that. Everything appeared to be in order. Even now, all seems to be progressing as it should be, unadulterated."

"Okay," said Kallen, sounding unconvinced.

He leaned in and whispered in Johnson's ear, "Can I speak with you for a minute outside?"

The two of them proceeded to step out of the room. Johnson asked, "What's up?"

"You did incorporate that little provision into the plea deal like we talked about, didn't you?"

"Absolutely. He knows that, if he does anything to hinder the investigation, he will have effectively plead 'guilty' to Capital Treason and will go straight to the gallows."

"Let's hope that is incentive enough," remarked Kallen. "Let me ask you this, doesn't it seem strange that he knows absolutely nothing about what Peck might have planned in connection with the ISS? That he was only the 'computer guy'?"

"Not really," answered Johnson. "If Peck is planning something on a scale we believe he is, it is better to keep a small inner circle. The fewer individuals that know the ultimate plan, the better. It allows for plausible deniability for the underlings, such as Cain, while at the same time, limits the chances for a leak." Johnson looked at Kallen, who still did not seem convinced. "In any case, if he cooperates and can effectively disable the SatCom satellite and the excess electricity it is providing, then we can focus on Peck and his intentions later without simultaneously worrying about a national catastrophe at the same time."

"I guess so," said Kallen, shrugging his shoulders before heading back into the computer room, accompanied by Johnson.

Chapter Seventy-Three
August 2, 2017

Redwood City, California

Because he still had not rebuilt the bunker beneath the building following the FBI raid, Peck was using his handheld satphone in a park near the Healthmed facilities. What he did not know, however, was that the FBI, using a low earth orbiting (LEO) satellite, was tracking Peck's location to within a few meters.

More importantly, even though most satphones are encrypted to prevent eavesdropping, a team of academic security researchers, in 2012, reverse-engineered the two major proprietary encryption algorithms, and later cryptanalyzed a third algorithm. The result was that, unbeknownst to Peck, the FBI was now listening in on this conversation.

"We agree that the time frame should be advanced," said the voice on the other end of the line. The voice was a familiar one, not the one they had heard over the past few conversations.

"Okay, have all parties been so advised," asked Peck. "Yes," came the response.

Meanwhile, the FBI was running the voice on the other end of the line through a voice recognition program. When it came back with a hit, Johnson's face instantly revealed shock and disbelief. "Can this be right?" he immediately asked the agent in charge of the program. "Within a .01 margin of error," answered the agent.

The conversation continued. "And just what time frame are we talking about," inquired Peck.

"Forty-eight hours."

Apparently, the FBI was not the only one tracking Peck's location because a moment later, the voice on the other end of the line abruptly asked, "Wait, where are you calling from?"

"What do you mean," Peck asked. "Don't worry, I am on a secure satphone near my headquarters."

Click was the next thing Peck, and the agents, heard as the line went dead.

Apparently, Peck had gotten sloppy. Based upon the results of the voice recognition program, however, there were far more serious issues.

The Oval Office, White House, Washington, D.C.

"Forty-eight hours!" exclaimed the President who FBI Director Stephens was presently briefing, along with the rest of his National Security team, about the recent satphone call Peck placed to an unknown number in an unknown location. And, despite the FBI's ability to track the source of the call to Peck in Redwood City, they had not been as fortunate in tracking the location of the other participant to the call.

"So, all we have is a time frame, and not much else to go on?" asked Fitzpatrick.

"Correct, sir, and I might add, having been over this transcript dozens of times now, there is nothing incriminating in the conversation, or anything that might remotely suggest they are referring to a terrorist attack," answered Director Stephens.

"But it does suggest a conspiracy, doesn't it?" asked the President.

"It does, Mr. President."

"Do we have any idea who those other individuals might be other than this Cain fellow?" inquired the Vice President who was also attending this meeting.

"Well, that is the interesting thing, sir," responded the FBI Director. "Our voice recognition program suggests that the other participant is none other than al-Fazeh himself." The President and Fitzpatrick immediately turned to their National Security team who responded in unison that they had no new information on the drone attack that purportedly killed al-Fazeh a month earlier.

"Damn it, I want al-Fazeh, and I want him now," demanded the President. "Next time, I want the drone strike to be very real and want there to be no question about who was responsible for it. Am I making myself clear?" the President instructed his National Security team.

Changing gears, a bit, the President next asked the FBI Director, "How about Peck? Do we have enough to bring him in?"

"Not really, but technically, we have 72 hours after his arrest before we have to charge him with a crime, which would effectively prevent him from participating in whatever is planned over the course of the next forty-eight hours."

"Do it," instructed the President. "Yes, sir, Mr. President."

Secure Computer Room, Kennedy Space Center, Merritt Island, Florida

Having hit a glitch, a team of the best computer hackers from the NSA were brought in to assist Cain while a team of analysts from the OIG Computer Crimes Division (CCD) and FBI looked on, as well.

"Damn it, that line of code is not supposed to be there," cursed Cain. "Try this," one of the hackers said reaching over Cain's shoulder. Cain just glared at him wishing he could twist the scrawny arm reaching over him at that very moment and break it in two. Instead, he just watched as the computer geek performed his magic, which seemed to work, at least temporarily; that is, they had the same problem a few moments later.

Kallen stared hard at Cain.

"I thought you said you debugged the program," he said.

"No, what I said was that I had programmed a safety net preventing him from creating a firewall to keep me out. However, it appears that Peck has, unbeknownst to me, inserted various lines of source code throughout the program which has effectively reconfigured it."

All of a sudden, the NSA computer hacker, who had taken over the keyboard turned and looked at Cain and yelled, "You son of a bitch."

"It was not Peck, it was him who has been inserting it," explained the hacker. Cain immediately threw an elbow at the hacker's face which was intercepted by Kallen's forearm preventing Cain from striking the hacker. Meanwhile, Cain simultaneously lunged for Frank Johnson's sidearm while a single shot rang out, striking Cain in the middle of the forehead. As he collapsed to the floor, all eyes turned to the FBI agent holding the smoking firearm.

"Guess, he is not going to the gallows after all," Kallen said, half joking, as he wiped blood, and brain splatter, off him.

"I don't believe it," said Frank Johnson, just shaking his head. "What the hell did you just do, Agent Collins?"

"I am sorry, sir. It was a combination of instinct, reaction and training," responded Agent Collins trying to explain herself, obviously oblivious to the full extent of the damage she had just done. Frank Johnson just held up his hands to quiet her down. "You just killed our best chance at stopping Peck and whatever his buddies are up to," Johnson said, hopelessly, in despair.

Then, suddenly, a small squeaky voice spoke up. "I got this," he said. All heads turned from Agent Collins to the NSA hacker who was sitting at the computer where Cain was sitting just moments ago, and who was now furiously typing away at the keyboard.

Johnson and Kallen approached the hacker and the computer screen.

"I thought Cain said the program was reconfigured to prevent interference with its intended purpose," asked Johnson and Kallen almost simultaneously.

"It has been," answered the hacker. "We just need to re-program it to do what we want it to do. The key is that we are finally in. Before we ever secured Cain's cooperation," he said raising his eyebrows as to the questionable nature of that cooperation. "The NSA was working on hacking the program, but the problem was always accessing the source code itself. You see, they had installed a Dallas Semiconductor chip to the computer board which prevented us from reading or accessing the code at the risk of being completely shut out after a certain number of attempts. Once Cain opened the program, however, he input the security code for the chip which freed up access to the source code. Now that we are in, we can deactivate the old application deleting the bad lines of code and reprogramming the source code to tell it to do what we want it to do, but it's going to take some time."

"Time is a luxury we do not have," said Johnson. "How much time are you talking about?"

"Working around the clock, maybe a few days," estimated the computer hacker.

"You have forty-eight hours," said Johnson.

Chapter Seventy-Four
August 3, 2017

San Mateo, California

As the Bentley limousine headed north on Highway 101 to San Carlos Airport, four black SUVs suddenly surrounded it, with sirens flashing through the darkened windshields. Peck's driver immediately exited the highway at the approaching off-ramp and pulled over to the side of the road. The FBI ordered Peck out of the vehicle. He instructed his driver to call his lead attorney, and Peck was then taken into FBI custody. He was transported to a holding cell in the Federal Building on 7th Street in the South of Market District in San Francisco.

Despite pleas to see his attorney, Peck was left to sit with his thoughts alone in his solitary cell. Since they were not interrogating him, and ultimately knew they would not be charging him due to lack of evidence, they were not going to accommodate his request any time soon, and certainly, not anytime within the next forty-eight hours. Besides, those were the orders from the FBI Director himself.

It didn't much matter, thought Peck to himself. Within the next couple days, the plan would go into effect, and he would be free soon enough. It was a good thing he had come up with a backup plan since it now appeared he would be indisposed at the crucial hour.

Secure Computer Room, Kennedy Space Center, Merritt Island, Florida

The teams of computer analysts were all frantically typing away, deleting unnecessary lines of code to begin reprogramming the SatCom satellite. Before they could reprogram it, however, they needed to know what to tell it to do.

After all, they still did not know what it was programmed to do, nor did they have enough time to determine what was planned through the intermittent lines of false code. As a result, it was going

261

to take quite some time to clean up the mess Cain created during the last few hours of his life.

"How is it going?" asked Johnson to the NSA programmer who came up with 'the fix' in the first place. He had now assumed the position as lead programmer for the team. His name was Gene Betel.

"Slowly. We won't even begin to have an idea as to what they are up to until we delete all the lines of bad code. That could be another half a day or so," explained the programmer.

"Even with all of this help you have here?" asked Johnson, waiving his hand around the room.

"You have to understand, coordinating the code input amongst all these different computers also takes time."

"Once again, time is something we do not have at this point," said Johnson.

National Reconnaissance Office, Chantilly, Virginia

In the bowels of the highly secretive intelligence agency, the National Reconnaissance Office (NRO), whose very existence was classified until just recently, analysts were poring over satellite images over Southeastern Syria in an effort to find the ever-elusive Nassir al-Fazeh. Although the FBI was able to track Peck's location using the GEO satellites, they had not been able to do so for al-Fazeh due to highly sophisticated scrambling devices employed on his end of the sat phone call. Using intel from other sources, however, the NRO analysts believed al-Fazeh to be in this general location. Using satellite imagery hundreds of miles above the Earth's surface, the analysts could focus in on a cigarette in a man's hand and enlarge it to such a degree that they could literally see the ashes flicker to the ground. They just needed to know where to look; that was the only thing. Right now, based upon intelligence they received from the CIA, working in conjunction with Israel's Mossad, they were focusing on a small Bedouin camp in Southeastern Syria.

"There, do you see him?" one analyst asked the other excitedly.

"Who?" asked the other.

"Right there," said the first one pointing to an elderly man wearing a Hijab exiting a dark Toyota Subaru.

"Can you get enough of his face for FaceVACS to do its thing?" asked the second analyst, referring to the NRO's advanced facial recognition program.

"I'll try," said the first analyst, manipulating the angle from the satellite, and enlarging the image on the screen. "Bingo," he exclaimed.

A moment later, they had their answer.

Chapter Seventy-Five
August 3, 2017

The Oval Office, White House, Washington, D.C.

"Mr. President, the Vice President is here to see you," announced Nora Summers. "Oh, and by the way, maintenance called earlier, and said they were working on an issue with the White House recording system. As a result, the system could be down sporadically over the next couple of hours," she added.

That's odd that the Vice President would just show up without an appointment, thought the President, who did not share the same relationship with the current Vice President as he did with his predecessor.

"That's fine. Send him in," said the President.

The Vice President entered the Oval Office. Almost immediately, the President sensed an aura of confidence in the Vice President he had not previously seen before.

"Good Morning Jed, what can I do for you?"

"It's not so much what you can do for me, but more appropriately, what you can do for the people of this great Nation."

"I am sorry, I don't understand," said the President.

"No, of course not, why would you?" said the Vice President slowly, calculating and condescendingly. "Let's back up a moment, shall we. You asked what you could do for me, right," he said rhetorically. "You can begin by stepping down from Office, effective immediately."

"Excuse me, what did you just say?" the President asked, hoping he misheard the Vice President, or that this was some type of terrible joke.

"You heard me correctly," said the Vice President, grinning one of the evilest smiles ever seen.

"Why on Earth would I ever do that?" asked the President.

"Well, it is interesting that you should bring up 'Earth', Mr. President," said the Vice President. "The reason you will be stepping down has nothing to do with Earth, I am afraid to say, but more appropriately, with Space. You see, you wanted to be the 'Space President.' Well, now you get your chance," said the Vice President mockingly.

The Vice President continued, "As you know by now, your buddy, Bob Peck recently sent a satellite into space, which combined with cloud computing capabilities, has the ability to destabilize much of the entire Country. Until now, the million-dollar question has always been what he intended to do with such capabilities." The Vice President continued unabated, "Well, let me answer that for you, my friend. The answer lies in the way Peck made his fortune in the first place." He paused, for effect.

"Pacemakers," exclaimed the Vice President. "You see, Mr. President, unless you step down effective immediately, we will use the payload aboard the SatCom satellite to shut down the power in every pacemaker in the United States thereby effectively killing every person with a pacemaker in the United States." Abel could see the horrific look of shock evident upon the President's face. Nonetheless, he just kept going, "Oh, and let me save you the trouble of doing the math, Jack, there are presently about 800,000 people, give or take, with pacemakers in the United States. With one switch of a button, they will all die. Think about it, Jack! Rich Hillary was no accident."

At that point, the President had enough. He lunged across the table at the Vice President. "You son of a bitch," he yelled. The Vice President caught the brunt of the President full force, and the two tumbled backwards onto the ground while two Secret Service agents immediately burst into the Oval Office.

As they did so, the Vice President whispered into the President's ear, "By the way, if anything happens to me or there are any efforts to undo what we have undertaken, the result will be the same."

Observing the President and Vice President rolling around on the ground, one of the Secret Service agents asked the President quizzically, "Is everything alright, sir?"

It took almost everything the President had for him not to have the Vice President arrested, but in the end, the President played it smart. He said simply, "No, everything is fine, Stan. I tripped, and the Vice President caught me."

"Uh, okay," said the agents, helping the two men to their feet.

"It's okay, Stan. Really, everything is fine," the President reassured the agents.

Once they had left the room, the Vice President continued, "Like I was saying before, if there are any attempts to expose our little scheme, people will die, Jack. We have our people strategically placed throughout the highest levels of government, including some even in your own Administration. It does not matter that you have Peck or Cain in custody. Precautions were taken for both circumstances," Abel assured the President. That signaled to the President that he did not know what happened to Cain, which possibly the President could use later to his advantage, he figured.

"Oh, and you are not to say a word to that little puppet of yours, Fitzpatrick," he instructed.

That was another good sign, thought the President. It meant that one of his closest friends and confidants was not involved with the plot. "Just tell him, and the American people, that you are stepping down for sudden health reasons," suggested Abel.

The President glared at him.

Abel shook his head, and said, "You have to understand, Jack, this is bigger than both of us. It goes back to before either you or I were born."

"Can I ask you something?" asked the President. "What is it you intend to do once you are President?"

"First, and foremost, I will pull the United States out of the Middle East entirely, leaving Israel to confront its Arab neighbors on its own. Oh, and to make it a level playing field against those Zionist pigs, I fully intend to arm my Sunni brethren with the greatest weapon of all."

"What are you talking about? Arming ISIS with nuclear weapons?"

"Precisely," he said, grinning that crazy evil smile once again.

"Christ, you truly are crazy," exclaimed the President.

Unfazed by the personal attack, the Vice President simply proceeded to instruct the President, "You will make the announcement tomorrow morning from the Rose Garden."

"Don't you think that is a little too soon. The American people are not idiots, after all. They are bound to suspect something."

"They can suspect all they want. All the matters is, that after tomorrow, I will be President of the United States. Oh, and by the way, while you heard that the White House taping system was under maintenance, I fully suspect that it has been turned back on by now."

He smiled before leaving the room, and said, "I will be listening to the back-ups, just in case, of course. Oh, and I will need access to the Situation Room for the next couple of hours." Then he left while the President just sat there, stunned and speechless.

Chapter Seventy-Six
August 3, 2017

The Personal Residence of the White House, Washington, D.C.

Twenty-One Hours Until the Deadline: 11:00 A.M.

"Incredible," was all the First Lady could muster after the President disclosed Abel and Peck's little plot to her. She was as equally stunned as the President.

"So, what are you going to do?" she asked. "What can I do," he said, defeated.

"Stall," she offered.

"That may only postpone the inevitable, and he could trigger a partial shutdown killing thousands, just to show us how serious and capable they are."

"I am sorry to say this, honey, but wasn't that, at least in part, why they killed Rich?"

"Yes, but I fear it could be on a much grander scale now, especially if they believe we are just buying time."

"You have to try, don't you? Didn't you say you have that team of computer analysts working around the clock to break the Code?"

He nodded.

"What does Teddy think?" she asked.

Taking one look at him, she instantly knew the answer. "You haven't spoken to him about it, have you. Why not? You don't think he is involved, do you?"

"No, Abel said not to discuss it with him, which confirms he is not involved."

"Are you sure he did not say that as a diversionary tactic, just to test the waters to see how much he can trust you not to say anything?"

Now, it was the President's turn to stare at the First Lady. "We are talking about a man I have known and trusted now for well over a quarter of century, I don't think so, honey," he said shaking his head.

"Then, why haven't you spoken to him yet?"

"I will speak with him later. I just wanted to talk to you first."

"I appreciate that honey, but we are running out of time and you need to figure this out, right away. Go talk to Teddy!"

The Rose Garden, the White House, Washington, D.C.
Twenty Hours and Forty Minutes Until the Deadline: 11:20 A.M.

Twenty minutes later, the President and Teddy Fitzpatrick were walking in the Rose Garden. Once he heard everything, Fitzpatrick snarled in disbelief, "You are serious?"

The President just stared at him hard, and said, "Believe me Teddy, I wish it were all a bad joke, but we both know this threat is all too real. We should have seen it coming sooner."

"What do you mean? How?" exclaimed Fitzpatrick. "Believe me Jack, other than the First Lady, and maybe Jonas, I have spent more time with him than anyone over the last few weeks and he had us all fooled. For Christ's sake, he even had the Speaker fooled."

"Wait a minute, what was that you just said," asked the President. "What, about the Speaker?"

"No, about Jonas," clarified the President. "What about Jonas?"

"Do you think he had anything to do with this? Could he be the inside source to which Abel was referring?"

Fitzpatrick was immediately about to reject the idea out of hand when the more he thought about it, the more it made sense. Jonas was there right from the beginning; when they first learned about the NASA investigation, throughout the search for a Vice Presidential successor, and all of those late-night prep sessions with the ultimate Nominee, whom he seemed unquestionably determined to have both Houses confirm. Now, it seems his true motives may be in question. Fitzpatrick's face immediately soured. Begrudgingly, he agreed to contact Director Stephens and have an FBI tail placed on Jonas Frank.

"In the meantime, you should act as it is business as usual with him, Teddy. Include him on all important issues, but of course, nothing having to do with what we just discussed, okay? We don't want him to get suspicious."

Fitzpatrick reluctantly agreed. "What are you going to do?" he asked.

"What can I do?" asked the President rhetorically. "Stall," he said, answering his own question. "We have to buy time for our computer analysts to reprogram that satellite," he continued.

"How are you going to do that?"

"That's the problem. I don't know just yet, but as I said, we can't let them get suspicious in the meantime. So, we must proceed as if I am planning on making that ridiculous announcement tomorrow. I have scheduled a Press Conference for undisclosed reasons for 8:30 tomorrow morning and am having Nora contact Dr. Allenstein about planning on being in attendance for the Press Conference. That way, if they are truly monitoring the situation, they will see that things are progressing as they planned."

Secure Computer Room, Kennedy Space Center, Merritt Island, Florida
Nineteen Hours Until the Deadline: 1:00 P.M.

"The good news is now that we know what the satellite's intended purpose is, it will take less time to reprogram the satellite once we deactivate the old application. The bad news is that it is taking much longer to deactivate the old application than expected. You see, before we figured out what he was up to, Cain managed to insert an algorithm that generated thousands of unnecessary lines into the source code, making it difficult and time consuming to deactivate the application. He also set up various firewalls and traps throughout the program which causes it to switch to a different user system, temporarily suspending all functions, making it take longer than it should," explained NSA computer analyst Gene Betel to Agent Johnson. Johnson just looked at him.

"Okay, in English, what does that all mean?"

"It means it is taking us far longer to reprogram the source code than originally anticipated. The damage Cain managed to do during those last few hours is truly devastating."

"I don't understand," said Johnson, shaking his head. "A team of FBI computer analysts was watching him the entire time."

"What can I say?" said the analyst shrugging his shoulders.

"So, what is the time frame we are talking about for fixing this whole mess?" asked Johnson.

"I don't know, could be a couple of days, I guess."

"We don't have a couple of days. Get more analysts in here if you need them, but this has to be done within the next twelve hours," he said, leaving himself some extra time, just in case they needed it.

Chapter Seventy-Seven
August 3, 2017

The Situation Room, the White House, Washington, D.C.
Eighteen and a Half Hours Until the Deadline: 1:30 P.M.

With Peck indisposed, the Vice President had to take initiative. So, he contacted his uncle using a secure videoconferencing line in one of the many whisper rooms that comprise the 'Situation Room' beneath the Oval Office. In fact, it was rumored to be the same line that President Bush routinely used to communicate with Iraqi Prime Minister al-Maliki during his Presidency.

"Is everything in order?" asked the Vice President, seeing his uncle for the first time in his life. For being dead, he looked pretty good, thought the Vice President.

"It is," was his uncle's response. Al-Fazeh was noticeably uncomfortable using the video conferencing system, avoiding eye contact the entire time.

Following up, Abel asked, "Are you sure Walker knows what to do?"

"He does."

"How will he access the Facility?"

"Leave that to us."

"Will he know how to use the Program once inside the facility?"

"Don't worry, he has been properly prepared. You are to proceed as planned," al- Fazeh instructed the Vice President. "The time table remains the same," al-Fazeh said gruffly, as he abruptly ended the call.

For the Vice President, however, the call ended much the same way it began, with the Vice President feeling uneasy about retired Chief Warrant Officer, U.S. Army (Ret.) Mark Walker, aka Rick Marshall, being able to successfully perform that which Cain was initially assigned to complete. Although he was sufficiently trained in computers, Walker certainly did not have the same skill set that Cain possessed. *If anything went wrong with the computer hook up to the satellite, the entire plan could be foiled*, he suddenly worried. *While it is true they had taken precautions, would those ultimately prove to be enough when all was said and done*, he now wondered.

Lyndon B. Johnson Space Center, Houston, Texas
Seventeen and a Half Hours Until the Deadline: 2:30 P.M.

Aaron Harbath was speaking with Commander Thorson through a secure videoconferencing link between the ISS and Johnson Space Center.

"As you know Commander, we have been preparing you over the last few weeks to reprogram the electrical system aboard the ISS to diffuse a potential terrorist threat. As it turns out, that threat level has gone from 'potential' to 'actionable.' The FBI and NSA have been working on debugging the satellite through the actual program itself, but we may still need you to be prepared to disconnect the battery charge/discharge unit in the JEM-EF, if necessary, okay?"

"Copy that," replied Thorson. "I have been studying and working intermittently on the power management and distribution subsystem."

"Great. Oh, and Jim, we don't want you to say anything to Korbatov about it, at least not yet."

This request was based, in part, on Kallen's prior determination that Korbatov had been with Russia's FSB, in charge of spy satellites, before becoming a Cosmonaut. As such, it was determined that he could not be trusted with information concerning one of the greatest national security threats to this Country in modern history.

"Don't you think he will become suspicious when all the power goes out?" asked Commander Thorson.

"Not necessarily. Remember Jim, we only want you to shut down the battery source in the JEM-EF, where the SatCom satellite is housed, to deactivate the EM Drive aboard the satellite itself. So, if Korbatov is in a different part of the ISS, he should not notice anything out of the ordinary. We will speak again soon once I have more information."

"Copy that," said Thorson, signing off.

The Budget Motel, Titusville, Florida
Sixteen Hours Until the Deadline: 4:00 P.M.

Having carefully eluded the authorities, Mark Walker checked into the same room Cain had used only a few days earlier. He never much liked Cain; in fact, he always thought he was a bit of an arrogant son of a bitch. *For such a little man, he should have been humbler,* Walker figured. It was not so much that Cain was a little man, but more that Mark Walker was a hulking mass of a man, standing six feet seven inches tall and weighing about two hundred ninety pounds. His humongous biceps were covered in tattoos, from back when he was in the Army. The rule, back in the day, was nothing below your elbow so he had elbow length sleeve tattoos of serpents, representing Operation Gothic Serpent in Mogadishu, Somalia in 1993, which Walker had fought in, and which was considered one of the bloodiest battles involving US Special Forces since Vietnam.

The minute Walker entered Room 102, he was smacked in the face with the stench of fast food even though the room should have been cleaned several times since Cain last used it; *another disgusting habit of Cain's,* Walker thought.

He immediately placed his bag on the luggage rack, if you could call it that, having been converted from a used TV stand, apparently. He pulled his backpack from his bag, and then spread the map out on the Formica table in the corner of the room. Peck had given strict instructions. Should Cain become compromised, for whatever reason, the job would fall to Walker to program the satellite. He knew this day would come.

The authorities were all over the place so he carefully considered his options, and decided to enter Kennedy through the North entrance instead of the East Entrance that Cain had previously used. Once inside, he would use the security pass and contact lenses he had been provided to bypass the internal security procedures. Then, he would proceed to the central stairwell, where he would descend to the Engineering Room where Cain had initially made the remote connection to the ISS. Because security was much greater now, however, he would use the utility closet next to the Engineering Room instead of the Engineering Room itself and would use an extender to make the connection. Also, he knew that, at the same time he entered the Facility, the authorities and NASA security personnel would be busy responding to more serious issues allowing him time to enter relatively unnoticed. Such distractions should also provide sufficient time for Walker to establish a connection with the ISS to make the satellite operational once he received confirmation from the Vice President.

Chapter Seventy-Eight
August 3, 2017

Max Kallen's Office, Kennedy Space Center, Merritt Island, Florida

Fifteen and a Half Hours Until the Deadline: 5:00 P.M.

Max Kallen was on a secure conference call with his boss, Inspector General, Mark Weisburg, and Special Agent, Frank Johnson, going over the necessary security measures to be implemented within the next few hours at both NASA facilities.

"We will need around the clock monitoring of all security systems. I want the entry records monitored visually every 30 seconds so that we know everybody who is coming and going at each facility at every minute," barked Weisburg.

"Yes, I am putting additional security teams together as we speak," advised Kallen. "Is it possible we could get a few extra Special Agents to assist with security at each facility?" Kallen asked Johnson, who immediately responded, "Done."

"Also, Agent Johnson, can you contact the local PD and have them send some extra squad cars to the sites?" asked Weisburg. "I want a heavy security present at both facilities. We know, after all, that they will ultimately have to enter one of the facilities to access the satellite remotely."

"Will do," responded Johnson. "By the way, I will be in the Computer Room on and off for the next few hours and may be inaccessible through normal channels, but Max has my secure cell phone," Johnson noted.

"Okay, we should periodically stay in touch as we will need updates from you as well as to what is going on from your end of things," noted Kallen.

"Will do," Frank Johnson agreed.

"In the meantime, I understand that ISS Mission Control Director, Aaron Harbath, has been in contact with Commander

Thorson who is prepared to shut down the battery charge/discharge unit, or BCDU, in the JEM-EF as a backup measure. Just to let you guys know, however, our electrical engineers don't believe such measures will even work since the satellite has its own EM Drive, which combined with the Station-to-Shuttle Power Transfer System, could still allow the satellite to access the energy generated from the Solar Array Wing. A more thorough overhaul of the entire electrical system aboard the ISS, akin to what Commander Boucher was training for, would be required to effectively shut the EM down as an alternative power source. Also, the Power Transfer Unit of the ISS could allow for the transfer of up to 8 kilowatts of power from the space station to the satellite, thereby still providing a sufficiently large power base. Because the EM readings at the time of the SatCom launch were almost two and half times those initially disclosed in the RIO Disclosure, our engineers believe that the EM Drive itself could prove to be an effective alternative source of energy to power the program even if Thorson successfully shuts down the BCDU in the JEM-EF Module."

"No doubt," responded Kallen. "I mean, they would not have gone to all this trouble if all we needed to do to foil their plan was flip a switch."

Johnson agreed, and the call ended shortly thereafter.

The Truman Balcony, the White House, Washington, D.C.
Twelve and a Half Hours Until the Deadline: 7:30 P.M.

Standing on the second-floor balcony of the Executive Residence of the White House, the President and Fitzpatrick spoke in hushed tones. The President had just finished detailing his plans to buy additional time before he was supposed to give the dreaded Rose Garden announcement. "It could work," said Fitzpatrick, considering what the President had just told him.

"You are sure no one will get hurt or be in danger, at any time?" Fitzpatrick asked, obviously gravely concerned.

"If properly executed with the necessary precision, that is the idea."

"And how much extra time will that really buy us?"

"Maybe an additional six to eight hours."

"The Vice President will not suspect anything?" Teddy asked.

"That is the beautiful part about it," said the President. "Even if he does, he will be in no position to do anything about it."

Fitzpatrick thought about it for a moment and realized that the President was right. "It seems we do not have many other options at this point," he said.

The President sadly agreed. "Let's hope it works, Teddy, and buys us enough time for those NSA and FBI programmers to debunk that satellite."

Fitzpatrick shook his head, and said, "God help us all if it doesn't."

Chapter Seventy-Nine
August 3, 2017

Secure Computer Room, Kennedy Space Center, Merritt Island, Florida Twelve Hours Until the Deadline: 8:00 P.M.

Johnson was hunched over Betel's shoulder. "How is it coming?" he asked.

"Not any faster with you looking over my shoulder the whole time," Betel responded. "Again, we keep finding new traps that are taking us longer than expected to deactivate the application."

"So, how long do you estimate it is going to take until we are able to begin entering the new code into the Program?"

"At least twelve to fourteen hours."

"And how long do you estimate it will take to reprogram it after that?"

"It depends upon what you guys want it to do. Probably, at least another five to six hours after that, I would imagine."

"We don't have that much time! Get moving," exclaimed Johnson.

Early Morning Hours of August 4, 2017 the Pentagon, Washington, D.C.
Seven and Half Hours Until the Deadline: 12:30 A.M.

"You want us to do what?" exclaimed the Chairman of the Joint Chiefs of Staff to the President of the United States, somewhat incredulously.

The President went over his plan again in detail. When he finished, the President asked, "Well, can it be done?"

The Chairman turned to the Five Star Air Force General whose presence the President had also requested at this top-secret meeting, which only the men present in the room knew about. It was just past midnight in a room beneath the Pentagon akin to the White House's

Situation Room. At first, the Generals and Secretary of Defense thought it was odd that the President had requested the meeting here instead of the White House Situation Room, but now they understood why.

The Air Force General shrugged his shoulders and said, "I suppose so."

"Without the risk of injury to any civilians or staff?" the President pressed further.

At this point, the Chairman interjected himself back into the conversation explaining, "As you know, Mr. President, ever since 9/11, a distributed and networked medium to long range air-defense system, known as NASAMS or Norwegian Advanced Surface to Air Missile System, has been in place protecting the air space over Washington D.C., and the White House. It is possible, Mr. President, in fact, I would say likely, that the F1 Sentinel air defense radar system of NASAMS would detect the incoming ordinance and fire an AMRAAM missile at it. This could, of course, result in collateral damage on the ground, sir."

"What would the Collateral Damage Estimate (CDE) be?" asked the President. "Based upon the Collateral Effects Radius, or CER, I would estimate somewhere around a CDE Level 1 of less than 10%, with no potential casualties."

"So, we are talking about just structural damage then?" "Correct, sir."

"And, if we were to do it during the early morning hours, what effect would that have on that estimate?"

"It would of course reduce it even greater, sir."

"How long before something like this could be operational?" asked the President. "Since no ground personnel is necessarily involved, Mr. President, we could be operational within a matter minutes, if even that," answered the Chairman of the Joint Chiefs. "Great, for security reasons, that may be all we have."

"Yes, sir, Mr. President," came the response from everyone in the room, acknowledging the short leash under which they would be operating.

"Sir, there is another issue," announced the Chairman of the Joint Chiefs.

"Yes, what is it?"

"The NRO confirmed the location of an individual they believe to be Nassir al-Fazeh in Southern Syria, sir."

"Can we do a drone strike?"

"We can, Mr. President. The only question is how the nearby pro-Assad backed Russian forces might react."

"Do it," instructed the President. "I'll deal with Putin, later."

John F. Kennedy Space Center, Merritt Island, Florida
Three and a Half Hours Until the Deadline: 4:30 A.M.

While conducting surveillance, Walker noted the heavy police presence, which he fully expected. He had just finished circling the outer perimeter of the industrial section of the Kennedy Space Center for the third time. That is where the Central Instrumentation Facility (CIF) is located. Each time, he used a different vehicle that he had rented from three different rental agencies, using fake credit cards.

Once he determined it was safe to act, Mark Walker made his move. He knew that he would receive heightened scrutiny from the guards at the North gate, and that security personnel inside the facility would be simultaneously recording and analyzing his entrance. Nevertheless, he figured that, soon enough, they would have far greater issues to worry about than a lowly janitor entering the North Entrance of Kennedy Space Center.

As expected, Walker encountered additional screening from the guards at the North Gate. Once his credentials passed muster, however, he was permitted entry into the facility, and parked in his designated spot next to the CIF.

Just as he was pulling into his parking spot, there was suddenly a bright flash, accompanied by a thunderous roar of an explosion in the direction of the nearby Launch Complex 39. Instantly, sirens could be heard wailing, and sirens seen flashing, in the distance. Alarms sounded all throughout the facility. Walker nonetheless proceeded calmly, unfazed by the sudden frenzy of activity all around him. He entered the CIF, using the secure key card he was given after Cain's capture. He was assured it had been reprogrammed appropriately. Sure enough, it worked. Thankfully, once inside, he was not greeted by a legion of security personnel pointing M-16s at him, like Cain.

Walker next proceeded to the eye scanner, carefully placing his right eye directly up to the scanner. That was, of course, the eye specially fitted with the computer programmed contact lenses. Like clockwork, it worked too. A minute later, he was descending the central staircase in the CIF heading for the Engineering Room and its attached maintenance closet.

Once in front of the Engineering Room, Walker positioned himself directly in front of the door with his back to the door. He had the key card in his hand but knowing that the video cameras were on a timed feed, switching from various locations, at different intervals, he waited precisely thirty seconds before slipping the key card into the door, and flipping the door open. Backing in, he pushed the door quickly closed. This took no more than a matter of seconds, and if anybody was watching the security video at the time, all they would see is a man standing in the hall one minute, and when the next feed appeared, that same individual would be gone, leaving the security personnel only to speculate as to where he might have gone.

Again, all security personnel would likely be dealing with the explosion at Launch Complex 39, and hopefully, would not be paying attention to the monitor at that time he entered, he figured. As a result, it should be several hours before security staff got around to reviewing the video feeds for other locations throughout the facility during the time of the explosion. In other words, by that time, it would be too late even if someone did see the suspicious video footage.

Once inside, Walker quickly made his way to the adjoining maintenance closet. After moving several items around inside the closet, Walker made himself comfortable. He settled in for the next few hours, until he was given the green light from the Vice President, or as a backup, the mysterious caller whom he only heard about, but with whom, he never had any prior dealings.

Lyndon B. Johnson Space Center, Houston, Texas
Three and a Half Hours Until the Deadline: 4:30 A.M.

Meanwhile, at precisely that same time, the black Ford F350 sped down Second Street on the grounds of the Johnson Space Center before turning left on the Delta Link and turning left through the parking area. It headed straight for the Christopher C. Craft, Jr. Mission Control Center.

At the very last minute, however, two security vehicles intercepted the vehicle just as it was about to crash into the Mission Control Center, causing a huge explosion, instantly killing all inside the three vehicles. As a result, a section within the Mission Control

Center had to be shut down while emergency response units responded to the scene. This resulted in a temporary delay of communications between the Johnson Space Center and other NASA facilities. Consequently, security personnel at Johnson Space Center had no knowledge about the attack at Kennedy Space Center, and vice versa.

Chapter Eighty
August 4, 2017

John F. Kennedy Space Center, Merritt Island, Florida
Three and a Half Hours Until the Deadline: 4:30 A.M.

The ominous flash and thunderous roar of an explosion rippled throughout the area surrounding Launch Complex 39. Max Kallen, who was scanning the security monitors at the time, yelled, "Jesus, what the hell was that?"

He immediately instructed the security analysts in the room, "Don't take your eyes off the monitors!"

As it turns out, however, the explosion at Launch Complex 39 proved to be a sufficient distraction for the security analyst who, at the time, had a picture of the hallway outside the Engineering Room on his monitor. As a result, the man standing with his back in front of the Engineering Room door proceeded to go unnoticed.

"Get me JSC on the line now," ordered Kallen, referring to Johnson Space Center. "I am sorry, sir, but all communications with JSC appear to be temporarily suspended.

We are looking into why right now, sir."

At that very moment, the Inspector General burst into the room. "What the hell is going on?" he demanded.

"Sir, I just received a secure text that there was an explosion near the Craft Mission Control Center at JSC, and as a result, all communications have temporarily been suspended while emergency response crews respond to the scene."

"Christ, we are under attack!" Inspector General Mark Weisburg hollered. "Get Administrator Redwell on his cell phone now," he bellowed.

SOCOM, Creech Air Force Base, Outside Las Vegas, Nevada
Two Hours and Forty Minutes Until the Deadline: 5:30 A.M.

The Captain was piloting the MQ-1 Predator Drone over Southern Syria, with her newly minted Lieutenant at her side. The coordinates that the NRO provided turned out to be accurate. The Captain, and Lieutenant, were awaiting facial confirmation of the high value target, using the military approved facial recognition program, which came minutes later. The Captain then entered the precise coordinates which her Lieutenant confirmed.

Next, they both visually confirmed the computer enhanced facial features of the subject before entering the final command to fire. Once confirmed, the captain pushed a button, and an AGM-114 Hellfire Air to Surface Missile was launched from the Predator Drone in the sky above the Camp where Nassir al-Fazeh was busy finalizing the last-minute details of his Grand Plan with other Sunni Jihadists.

Minutes later, the kill was confirmed.

Secure Computer Room, Kennedy Space Center, Merritt Island, Florida
Two and a Half Hours Until the Deadline: 5:30 A.M.

"Done," exclaimed Betel, with sheer relief, as he deleted the final line of 'bad' code.

He was exhausted, having worked through the night non-stop; a feat he had not achieved since he had attended his last day in college.

Agent Frank Johnson ran over to him. "Great, so you can shut it down now?" asked Johnson expectantly.

"No, we can start programming it to do that now. Again however, it is going to take some time. We just finished deleting all the old application and getting rid of all the traps. We can now finally begin to tell it what to do. What do you want it to do?" asked Betel.

After consulting with the powers that be, Johnson advised Betel to 'shut down its remote capabilities'.

"How long will it take?" asked Johnson.

"At least five to six hours," Betel responded.

"You don't get it, do you?" Johnson said, shaking his head. "You have two and half hours. Get it done now!"

Chapter Eighty-One
August 4, 2017

The White House, Washington, D.C.
Two Hours and Twenty-Five Minutes Until
the Deadline: 5:35 A.M.

In accordance with the President's instructions, the Predator Drone hovered several thousand meters above the White House and Washington D.C. before the General gave the final order to fire the unarmed missile in the least traveled area of the White House grounds, with the heaviest vegetation.

NASAMS worked perfectly, as expected, firing one AMRAAN missile at the approaching unarmed Hellfire missile, causing explosion several hundred feet above the White House resulting in debris in the planned Collateral Effects Radius (CER). Because the Hellfire missile was unarmed, the resulting explosion and collateral damage was minimal. Most importantly, there were no known casualties or injuries reported as a result of shrapnel falling from the sky.

Equally important, the attack triggered the evacuation of the President and Vice President to the President's Emergency Operations Center (PEOC), which is a bunker-like structure that lies underground, beneath the East Wing of the White House. It serves as a secure shelter for the President of the United States and other protectees in case of an emergency. In fact, it was there where Vice President Dick Cheney, Condoleezza Rice, Scooter Libby, and others were sequestered during the attacks on 9/11. This is where the President, the Vice President, and others would be now too, thereby effectively depriving the Vice President of access to any viable communications that could trigger the attack, at least temporarily, just as the President planned.

The United States Naval Observatory, Washington, D.C.
Two Hours and Twenty-Three Minutes Until the Deadline: 5:37 A.M.

As he prepared for the day ahead of him, the Vice President was beaming with confidence, satisfied that all had finally come together, as originally planned over half a century ago. He had confirmed that the President had indeed scheduled a Press Conference for 8:30 a.m. later that morning, and the White House Doctor, Reuben Allenstein, was scheduled to be in attendance, as well. He could hardly believe that, in only a matter of hours, he would be President of the United States. He stared at his own reflection in the mirror, impressed with himself and all that he had achieved, and would accomplish in the future.

Then, all of a sudden, he heard a loud thundering boom in the distance. A minute later, there was a heavy knock at the door.

When he opened it, the head of his Secret Service detail greeted him.

"I'm sorry, sir, you will have to come with us. There has been an attack on the White House," advised the Secret Service Agent.

"What are you talking about," exclaimed the Vice President.

"Moments ago, there was a drone attack on the White House grounds. We have been ordered to bring you to PEOC immediately, sir," said the agent. "Please, sir, we do not have much time. You must come with me now," instructed the agent. The Vice President simply had no alternative but to comply.

Lyndon B. Johnson Space Center, Houston, Texas
Two Hours Until the Deadline: 6:00 A.M.

Once the communications at JSC was reestablished, ISS Mission Control Director Aaron Harbath immediately got in touch with Commander Thorson at the ISS. "Jim, we are going to need you to shut down the battery charge/discharge units in the JEM-EF, effectively shutting down the power to the SatCom satellite," he advised.

"Okay, when?"

"At approximately zero eight hundred."

"Okay, that is only a couple of hours from now."

"Yes, and again Commander," Harbath said, "it must be done discreetly without alerting Korbatov, if possible."

"Understood."

"Once shut down, please communicate only directly through this secure line, understood?"

"Yes, sir."

"Okay, signing off for now."

"Copy that," responded Thorson.

Chapter Eighty-Two
August 4, 2017

The President's Emergency Operations Center, Washington, D.C.
Two Hours Until the Deadline: 6:00 A.M.

Immediately upon his arrival to PEOC, the President, his Chief of Staff, and Deputy Chief of Staff, Jonas Frank, greeted the Vice President before being ushered into a separate chamber of PEOC, using the tunnels beneath the White House.

"You've been advised about the attack?" the President asked the Vice President. "I was told there was a drone attack on the White House," responded the Vice President, suspiciously.

"That is correct," said the President.

"And, as it turns out, Major Pollock, the PEOC Director, advises me that the communications center here has been temporarily compromised because of the attack. Therefore, for additional security reasons, all communications have been temporarily shut down here in PEOC," advised the President.

Now, the Vice President was even more suspicious, raising an eyebrow subtly. The President could only grin.

"I guess, you will have to settle in for the next few hours, until we are cleared to return to the White House," he said.

"I know what you are up to," whispered the Vice President in the President's ear. "It's not going to work. There are others who can trigger the satellite if I, or others, are indisposed," he advised the President.

Again, the President could only smile and act as if he had no idea what the Vice President was talking about before the Vice President was escorted into a different chamber, separate and apart from that of the President.

Meanwhile, the President was a bit concerned that he had not yet received confirmation of the drone strike on al-Fazeh before he was ushered into PEOC. With the communications now shut down in PEOC (albeit at his request), there was no way to confirm whether the attack on al-Fazeh was successful or not. Although he did have his secure cell phone, he, like Obama at the end of his second term, rarely used it, for security reasons, after the whole Hillary Clinton fiasco. Besides, he could probably not even get service in here if he tried.

In any case, that was apparently the one ace in the hole they now held since it appeared that the Vice President was unaware of his uncle's untimely demise if that were in fact the case. Hopefully, that avenue was now closed, and with the Vice President sequestered in PEOC for the next couple of hours, the computer programmers could do their thing and shut down the SatCom satellite once and for all before the plan went operational.

John F. Kennedy Space Center, Merritt Island, Florida
One and a Half Hours Until the Deadline: 6:30 A.M.

Kallen and Weisburg were on the phone with Administrator Redwell who was updating them as to the status of the attack at JSC. Communications at the Craft Mission Control Center had finally been restored following the attack. The vehicles involved in the collision were doused with chemical retardant to control the unusually hot flames. Apparently, the truck at JSC had a flatbed full of chemical explosives which instantly ignited upon impact causing a humongous explosion. HazMat was called in, and still had not cleared the area in the immediate vicinity of the Mission Control Center. The Administrator was calling from his office in the Headquarters Building at JSC.

Now, it was Kallen's turn to update Redwell. "The MO appears to be the same for the attack here as well," explained Kallen. "Except, here, instead of a moving vehicle, an IED appears to have been strategically placed just behind Launch Complex 39 and was triggered to go off at the same time as the breach at JSC. Based upon what you just described, sir, and what we observed here, I think it is safe to say that both attacks appear to be simply diversionary tactics."

"What about JPL?" asked the Administrator, referring to the Jet Propulsion Laboratory in La Canada, California, which although privately owned, is also technically considered to be one of the many NASA facilities across the country.

"We checked with Security there, sir, and all has been quiet. So, only JSC and KSC appear to have been targeted in these attacks, which means, right now, our mysterious computer hacker must be at one of those two facilities," speculated Kallen.

"As a result, I have ordered a security sweep of each of the two facilities by all security personnel at each facility, sir," advised Inspector General Weisburg. "However, as you know, sir, we are talking about dozens and dozens of square miles between the two facilities, so it could take some time."

"I have also ordered a review of all security monitors at both facilities during the time of the Launch Complex 39 explosion and breach at JSC. Of course, we will continue to keep you posted of our progress, sir," advised Kallen.

"I want updates every five minutes," demanded Administrator Redwell.

"I was supposed to brief the President a half hour ago, but for some reason, I have been unable to reach him. Nevertheless, I want up to the minute updates regularly, so I can adequately brief him as to the status of things the minute I am able to speak with the President."

"Understood, sir," responded both Kallen and Weisburg, simultaneously.

Chapter Eighty-Three
Finale
August 4, 2017

Secure Computer Room, Kennedy Space Center, Merritt Island, Florida
Half an Hour Until the Deadline: 7:30 A.M.

"We are making better progress than expected, sir, but there is no way we will finish within the next half an hour," Betel advised Agent Johnson.

"What is your best estimate," asked Johnson.

"Maybe a couple of hours, sir, if we are lucky," estimated Betel.

"Do your best to get it done within the next hour," instructed Johnson.

"Sir, we are doing the best we can, but the additional code you requested about tracking access points is taking a bit longer than expected since it is more complex code."

"One hour," repeated Johnson.

"If need be, delete the additional Code, and just ensure it is non-operational." Johnson walked out of the room to call Max Kallen. Kallen picked up on the first ring.

"They are estimating another couple of hours. I told them they could have one," advised Johnson. "How is it going on your end?"

"Following the attacks on JSC and KSC, we have instituted an all points search of both facilities, and I have ordered a review of all video footage, from all feeds. I am also having a manual review of entry logs and video footage for all gates performed. We will keep you apprised of our progress."

"Same here," responded Johnson. "Oh, and Max, good luck!"

"Yeah, you too, Frank," said Kallen, gravely.

International Space Station
Half an Hour Until the Deadline: 7:30 A.M.

Following Harbath's instructions, Commander Thorson maneuvered himself to the JEM-EF through the Internal Truss Structure. Once inside, he quickly found the battery charge/discharge unit (BCDUs) for the JEM-EF Module, flipped a couple of switches, and entered a few different codes into the nearby computer screen. Then, as NASA electricians instructed, he switched some of the wiring inside the box. Suddenly, the lighting in the JEM-EF flickered on and off a bit before it went completely dark. Feeling his way through the darkness, Commander Thorson made his way out of the JEM-EF, and back into the main corridor of the Internal Truss Structure of the ISS.

The Rose Garden, the White House, Washington, D.C.
The Deadline: 8:00 A.M.

The deadline came and went without much ado. The Press Conference was abruptly cancelled, and rescheduled to later in the morning, following the temporary evacuation of White House staff after what was now being described as a non-threatening action, but would later be attributed to a rogue nation.

The White House, Office of the Secret Service, Washington, D.C.
Half an Hour After the Deadline: 8:30 A.M.

The last two agents finished making the rounds of the outer perimeter of the White House. "Code 4, sir," they reported, indicating everything was all clear.

"Have the chemical response teams completed their reports?" asked the Secret Service supervisory agent.

"They should be here in the next twenty minutes. Should I notify PEOC?" asked one of the agents.

"Not yet, I want to see those reports, as well as an aerial surveillance report before we give the all clear to PEOC. Also, get me the present F1 Sentinel radar readings for NASAMS. I am not releasing the President and Vice President until we know for sure it is safe to do so," said the Secret Service agent in charge.

International Space Station
Thirty-Five Minutes After the Deadline: 8:35 A.M.

Thorson could not make sense of it. Despite his best efforts, and the fact that he confirmed he had effectively shut down all power to the JEM-EF, the computer readings showed that the SatCom satellite was up and running, and the levels of electricity it was generating were astronomical.

John F. Kennedy Space Center, Merritt Island, Florida
One Hour Ten Minutes After the Deadline: 9:10 A.M.

"There," shouted the security analyst, pointing at the monitor, as he was re-reviewing the security footage. Kallen saw it immediately and stopped the footage. He paused the computer mid-frame and enlarged it 500 percent. Kallen thought it could be Walker. He ordered two sets of security teams, of four men each, to approach the Engineering Room door with guns drawn.

Secure Computer Room, Kennedy Space Center, Merritt Island, Florida
One Hour and Twelve Minutes After the Deadline: 9:12 A.M.

"Done," yelled Betel, as he typed the last line of code into the computer before collapsing to the ground from exhaustion.

Johnson ran to the computer screen. He looked down at Betel on the ground. "So, it will effectively deny access to anyone trying to access the SatCom satellite remotely?" he asked excitedly.

Betel shrugged his shoulders, and said, "Who knows? It should."

"God help us all if it doesn't," mumbled Johnson to himself.

Engineering Room Maintenance Closet, Kennedy Space Center, Florida
One Hour and Twelve Minutes, Thirty Seconds After the Deadline: 9:12:30 A.M.

Walker was looking at his watch now for the last hour and half every thirty seconds. To say he was worried would be an understatement. The call should have come over an hour ago. Fearing that both the Vice President and the mysterious caller may have been compromised, Walker was determined to show initiative. He would stay the course. So, he opened his laptop, powered it up, found the program to access the satellite in the bottom corner of his Desktop, and scrolled his mouse over to the icon. But just as he was about to click on the icon, the Engineering Room closet door flung open and a small contingent of security personnel appeared, leveling their laser pointed guns directly at the middle of his forehead. He had just enough time to click on the icon. The computer program sprang to life with a spinning circle in the corner of the screen, indicating it was being downloaded. Walker grinned an evil grin, and then suddenly, the screen went blank. The Blue Screen of Death appeared on the computer screen, repeating 'system failure', over and over, line after line.

"No!" yelled Walker.

The President's Emergency Operations Center, Washington, D.C.
One Hour and Thirteen Minutes After the Deadline: 9:13 A.M.

Having just received word from the Secret Service that the grounds of the White House were secure, and there was no known impending threat, PEOC Director Major Pollock began initiating the procedure for release of all protected from the President's Emergency Operations Center. The entire process should last no more than three to five minutes.

Meanwhile, the President still had no way of knowing whether the computer analysts had successfully debugged the program or whether the drone attack on Nassir al-Fazeh was successful, both of which left open viable avenues of attack. In other words, the President still did not know whether he would be giving a speech later that morning stepping down from Office, thereby effectively putting a mad man into power. He was damned if he was going to let that happen. The President grabbed the Major's sidearm and fired a single shot into the back of the Vice President, who collapsed to the floor. Immediately, Secret Service agents swarmed both the President and Vice President.

Epilogue

The initial shock and confusion over the events which unfolded in the President's Emergency Operations Center (PEOC) was resolved shortly after the arrest and capture of Chief Warrant Officer, U.S. Army (Ret.) Mark Walker, from the Engineering Room maintenance closet at Kennedy Space Center. Mark Walker was ultimately tried, and convicted, of treason. The Government chose not to seek the death penalty in exchange for his testimony against J. Robert Peck.

Shortly after the events that transpired in PEOC, the President was released from Secret Service custody, and the Vice President was immediately taken into custody, and transported to George Washington Medical Center; ironically, just like his predecessor. The only difference was that this time, the Vice President was chained to his hospital bed, and had round the clock FBI agents stationed outside his room. And, instead of suffering a heart attack, the doctors later advised this Vice President that he would never walk again because of the bullet severing his spine.

Following the Vice President's impeachment in the House and Senate, the President nominated Senator Henry McClintock to serve as the next Vice President, who after having his name cleared, gladly accepted the nomination. He was confirmed by a vote of sixty-one to thirty-nine in the Senate, and two hundred ninety-nine to one hundred thirty-six in the House of Representatives.

Needless to say, the American public viewed the President as a true hero and he easily won re-election in 2020. Teddy Fitzpatrick remained as White House Chief of Staff, and the President's best friend, until he died of lung cancer in 2022.

Jonas Frank was arrested shortly after the capture of Mark Walker when he tried to access the program to the SatCom satellite from his White House Office and the tracer part of Betel's new program worked brilliantly, leading the authorities to directly to Frank, thereby confirming the President and Teddy Fitzpatrick's worst fears as to the source of the internal White House leak. Jonas Frank was sentenced to fifty years at Leavenworth. He committed suicide after just two years there.

J. Robert Peck remained in FBI custody. He was subsequently prosecuted for, and convicted, of treason, based in part upon testimony from the Government's key witness, former Chief Warrant Officer Mark Walker. Peck was sentenced to death and was the first person to be executed by the Federal Government since Timothy McVeigh.

Max Kallen's 'Top Secret' security clearance was reestablished, and he was offered the job of the guy he had hit in the face many years ago, the Deputy Director of the CIA, which he gladly accepted, happy to be back in the company of spies again. Thereafter, Kallen's influence in the government intelligence community grew as he ultimately rose to the level of Director of National Intelligence and one of the President's most trusted advisors.

Judge Stephens retired as Director of the FBI, settling for retirement in Montana, spending afternoons fly fishing and watching sunsets. *Long overdue*, he determined. Special Agent in Charge of the D.C. Office, Frank Johnson, was promoted to FBI Director, overstepping his boss, the current Deputy Director, largely because of role in *Heart Attack* (as it was later dubbed by the FBI and Secret Service).

Nassir al-Fazeh was a 'confirmed kill' in the drone attack in Southern Syria. Two weeks later, U.S. Special Forces raided a Sunni terrorist camp in Southern Syria, killing all there.